This Signed First Edition Has Been
Specially Bound And Produced
By The Publisher

LIANE MORIARTY

FLATIRON
BOOKS
NEW YORK

Truly
Madly
Guilty

Also by Liane Moriarty

Big Little Lies
The Husband's Secret
The Hypnotist's Love Story
What Alice Forgot
The Last Anniversary
Three Wishes

Liane Moriarty

Truly Madly Guilty

FLATIRON
BOOKS
NEW YORK

This is a work of fiction. All of the characters, organizations, and events portrayed in this novel are either products of the author's imagination or are used fictitiously.

TRULY MADLY GUILTY. Copyright © 2016 by Liane Moriarty. All rights reserved. Printed in the United States of America. For information, address Flatiron Books, 175 Fifth Avenue, New York, N.Y. 10010.

www.flatironbooks.com

Designed by Anna Gorovoy

The Library of Congress Cataloging-in-Publication Data is available upon request.

ISBN 978-1-250-06979-5 (hardcover)
ISBN 978-1-250-11273-6 (international, sold outside the U.S., subject to rights availability)
ISBN 978-1-250-09901-3 (signed edition)
ISBN 978-1-250-06981-8 (e-book)

Our books may be purchased in bulk for promotional, educational, or business use. Please contact your local bookseller or the Macmillan Corporate and Premium Sales Department at 1-800-221-7945, extension 5442, or by e-mail at MacmillanSpecialMarkets@macmillan.com.

First U.S. Edition: July 2016
First International Edition: July 2016

10 9 8 7 6 5 4 3 2 1

For Jaci

Music is the silence between the notes.

Claude Debussy

Truly
Madly
Guilty

1

"This is a story that begins with a barbecue," said Clementine. The microphone amplified and smoothed her voice, making it more authoritative, as if it had been photoshopped. "An ordinary neighborhood barbecue in an ordinary backyard."

Well, not exactly an *ordinary* backyard, thought Erika. She crossed her legs, tucked one foot behind her ankle, and sniffed. Nobody would call Vid's backyard ordinary.

Erika sat in the middle of the back row of the audience in the event room that adjoined this smartly renovated local library in a suburb *forty-five* minutes out of the city, not thirty minutes, thank you very much, as suggested by the person at the cab company, who you would think would have some sort of expertise in the matter.

There were maybe twenty people in the audience, although there were foldout chairs available for twice that many. Most of the audience were elderly people, with lively, expectant faces. These were intelligent, informed senior citizens who had come along on this rainy (yet again, would it ever end?) morning to collect new and fascinating information at their local Community Matters Meeting. "I saw the most interesting woman speak today," they wanted to tell their children and grandchildren.

2 | Liane Moriarty

Before she came, Erika had looked up the library's website to see how it described Clementine's talk. The blurb was short, and not very informative:

Hear Sydney mother and well-known cellist Clementine Hart share her story: "One Ordinary Day."

Was Clementine really a "well-known" cellist? That seemed a stretch.

The five-dollar fee for today's event included two guest speakers, a delicious homemade morning tea and the chance to win a lucky door prize. The speaker after Clementine was going to talk about Council's controversial redevelopment plan for the local pool. Erika could hear the distant gentle clatter of cups and saucers being set up for the morning tea now. She held her flimsy raffle ticket for the lucky door prize safe on her lap. She couldn't be bothered putting it in her bag and then having to find it when they drew the raffle. Blue, E 24. It didn't have the look of a winning ticket.

The lady who sat directly in front of Erika had her gray, curly-haired head tipped to one side in a sympathetic, engaged manner, as if she were ready to agree with everything Clementine had to say. The tag on her shirt was sticking up. Size twelve. Target. Erika reached over and slid it back down.

The lady turned her head.

"Tag," whispered Erika.

The lady smiled her thanks and Erika watched the back of her neck turn pale pink. The younger man sitting next to her, her son perhaps, who looked to be in his forties, had a bar code tattooed on the back of his tanned neck, as if he were a supermarket product. Was it meant to be funny? Ironic? Symbolic? Erika wanted to tell him that it was, in point of fact, idiotic.

"It was just an ordinary Sunday afternoon," said Clementine.

Noticeable repetition of the word "ordinary." Clementine must have decided that it was important she appear "relatable" to these ordinary people in the ordinary outer suburbs. Erika imagined Clementine sitting at her small dining room table, or maybe at Sam's unrestored antique desk, in her shabby-chic sandstone terrace house with its "water glimpse," writing her little community-minded speech while she chewed on the end of her pen and pulled all that lavish, dark hair of hers over one shoulder to caress in that sensual, slightly self-satisfied way she had, as if she were Rapunzel, thinking to herself: Ordinary.

Indeed, Clementine, how shall you make the ordinary people understand?

"It was early winter. A cold, gloomy day," said Clementine.

What the . . . ? Erika shifted in her chair. It had been a beautiful day. A "magnificent" day. That was the word Vid had used.

Or possibly "glorious." A word like that, anyway.

"There was a real bite in the air," said Clementine, and she actually shivered theatrically, and surely unnecessarily, when it was warm in the room, so much so that a man sitting a few rows in front of Erika appeared to have nodded off. He had his legs stretched out in front of him and his hands clasped comfortably across his stomach, his head tipped back as if he were napping on an invisible pillow. Perhaps he'd died.

Maybe the day of the barbecue had been cool, but it was definitely not *gloomy*. Erika knew that eyewitness accounts were notoriously unreliable because people thought they just pressed Rewind on the little recorder installed in their heads, when in fact they constructed their memories. They "developed their own narratives." And so, when Clementine remembered the barbecue, she remembered a cold, gloomy day. But Clementine was wrong. Erika remembered (she *remembered*; she was absolutely not constructing) how on the morning of the barbecue, Vid had bent down to lean into her car window. "Isn't it a magnificent day!" he said.

Erika knew for an absolute fact that was what he'd said.

Or it may have been "glorious."

But it was a word with positive connotations. She could be sure of that.

(If only Erika had said, "Yes, Vid, it certainly is a magnificent/glorious day," and put her foot back on the accelerator.)

"I remember I'd dressed my little girls extra warmly," said Clementine.

Sam probably dressed the girls, thought Erika.

Clementine cleared her throat and gripped the sides of the lectern with both hands. The microphone was angled too high for her, so it seemed as though she were on tippy-toes trying to get her mouth close enough. Her neck was elongated, emphasizing the new skinniness of her face.

Erika considered the possibility of discreetly edging her way around the side of the room and zipping over to adjust the microphone. It would only take a second. She imagined Clementine shooting her a grateful smile. "Thank God you did that," she would say afterwards, while they had coffee. "You really saved the day."

Except that Clementine didn't really want Erika there today. Erika hadn't missed the horrified expression that flashed across her face when Erika had suggested she'd like to come along to hear her speak, although Clementine had quickly recovered herself and said it was fine, lovely, how nice, they could have coffee in the local food court afterwards.

"It was a last-minute invitation," said Clementine. "The barbecue. We didn't know our hosts that well. They were, well, they were friends of friends." She looked down at the lectern as if she'd lost her place. She'd carried a little pile of handwritten palm-sized index cards with her when she walked up to the lectern. There was something heartbreaking about those cards, as if Clementine had remembered that little tip from their oratory lessons at school. She must have cut them up with scissors. Not her grandmother's pearl-handled ones. They'd gone missing.

It was odd seeing Clementine "onstage," so to speak, without her cello. She looked so conventional, in her blue jeans and "nice" floral top. Suburban mum outfit. Clementine's legs were too short for jeans, and they looked even shorter with flat ballet shoes like she was wearing today. Well, it was just a fact. She had looked almost—even though it seemed so disloyal to use the word in relation to Clementine—*frumpy*, when she'd walked up to the lectern. When she performed, she put her hair up and wore heels and all black: long skirts made out of floaty material, wide enough so she could fit the cello between her knees. Seeing Clementine sit with her head bowed tenderly, passionately toward her cello, as if she were embracing it, one long tendril of hair falling just short of the strings, her arm bent at that strange, geometric angle, was always so sensual, so exotic, so *other* to Erika. Each time she saw Clementine perform, even after all these years, Erika inevitably experienced a sensation like loss, as though she yearned for something unattainable. She'd always assumed that sensation represented something more complicated and interesting than envy, because she had no interest in playing a musical instrument, but maybe it didn't. Maybe it all came back to envy.

Watching Clementine give this halting, surely pointless little speech in this little room, with a view of the busy shopping center parking lot instead of the hushed, soaring-ceilinged concert halls where she normally performed, gave Erika the same shameful satisfaction she felt seeing a movie star in a trashy magazine without makeup: You're not that special after all.

"So there were six adults there that day," said Clementine. She cleared her throat, rocked back onto her heels and then rocked forward again. "Six adults and three children."

And one yappy dog, thought Erika. *Yap, yap, yap.*

"As I said, we didn't really know our hosts, but we were all having a nice time, we were enjoying ourselves."

You were enjoying yourself, thought Erika. *You* were.

She remembered how Clementine's clear, bell-like laughter rose and fell in tandem with Vid's deep chuckle. She saw people's faces slip in and out of murky shadows, their eyes like black pools, sudden flashes of teeth.

They'd taken far too long that afternoon to turn on the outdoor lights in that preposterous backyard.

"I remember at one point we were listening to music," said Clementine. She looked down at the lectern in front of her, and then up again, as if she were seeing something on the horizon far in the distance. Her eyes were blank. She didn't look like a suburban mum now. "'After a Dream' by the French composer Gabriel Fauré." Naturally she pronounced it the proper French way. "It's a beautiful piece of music. It has this exquisite mournfulness to it."

She stopped. Did she sense the slight shifting in seats, the discomfort in her audience? "Exquisite mournfulness" was not the right phrase for this audience: too excessive, too arty. Clementine, my love, we're too *ordinary* for your highbrow references to French composers. Anyway, they also played "November Rain" by Guns N' Roses that night. Not quite so arty.

Wasn't the playing of "November Rain" somehow related to Tiffany's revelation? Or was that before? When exactly did Tiffany share her secret? Was that when the afternoon had turned to liquid and begun to slip and slide away?

"We had been drinking," said Clementine. "But no one was drunk. Maybe a little tipsy."

Her eyes met Erika's, as though she'd been aware of exactly where she was sitting the whole time and had been avoiding looking at her, but had now made a deliberate decision to seek her out. Erika stared back and tried to smile, like a friend, Clementine's closest friend, the godmother of her children, but her face felt paralyzed, as if she'd had a stroke.

"Anyway, it was very late in the afternoon and we were all about to have dessert, we were all laughing," said Clementine. She dropped Erika's gaze to look at someone else in the audience in the front row, and it felt dismissive, even cruel. "Over something. I don't remember what."

Erika felt light-headed, claustrophobic. The room had become unbearably stuffy.

The need to get out was suddenly overpowering. Here we go, she thought. Here we go again. Fight-or-flight response. Activation of her sympathetic nervous system. A shift in her brain chemicals. That's what it was. Perfectly natural. Childhood trauma. She'd read all the literature. She knew exactly what was happening to her but the knowledge made no difference. Her body went right ahead and betrayed her. Her heart raced. Her hands trembled. She could *smell* her childhood, so thick and real in her nostrils: damp and mold and shame.

"Don't fight the panic. Face it. Float through it," her psychologist had told her.

Her psychologist was exceptional, worth every cent, but for God's sake, as if you could float when there was no room, no space anywhere, above, below, when you couldn't take a step without feeling the spongy give of rotting *stuff* beneath your feet.

She stood, pulling at her skirt, which had gotten stuck to the backs of her legs. The guy with the bar code glanced over his shoulder at her. The sympathetic concern in his eyes gave her a tiny shock; it was like seeing the disconcertingly intelligent eyes of an ape.

"Sorry," whispered Erika. "I have to—" She pointed at her watch and shuffled sideways past him, trying not to brush the back of his head with her jacket.

As she reached the back of the room, Clementine said, "I remember there was a moment when my friend screamed my name. Really loud. I'll never forget the sound."

Erika stopped with her hand on the door, her back to the front of the room. Clementine must have leaned toward the microphone because her voice suddenly filled the room: "She shouted, *Clementine!*"

Clementine had always been an excellent mimic; as a musician she had an ear for the precise intonations in people's voices. Erika could hear raw terror and shrill urgency in just that one word, "Clementine!"

Erika knew she was the friend who had shouted Clementine's name that night but she had no memory of it. There was nothing but a pure white space where that memory should have been, and if *she* couldn't remember a moment like that, well, that indicated a problem, an anomaly, a discrepancy, an extremely significant and concerning discrepancy. The wave of panic peaked and nearly swept her off her feet. She pushed down the handle of the door and staggered out into the relentless rain.

2

B een at a meeting then?" said the cabdriver taking Erika back into the city. He grinned paternally at her in the rearview mirror as if it was kind of cute the way women worked these days, all dressed up in suits, almost like they were proper businesspeople.

"Yes," said Erika. She gave her umbrella a vigorous shake on the floor of the cab. "Keep your eyes on the road."

"Yes, ma'am!" The cabdriver tapped two fingertips to his forehead in a mock salute.

"The rain," said Erika defensively. She indicated the raindrops pelleting furiously against the windshield. "Slippery roads."

"Just drove this goose to the airport," said the cabdriver. He stopped talking as he changed lanes, one meaty hand on the wheel, the other arm slung casually along the back of the seat, leaving Erika with the image of an actual large white goose sitting in the backseat of the taxi.

"He reckons all this rain is related to climate change. I said, mate, mate, I said, it's nothing to do with climate change. It's La Niña! You know about La Niña? El Niño and La Niña? Natural events! Been happening for thousands of years."

"Right," said Erika. She wished Oliver were with her. He'd take on this conversation for her. Why were cabdrivers so insistent on educating their passengers?

"Yep. La *Niña*," said the cabbie, with a sort of Mexican inflection. He obviously enjoyed saying "La Niña." "So, we broke the record, hey? Longest consecutive run of rainy days in Sydney since 1932. Hooray for us!"

"Yes," said Erika. "Hooray for us."

It was 1931, she never forgot a number, but there was no need to correct him.

"I think you'll find it was 1931," she said. She couldn't help herself. It was a character flaw. She knew it.

"Yep, that's it, 1931," said the cabbie, as if that's what he'd said in the first place. "Before that it was twenty-four days in 1893. Twenty-four rainy days in a row! Let's hope we don't break that record too, hey? Think we will?"

"Let's hope not," said Erika. She ran a finger along her forehead. Was that sweat or rain?

She'd calmed down as she waited in the rain outside the library for the cab. Her breathing was steady again, but her stomach still rocked and roiled, and she felt exhausted, depleted, as if she'd run a marathon.

She took out her phone and texted Clementine: *Sorry, had to rush off, problem at work, you were fantastic, talk later.*

She changed "fantastic" to "great." Fantastic was over the top. Also inaccurate. She pressed Send.

It had been an error of judgment to take precious time out of her working day to come and listen to Clementine's talk. She'd only gone to be supportive, and because she wanted to get her own feelings about what had happened filed away in an orderly fashion. It was as though her memory of that afternoon was a strip of old-fashioned film, and someone had taken a pair of scissors and removed certain frames. They weren't even whole frames. They were slivers. Thin slivers of time. She just wanted to fill in those slivers, without admitting to anyone, "I don't quite remember it all."

An image came to her of her own face reflected in her bathroom mirror, her hands shaking violently as she tried to break that little yellow pill in half with her thumbnail. She suspected the gaps in her memory were related to the tablet she'd taken that afternoon. But it was a *prescription* pill. It wasn't like she'd popped an Ecstasy tablet before going to a barbecue.

She remembered feeling odd, a little detached, before they went next door to the barbecue, but that still didn't account for the gaps. Too much to drink? Yes. Too much to drink. Face the facts, Erika. You were affected by alcohol. You were *drunk*. Erika couldn't quite believe that word could apply to her but it seemed to be the case. She had been unequivocally drunk for the first time in her life. So, maybe the gaps were alcoholic *blackouts*? Like Oliver's mum and dad. "They can't remember whole decades of their life," Oliver said once in front of his parents, and they'd both laughed delightedly and raised their glasses even though Oliver wasn't smiling.

"So what do you do for a quid, if you don't mind me asking?" said the cabbie.

"I'm an accountant," said Erika.

"*Are* you now?" said the cabbie with far too much interest. "What a coincidence, because I was just thinking—"

Erika's phone rang and Erika startled, as she did without fail whenever her phone rang. ("It's a phone, Erika," Oliver kept telling her. "That's what it's meant to do.") She could see it was her mother, the very last person in the world she wanted to talk to right now, but the cabdriver was shifting in his seat, his eyes on her instead of the road, virtually licking his lips in anticipation of all the free tax advice he was about to get. Cabdrivers knew a little bit about everything. He'd want to tell her about an amazing loophole he'd heard about from one of his regular customers. Erika wasn't that kind of accountant. "Loophole" was not a word she appreciated. Maybe her mother was the lesser of two evils.

"Hello, Mum."

"Well, *hello*! I didn't expect you to answer!" Her mother sounded both nervous and defiant, which didn't bode well at all. "I was all prepared to leave a voice mail message!" said Sylvia accusingly.

"Sorry I answered," said Erika. She was sorry.

"Obviously you don't need to be sorry, I just need to recalibrate. Tell you what, why don't you just listen while I pretend to leave you the message I had all prepared?"

"Go ahead," said Erika. She looked out at the rainy street, where a woman battled with an umbrella that wanted to turn itself inside out. Erika watched as the woman suddenly, marvelously lost her temper and jammed the umbrella into a rubbish bin without losing stride and continued walking in the rain. Good on you, thought Erika, exhilarated by this little tableau. Just throw it out. Throw the damned thing *out*.

Her mother's voice got louder in her ear as if she'd repositioned her phone. "I was going to start like this: 'Erika, darling,' I was going to say. 'Erika, darling, I know you can't talk right now because you're at work, which is such a pity, being stuck in an office on this beautiful day, not that it *is* a beautiful day, I must admit, it's actually a terrible day, a horrendous day, but *normally* this time of year we have such glorious days, and whenever I wake up and have a peek outside at the blue sky, I think, oh *dear*, oh what a *pity*, poor, poor old Erika, stuck in her office on this beautiful day, that's what I think, but that's the price you pay for corporate success! If only you'd been a park ranger or some other outdoorsy job.' I wasn't actually going to say the park ranger part, that just came to me then, and actually I know why it came to me, because Sally's son has just left school and he's going to be a park ranger, and when she was telling me, I just thought to myself, you know, what a marvelous job, what a clever idea, instead of being trapped in a little cubicle like you are."

"I'm not trapped in a cubicle," sighed Erika. Her office had harbor views and fresh flowers bought each Monday morning by her secretary. She loved her office. She loved her job.

"It was Sally's idea, you know. For her son to be a park ranger. So clever of her. She's not conventional, Sally, she thinks outside the box."

"Sally?" said Erika.

"Sally! My new hairdresser!" said her mother impatiently, as if Sally had been in her life for years, not a couple of months, as if Sally were going to be a lifelong friend. Ha. Sally would go the way of all the other wonderful strangers in her mother's life.

"So what else was your message going to say?" said Erika.

"Let's see now, then I was going to say, sort of casually, as if I'd only just thought of it: 'Oh, listen, darling, by the *way*!'"

Erika laughed. Her mother could always charm her, even at the worst times. Just when Erika thought she was done, that was it, she could take no more, her mother charmed her back into loving her.

Her mother laughed too, but it sounded hectic and high-pitched. "I was going to say: 'Listen, darling, I was wondering if you and Oliver would like to come to lunch at my place on Sunday?'"

"No," said Erika. "No."

She breathed in like she was breathing in through a straw. Her lips felt wonky. "No, thank you. We'll be at your place on the fifteenth. That's when we'll come, Mum. No other time. That's the deal."

"But, darling, I think you'd be so proud of me because—"

"No," said Erika. "I'll meet you anywhere else. We can go out to lunch this Sunday. To a nice restaurant. Or you can come to our place. Oliver and I don't have anything on. We can go anywhere else, but we are not coming to your house." She paused and said it again, louder and more clearly, as if she were speaking to someone without a good grasp of English. "We are not coming to your house."

There was silence.

"Until the fifteenth," said Erika. "It's in the diary. It's in both our diaries. And don't forget we've got that dinner with Clementine's parents on Thursday night! So we've got that to look forward to as well." Yes, indeed, that was going to be a barrel of laughs.

"I had a new recipe I wanted to try. I bought a gluten-free recipe book, did I tell you?"

It was the flip tone that did it. The calculated, cruel brightness, as if she thought there was a chance Erika might join her in playing the game they'd played for all those years, where they both pretended to be an ordinary mother and daughter having an ordinary conversation, when she *knew* that Erika no longer played, when they'd both agreed the game was over, when her mother had wept and apologized and made promises they both knew she'd never keep, but now she wanted to pretend she'd never even made the promises in the first place.

"Mum. Dear God."

"What?" Faux innocence. That infuriating babyish voice.

"You *promised* on Grandma's grave that you wouldn't buy another recipe book! You don't cook! You don't have a gluten allergy!" Why did her voice tremble with rage when she never expected those melodramatic promises to be kept?

"I made no such promise!" said her mother, and she dropped the baby voice and had the audacity to respond to Erika's rage with her own. "And as a matter of fact, I have been suffering quite dreadful bloating lately. I have gluten intolerance, thank you very much. Excuse me for worrying about my health."

Do not engage. Remove yourself from the emotional minefield. This was why she was investing thousands of dollars in therapy, for exactly this situation.

"All right then, well, Mum, it was nice talking to you," said Erika rapidly, without giving her mother a chance to speak, as if she were a telemarketer, "but I'm at work, so I have to go now. I'll talk to you later." She hung up before her mother could speak and dropped the phone in her lap.

The cabdriver's shoulders were conspicuously still against his beaded seat cover, only his hands moving on the bottom of the steering wheel, pretending that he hadn't been listening in. What sort of daughter refuses to go to her mother's house? What sort of daughter speaks with such violence to her mother about buying a new recipe book?

She blinked hard.

Her phone rang again, and she jumped so violently, it nearly slid off her lap. It would be her mother again, ringing to shout abuse.

But it wasn't her mother. It was Oliver.

"Hi," she said, and nearly cried with relief at the sound of his voice. "Just had a fun phone call with Mum. She wanted us to go over for lunch on Sunday."

"We're not due there until next month, are we?" said Oliver.

"No," said Erika. "She was pushing her boundaries."

"Are you okay?"

"Yep." She ran a fingertip under her eyes. "Fine."

"You sure?"

"Yes. Thank you."

"Just put her straight out of your mind," said Oliver. "Hey, did you go to Clementine's talk at that library out in wherever it was?"

Erika tipped back her head against the seat and closed her eyes. Dammit. Of course. That's why he was calling. Clementine. The plan had been that she would chat to Clementine after her talk, while they had coffee. Oliver had not been overly interested in Erika's motivation for attending Clementine's talk. He didn't understand her obsessive desire to fill in the blank spots of her memory. He found it irrelevant, almost silly. "Believe me, you've remembered everything you're ever going to remember," he'd said. (His lips went thin, his eyes hard on the words: "Believe me." Just a little flash of pain he could never quite repress, and that he would probably deny feeling.) "Blank spots are par for the course when you drink too much." They weren't par for *her* course. But Oliver had seen this as the perfect opportunity to talk to Clementine, to finally pin her down.

She should have let him go to voice mail too.

"I did," she said. "But I left halfway through. I didn't feel well."

"So you didn't get to talk to Clementine?" said Oliver. She could hear him doing his best to conceal his frustration.

"Not today," she said. "Don't worry. I'm just finding the right time. The food court wouldn't have been the best spot anyway."

"I'm just looking at my diary. It has been two months now since the barbecue. I don't think it's offensive or insensitive, or whatever, to just ask the question. Just ring her up. It doesn't need to be face-to-face."

"I know. I'm sorry."

"You don't need to be sorry," said Oliver. "This is difficult. It's not your fault."

"It was my fault we went to the barbecue in the first place," she said. Oliver wouldn't absolve her of that. He was too accurate. They'd always had that in common: a passion for accuracy.

The cabbie slammed on his brake. "Ya bloody idiot driver! Ya bloody goose!" Erika put her hand flat against the front seat to brace herself as Oliver said, "That's not relevant."

"It's relevant to me," said Erika. Her phone beeped to let her know that another call was coming through. It would be her mother. The fact that it had taken her a couple of minutes to call back meant that she had chosen tears over abuse. Tears took longer.

"I don't know what you want me to say about that, Erika," said Oliver worriedly. He thought there was an actual correct response. An answer at the back of the book. He thought there was a secret set of relationship rules that she must know, because she was the woman, and she was deliberately withholding them. "Just . . . will you talk to Clementine?" he said.

"I'll talk to Clementine," said Erika. "See you tonight."

She turned her phone to silent and put it in her bag, at her feet. The taxi driver turned up the radio. He must have given up on asking her accounting advice now, probably thinking that judging from her personal life, her professional advice couldn't be trusted.

Erika thought of Clementine, who would be finishing up her little speech at the library by now, presumably to polite applause from her audience. There would be no *bravos!*, no standing ovations, no bouquets backstage.

Poor Clementine, feeling she had to virtually *abase* herself in this way.

Oliver was right: the decision to go to the barbecue was of no relevance. It was a sunk cost. She put her head back against the seat, closed her eyes and remembered a silver car driving toward her, surrounded by a swirling funnel of autumn leaves.

3

The Day of the Barbecue

Erika drove into her cul-de-sac and was greeted by a strange, almost beautiful sight: someone was finally driving the silver BMW that had been parked outside the Richardsons' house for the last six months, and whoever was driving hadn't bothered to brush away the layer of red and gold autumn leaves that had accumulated on the car's hood and roof, so that as they drove (much too fast for a residential area), a whirling vortex of leaves was created, as if the car were being followed by a mini-tornado.

As the leaves cleared, Erika saw her next-door neighbor, Vid, standing at the end of his driveway, watching the car drive away while a single ray of sunlight bounced off his sunglasses, like the shimmer of a camera flash.

Erika braked next to him, opening her passenger-side window at the same time. "Good morning," she called out. "Someone finally moved that car!"

"Yes, they must have finished their drug dealing, what do you reckon?" Vid leaned down toward the car, pushing his sunglasses up onto his head of luxuriant gray hair. "Or maybe it was the Mafia, you know?"

"Ha ha!" Erika laughed unconvincingly because Vid looked kind of like a successful gangster himself.

"It's a cracker of a day, you know. Look! Am I right?!" Vid made a satis-fied gesture at the sky, as if he'd personally purchased the day and paid a premium price for it, and got the quality product he deserved.

"It is a beautiful day," said Erika. "You off for a walk?"

Vid reacted with faint disgust to this suggestion. "Walk? Me? No." He indicated a lit cigarette between his fingers and the rolled-up, plastic-wrapped Sunday paper in the other hand. "I just came down to collect my paper, you know."

Erika reminded herself not to count the number of times Vid said "you know." Recording someone's conversational tic bordered on obsessive-compulsive. (Vid's current record: eleven times in a two-minute diatribe about the removal of the smoked pancetta pizza from the local pizzeria's menu. Vid could not believe it, he just could not believe it, you know. The "you know's" came thick and fast when he got excited.)

Erika was very aware that some of her behaviors could potentially be classified as obsessive-compulsive. "I wouldn't get too caught up with labels, Erika," her psychologist had said with the constipated smile she tended to give when Erika "self-diagnosed." (Erika had taken out a subscription to *Psy-chology Today* when she started therapy, just to educate herself a little about the process, and it was all so fascinating, she'd recently begun working her way through the first-year reading list for a psychological and behavioral sciences undergraduate degree at Cambridge. Just for interest, she'd told her psychologist, who didn't look threatened by this, but didn't look exactly thrilled by it either.)

"Bloody revhead kid hoons up the street and throws it from his car like he's throwing a grenade in bloody Syria, you know." Vid made a grenade-throwing gesture with the rolled-up paper. "So what are you up to? Been grocery shopping?"

He looked at the little collection of plastic bags on Erika's passenger seat and drew deeply on his cigarette, blowing a stream of smoke out the side of his mouth.

"Not exactly grocery shopping, just some, um, bits and bobs I needed."

"Bits and bobs," repeated Vid, trying out the phrase as if he'd never heard it before. Maybe he hadn't. He looked at Erika in that searching, almost disappointed way he had, as if he'd been hoping for something more from her.

"Yes. For afternoon tea. We've got Clementine and Sam coming over later for afternoon tea, with their little girls. My friends, Clementine and Sam? You met them at my place?" She knew perfectly well that Vid remembered them. She was giving him Clementine to make herself more interesting. That's all she had to offer Vid: Clementine.

Vid's face lit up instantly. "Your friend, the cellist!" said Vid delightedly. He virtually smacked his lips on the word "cellist." "And her husband. Tone-deaf! What a waste, eh?"

"Well, he likes to say he's tone-deaf," said Erika. "I think technically he's—"

"Top bloke! He was a—what do you call it?—a *marketing manager for an FMCG company*, and that stands for a fast-moving . . . don't tell me, don't tell me, a *fast-moving consumer good*. Whatever the hell that means. But how's that? Good memory, eh? I've got a mind like a steel trap, that's what I tell my wife."

"Well, he's actually changed jobs, now he's at an energy drink company."

"What? Energy drinks? Drinks that give you energy? Anyway, Sam and Clementine, they're good people, great people, you know! You should all come over to our place, for a barbecue, you know! Yes, we'll do a barbecue! Enjoy this amazing weather, you know! I insist. You must!"

"Oh," said Erika. "It's nice of you to offer." She should say no. She was perfectly capable of saying no. She had no problem saying no to people—in fact, she took pride in her ability to refuse—and Oliver wouldn't want her to change the plans for today. It was too important. Today was crucial. Today was potentially life-changing.

"I'll roast a pig on the spit! The Slovenian way. Well, it's not really the Slovenian way, it's my way, but it's like nothing you've ever tasted before. Your friend. Clementine. I remember. She's a foodie, you know. Like me." He patted his stomach.

"Well," said Erika. She looked again at the plastic bags on her passenger seat. All the way home from the shops, she'd kept glancing over at her purchases, worried that she'd somehow not gotten it quite right. She should have bought more. What was wrong with her? Why hadn't she bought a *feast*?

Also the crackers she'd chosen had sesame seeds on them, and there was some significance to sesame seeds. Did Clementine love sesame seeds or hate them?

"What do you say?" said Vid. "Tiffany would love to see you."

"Would she?" said Erika. Most wives wouldn't appreciate an unplanned barbecue, but Vid's wife did appear to be almost as sociable as Vid. Erika thought of the first time she'd introduced her closest friends to her extroverted next-door neighbors, when she and Oliver hosted Christmas drinks at their place last year in a fit of mutual "let's pretend we're the sort of people who entertain and enjoy it" madness. She and Oliver had both hated every moment. Entertaining was always fraught for Erika, because she had no experience of it, and because part of her would always believe that visitors were to be feared and despised.

"And they've got two little girls, right?" continued Vid. "Our Dakota would love to play with them."

"Yes. Although, remember, they're much younger than Dakota."

"Even better! Dakota loves playing with little girls, you know, pretending she's the big sister, you know. Plaiting their hair, painting their nails, you know, fun for all of them!"

Erika ran her hands around the steering wheel. She looked at her house. The low hedge lining the path to the front door was freshly trimmed with perfect, startling symmetry. The blinds were open. The windows were clean and streak-free. Nothing to hide. From the street, you could see their red Veronese table lamp. That's all. *Only* the lamp. An exquisite lamp. Just seeing that lamp from the street when she drove home gave Erika a sense of pride and peace. Oliver was inside now, vacuuming. Erika had vacuumed yesterday, so it was overkill. Excessive vacuuming. Embarrassing.

When Erika first left home, one of the many procedural things that worried her about domestic life was trying to work out how often normal people vacuumed. It was Clementine's mother who'd given her a definitive answer: Once a week, Erika, every Sunday afternoon, for example. You pick a regular time that suits you, make it a habit. Erika had followed Pam's rules for living religiously, whereas Clementine willfully ignored them. "Sam and I always forget that vacuuming is even a *thing*," she'd once told Erika. "We always feel better, though, once it's done, and then we say: Let's vacuum more often! It's kind of like when we remember to have sex."

Erika had been astonished, both by the vacuuming and the sex. She knew that she and Oliver were more formal with each other in public than other couples, they didn't really tease each other (they liked things to be clear, not open to misinterpretation), but gosh, they'd never *forget to have sex.*

A vacuumed house wasn't going to make a difference to the outcome of today's meeting, any more than sesame seeds were.

"Pig on the spit, eh?" said Erika to Vid. She put her head on one side, coquettishly, the way Clementine would in a situation like this. She sometimes borrowed Clementine's mannerisms for herself, although only when Clementine wasn't there, in case they were recognized. "You mean to say you've got a spare pig just lying around waiting to be roasted?"

Vid grinned, pleased with her, winked and pointed his cigarette at her. The smoke drifted into the car, bringing in another world. "Don't you worry about that, Erika." He put the emphasis on the second syllable. Erika. It made her name sound more exotic. "We'll get it all sorted, you know. What time is your cellist friend coming over? Two? Three?"

"Three," said Erika. She was already regretting the coquettishness. Oh, God. What had she done?

She looked past Vid and saw Harry, the old man who lived alone on the other side of Vid, in his front yard, standing next to his camellia bush with a pair of garden shears. Their eyes met, and she raised her hand to wave, but he immediately looked away and wandered off out of sight into the corner of the garden.

"Our mate Harry lurking about?" said Vid, without turning around.

"Yes," said Erika. "He's gone now."

"So three o'clock then?" said Vid. He gave the side of her car a decisive rap with his knuckles. "We see you then?"

"All right," said Erika weakly.

She watched Oliver open their front door and step onto the front porch with a bag of rubbish. He was going to be furious with her.

"Perfect. Outstanding!" Vid straightened from the car and caught sight of Oliver, who smiled and waved.

"Mate!" bellowed Vid. "We'll see you later today! Barbecue at our place!"

Oliver's smile disappeared.

4

Clementine drove out of the library parking lot in a mild panic, one hand on the steering wheel, the other fiddling with her de-mister because her windshield had suddenly, cruelly, fogged over so that it was virtually opaque in places. She was twenty minutes later leaving than she'd planned to be.

After she finished her talk, to the usual hesitant, muted applause, as if people weren't sure if it was quite appropriate to clap, she'd kept getting caught in conversation as she tried to reach the door (so close but yet so far) through the small but impenetrable group of people now tucking into their complimentary, homemade morning tea. One woman wanted to hug her and pat her cheek. A man, who she later noticed had a bar code tattooed on the back of his neck, was keen to hear her thoughts on the Council plans for the swimming pool redevelopment and didn't seem to believe her when she said she wasn't local and therefore really couldn't comment. A tiny white-haired lady wanted her to try a piece of carrot cake wrapped in a pink paper napkin.

She ate the carrot cake. It was very good carrot cake. So there was that.

The windshield cleared like a small gift and she turned left out of the lot, because left was always her default turn when she had no idea where she was going.

"Start talking," she said to her GPS. "You've got one job. Do it."

She needed the GPS to direct her home fast so she could pick up her cello before rushing over to her friend Ainsley's place, where she was going to play her pieces in front of Ainsley and her husband Hu. The audition was in two weeks' time. "So you're still going for this job?" her mother had said last week, in a tone of surprise and possibly judgment, but Clementine heard judgment everywhere these days, so she might have imagined it.

"Yes, I'm still going to audition," she'd said coldly, and her mother had said nothing further.

She drove slowly, waiting for instructions, but her GPS was silent, mulling things over.

"Are you going to tell me where to go?" she asked it.

Apparently not. She got to a set of lights and turned left. She couldn't just *keep* turning left, because otherwise she'd be turning in a circle. Wouldn't she? Once she would have gone home and told Sam about this and he would have laughed and teased and sympathized and offered to buy her a new GPS.

"I hate you," Clementine told the silent GPS. "I hate and despise you."

The GPS ignored her, and Clementine peered out the window through the rain, looking for a sign. She could feel the beginnings of a headache because she was frowning so hard.

She shouldn't be here, driving all the way to the other side of Sydney in the rain in this flat, gray, unfamiliar suburb. She should have been at home, practicing. That's what she *would* have been doing.

Wherever she went, whatever she did, part of her mind was always imagining a hypothetical life running parallel to her actual one, a life where, when Erika rang up and said, "Vid has invited us to a barbecue," Clementine answered, "No, thank you." Three simple words. Vid wouldn't have cared. He barely knew them.

It was not Vid at the symphony last night. It was her mind playing cruel tricks, placing that big head smack-bang in the middle of a sea of faces.

At least she'd been prepared to see Erika today in the audience, although her stomach had still lurched when she'd first caught sight of her, sitting so rigidly in the back row, like she was at a funeral, a flicker of a smile when she caught Clementine's eye. Why had she asked to come? It was weird. Did she think it was like seeing Clementine perform? Even if she did think that, it was still out of character for Erika to take time out of her workday to drive all the way out here from North Sydney to hear Clementine share a story she already knew. And then she'd gotten up and left halfway through! She'd texted to say there was a problem at work, but that seemed unlikely. Surely there was no accounting problem that couldn't wait twenty minutes.

It had been a relief when she left. It had been disconcerting trying to speak with that small intense face pulling her attention like a magnet. At one point, the irrelevant, distracting thought had crossed her mind that Erika's fair hair was cut in an identical style to Clementine's mother's. A no-nonsense symmetrical shoulder-length style with a long fringe cut dead straight just above the eyebrows. Erika idolized Clementine's mother. It was either a deliberate or a subconscious imitation, but surely not a coincidence.

She saw a sign pointing toward the city and quickly changed lanes just as the GPS woke up and directed her to the "right turn ahead" in a plummy female English accent.

"Yes, I worked it out myself, thanks anyway," she said.

The rain started again and she flicked on the wipers.

A piece of rubber on one of the wipers had made its way free, and on every third swipe it made a high-pitched screech, like a door slowly opening in a horror movie.

Scre-eech. Two. Three. Scre-eech. Two. Three. It made her think of zombies in a lumbering waltz.

She would call Erika today. Or tomorrow morning. Erika was owed an answer. Enough time had passed. There was only one answer, of course, but Clementine had been waiting for the appropriate time.

Don't think about that now. Think only about the audition. She needed to *compartmentalize*, as the Facebook articles suggested. Men were supposedly good at compartmentalizing, they gave their full attention to whatever they were doing, although in fact, Sam had never had a problem multitasking. He could make a risotto while unpacking the dishwasher and simultaneously playing some good-for-their-brains game with the girls. *Clementine* was the one who wandered off, picked up her cello and then forgot she had something in the oven. *She* was the one who had once (mortifyingly) forgotten to pick Holly up from a birthday party, something Sam would never do.

"Your mother walks around in a permanent daze," Sam used to say to the girls, but he said it fondly, or she thought he had. Maybe she'd imagined the fondness. She could no longer be sure what anyone truly thought of her: Her mother. Her husband. Her friend. Anything seemed possible.

She thought again of her mother's comment: "So you're still going for this job?" She'd never put in this many practice hours for an audition, even before the children were born. All that self-indulgent whining she used to do: *I'm a working mother with two small children! Woe is me! There just aren't enough hours in my day!* In fact, there were plenty more hours in the day if you just slept less. Now she went to bed at midnight instead of 10 P.M., and got up at five instead of seven.

Living on less sleep gave her a not-unpleasant, mildly sedated feeling. She felt detached from all aspects of her life. She had no time anymore to *feel*. All that time she used to waste *feeling*, and analyzing her feelings, as if they were a matter of national significance. *Clementine feels extremely nervous about her upcoming audition! Clementine doesn't know if she's good enough.* Well, hooly-dooly, stop the presses, let's research audition nerves, let's talk earnestly with musician friends, let's get constant reassurance.

Stop it. The endless self-mockery of the person she used to be was not especially productive either. Spend your time focusing on questions of technique. She searched her mind for a distracting technical problem—for example, the fingering for the opening arpeggio of the Beethoven. She kept changing her mind. The trickier option could pay off with a better musical result, but the risk was that she'd make a mistake when she was under pressure.

Was that a traffic jam ahead? She must not be late. Her friends were giving up their time to do this for her. There was nothing in it for them. Pure altruism. She looked at the stopped traffic, and once again she was in Tiffany's car, trapped in a sea of red brake lights, the seat belt like a restraint pulled tight against her neck.

The traffic kept moving. It was fine. She heard herself exhale, although she hadn't been aware she was holding her breath.

She would ask Sam tonight when they were out for dinner if his mind kept getting stuck in the same pointless "what if" groove as hers. Maybe it would open up a conversation. A "healing conversation." That was the sort of phrase her mother would use.

They were going out tonight on a "date night." Another modern term her mother had picked up. "What you kids need is a date night!" She and Sam both abhorred the term "date night," but they were going on one, to a restaurant suggested by Clementine's mother. Her mother was babysitting and had even made the booking.

"Forgiveness is the attribute of the strong. I think it was Gandhi who said that," her mother told her. Her mother's refrigerator door was covered with inspirational quotes scrawled on little pieces of paper held up by fridge magnets. The fridge magnets had quotes on them too.

Maybe tonight would be okay. Maybe it would even be fun. She was trying to be positive. One of them had to be. Her car drifted close to the gutter, and a gigantic wave of water whooshed up the side of her car. She swore, far more viciously than was warranted.

It felt like it had been raining ever since the day of the barbecue, although she knew this wasn't true. When she thought of her life before the barbecue, it was suffused with golden sunlight. Blue skies. Soft breezes. As if it had never rained before.

"Turn left ahead," said the GPS.

"What? Here?" said Clementine. "Are you sure? Or do you mean the next one? I think you mean the next one."

She kept driving.

"Turn around when possible," said the GPS with the hint of a sigh.

"Sorry," said Clementine humbly.

5

The Day of the Barbecue

Sunlight flooded the kitchen where Clementine ran in place in her pajamas while her husband Sam yelled sergeant major style, "Run, soldier, run!"

Her two-year-old daughter, Ruby, also in her pajamas, her hair a tangled blond bird's nest, ran alongside Clementine, bobbing about like a puppet on a string and giggling. She had a soft, soggy piece of croissant clamped in one pudgy hand and a metal whisk with a wooden handle in the other, although nobody thought of Whisk as merely a kitchen utensil anymore; Whisk was fed, bathed and put tenderly to bed each night by Ruby in his/her (Whisk's gender was fluid) tissue paper–lined shoe box.

"*Why* am I running?" panted Clementine. "I don't like running!"

This morning Sam had announced, with an evangelical look in his eye, that he'd developed a foolproof plan to help her "nail this audition, baby." He'd been up late last night getting his plan ready.

First she needed to run in place for five minutes as fast as she could.

"Don't ask questions, just follow orders!" said Sam. "Lift those knees! You've got to be puffing."

Clementine tried to lift her knees.

He must have Googled "tips for your orchestral audition," and tip number one was something delightfully trite like: "Exercise! Make sure you're in peak physical condition."

This was the problem with being married to a non-musician. A musician would have known that the way to help her prepare for her audition was *by taking the girls out this morning so she had time to practice before they had to go over to Erika's place.* It's not rocket science, soldier.

"Two minutes more!" Sam studied her. He was unshaven, in his T-shirt and boxers. "Actually, you might only need one minute more, you're not very fit."

"I'm stopping," said Clementine, slowing to a jog.

"No! You mustn't stop. It's to simulate your audition nerves by making your heart rate go up. Once it's up you have to launch straight into playing your excerpts."

"What? No, I'm not going to play now." She needed to spend time meticulously *preparing* her excerpts. "I want another coffee."

"Run, soldier, run!" shouted Sam.

"Oh, for God's sake." She kept running. It wouldn't hurt her to do some exercise, although actually, it was already hurting quite a lot.

Their five-year-old ("and three-quarters," it was important to clarify) daughter, Holly, clip-clopped into the living room, wearing her pajama pants, an old ripped *Frozen* dress and a pair of Clementine's high heels. She put her hand on her jutted hip as though she was on the red carpet and waited to be admired.

"Wow. Look at Holly," said Sam dutifully. "Take those shoes off before you hurt yourself."

"Why are you both . . . 'running'?" said Holly to her mother and her sister. She hooked her fingers in the air to make exaggerated quotation marks on the word "running." It was a new sophisticated habit of hers, except she thought you could just pick any word at random and give it quotation marks. The more words the better. She frowned. "Stop that."

"Your father is making me run," gasped Clementine.

Ruby had suddenly had enough of running and plopped down on her bottom. She carefully laid her piece of croissant on the floor for later and sucked hard on her thumb, like a smoker in need of a drag.

"Daddy, stop making Mummy run," demanded Holly. "She's breathing funny!"

"I am breathing funny," agreed Clementine.

"Excellent," said Sam. "We need her breathless. Girls! Come with me! We've got an important job to do! Holly, I told you, shoes off before you hurt yourself!"

He grabbed Ruby up off the floor and held her under one arm like a football so she shrieked with delight, and ran down the hallway. Holly ran behind, ignoring his directive about the shoes.

"Keep running until we call for you!" shouted Sam from the living room.

Clementine, as disobedient as Holly, slowed down to a shuffle.

"We're ready for you!" called Sam.

She walked into the living room, half-laughing, breathing heavily. She stopped at the doorway. The furniture had been pushed to the corners of the room, and a solitary chair stood in the middle of the room, behind her music stand. Her cello leaned against the chair, the endpin jammed firmly into the hardwood floor, where it would leave another tiny hole. (They'd agreed to call the holes "character" rather than "damage.") A queen-sized bedsheet hung from the ceiling, dividing the room. Holly, Ruby and Sam sat behind it. She could hear Ruby giggling.

So this was what Sam was so excited about. He'd set the room up to look like an audition. The white bedsheet was meant to represent the black screen where the audition panel sat behind like an invisible firing squad, judging and condemning, faceless and silent (except for the occasional intimidating rustle or cough and the loud, bored, superior voice that could at any moment interrupt her playing with, "That will do, thank you").

She was surprised and almost embarrassed by her body's automatic visceral response to the sight of that lonely chair.

Every audition she'd ever done rushed back into her head: a cascade of memories. The time there was only the one warm-up room for everyone, a room so astonishingly hot and airless and noisy, so crowded with extraordinarily talented-seeming musicians, that everything had begun to spin like a merry-go-round, and a French cellist had reached out a languid hand to save Clementine's cello as it slipped from her grasp. (She was a champion fainter.)

The time she'd done a first-round audition and played exceptionally well except for a mortifying slipup in her concerto, not even in a tricky passage, a mistake she'd never made in concert and never made again. She'd been so crushed, she'd cried for three hours straight in a Gloria Jean's coffee shop, while the lady at the next table passed her tissues and her boyfriend at the time (the oboist with eczema) said over and over, "They forgive you one wrong note!" He was right, they forgave her the one wrong note, she'd gotten the callback that afternoon, but by then she was so spent from all that crying, she played with a bow arm so fatigued it felt as limp as spaghetti, and missed out on the final round.

"Sam," she began. It was sweet of him, it was really, really sweet of him and she adored him for doing it, but it was not helping.

"Hello, Mummy!" said Ruby clearly from behind the sheet.

"Hello, Ruby," said Clementine.

"Shh," said Sam. "No talking."

"Why isn't Mummy 'playing'?" said Holly. You didn't need to see her to know she was doing her air quotes.

"I don't know," said Sam. "We won't give this applicant the job if she doesn't play, will we?"

Clementine sighed. She'd have to go along with the game. She went and sat on the chair. She tasted banana. Every time she did an audition, she ate a banana in the car on the way in because bananas supposedly contained natural beta-blockers to help with her nerves. Now she couldn't eat bananas at any other time because they made her think of auditions.

Maybe this time she could try real beta-blockers again, although the one time she had, she hadn't liked that cotton-mouth feeling and her brain had felt kind of blasted clean, as if something had exploded in the center of her head.

"Mummy already has a job," said Holly. "She already *is* a cellist."

"This is her dream job," said Sam.

"Kind of," said Clementine.

"What's that?" said Sam. "Who was that? We didn't hear the applicant talk, did we? She doesn't talk, she just plays."

"That was Mummy," said Ruby. "Hello, Mummy!"

"Hello, Ruby!" called back Clementine as she rosined her bow.

"Dream job" was maybe excessive (if she were dreaming, she may as well be a world-famous soloist), but she very, very badly wanted this job: principal cellist with the Sydney Royal Chamber Orchestra. A permanent position with colleagues and holidays and a schedule. Life as a freelance musician was flexible and fun, but it was so cobbled together, so fragmented and bitsy, with weddings and corporate gigs and teaching lessons and subbing and whatever else she could take. Now that the girls were settled in school and day care, she wanted to get her career back on track.

She already knew everyone in the string section of the SRCO because she often played for the orchestra casually. ("So you shouldn't have any trouble getting this job then, right? Because you're already *doing* it!" her mother had said last night, cheerfully oblivious to the fierce competitiveness of Clementine's world. Clementine's two older brothers were both working overseas, as engineers. Ever since university, their careers had moved forward in a logical, linear fashion. They never wailed, "I just feel like I can't engineer today!")

Her closest friends in the orchestra, Ainsley and Hu, a married cellist and double bassist, who would be part of the panel sitting behind the screen deciding her fate, were being particularly encouraging. Rationally, Clementine knew she had a shot. It was only her debilitating audition phobia that prevented her making her perfect life a reality. Her terror of the terror.

"Preparation is the solution," Sam had told her last night, as if this were groundbreaking advice. "Visualization. You need to visualize yourself winning your audition."

It was disloyal of her to think that one didn't "win" an orchestral audition and preparing for one was not in the same league as, say, preparing a PowerPoint presentation about sales and marketing plans for a new anti-dandruff shampoo, as Sam's last job had required him to do. Maybe it was the same. She didn't know. She couldn't imagine what people actually did in office jobs, sitting at their computers all day long. Sam was peppy right now, he was leaving for work each day looking very *chipper*, because he'd just gotten a new job as marketing director for a bigger, "more dynamic" company that made energy drinks. There were lots of twentysomethings at his new office. Sometimes she could hear their drawling speech inflections creeping into his voice. He was still in the honeymoon stage. Yesterday he'd said something about the "forward-thinking corporate culture," and he'd said it *non-ironically*. He'd only started a week ago. She'd give him a grace period before she started teasing him about it.

"Can I go play on the iPad?" said Holly from behind the sheet.

"Shh, your mother is auditioning," said Sam.

"Can I have something to eat then?" said Holly, and then, outraged, "Ru*by*!"

"Ruby, please stop licking your sister," sighed Sam.

Clementine looked up and tried not to think about how the sheet was attached to the ceiling. He wouldn't have stuck thumbtacks in their original decorative ceiling, would he? No. He was the sensible one. She picked up her bow and positioned her cello.

The excerpts were on her music stand. There had been no real surprises when she'd gone through them yesterday. The Brahms would be fine. The Beethoven, okay, as long as she phrased the opening convincingly. *Don Juan*, of course, her nemesis, but she just needed to put the time in. She'd been happy to see the Mahler: fifth movement of Symphony No. 7. Maybe she'd play Sam the Mahler now, keep him happy and make him think this was helping.

As she tuned, she heard Marianne's German-accented voice in her head giving her audition advice: "First impressions count! Even when you are tuning! You must tune quickly, quietly and calmly." She felt a sudden fresh wave of grief for her old music teacher, even though it had been ten years since she died.

She remembered a time when she'd started to panic because she'd felt she was taking an inordinately long time to tune and she'd thought she could sense the impatience emanating from the other side of the screen. It was in Perth, and she'd had to carry her perfectly tuned cello across a quadrangle in the most extraordinarily searing heat and into a frosty concert hall.

All auditions had a nightmarish quality to them but that one had been particularly traumatic. The monitor had asked her to take off her shoes before she went on, so that her high heels couldn't be heard clicking across the stage and give away her gender. He'd also suggested she try to avoid coughing or clearing her throat, as that too could give away her gender. He was kind of obsessed with it. As she'd walked onstage, one of her stockinged feet had slipped on the stage (black stockings! On a 103-degree day!) and she'd shrieked in a very gender-specific way. By the time she'd finally tuned the cello, she was a mess. All she could think about as she quivered and sweated and shivered was how much she'd wasted on flights and accommodation for an audition she wouldn't get.

My God, she hated auditions. If she got this job, she never, ever wanted to audition again.

"Ruby! Come back! Don't touch!"

The bedsheet suddenly fell from the ceiling to reveal Sam sitting on the couch with Holly on his lap and Ruby sitting on the floor, looking both guilty and thrilled at what she'd achieved, the sheet pooled around her.

"Whisk did it," said Ruby.

"Whisk did not do it!" said Holly. "*You* did it, Ruby!"

"Okay, okay," said Sam. "Relax." He gave Clementine a wry shrug. "I got this idea in my head that we'd do a mock audition every Sunday morning after breakfast. I thought it would just be fun and maybe even . . . helpful, but it was probably a bit lame, sorry."

Holly climbed off Sam's lap and went and pulled the sheet over her head. Ruby climbed under with her and they whispered to each other.

"It wasn't lame," said Clementine. She thought of her ex-boyfriend Dean, a double bass player who was now playing with the New York Philharmonic. She remembered practicing for him and how he'd cry *"Ne-ext!"* and point to the door to indicate her playing wasn't up to scratch, and how she'd burst into tears. "Fuck, this self-doubt of yours is a bore," Dean would yawn. Fuck, you were a pretentious twat, Dean, and you weren't even that good, buddy.

"I'll take the girls out for the morning so you can practice," said Sam.

"Thank you," said Clementine.

"You don't need to thank me," said Sam. "You don't need to feel grateful. Seriously. Get that grateful look off your face."

She made her face exaggeratedly blank, and Sam laughed, but she did feel grateful, and that was the problem because she knew it was the first step in a convoluted journey that ended in resentment, irrational but heartfelt resentment, and maybe Sam intuited this and that's why he was preempting her gratitude. He'd been here before. He knew how the audition was going to affect their lives for the next ten weeks as she slowly lost her mind from nerves and the strain of trying to scrounge precious practice time from an already jam-packed life. No matter how much time poor Sam gave her, it would never be quite enough, because what she actually needed was for him and the kids to just temporarily not exist. She needed to slip into another dimension where she was a single, childless person. Just between now and the audition. She needed to go to a mountain chalet (somewhere with good acoustics) and live and breathe nothing but music. Go for walks. Meditate. Eat well. Do all those positive-visualization exercises young musicians did these days. She had an awful suspicion that if she were to do this in reality, she might not even miss Sam and the children that much, or if she did miss them, it would be quite bearable.

"I know I'm not much fun when I've got an audition coming up," said Clementine.

"What are you talking about? You're adorable when you've got an audition coming up," said Sam.

She pretended to punch him in the stomach. "Shut up."

He caught her wrist and pulled her to him in a big bear hug. "We'll work it out," he said. She breathed in his scent. He'd washed himself with the girls' No More Tears baby shampoo again. His chest hair was as soft and fluffy as a baby chick. "We'll get there."

She loved the fact that he said "we." He always did this. Even when he was working on some renovation project around the house, a project where she was contributing absolutely nothing except staying out of the way, he'd survey his work, wipe his dusty, sweaty face and say, "We're getting there."

Unselfishness came naturally to him. She kind of had to fake it.

"You're a good man, Samuel," said Clementine. It was a line from some TV show they'd watched years ago and it had become her way of saying, Thank you and I love you.

"I am a very good man," agreed Sam, releasing her. "A fine man. Possibly a great man." He watched the little Holly and Ruby shapes move about under the sheet. "Have you seen Holly and Ruby?" he said loudly. "Because I thought they were right here, but now they seem to have disappeared."

"I don't know. Where *could* they be?" said Clementine.

"We're here!" trilled Ruby.

"Shh!" Holly took games like this very seriously.

"Hey, what time is this afternoon tea at Erika's place?" said Sam. "Maybe we should cancel." He looked hopeful. "Give you a full day of practice?"

"We can't cancel," said Clementine. "Erika and Oliver want to, how did she put it? She wants to *discuss something*."

Sam winced. "That sounds ominous. They didn't use the words *investment opportunity*, did they? Remember when Lauren and David asked us over for dinner and it was all a ploy to try to get us into their bloody environmentally friendly washcloth business or whatever the hell it was?"

"If Erika and Oliver offered us an investment opportunity, we'd *take* it," said Clementine. "We'd definitely take it."

"Good point," said Sam. He frowned. "I bet they want us to join them on a 'fun run.'" He put Holly's air quotes on the words "fun run." "For a worthy charity. So we'll feel obliged."

"We'd slow them down too much," said Clementine.

"Yeah, we would, or you would. My natural athletic ability would get me through." Sam frowned again and scratched his cheek thoughtfully. "Oh jeez, what if they want us to go *camping*? They'll say it's good for the children. Get them outdoors."

Erika and Oliver were childless by choice, but although they had no interest in having children of their own, they took an active, almost proprietary interest in Holly and Ruby. It was almost as if it were good for them, as if it were part of a systematic approach they were taking to being well-rounded, self-actualized people: We exercise regularly; we go to the theater; we read the right novels, not just the Man Booker short list but the Man Booker *long* list; we see the right exhibitions; and we take a real interest in international politics, social issues and our friends' cute children.

That was unfair. Probably monstrously unfair. Their interest in the children wasn't just for show, and Clementine knew that the reasons they kept their lives in such tight, tidy control had nothing to do with competitiveness.

"Maybe they want to set up trust funds for the girls," said Sam. He considered this, shrugged. "I could live with that. I'm man enough."

"They're not *that* kind of wealthy," laughed Clementine.

"You don't think one of them has some terribly rare genetic disease, do you?" said Sam. "Imagine how bad I'll feel then." He winced. "Oliver looked kind of skinny the last time we saw them."

"The marathon running makes them skinny. I'm sure whatever it is, it will be fine," said Clementine distractedly, although she did feel a mild sense of unease about today, but that was probably just the audition, already tainting everything, creating a permanent undertone of low-level fear for the next ten weeks. There was nothing to be frightened about. It was just afternoon tea on a beautiful sunny day.

6

A kid in a shiny wet black raincoat stood poised on the edge of the ferry, a coil of thick heavy rope looped over one arm. Sam watched him from his seat by the ferry window. The kid squinted through the torrential rain to see the wharf emerging in the gray mist. His young, unlined face was covered with raindrops. The ferry rolled and pitched. Cold, salty air filled Sam's nostrils. The boy lifted the noose at the end of the rope and held it high like a cattle wrangler astride a horse. He threw it, snagging the bollard first try. Then he leaped from the ferry to the wharf and pulled tight, as though he were dragging the ferry to him.

The kid looked like he was no more than fifteen, and yet there he was effortlessly snaring a ferry wharf. He made some sort of signal to the ferry captain and called out, "Circular Quay!" to the waiting passengers with their umbrellas and raincoats, and then he wrenched the gangway from the ferry to the wharf with a serious metal *bang clang*. The passengers hurried across it onto the ferry, shoulders hunched and huddled against the rain, while the boy stood tall and fearless.

See, now, that was a good honest job. Wrangling wharves. Herding office workers on and off ferries. He was only a kid, but he looked like a man, standing there in the rain. He made Sam feel soft and doughy, sitting docilely in his damp wool trousers, his pin-striped shirt. The kid probably hated the idea of an office job. He'd say, "No way, I'd feel like a trapped rat."

A rat pushing a lever to get cheese. Like those old experiments. Yesterday Sam had sat at his desk like a rat using his little finger to push the letter *p* on his keyboard and his thumb to push the space bar over and over, with a space in between each *p*, until his screen was filled with nothing but *p p p p p p p p*. He did that for maybe twenty minutes. Maybe even half an hour. He wasn't sure. That had been his biggest achievement at work yesterday. A screen filled with the letter *p*.

He watched the group of passengers streaming onto the ferry shaking their umbrellas, their faces grumpy and over it before the day had even begun.

The kid probably didn't realize that a white-collar worker could spend a whole day in his office doing nothing, literally sweet fuck-all, and still get paid for it. Sam felt himself break out in a cold sweat at the thought of how little he was achieving at work. He had to get something *done* today. This couldn't go on much longer. He was going to lose his job if he didn't find a way to focus his mind. He was still in his trial period. They could sack him without too much paperwork or stress. At the moment, he was getting away with it because of his team. He had four tech-savvy, everything-savvy twentysomethings reporting directly to him. They were all smarter than him. He wasn't managing them, they were managing themselves, but that couldn't go on forever.

If Sam had had a blue-collar job, he would have lost it weeks ago. He thought of his dad. Stan the Man couldn't go out to a plumbing job and just sit there staring into space, could he? He couldn't mindlessly bang a wrench against a pipe for twenty minutes. If Sam had been a plumber, then he would have been forced to focus and his mind wouldn't be slowly unraveling, or whatever the hell was happening to him. Wasn't there a great-aunt somebody or other on his dad's side who'd had a (hushed voice) "nervous breakdown"? Maybe he was having one of those. His nerves were disintegrating, crumbling to dust like porous sandstone.

The ferry lurched off, back across the harbor to deliver everyone to their jobs, and as Sam looked at his fellow passengers, it occurred to him that he'd never really belonged. He wasn't one of these corporate people. He'd always liked his work well enough, it was a relatively stimulating way to pay the bills, but there been those times, as he stood at the front of the room with his PowerPoint presentation for example, when he'd feel, just for a moment, like it was all an act, an elaborate act, like he was just pretending he was the "businessman" his mother had always dreamed he would be. Not a doctor or a lawyer, but a *businessman.* Joy had no idea what a businessman actually did all day, except that he wore a tie, not overalls, and his fingernails were clean, and that if Sam got good marks at school, which he had, then the glamorous life of business would be his reward. He could have insisted he do a trade like his father and brothers—his mother wasn't domineering, just enthusiastic—but instead his teenage self had dopily, sleepily gone along with it, without ever really considering what he actually wanted, what would give him satisfaction, and now here he was, stuck in the wrong life, a middlingly good middle manager, pretending to be passionate about marketing energy drinks.

So what? Suck it up. What percentage of people on this ferry felt passionate about their jobs? It wasn't a God-given right that you would love your job. People said to Clementine all the time: "You're so lucky to do what you love." She wasn't grateful enough for that privilege. Sometimes she'd answer, "Yes, but I've always got the fear of wondering if I'm good enough." Her neuroticism about her music had always baffled and bugged him—just play the damned thing—but now for the first time he understood what she meant when she said, "I just feel like I can't play today." He saw again his computer screen filled with the letter p and felt the panic rise. He couldn't afford to lose his job, not with their mortgage. You have a family. A family to protect. Be a man. Pull yourself together. You had it all and you risked it all for what? For nothing. He looked out the window as the ferry dipped into a swell of green-gray water laced with white froth and he heard himself make a sound: a mortifying high-pitched squeak of distress, like a little girl. He coughed, so people would think he'd just been clearing his throat.

He found himself remembering the morning of the barbecue. It was like remembering someone else, a friend, or someone he'd seen playing the role of a father in a movie. Surely it had been somebody else, not him, strolling about, *strutting* about his sunlit house, so sure of himself and his place in the world. What happened that morning? Croissants for breakfast. He'd tried to set up the mock audition for Clementine. It hadn't really worked.

What happened next? He had meant to take the girls out so Clementine could practice. They couldn't find Ruby's shoe with the flashing sole. Did they *ever* find that damned shoe?

If someone had asked him that morning about how he felt about his life, he would have said he was happy. Pleased about the new job. Actually kind of psyched about the new job. He was all smug about how he'd negotiated flexible hours so he could continue being a hands-on dad, the dad his own father never got to be, and didn't he just lap up all the praise he got for being such an involved father, and laugh sympathetically, but enjoyably, over the fact that Clementine never got any praise for being an involved mother?

He might have had doubts about his role in the corporate world but he'd never had doubts about his role as a father. Clementine always said that she could tell when Sam was talking to his dad on the phone because his voice went down a notch. He knew he was more likely to tell his dad about some *manly* DIY project he'd completed around the house than a promotion he'd gotten at work, but he didn't care about the bemused expression his dad got when Clementine said what a great job Sam did doing Holly's hair for ballet (better than her) or when he took Ruby off to change or bathe her. Sam was 100 percent secure in his role as a husband and a father. He thought his own father didn't know what he'd missed.

If someone had asked him about his dreams on the morning of the barbecue, he would have said that he didn't want for much, but he wouldn't mind a lower mortgage, a tidier house, another baby—ideally a son, but he'd take another girl no problem at all—a big motherfucking boat if it were up for grabs, and more sex. He would have laughed about the sex. Or smiled at least. A rueful smile.

Maybe the smile would have been exactly halfway between rueful and bitter.

He found he was smiling bitterly now, and a woman sitting across the aisle from him caught his eye and looked away fast. Sam stopped smiling and watched his hands resting on his knees clench into fists. He made himself unclench them. Look normal.

He picked up a newspaper someone had left behind on the seat next to him. It was yesterday's issue. ENOUGH ALREADY was the headline above an arty-looking picture taken through a rain-spattered window of Sydney's rainy skyline. Sam tried to read the article. Warragamba Dam was expected to spill at any moment. Flash floods across the state. The sentences started jumping around, the way they did now. Maybe he needed his eyes checked. He could no longer read for a sustained period of time before he felt twitchy and anxious. He would look up in sudden terror as if he'd missed something important, as if he'd fallen asleep.

He looked up and caught the eye of the woman again.

For fuck's sake, I'm not trying to look at you. I'm not trying to pick you up. I love my wife.

Did he still love his wife?

He saw Tiffany's face in that gold-lit backyard. *Come on, Muscles.* That smile like a caress. He turned his head toward his ferry window, as if he were facing away from Tiffany's physical presence, not just the thought of her, and looked instead at the bays and inlets of Sydney Harbour under a low gray forbidding sky. Everything had an apocalyptic feel to it.

There were things he could say to Clementine. Accusations he wanted to hurl, except he knew as soon as they left his mouth he'd want to snatch them right back, because he deserved far worse. Yet still the accusations hovered, not on the tip of his tongue but at the back of his throat, lodged there, like an undigested lump of food, so he sometimes felt he couldn't swallow properly.

Today she was doing another one of those senseless community talks she now did. At some library way out in the distant suburbs. Surely nobody would turn up in this weather. Why did she do it? She was turning down gigs to do this unpaid work. It was incomprehensible to Sam. How could she *choose* to relive that day when Sam spent his days trying so hard to stop the flashes of shameful memory flickering over and over in his head?

"Excuse me?"

Sam jumped. His right arm flew out violently as if to catch something falling. He shouted, "Where?"

A woman in a beige raincoat stood in the aisle, stared at him with wide Bambi eyes, both her hands crossed protectively over her chest. "I'm so sorry. I didn't mean to scare you."

Sam felt pure, unadulterated rage. He imagined leaping at her, putting his hands around her throat, shaking her like a rag doll.

"I just wondered if that was yours? If you were finished with it?" She nodded her head at the newspaper.

"Sorry," said Sam hoarsely. "I was just deep in thought." He handed her the paper. It shook in his hand. "It's not mine. There you go."

"Thank you. So sorry about that," said the woman again.

"No, no." She backed away. She thought he was crazy. He *was* crazy. As the days went by he was getting crazier and crazier.

Sam waited for his heart to slow.

He turned his head to face the window again. He saw the Overseas Passenger Terminal and remembered that he and Clementine were meant to be going to a restaurant there tonight. A fancy, overpriced restaurant. He didn't want to go. He had nothing to say to her.

The thought crossed his mind that they should break up. Not break up, *separate*. This is a marriage, buddy, you don't just break up like boyfriend and girlfriend, you separate. What a load of shit. He and Clementine weren't going to separate. They were fine. And yet there was something strangely appealing about that word: "separate." It felt like a solution. If he could just separate himself, detach himself, remove himself, then he could get relief. Like an amputation.

He stood suddenly. He held on to the backs of seats to balance himself as the ferry rocked, and went to stand outside on the deserted deck. The cold rainy air slapped his face like an angry woman, and the kid in the raincoat looked at him with disinterest, and then his gaze slid slowly away, as if Sam were just another feature of the dull, gray landscape.

Sam clung on to the slippery railing that ran along the edge of the ferry. He didn't want to be here, he didn't want to be at home. He didn't want to be anywhere, except back in time, in that ludicrous backyard, at that moment in the hazy twilight, the fairy lights twinkling in his peripheral vision when that *Tiffany*, a woman who meant nothing to him, nothing at all, was laughing with him, and he wasn't looking at the outrageous Jessica Rabbit curves of her body, he was not looking, but he was aware of them, he was very aware of them. "Come on, Muscles," she'd said.

Right there. That's where he needed to press Pause.

All he needed was the next five minutes after that. Just one more chance. If he could just have one more chance, he'd act like the man he'd always believed himself to be.

7

The Day of the Barbecue

L et's just forget it," said Clementine.

It was nearly one o'clock, they were expected at Erika's house for afternoon tea at three and Sam and the girls still hadn't managed to actually leave the house to give her the promised practice time. It wasn't going to happen.

"No," said Sam. "I will not be defeated by one small shoe."

One of Ruby's brand-new, remarkably expensive, flashing-soled runners had gone missing and due to a recent growth spurt, those were the only shoes that fit her at the moment.

"What's that poem?" said Clementine. " 'For want of a nail the shoe was lost / For want of a shoe the horse was lost' . . . and then something, until the kingdom is lost."

"What?" grunted Sam. He lay flat on his stomach on the floor, looking under the couch for the shoe.

"For want of a shoe my audition was lost," murmured Clementine as she pulled off cushions from the same couch to reveal crumbs, coins, pencils, hair clips, a sports bra and no shoe.

"*What?*" said Sam again. He stretched out his arm. "I think I see it!" He pulled out a dust-covered sock.

"That's a *sock*," said Holly.

Sam sneezed. "Yes, I know it's a sock." He sat back on his haunches, massaging his shoulder. "We spend half our lives trying to *locate possessions*. We need better systems. Procedures. There must be an app for this. A 'where's our stuff?' app."

"Shoe! Where are you! Shoe!" called out Ruby. She walked about lopsidedly, wearing one shoe, stamping it occasionally to make the colored lights flash.

"Shoes do not have ears, Ruby," said Holly contemptuously.

"Erika says we need a shoe rack by the door." Clementine replaced the cushions on top of all the detritus. "She says we should train the children to put their shoes there as soon as they come in."

"She's right," said Sam. "That woman is always right."

For someone who didn't want children, Erika had a wealth of parenting expertise she felt obliged to share. You couldn't say, "How would you know?" because she always cited her sources. "I read an article in *Psychology Today*," she would begin.

"She sounds like one of those toxic friends," Clementine's friend Ainsley had once said. "You should cull her."

"She's not toxic," Clementine had said. "Don't you have friends who annoy you?" She thought everyone had friends who felt like obligations. There was a particular expression her mother got when she picked up the phone, a stoic "here we go" look, which meant her friend Lois was calling.

"Not the way that chick bugs you," said Ainsley.

Clementine could never, would never, *cull* Erika. She was Holly's godmother. The moment, if there had ever been such a moment, where she could have ended their friendship was long gone. You couldn't do that to a person. Were there even words for it? Erika would be devastated.

Anyway, over recent years, since Erika had met and married the lovely, serious Oliver, their friendship had become much more manageable. Although Clementine had cringed at Ainsley's use of the word, "toxic" was actually an accurate description of the feelings Clementine had so often felt in Erika's presence: the intense aggravation she had to work so hard to resist and conceal, the disappointment with herself, because Erika wasn't evil or cruel or stupid, she was simply annoying, and Clementine's response to her annoyingness was so completely disproportionate, it embarrassed and confounded her. Erika loved Clementine. She'd do anything for her. So why did she inflame Clementine so? It was like she was allergic to her. She'd learned over the years to limit the time they spent together. Like today, for example, when Erika had suggested lunch, Clementine had automatically said, "Let's make it afternoon tea." Shorter. Less time to lose your mind.

"Please can I have a cracker, Daddy?" said Holly.

"No," said Sam. "Help look for your sister's shoe."

"You girls make sure you say please and thank you to Erika and Oliver at afternoon tea today, won't you?" said Clementine to the girls as she tried behind the curtains for the missing shoe. "In a nice, big loud voice?"

Holly was outraged. "I *do* say please and thank you! I just *said* please to Daddy."

"I know," said Clementine. "That's what made me think of it. I thought, 'What good manners!'"

If Holly or Ruby were ever going to forget to say please or thank you, it would be with Erika, who had a habit of pointedly reminding the girls of their manners in a way that Clementine found to be kind of unmannerly. "Did I hear a thank you?" Erika would say the moment she handed over a glass of water, cupping her hand around her ear, and Holly would answer, "No, you didn't," which came across as precocious, even though she was just being her literal self.

Holly took off her shoes, climbed on the couch, balanced on her socks on the side with her arms held out wide like a skydiver and then let herself fall, face-first, onto the cushions.

"Don't do that, Holly," said Sam. "I've told you before. You could hurt yourself."

"Mummy lets me do it," pouted Holly.

"Well, she shouldn't," said Sam. He shot Clementine a look. "You could break your neck. You could hurt yourself very, *very* badly."

"Put your shoes back on, Holly," said Clementine. "Before they get lost too." Sometimes she wondered how Sam thought she managed to keep the children alive when he wasn't there to point out all the perilous hazards. She let Holly do that face-first dive off the side of the couch all the time when he was at work. Mostly the girls were good at remembering the different rules that applied when Daddy was at home, not that those different sets of rules were ever actually acknowledged out loud. It was just an unspoken way of keeping the peace. She suspected different rules about vegetables and teeth-cleaning applied when Mummy wasn't home.

Holly got down off the couch and slumped back. "I'm bored. *Why* can't I have a cracker? I'm *starving.*"

"Please don't whine," said Clementine.

"But I'm so hungry," said Holly, while Ruby wandered off into the hallway hollering "SHOE! WHERE ARE YOU, MY DARLING SHOE?"

"I actually really do need a cracker. Just *one* cracker," said Holly.

"Quiet!" shouted Clementine and Sam simultaneously.

"You are both so mean!" Holly turned on her heel to leave the room and kicked her toe on the leg of the couch, which Sam had dragged sideways looking for the shoe. She screamed in frustration.

"Oh dear." Clementine automatically bent down to hug her, forgetting that Holly always needed a minute to process her rage at the universe before she accepted comfort. Holly threw back her head and gave Clementine a painful blow on the chin.

"Ow!" Clementine grabbed her chin. "*Holly!*"

"Bloody hell," said Sam. He stomped out of the room.

Now Holly wanted a cuddle. She launched herself into Clementine's arms, and Clementine hugged her, even though she wanted to shake her, because her chin really hurt.

She murmured sympathetic words of comfort and rocked Holly back and forth while she stared longingly at her cello, sitting quiet and dignified up against her pretend audition chair. No one warned you that having children reduced you right down to some smaller, rudimentary, primitive version of yourself, where your talents and your education and your achievements meant nothing.

Clementine remembered when Erika, at the age of sixteen, had casually mentioned that she never wanted children, and Clementine had felt strangely put out by this, and it had taken her a while to work out the reasons for her aggravation (all her life, there had always been so many varied, complex reasons why Erika aggravated her) and she'd eventually realized it was because *she wished she'd thought of saying it first.* Clementine was meant to be the crazy, creative, bohemian one. Erika was the conservative one. The rule follower. The designated driver. Erika dreamed of getting enough marks to do a Bachelor of Business degree with a double major in accounting and finance. Erika dreamed of home ownership and a stock portfolio and a job at one of the big six accounting firms with a fast track to partnership. Clementine's dream was to study at the Conservatorium of Music, to play extraordinary music and experience extraordinary *passion* and then, sure, to settle down one day, and have babies with a nice man, because didn't everyone want that? Babies were cute. It had seemed to indicate a failure of the imagination that it had never occurred to Clementine that you could choose not to have children.

But that was the thing with Erika. She refused to be typecast. When they were seventeen, Erika had gone through a Goth stage. *Erika*, of all people. She'd dyed her hair black, worn black nail polish, black lipstick, studded wristbands and platform boots. "What?" she'd said defensively, the first time Clementine saw her new look. Erika's rock-star style got them into the cool clubs, where she stood at the back scowling, drinking mineral water and looking like she was thinking dark Gothic thoughts when she was probably just thinking about her homework, while Clementine got drunk and danced and kissed inappropriate boys and then cried all the way home, because, you know, *life*.

Now Erika wore clothes you didn't notice or remember: plain, sensible, comfortable clothes. She had her job at one of the big accounting firms (now one of the big four, not the big six) and her neat, probably mortgage-free three-bedroom house not far from where they both grew up. And now, of course, Clementine didn't regret her decision to have children. She loved them senseless, of course she did, it was just that sometimes she regretted their timing. It would have made sense to put off kids until they'd paid off more of the house, until her career was better established.

Sam wanted a third child, which was ludicrous, impossible. She kept changing the subject every time he brought it up. A third child would be like sliding down a snake in a game of Snakes and Ladders. He couldn't be serious. She was hoping that eventually he'd see sense.

Sam reappeared at the doorway and held out a packet of crackers toward Holly. Holly jumped off Clementine's knee, magically cured, at the same time as Clementine's phone, which was sitting on one of the bookshelves, began to ring.

"It's Erika," said Clementine to Sam as she picked it up.

"Maybe she's canceling," said Sam hopefully.

"She never cancels," said Clementine. She put the phone to her ear. "Hi, Erika."

"It's Erika," said Erika in that querulous way, as if Clementine had already let her down.

"I know," said Clementine. "This newfangled technology is amazing, it—"

"Yes, very funny," interrupted Erika. "Look. About today. I was on my way back from the shops and I ran into Vid. You remember Vid, from next door?"

"Of course I do. How could I forget Vid from next door," said Clementine. "The big electrician. Like Tony Soprano. We love Vid from next door." Erika sometimes brought out this kind of frivolity in Clementine. "Married to the smoking-hot Tiffany." She drew out the word "Tiff-an-y." "Sam just loves Tiffany from next door."

She looked over at Sam to see if he recognized the name. Sam used his hands to indicate Tiffany's spectacularly memorable figure, and Clementine gave him a thumbs-up. They had met Erika's neighbors just once, at an awkward drinks party at Erika's place last Christmas. They were maybe a decade older than Clementine and Sam but they seemed younger. They'd saved the night as far as Sam and Clementine were concerned.

"Well, anyway," said Erika. "I told Vid you were coming over today and he invited us all over for a barbecue. They've got a daughter, Dakota, who is about ten, and he seemed to think she'd like to play with your girls."

"Sounds great," said Clementine, aware of spirits lifting, even soaring. She moved to the window and studied the brilliant blue sky. The day suddenly felt festive. A barbecue. No need to cook dinner tonight. She'd take along that bottle of champagne Ainsley had given her. She'd find time to practice tomorrow. She quite liked this aspect of her personality: the way her mood could change from melancholy to euphoric because of a breeze or a flavor or a beautiful chord progression. It meant she never had to feel too down about feeling down. "Man, you're a strange girl, it's like you're on drugs," her brother Brian once said to her. She always remembered that comment. It made her feel proud. Yeah, I'm so *crazy*. Although probably that was evidence of her lack of craziness. Truly crazy people were too busy being crazy to think about it.

"Vid sort of railroaded me into this barbecue," said Erika defensively, and oddly, because Clementine had never known Erika to be railroaded into anything.

"We don't mind," said Clementine. "We liked them. It will be fun." She smiled as she watched Holly waltz around the room with a cracker held ecstatically high like a trophy. Holly had inherited Clementine's temperament, which was fine except for when their moods didn't synchronize. Ruby was more like Sam, pragmatic and patient. Yesterday Clementine had walked into their bedroom to find Ruby sitting on the floor next to Holly, gently patting her shoulder while Holly lay flat on her stomach prostrate with grief because her drawing of a panda bear *didn't look like a panda bear*. "Twy again!" Ruby said with a perplexed expression on her face just like Sam's, an expression that said: "Why make life so hard for yourself?"

"Okay, well, good. Fun, yes," said Erika. She sounded disappointed, as if she hadn't actually planned for the day to be *fun*. "It's just that—Oliver is kind of cranky with me for accepting Vid's invitation because, ah, as I mentioned, we'd love to discuss, this, ah, proposal we have, and he thinks we won't have the chance now. I was thinking maybe after the barbecue you could come back to our place for coffee. If there is time."

"Of course," said Clementine. "Or even beforehand if you like. Whichever. It's all very mysterious, Erika. Can you give me a hint?"

"Oh, well, no, not really." Now she sounded almost agitated.

"Fine then," soothed Clementine. "We'll talk about this mysterious whatever-it-is after the barbecue."

"Or before," said Erika. "You just said—"

"Or before," agreed Clementine just as Ruby toddled into the room carrying a tiny plastic pink gumboot in each hand and looking pleased with herself. "Oh clever *girl*, Ruby, you can wear your gumboots! That's a great idea."

"I beg your pardon?" said Erika, who could never bear it when Clementine spoke to her kids when she was on the phone to her. She seemed to think it was a breach of etiquette.

"Nothing. Sure. Let's talk *before* the barbecue."

"See you then," said Erika brusquely, and she hung up in that infuriatingly abrupt way of hers, as if Clementine were her lowly intern.

It didn't matter. A barbecue with Erika's charming neighbors on this sunny winter's day would be fun. What could be nicer?

8

The rain eased slightly, although of course it didn't stop, it would freaking well never stop, so Tiffany took the opportunity to grab an umbrella and drag their recycling bin, rattling indiscreetly with wine and beer bottles from the previous night, down her driveway.

She was thinking about Dakota and the smile she'd given Tiffany when she'd dropped her off at school this morning: a cool, *polite* smile, as if Tiffany were someone else's mother.

There was something going on with Dakota. It was subtle, this thing. It might be nothing, or it might be something. It wasn't that she was misbehaving. Not at all. But there was something spookily distant about her. It was like she was encased in an invisible glass bubble.

For example, this morning at breakfast Dakota had sat straight-backed at the table, chewing daintily on her toast, her eyes flat and unreadable. "Yes, please. No, thank you." Why was she being so polite? It was creepy! It was like they had a well-mannered foreign exchange student boarding with them. Eating disorder? But she was still eating, although not with much enthusiasm.

Tiffany couldn't get to the bottom of it, no matter how hard she tried or what questions she asked.

"I'm fine," Dakota kept saying in her mechanical new way.

"She's fine, leave the kid alone!" Vid said. It made Tiffany want to scream. Dakota was not fine. She was ten years old. A ten-year-old shouldn't smile politely at her mother.

Tiffany was determined to smash right through this freaking glass bubble thing Dakota had going on. Even if she was imagining it.

She was nearly out on the street when she saw Oliver bringing out his recycling bin too, although it wasn't rattling as much as hers.

"Morning, Oliver!" she called out. "How are you? Isn't this rain terrible!"

Shit. Every time she saw her neighbors now, ever since the barbecue, her stomach muscles tensed, as if she were doing a Pilates crunch.

She'd always liked Oliver. He was so straightforward and polite; a bit of a dork, with his black hair and spectacles, like a grown-up Harry Potter. He had a very small head, she couldn't help but notice. There was nothing to be done about his pea-head, but Tiffany should tell Erika to buy Oliver some of those vintage, black-rimmed glasses; transform her husband into a cute hipster in just one move. (Vid had a massive head. You couldn't get a baseball cap to fit him. Not that he'd ever wear a baseball cap.)

"How are you, Tiffany?" called back Oliver. He neatly pulled his bin to a noiseless stop, while Tiffany grunted as she hauled hers over the curb. "Need a hand?"

"No, no, I've got it. Aren't you nice to offer! Don't hear Vid offering! *Oomph.* That's my workout done for the day!" (It wasn't. She was going to the gym later.) "What are you doing home at this hour? Taking a sickie?"

She walked over to within chatting distance and noted Oliver's terrified glance at her cleavage. He fixed his eyes desperately on her forehead as if she were a test. Yeah, buddy, I'm a test, but you pass every time.

"I am, actually. Getting over a bit of a flu thing." Oliver put his fist over his mouth and coughed.

"How's Erika?" said Tiffany. "I haven't seen her much lately."

"She's fine," said Oliver shortly, as if that were personal.

Jeez Louise, ever since the barbecue, every conversation with Erika and Oliver felt as strained and difficult as if she were talking to an ex-boyfriend straight after a breakup. A breakup that was her fault. A breakup where she'd cheated.

"And, um, so we haven't seen you much since—" she said to Oliver. "How *are* Clementine and Sam?"

Oliver coughed. "They're okay," he said. He frowned off into the distance over Tiffany's shoulder.

"And how is—?"

"You know, it seems like a while since Harry has had his bin out," interrupted Oliver. Tiffany turned and looked at the empty spot on the road in front of Harry's house. Or Mr. Spitty's house, as Dakota called him, because of his habit of spitting with disgust at all the things that disgusted him, like *Dakota*. Sometimes he looked at Tiffany's beautiful daughter and spat, as if her very existence offended him.

"He doesn't put it out every week," said Tiffany. "I don't think he creates a lot of rubbish."

"Yeah, I know," said Oliver. "But it feels like it's been weeks since I've seen him. I wonder if I should go bang on his door."

Tiffany turned back to look at Oliver. "He'll probably just yell abuse at you."

"He probably will," agreed Oliver ruefully. He really was a nice guy. "It's just that it feels like it's been a long time between abusive tirades."

Tiffany looked at Harry's dilapidated, two-story, redbrick Federation house. It was always kind of depressing to look at: the paint peeling off the window frames, the faded red roof tiles in need of repair. Gardeners came once a month to mow the lawns and trim the hedges, so it wasn't like it was derelict, but ever since they'd moved here, and Harry came over to greet them to the neighborhood with a demand that they do something about their oak tree, it had been a sad, lonely-looking old house.

"When did I see him last?" said Tiffany. She searched her mind for unpleasant incidents. A few times Harry had stood in his front yard and yelled at Dakota, and made her cry, and that had made Tiffany lose her temper and yell back at Harry in a way that made her feel ashamed afterwards because he was an old man, and probably had dementia, so she should have shown more respect and self-control. What was the last thing one of them had done wrong to upset Harry?

Then she remembered.

"You're right," she said slowly to Oliver, her eyes on the house. "It has been a while since I saw him."

In fact, she knew exactly when she'd seen Harry last. It was the morning of the barbecue. That goddamned nightmare of a barbecue she'd never wanted to host in the first place.

9

The Day of the Barbecue

It was quiet. It was always especially quiet the moment directly after Vid left the room. It was like the moment after a band stopped playing when the silence roared in your ears. Tiffany could hear the tick of the clock. She never heard the clock ticking when Vid was in the room.

Tiffany sat at the kitchen table catching up on email on her laptop and eating Vegemite on toast. Vid had gone down the driveway to collect the paper, muttering about how he had to hunt for it each day in the garden and he was going to cancel the delivery.

"Read it electronically like the rest of the world," Tiffany always told him, but although Vid was generally enthusiastic about trying new things, he was also extremely loyal, and his loyalty to certain habits and personal rituals, products and people was unshakable.

"Isn't it quiet when Daddy leaves the room?" Tiffany said to Dakota, who lay on her side on the long bay window seat, curled up like a cat in a rectangle of quivering morning sunlight. Barney, their miniature schnauzer, lay next to Dakota, his nose and paws resting on Dakota's arm, his eyes shut so all you could see were his big, bushy eyebrows. Barney was a dog who napped like a cat.

Dakota was reading, of course. She was always reading, disappearing into different worlds where Tiffany couldn't follow. Well, she *could* follow, if she could be bothered to pick up a book, but reading made Tiffany restless. Her legs started to twitch impatiently after one page. TV made her restless too, but at least she could fold laundry or pay bills while she watched. At Dakota's age Tiffany never would have picked up a book for pleasure. She was into makeup and clothes. The other day Tiffany had offered to paint Dakota's nails and Dakota had responded with a kind, vague: "Uh, maybe later, Mum." It was her karma for all the times her own sweet, domestic mother had suggested that Tiffany might like to help her bake something and Tiffany had apparently said, according to family folklore: "Will you pay me?" "You were always so keen to be *compensated*," her mother said.

Well, time is money.

"It's quiet, isn't it?" said Tiffany when Dakota didn't answer.

"What?" said Dakota.

"You mean, pardon?" said Tiffany.

There was a beat. "What?" said Dakota again, and she turned a page.

Tiffany snorted.

She opened a new email. It was from Saint Anastasias, the super-posh private school that Dakota would be attending next year. Tiffany wouldn't be able to follow her daughter into that new world either. Vid's three older daughters from his first marriage, Dakota's three older stepsisters, had all attended Saint Anastasias, which wasn't a great advertisement as far as Tiffany was concerned, but the school did have a stellar reputation (it freaking well ought to have for what it charged) and Vid had wanted to send Dakota from kindergarten. Tiffany thought that was ridiculous, when there was a great little public school just down the road. Year 5 was the compromise.

There was to be an Information Morning in August. Two months away. It was "compulsory" for all students and "both parents" to attend. Compulsory. Tiffany felt her hackles rise at the email's officious tone and quickly closed it. She wasn't going to fit in at this place. She felt a real resistance to attending the Information Morning and even a certain level of nerves. As soon as she registered the feeling as fear she was disgusted with herself. Furious. She snapped the laptop shut, refusing to even think about it. It was Sunday. They had the day free. She had a huge week ahead of her.

"Good book?" she asked Dakota.

"What?" said Dakota. "I mean, pardon?"

Tiffany said, "I love you, Dakota."

Long pause. "What?"

The front door banged. There was a mark on the wall from where Vid threw it open each time he came into the house as if he were making a grand return from an epic journey.

"Where are you, women?" he shouted.

"Where you left us, you peanut!" called back Tiffany.

"I am not a peanut! Why do you keep calling me that? It doesn't even make sense! Now, listen to me, I have news!" He came in swinging his rolled-up paper like a baton. He looked energized. "I just invited the neighbors over for a barbecue. Ran into Erika in the street."

"Vid, Vid, *Vid.*" Tiffany rested her head on her hand. "Why would you do that?"

Erika and Oliver were nice enough, but they were so freaking shy and serious. It was hard work. It was better to invite them over when other people were going to be there so you could pass them on when you got tired of all the seriousness.

"You promised we'd have just one Sunday relaxing," she said.

She had such a busy week ahead of her: a property going to auction on Tuesday night, a fight with a local council at the Land and Environment Court on Wednesday and a painter, a tiler and an electrician (well, Vid) were all waiting on her to make decisions. She needed a break.

"What are you talking about? That's what we're doing! Relaxing on this beautiful day!" protested Vid, looking genuinely puzzled. "What's more relaxing than a barbecue? I'm going to call Drago. Organize a pig. Oh, and their friends are coming. Remember the cellist? Clementine. Clementine and her husband. What was his name?"

"Sam," said Tiffany, perking up. She'd liked Sam. He had that short, broad-chested blond surfer boy look she used to go for before Vid, and he was funny and easygoing. They'd met them just the once when Erika and Oliver had hosted Christmas drinks at their place last year. That had been such a strange night. Vid and Tiffany had never been to a drinks party like it. All these people standing about, talking so quietly, as if they were in a library or church. One woman was drinking *a cup of tea.*

"Where's the food?" Vid kept whispering too loudly to Tiffany while Oliver and Erika seemed to spend an inordinate amount of time worriedly wiping down already clean kitchen countertops with dish towels, as if to make it clear their guests were making a mess but they were on top of it. It had been such a relief when they got introduced to Clementine and Sam. Vid, who loved classical music, had been so excited to learn that Clementine was a cellist, it was almost embarrassing, but then Tiffany and Sam got talking politics and had an enjoyable argument. (He was a bleeding heart but she forgave him that.) "Do you think we could order a pizza?" Sam had whispered at one point, and Vid had roared laughing, although then they all had to stop him from pulling out his mobile phone and actually ordering one. Clementine found a chocolate bar in the bottom of her handbag and surreptitiously divided it up among the four of them while poor Erika and Oliver were busy polishing their countertops. It was like they had all been marooned on a desert island, and had done what they could to survive.

"They've got two little girls," said Vid.

"I remember they said they had little kids," said Tiffany. "Cutesy little names."

"I don't remember their *names,*" said Vid. "Anyway, Dakota can play with them, you know, can't you, Dakota?" He looked hopefully at Dakota.

"Uh, guys, there's someone at the front door," said Dakota without looking up from her book, as Barney, eyes alert, lifted his head from her arm and leaped to the floor, where he ran around in circles, yapping delightedly. Barney liked guests nearly as much as Vid.

Someone was thumping over and over again on the front door, ignoring the doorbell.

"You didn't invite them right this very minute, did you?" said Tiffany. "*Shh,* Barney. Vid, did you?"

Vid was standing at the pantry, pulling out ingredients. "Of course I did not," he said distractedly, although he was perfectly capable of doing that.

Tiffany went to answer the door, Barney zigzagging excitedly in front of her, almost tripping her up, and found Harry, the old man who lived next door, standing on the front porch, glowering at her, as usual, in his normal outfit of old gray suit trousers (from his old job maybe?) and a white business shirt going yellow around the collar. White tufts of hair spurted from the top button of his shirt. He had white bushy eyebrows just like Barney.

"Hello, Harry," said Tiffany, smiling as nice a smile as she could muster while thinking, And how have we freaking well offended you today, my elderly friend? "How are you?"

"This keeps happening!" shouted Harry. "It's unacceptable!" He handed her a letter addressed to Vid. "I've spoken to you about it before. I don't want your mail. I shouldn't have to deliver your mail. It's nothing to do with me."

"It's the postman, Harry," said Tiffany. "He accidentally put it in the wrong letter box. It happens."

"It's happened before!" said Harry belligerently.

"Yes, I think it did happen one other time," said Tiffany.

"Well, you need to put a stop to it! Are you *stupid*? It's not my responsibility!"

"Okay, Harry," said Tiffany.

"Harry, mate!" Vid strolled out into the hallway, stuffing a handful of purple grapes into his mouth. "You want to come to a barbecue later? We're having Erika and Oliver over! You know, from number seven."

Harry blinked at Vid. He put his hand inside his shirtfront and scratched. "What? No, I don't want to come to a *barbecue*."

"Ah, that's a pity," said Vid. He put his arm around Tiffany. "Maybe another time, but, Harry, you know, I don't want to hear you calling my wife 'stupid.' Okay, Harry? That's not nice. That's not neighborly."

Harry looked at them with his rheumy brown eyes. "I don't want any more of your letters," he muttered. "Not my responsibility. You've *got to take responsibility*."

"We take responsibility," said Vid. "Don't you worry about that."

"Get that dog away from me!" said Harry as Barney sniffed his shoe with fascination. Barney lifted his bearded little face, as if his feelings were hurt.

"Come on, Barney." Vid clicked his fingers at the dog.

"You know we're always here if you need us, Harry," said Tiffany. He suddenly seemed so heartbreaking, like a confused child.

"What?" Harry looked appalled. "Why would I need *you*? Just keep your damned letters out of my letter box." He shuffled off, shoulders bowed, shaking his head and muttering.

Vid shut the door. Harry was already forgotten. "Right," he said. "Do I feel like baking? Yes, I feel like baking! Will I make strudel? What do you think? Strudel? Yes. I think most definitely strudel."

10

Erika was back in the dry comfort of her office. The return cab fare from the library where Clementine had given her talk had been even more than the one out there. She'd just wasted 134 non-claimable dollars. She couldn't understand her own decision-making process. Listening to Clementine had certainly not filled in any gaps in her memory. All it had done was to stir up all sorts of uncomfortable feelings, and then she'd had to deal with the phone calls from both her husband and her mother on the way home in the taxi. She couldn't wait to throw herself into some complex work. It would clear her mind almost as well as going for a good, hard run with multiple hill sprints. Thank goodness she didn't have a job like Clementine's, where you needed to constantly draw upon the well of your own emotions. Work should be devoid of emotion. That was the joy of work.

She listened to her voice mail messages while she watched the rain falling outside the thick glass of her window. The weather had no relevance when you were safely ensconced in a high-rise office block. It was like it was happening in another dimension.

As she scrolled through her email inbox, her phone rang and she saw it was Oliver again. She'd only spoken to him less than half an hour ago. Surely he wasn't ringing to ask her again about talking to Clementine? He must have a good reason to call.

"Sorry to disturb you again," he said quickly. "I'll be fast. I just wondered if you'd seen Harry around lately?"

"Harry?" said Erika as she opened an email. "Who is Harry?"

"*Harry!*" said Oliver impatiently. "Our next-door neighbor!"

For heaven's sake. Harry was hardly a good friend. They barely knew the old man, and in point of fact, he wasn't their next-door neighbor, he lived on the other side of Vid and Tiffany.

"I don't know," said Erika. "I don't think so. Why?"

"I was talking to Tiffany when I took out the bins," said Oliver. He stopped to blow his nose, and Erika stiffened at the mention of Tiffany, her hand on her computer mouse. She hadn't wanted anything to do with Tiffany and Vid since the barbecue. They'd never had a real friendship anyway. It was proximity. Tiffany and Vid liked Clementine and Sam much more than them. If Erika hadn't mentioned Clementine that day, if she'd said they had the day free, would Vid still have asked them over for a barbecue? Unlikely.

"Anyway, I mentioned to her that I hadn't seen Harry in a while," said Oliver. "So we went over together and looked at his letter box, and it was pretty full. So, we took his mail up and knocked on his door but there was no answer. I tried to look in a window, but I don't know, I just have this feeling that something isn't right. Tiffany's calling Vid now to ask if he knows anything."

"Okay," said Erika. She had no interest in any of this. "Maybe he's gone away."

"I don't think Harry goes on *holiday*," said Oliver. "When was the last time you saw him?"

"I have no idea," said Erika. She was wasting time on this. "Not for a while."

"I'm wondering if I should call the police," fretted Oliver. "I mean, I don't want to embarrass him if he's fine, or waste police resources, but—"

"He'll have a spare key," said Erika. "There'll be one under a garden pot or something near the front door."

"How do you know?" said Oliver.

"I just know," said Erika. "He's of that generation." Erika's grandmother had always left a key under a pot of geraniums by the front door whereas Erika's mother would never have risked the horror of someone coming into her home without her permission. Her front door was double-deadlocked at all times. To protect the oh-so-precious contents of her home.

"Right," said Oliver. "Good idea. I'll try that."

He hung up abruptly and Erika put down the phone and found herself unwillingly and annoyingly distracted by the thought of her elderly neighbor. When *was* the last time she'd seen him? He would have been complaining to her about something. He didn't like anyone parking on the street outside his house, and he was always *full* of complaints about Vid and Tiffany: the noise (they liked to entertain; he'd called the police more than once), the dog (Harry said it dug up his garden; he'd put in an official complaint to the council), the general look of the place (looks like the bloody Taj Mahal). He seemed to genuinely hate Tiffany and Vid, and even Dakota, but he tolerated Erika, and seemed to quite like Oliver.

She stood up and walked over to her office window. Some people, like her managing partner, couldn't stand too close to the windows in this building—the way the windows were set gave you the sensation of standing at the edge of a cliff—but Erika enjoyed the drop in her stomach as she looked out at the streets snarled with rainy-day traffic below.

Harry. The last time she remembered seeing him was the morning of the barbecue.

It was when she rushed out to buy more crackers. She'd been worried about those sesame seeds. As she'd driven off down the street she'd looked in her rearview mirror and caught sight of Harry yelling at Vid and Tiffany's dog. He'd kicked out his foot, aggressively, but Erika was sure he hadn't actually made contact with the little dog. He'd just done it for effect. Vid had come out onto his front veranda, presumably to call for the dog. That's all she'd seen.

Erika didn't have a problem with Harry's grumpiness. Grumpiness was less time-consuming and tiring than cheeriness. Harry never wanted to stand around chatting for long.

She wondered if something had happened to him, if he was sick perhaps, or if he was fine, and poor, responsible Oliver was going to get his head snapped off for interfering.

A flash of lightning lit up the city skyline like a firework and Erika imagined how she would look to someone on the street below, if they happened to glance up at the rainy sky right at that moment and see her dark, solitary figure illuminated against the window.

The image carried a memory, perhaps it did, maybe it did, of hands pressed against glass, a face without features except for the idea of a mouth, a gaping mouth, but then the memory split and fractured into a thousand tiny pieces. Was it possible she'd done something irreparable and catastrophic to her *brain chemistry* that day?

She turned away from the window and hurried back to her desk to open a spreadsheet, any spreadsheet, as long as it made sense, it added up, and as the soothing figures filled her computer screen, she picked up her phone and rang her psychologist's number and said to the secretary, lightly, as if it didn't really matter, "I don't suppose you have any cancellations for tomorrow?" But then she changed her mind and begged, "Please?"

11

Oliver put down the phone from Erika and blew his nose hard. He picked up his umbrella. It was not the best for his health to be traipsing about in the pouring rain checking on elderly neighbors, but there was no way he could delay it a moment longer.

He had a terrible feeling about this. The last time he could remember seeing Harry was the day before the barbecue, before there was any plan of a barbecue, before Erika's curve ball, when it was still just afternoon tea with Clementine and Sam and the girls, *as per the plan.*

That Saturday afternoon Harry had ambled over for a chat and given Oliver some tips about the correct way to hold the edge trimmer. Some people didn't like being given unsolicited advice, but Oliver was always happy to learn from other people's experiences. Harry had complained about Vid and Tiffany's dog. Its barking kept him up at night, apparently. Oliver had found that hard to believe. Barney was such a little dog. Harry had said he was calling the police, or it might have been the local council, but frankly Oliver hadn't taken that much notice. Harry was always making official complaints through whatever official channels he could find. Making complaints was like a hobby for him. Everyone needed an interest when they retired.

That was two months ago now, and Oliver couldn't remember seeing Harry since then.

He opened his front door and jumped back when he saw Tiffany there, her umbrella tipped back on her shoulders as she stood on the shelter of their front veranda, her hand up as if she'd been just about to knock.

"Sorry," she said. "I know you're sick, but it's just that I've been thinking about Harry. I really think we should try to break in. Or call the police. Vid can't remember seeing him for weeks either."

"Neither can Erika," said Oliver. "I was just about to go over." He was suddenly frantic. It was as if every minute counted now. "Let's go." The wind picked up. "My God, this *rain*."

They held their umbrellas up and ducked behind them like riot shields as they hurried over the lawns and back onto the front veranda of Harry's house.

Tiffany dropped her umbrella in a soggy heap on the balcony and began banging on the door with a closed fist. "Harry!" she called over the noise of the rain. There was a panicky note in her voice. "Harry! It's just us! Just the neighbors!"

Oliver lifted up a heavy sandstone pot. No key underneath. There was a set of crappy old green plastic pots with very dead plants and dry crumbling soil. Surely, Harry wouldn't keep a key under one of them? But he lifted the first pot and there it was. A small gold key. Harry, old mate, thought Oliver. That's not great security.

"Tiffany." Oliver held up the key to show her.

"Ah," said Tiffany. She stood back as Oliver went to the front door and put the key in the lock.

"He might have gone away," she said tremulously. "To see family." But they both knew he hadn't gone away.

"Harry!" called out Oliver as he opened the door.

"Oh God, no, no, no," said Tiffany immediately. The smell took a fraction longer to get past Oliver's blocked nostrils, and then it was like he'd walked smack-bang into a wall of it. A wall of smell. Sweet, rotten smell. It was like someone had sprinkled cheap perfume over meat that had gone off. His stomach heaved. He looked back at Tiffany and he was reminded of the day of the barbecue, how in times of crisis a person's face is somehow stripped back to something essential and universally human: all those labels like "beautiful," "sexy," "plain" became irrelevant.

"Fuck," she said sadly.

Oliver pushed the door all the way open and took a step forward into the dim light. He'd never been inside before. All his interactions with Harry had taken place in front yards. Harry's front yard. His front yard.

A single light burned overhead. He could see a long hallway with a surprisingly beautiful red runner leading off into darkness. A staircase with a curved wooden banister.

At the bottom of the staircase lay a large unfamiliar object, and of course he knew already it had to be Harry's body, that exactly what he'd feared had happened, but still for a few seconds he stared, trying to puzzle it out, as if it were one of those tricky optical illusion pictures. It just didn't seem possible that cranky, stomping, spitting Harry was now that bloated, blackened, silent thing of horror.

Oliver registered certain things: Harry's socks weren't matching. One black. One gray. His glasses had sunk into his face as if they'd been pressed firmly by an unseen hand into soft, yielding flesh. His white hair was still as neatly combed as ever. A tiny swarm of busily buzzing flies.

Oliver's stomach recoiled. He stepped back on trembling legs and pulled the door shut while Tiffany vomited into the sandstone pot and the rain continued to fall and fall.

12

The Day of the Barbecue

Dakota sensed a flash of movement in her peripheral vision. She looked out the window and saw Barney streak across the lawn. The front door flew open with a bang and she heard her dad shout, "I've had just about enough of that man! Tiffany! Where are you? He's crossed a line! There is a line, Tiffany, a line! And this time that man has crossed it!"

She heard her mother from somewhere else in the house call out, "What?"

Pardon, thought Dakota.

"Dakota! Where is your mother? Where are you?"

Dakota was exactly where she had been all morning, reading her book on the window seat, but of course, her dad didn't notice details like that.

The house was so big they could never find each other. "You need a map to get around this place," Dakota's auntie said every single time she came over, even though she'd been here a million times and did not need a map at all. She even knew exactly where everything went in the kitchen cupboards better than Dakota did.

Dakota didn't answer her dad. Her mum had said she could finish the chapter before she had to help tidy up the house for the visitors. (As if the visitors were *her* choice.) She looked up, considering, because she'd actually sneaked just a little way into a new chapter, but she looked back down at the page, and just seeing the words was enough to pull her back in, she felt it like a pleasurable physical sensation, as if she were literally falling, straight back into the world of *The Hunger Games*, where Dakota was Katniss and she was strong and powerful and skilled, but also very pretty. Dakota was 100 percent certain that she'd be like Katniss and sacrifice herself in the Games for her cute little sister, if she had one. She didn't particularly *want* one (her friend Ashling's little sister was always there, hanging about, and poor Ashling could never get rid of her) but if Dakota did have a little sister, she'd totally die for her.

"Where are you, Dakota?" called out her mother this time.

"Here," whispered Dakota. She turned the page. "I'm right here."

13

Harry is dead," said Oliver, almost the moment Erika arrived home from work and put down her briefcase and umbrella. She touched her neck. Ice-cold raindrops were running down her back. Oliver was sitting on the couch surrounded by a little lake of squashed, used-up tissues.

"Seriously?" said Erika. She was focused on the tissues. "What happened?" The sight of the tissues made her heart rate pick up. Visceral response linked to childhood trauma. Perfectly natural. Three deep breaths. She just needed to get rid of those tissues.

"Tiffany and I found his body," said Oliver as Erika hurried to the cupboard under the kitchen sink to find a plastic bag.

"Where?" said Erika, scooping up tissues. "At his house, do you mean?"

She tied the handles of the plastic bag into a firm, satisfying knot and took it over to the bin and dropped it in.

"Yes," said Oliver. "You were right about the key. It was under a pot."

"So he was . . . dead?" said Erika as she stood at the sink, scrubbing her hands. People always asked if she'd been in the medical profession because of the way she washed her hands. When she was in public she tried to be less obviously rigorous, but now that she was home with Oliver, she could scrub and scrub without worrying that someone would diagnose her with OCD. Oliver never judged.

"Yes, Erika," said Oliver. He sounded aggravated. "He was very dead. He'd been dead for some time. Weeks and weeks, I'd say." His voice broke.

"Oh. I see. Oh dear." Erika turned from the sink. Oliver looked very pale. His hands lay limply on his knees and he sat upright, his feet flat on the floor, like a kid in the throes of terrible remorse, sitting outside the school principal's office.

She took a breath. Her husband was upset. Extremely upset, by the look of it. So he probably wanted and needed to "share." People with dysfunctional childhoods like hers didn't have the best interpersonal skills when it came to relationships. Well, it was just a fact. No one had modeled a healthy relationship for her. No one had modeled a healthy relationship for Oliver either. They had their dysfunctional childhoods in common. That's why Erika had invested close to six thousand dollars to date in high-quality therapy. The cycles of dysfunction and mental illness did not have to carry over from generation to generation. You just had to educate yourself.

Erika went and sat on the couch next to Oliver and indicated by her body language that she was ready to listen. She made eye contact. She touched his forearm. She would use hand sanitizer once they finished talking. She really didn't want to catch that horrible cold.

"Was he . . ." She didn't want to know the answers to any of the questions she knew she should ask. "Was he . . . what, in bed?" She thought of a manically grinning corpse sitting upright in a bed, one rotting hand on the coverlet.

"He was at the bottom of the stairs. As soon as I opened the door we could smell it." Oliver shuddered.

"God," said Erika.

Smell was one of her issues. Oliver always laughed at the way she'd drop rubbish in the bin and then jump back so the smell couldn't catch her.

"I only looked for one second, and then I just, I just . . . well, I slammed the door shut, and we called the police."

"That's awful," said Erika mechanically. "Horrible for you." She felt herself resist. She didn't want to hear about it, she didn't want him to *share* this experience with her. She wanted him to stop talking. She wanted to talk about dinner. She wanted to calm down after the day she'd had. She'd skipped lunch, and she'd stayed back at work to make up for the time she'd wasted going to Clementine's talk, so she was starving, but obviously after your husband tells you about finding a corpse, you can't then immediately follow it with, "Fancy some pasta?" No. She'd have to wait at least half an hour before she could mention dinner.

"The police said they think maybe he fell down the stairs," said Oliver. "And I keep thinking, I keep thinking . . ."

He made strange little breathy noises. Erika tried to keep the irritation off her face. He was going to sneeze. Every sneeze was a performance. She waited. No. He wasn't going to sneeze. He was trying not to cry.

Erika recoiled. She couldn't join him in this. If she allowed herself to feel sad and guilty about Harry, who she hadn't even *liked*, then who knew what could happen. It would be like uncorking a champagne bottle that had been vigorously shaken. Her emotions would fly all over the place. Messy. She needed order. "I need order," she'd told her psychologist. "Of course you need order," her psychologist had said. "You crave order. That's perfectly understandable." Her psychologist was the nicest person she knew.

Oliver took his glasses off and wiped his eyes. "I keep thinking what if he fell down the stairs and he couldn't move and he was calling and calling for help but nobody heard? We all just went about our daily lives, while Harry starved to death. What if that happened? We're like those neighbors you see on TV, and you think, how could you not have noticed? How could you not have cared? So what if he was a bit grumpy?"

"Well, you know, Vid and Tiffany are right next door to him," said Erika. She did not want to think about Harry lying on the floor. The sun rising and setting. Hearing the sounds of the neighborhood: lawn mowers, garbage trucks, the leaf blower he hated so much.

"I know. Tiffany is really upset too. But you know what? *I* was the one on the street he probably liked the most. He tolerated me, anyway. I mean, we had some civil conversations."

"I know," said Erika. "Like that time you were both so mad about that abandoned car outside the Richardsons'."

"I should have noticed he hadn't been out and about," said Oliver. He took a tissue from the box and blew his nose noisily. "I *did* think I hadn't seen him for a while, maybe a week or so ago, but then I just forgot about it."

"He wouldn't have *starved* to death," reflected Erika. "It would have been the lack of water that killed him. Dehydration."

"Erika!" Oliver winced. He dropped his scrunched-up tissue on the couch next to him and pulled another one from the box.

"What? I'm just saying he didn't lie there for *weeks* on end." She paused. "He should have had one of those emergency alarm things around his neck."

"Well, he didn't," said Oliver shortly. He blew his nose again.

"And I guess he had no family," said Erika. "No friends." Because he was such a nasty, vindictive old bastard. She wasn't going to let Oliver drag her into the morass of guilt into which he was sinking. Let Tiffany sink with him. Erika already lived with the permanent thrum of guilt.

"I guess he didn't," said Oliver. "Or if he did, we never saw them visit. That's why it was up to us to keep an eye out for him. These are the people who slip through the cracks of society. I mean, as a community, we have a moral obligation to—"

The landline rang and Erika leaped to her feet as though she'd won a prize. "I'll get it."

She picked up the phone. "Hello?"

"Erika, darling. It's Pam."

That well-bred, well-projected voice. The voice of good sense and good manners.

"Pam," said Erika. "Hi." She felt an instant softening and a ticklish feeling of imminent tears. She felt it whenever she spoke to Clementine's mother. That old childhood adoration, the dizzy, glorious feeling of relief, as if she'd been rescued at sea.

"I'm babysitting for Clementine and Sam," said Pam. "They've just left. They're going out for dinner at that new restaurant in the Overseas Passenger Terminal people have been raving about. I booked it for them. It's got three hats. Maybe even five hats? I don't know. An impressive number of hats. Hopefully they're having as nice a time as can be expected, although I wish it wasn't raining, but fingers crossed. They need it, the poor kids. To be frank, I'm worried about their marriage. That's talking out of school, I know, but, well, you're her best friend, so you probably know more than me about it."

"Oh, well, I don't know about that," said Erika. In actual fact, Erika knew nothing about Clementine's marriage problems. Surely Pam knew that the "best friends" label had been created by her, and for all those years Erika had clung to it while Clementine merely endured it.

"Anyway, Erika, darling, I know we're seeing you soon for our special dinner at my place, which I'm really looking forward to, but listen, the reason I thought I'd give you a call tonight . . ."

Erika heard the tentativeness in Pam's voice and her jaw clenched.

"Well, I had to go to Flower Power today, which meant I drove by your mum's house," said Pam. "I didn't stop." She paused. "Perhaps I should have, but your mum has really taken against me in recent years, hasn't she?" She didn't wait for an answer. "Erika, I know you stick to a schedule now with your visits and I think that's a really sensible idea for your own mental health, but I'm thinking perhaps you need to bring this month's visit forward."

Erika breathed out a long thin stream of air like she was blowing up a balloon. She looked at Oliver. He'd closed his eyes and let his head tip back against the couch, one hand pressed to his forehead.

"How bad?" she said to Pam.

"Pretty bad, darling, I'm afraid. Pretty bad."

14

How did your, ah, thing at the library go today? Your, um, what-do-ya-call-it, speech?" asked Sam in a strangled voice, as though the question were being forcibly squeezed from him.

"It went well—" began Clementine.

"Many people there?" interrupted Sam. He piano-played his fingertips on the white linen tablecloth and scanned the restaurant feverishly, as if there were someone or something he needed. "How many, would you say? Twenty? Thirty?"

"Less than twenty," said Clementine. "One of them was Erika."

She waited for a reaction and when none seemed forthcoming she said, "I didn't really understand why she *wanted* to come."

"Well, Erika is your biggest fan," said Sam with a faint smile.

That was kind of a joke. It gave her hope for the night that he was making a joke. Sam had been the first man she ever dated who immediately and instinctively grasped the complexities of her friendship with Erika. He'd never reacted with impatience or incomprehension; he'd never said, "I don't get it, if you don't like her, don't hang out with her!" He'd just accepted Erika as part of the Clementine package, as if she were a difficult sister.

"That's true," said Clementine, and she laughed too loudly. "Although she left halfway through."

Sam said nothing. He looked just to the right of her head, as if there were something interesting going on behind her.

"How was work today?" she said.

"Fine," said Sam coldly. "Same as usual."

("Your marriage is being tested, darling, but the best comes after the worst! Forgiveness and communication is the only way through!" Clementine's mother had said all this in a dramatic, passionate whisper to Clementine, as if she were imparting urgent words of wisdom before Clementine set off on some epic journey. They were standing together at the front door waiting for Sam, who had chosen that moment to sit down at the computer and answer an email that was apparently a matter of life and death, while the jarring sound of some terrible pop princess movie blared out from the television. Pam had made a tiny, unnecessary adjustment to the strap of Clementine's dress. "The two of you need to *talk*! Talk it out! Say what you feel!")

"So how's that 'forward-thinking corporate culture' working out for you?" said Clementine.

Once she could have said exactly those words and made him laugh, but now she could hear the thread of spite in her voice. Two musicians could play the same notes and sound entirely different. Intonation was everything.

"It's working out great for me." Sam looked at her with something like hatred.

Clementine dropped her eyes. Sometimes when she looked at him, she felt like there was a sleeping snake tightly coiled within her chest, a snake that would one day hiss to life and strike with unimaginable, unforgivable consequences.

She changed the subject.

"I have to admit I don't really enjoy doing these talks," she said. Each time she felt so nervous, but it was an entirely different sort of anxiety from the kind she felt before a performance or even an audition. Her audiences always clapped, but it was subdued applause, and often she sensed an undertone of disapproval.

She looked out the rain-dotted giant glass window revealing a blurry postcard view of Sydney Harbour complete with the white sails of the

Opera House, where she'd performed just two nights previously. "I sort of hate it."

She glanced back at Sam. An expression of intense aggravation crossed his face. He virtually shuddered with it. "Then stop," he said. "Just stop it. Why do you keep doing them? You're obsessed! You've got enough on your plate. You should be preparing for your audition. Are you even *going* to audition?"

"Of course I'm still going to audition!" said Clementine. Why did people keep asking her that? "I've been getting up at five A.M. to practice every day!" How could he not know that? She knew he'd been having trouble sleeping. She'd wake up sometimes in the middle of the night and hear his footsteps in the hallway or the muted sound of the television from downstairs. "Haven't you heard me?"

"I guess maybe I have heard you," said Sam uncomfortably. "I guess I didn't put two and two—I didn't realize you were practicing."

What did he think she was doing? Was the sound of the cello just irrelevant background noise to him? Or did he not care enough even to wonder?

She managed to keep the fractiousness she was feeling out of her voice. "And I went to Ainsley's place today to practice in front of her and Hu."

"Oh," said Sam. He seemed genuinely taken aback. "Well, great, I guess. How did it go?"

"Fine. It went fine."

It hadn't gone fine. It had been strange and awful. Hu and Ainsley had argued quite vehemently over her performance of the first movement of her concerto.

"Wonderful!" Hu had said as soon as she finished. "Bravo. Give the girl a job." He looked expectantly at his wife, but Ainsley wasn't smiling.

"Well," she said uncomfortably. "You've obviously been working really hard. It was technically perfect. It's just . . . I don't know, it didn't sound like you. If I was behind the screen, I would never have picked it was you."

"So what?" said Hu.

"It was *so* accurate. Every single note precisely where it should be. I would have guessed it was an arrogant twenty-year-old whiz kid, straight out of the Con."

"And I say again, so what? If she played like that, she'd absolutely get through to the next round," said Hu. "*I'd* put her through for sure. You would too. I know you would."

"Maybe, but I don't think it would get her through the second round. There was something almost—don't take this the wrong way, Clementine— but there was something almost *robotic* about it."

Hu said, "How can she not take that the wrong way?"

"We're here to be honest," said Ainsley. "Not kind." Then she'd looked at Clementine and said suddenly, "Are you sure you still want it? After . . . everything?"

"Of course she still wants it," said Hu. "What's wrong with you?"

Then their house phone had rung and Clementine never got to answer what should have been a straightforward question.

"How are Ainsley and Hu?" asked Sam. She could *see* the strain it cost him just to ask an ordinary civil question. It was like watching him do a chin-up. "I haven't seen them for a while."

But he was trying, so she'd try too.

"Good. They're good. Hey, I was telling Hu how you got me to run in place before practicing my excerpts and he said he had a teacher who made him do that!" Sam looked at her dully. You would think it was somebody else who had pinned the bedsheet to the ceiling all those weeks ago, who had yelled, "Run, soldier, run!" She plowed on. "His teacher also used to tell him to wake up and practice in the middle of the night, when he was still half asleep, and to play after he'd had a few drinks, speaking of which—oh, good, here comes somebody."

A young waiter approached their table and stood just a little too far back. "Would you like me to go through today's specials?" He squared his shoulders in the heroic manner of someone volunteering to do something perilous.

"Yes, but we're actually wondering about our drinks? We ordered two glasses of wine . . . um, a while ago." A million years ago.

Clementine tried to soften her words with a smile. The waiter was painfully young and sort of famished-looking. He'd be perfectly cast as a street urchin in *Les Misérables*.

"You haven't got your drinks yet?" The waiter looked alarmed, as if he'd never heard of such a thing.

Clementine gestured at their table to indicate: No drinks. Just their two mobile phones placed at precise angles in front of them, ready to be snatched up in case of crisis, because that's how they lived now, in readiness for crisis.

"Maybe they've been forgotten," suggested Clementine.

"Maybe," said the waiter. He glanced fearfully over his shoulder at the restaurant bar, where a pretty waitress dreamily polished wineglasses.

"You could check on them?" said Clementine. For the love of God. Why was this swanky restaurant employing children? Starving children? Feed him and send him home.

"Of course, right, it was two glasses of the . . ."

"The Pepper Tree shiraz," said Clementine.

She could hear a fishwifey, high-pitched note in her voice.

"Right. Um. Shall I just go through the specials first?"

"No," said Clementine at the same time as Sam said, "Sure, mate." He smiled up at the waiter. "Let's hear the specials."

He always snatched the Good Cop role for himself.

The waiter took a deep breath, clasped his hands choirboy style and recited, "For an entrée we have a confit of salmon cooked in coriander, orange and mint."

He stopped. His lips moved silently. Clementine pressed her fingertip against her phone. It lit up. No calls. Everything was fine.

Sam shifted in his chair and gave the waiter a tiny "you can do it" nod of encouragement, as though he were an affectionate parent in the audience at a poetry recital.

Watching her husband—the exasperating *humanity* of the man—Clementine felt an unexpected jolt of love, like one perfect, pure note. A velvety E-flat. But as soon as she registered the feeling, it was gone and she felt nothing but itchy irritability as the waiter haltingly made his way through the longest list of specials in the history of fine dining.

"A prosciutto and pepperoni, no wait, not pepperoni, a prosciutto and, um, a prosciutto and . . ." He rocked forward and studied his shoes, lips compressed. Clementine met Sam's gaze. Once Clementine would only have needed to fractionally widen her eyes to make Sam lose his composure, and in his desperation not to hurt the waiter's feelings his face would have turned red while his eyes filled with tears of mirth.

But now they just looked steadily at each other and then away again, as if levity were against the new rules for life where they trod so very carefully, where they checked and double-checked, where they knew better than to relax, even for a moment.

The waiter continued on his torturous way, and Clementine distracted herself by playing the Brahms excerpt in her head while using her forearm as a pretend fingerboard under the tablecloth. The Brahms had lots of mini-phrases linked in one extended line. It needed to have that beautiful lyrical feel. Was Ainsley right? Was she focusing too much on technical perfection? "If you concentrate on the music, the technical problems often solve themselves," Marianne used to tell her, but Clementine had come to believe she'd taken that advice too much to heart in every aspect of her life. She needed to be focused, to be *disciplined*, to clean up as she went, to pay her bills on time and follow the rules and grow the fuck up.

". . . with a beef and goat's cheese parfait!" The waiter finished his recital in the jubilant rush of a carol singer chorusing, *and a partridge in a pear tree!*

"All sounds delicious," said Sam.

"Do you want me to go back over anything?" said the waiter.

"Absolutely not," said Sam, and Clementine nearly laughed out loud. He'd always been good at delivering a dry, straight-faced line.

"Right. So, you have a think, and in the meantime I'll just check on your—?" The waiter looked at Clementine.

"Shiraz," supplied Clementine. "Pepper Tree shiraz."

"Too easy." The waiter snapped his fingers, jaunty with relief now that he'd gotten through the specials.

"So," said Sam, after the waiter had gone.

"So," said Clementine.

"What are you having?" Sam lifted the menu in front of him like a newspaper.

"Not sure," said Clementine, picking up her own menu. "It all looks good."

She needed to make a joke. A joke about the waiter. The specials. The non-arrival of the drinks. The girl behind the bar still obliviously polishing glasses. There was so much potential material. For a moment, it felt as though everything rested on this. If she could just make the right joke right now, she would save the night, save their marriage. Something about the girl taking a Buddhist approach to her job? Mindfully polishing her wineglasses? If only she'd mindfully pour their drinks? Dear God, when did she become the sort of person who mentally rehearsed flippant remarks?

Someone laughed in the restaurant. A man's laugh. A deep, distinctive baritone laugh.

Clementine's heart lurched. Sam's head jerked up from the menu.

Not Vid. Not here. Not tonight.

15

There it was again. Inappropriately loud for this soft-carpeted place.

Clementine swung her head to watch three men making their way through the restaurant. They all bore a superficial resemblance to Vid: the big bulletheads, giant shoulders, proud stomachs and that European way of walking, not quite a swagger.

But none of them was Vid.

Clementine exhaled. The man laughed again, but it didn't have the particular tone or depth of Vid's laugh at all.

She turned back to Sam. He had closed his menu and let it fall back against his chest.

"I thought it was Vid," he said. "It sounded exactly like him."

"I know," said Clementine. "I thought it was him too."

"Jesus. I just didn't want to see him." He took the menu and placed it back on the table. He pressed his hand to his collarbone. "I thought I was going to have a heart attack."

"I know," said Clementine again. "Me too."

Sam leaned forward, his elbows on the table. "It just brought it all back." He sounded close to tears. "Just seeing his face would—"

"The Margaret River shiraz!" Their young waiter triumphantly presented the bottle like a prize.

It was the wrong wine, but Clementine couldn't bear to see his face crumple. "That's it!" she said in a "well done, you" tone.

The waiter poured them overly generous glasses of wine, one hand behind his back. Red droplets stained the crisp white tablecloth. It might have been safer for him to use two hands.

"Are you ready to order?" The waiter beamed at them, flushed with success.

"Just a few more minutes," said Clementine.

"Of course! Too easy!" The waiter backed away.

Sam lifted his glass. His hand shook.

"I thought I saw Vid in the audience at the symphony the other night," said Clementine. "It gave me such a shock, I forgot to come in. It's lucky Ainsley was my stand partner."

Sam gulped a large mouthful of wine. He wiped the back of his hand across his lips. "So you didn't *want* to see him?" he said roughly.

"Well, of course I didn't want to see him. It would have been . . ." Clementine couldn't come up with the right word. She lifted her own glass. There was no tremor in her hand. She'd learned to control a shaking bow arm without beta-blockers, even while her heart thumped with excruciating stage fright.

Sam grunted. He reopened his menu but she could tell he wasn't reading it. He was busy reassembling himself, smoothing out his face, becoming bland again.

She couldn't bear it. She wanted him to crack again.

"Although, actually, Erika mentioned the other day that Vid is keen to see *us*," said Clementine. She didn't want yet another generic conversation about the view and the menu and the weather. A conversation like elevator music.

Sam glanced up at her, but his face was blank, his eyes were closed windows. She waited. There was that strange little pause before he answered. It was like a mechanical glitch. Nobody but her seemed to have noticed that Sam's timing was off when he spoke these days.

"Well, I'm sure we probably will run into him sometime," he said. His eyes returned to the menu. "I think I'll have the chicken risotto."

She couldn't bear it.

"Actually, 'desperate' was the word Erika used," she said.

His mouth twisted. "Yeah, well, he's probably desperate to see you."

"I mean it's inevitable that we'll run into them again, isn't it?"

"I don't see why," said Sam.

"When we're visiting Erika and Oliver? We can't avoid driving down their street again."

Although perhaps that's exactly what Sam intended. Maybe it was what she intended too. They could still see Erika and Oliver without going anywhere near their house. It would just be a matter of making the right excuse, deftly sidestepping Erika's invitations. They were never that keen on them in the first place.

She remembered the first time she'd seen Erika and Oliver's new house. "We're kind of dwarfed by our neighbors," Erika had said with a doubtful grimace at the castle-like mansion with its tizzy curls and curlicues. It looked especially over the top compared to Erika and Oliver's benign, beige bungalow: a safe, personality-less house that was so very *them*. Oh, but they couldn't laugh at Erika and Oliver like that anymore, could they? Their relationship had changed forever that day. The power balance had shifted. Clementine and Sam could never again make their superior "we're so easygoing, they're so uptight" digs.

Sam placed his menu carefully on the edge of the table. He readjusted the placement of his mobile phone. "Let's talk about something more pleasant," he said with the social smile of a stranger.

"I mean, it wasn't their fault," she said. Her voice was thick with inappropriate emotion. She saw him flinch. His color rose.

"Let's talk about something else," repeated Sam. "What are you having?"

"I'm not actually that hungry," said Clementine.

"Good," said Sam. "Neither am I." He looked businesslike. "Shall we just go?"

Clementine put her menu on top of his and squared up the corners. "Fine." She lifted her glass. "So much for 'date night.'"

"So much for date night," agreed Sam contemptuously.

Clementine watched him swirl his wine in his glass. Did he hate her? Did he actually hate her?

She looked away from him to their expensive rainy view. She let her eye follow the choppy water to the horizon. You couldn't hear the rain from in here. Lights sparkled and winked on the skyscrapers. Romantic. If she'd just made the right joke. If that damned man hadn't laughed like Vid.

"Do you ever think," she said carefully, without looking at Sam, her eyes on a keeling solitary yacht, the wind tugging angrily at its sail. Who would choose to sail in this weather? "What if we just hadn't gone? What if one of the girls had got sick, or I'd had to work, or you'd had to work, or whatever, what if we just hadn't gone to the barbecue? Do you ever think about that?"

She kept her eyes on the maniac in the yacht.

The too-long pause.

She wanted him to say: "Of course I think about it. I think about it every day."

"But we did go," said Sam. His voice was heavy and cold. He wasn't going to consider any other possibilities for their life than the one they were leading. "We went, didn't we?"

16

The Day of the Barbecue

Erika checked the time. Clementine and Sam were expected ten minutes ago, but that was normal for them, they seemed to think that anything within half an hour of the agreed-upon arrival time was acceptable.

Over the years, Oliver had come to accept their lateness, and no longer
suggested Erika call to check if there had been an accident. Right now, he
was pacing the hallway and at intervals making an unendurable squeaking
sound by sucking his lower lip beneath his top teeth.

Erika went to the bathroom, locked the door behind her, double-checked
and triple-checked it was locked and then pulled out a packet of pills from
the back of the bathroom cabinet. It's not that she was *hiding* them from
Oliver. They were right there in the bathroom cupboard for him to see if he
wanted, and Oliver would be sympathetic with her need for some sort of
anti-anxiety medication. It was just that he was so paranoid about anything
that went into his body: alcohol, pills, food that had passed its use-by date.
(Erika shared the obsession with use-by dates. According to Clementine,
Sam treated use-by dates as *suggestions*.)

Her psychologist had prescribed her this medication for those days when
she knew her anxiety symptoms (racing heart, trembling hands, overwhelm-

ing sense of panic and imminent danger, etcetera, etcetera) would be hard to control.

"Experiment a bit. Start out really low," her psychologist had said. "You might find even a quarter of a tablet is enough to get you through."

She took one tablet out of the blister pack and attempted to break it in half with her thumbnail. There was a deep groove down the middle of the tablet as if that was where you were meant to break it, but the design was faulty. It was impossible to break it in two. Her anti-anxiety medication was making her anxious. There was a not-especially-funny joke there somewhere.

Erika had planned to use the medication only when she visited her mother. She did feel nervous about today's discussion with Clementine, of course she did, but it was just normal-person anxiety that anyone would experience in a situation like this.

However, that was until she'd walked in the door after her conversation with Vid in the driveway to find her husband looking at her with incredulous disbelief, a feather duster hanging absurdly by his side. (Clementine couldn't believe they owned a feather duster. "Where's your feather duster?" Erika had said to her once when she visited, and Clementine had fallen about laughing and Erika had felt that familiar feeling of sick humiliation. Feather dusters were funny. Who knew? *How* did you know? Weren't they quite useful?)

"Why would you do that?" Oliver had said. "Why would you say yes to a *barbecue* with the neighbors today, of all days? We've had it all planned! We've been planning it for *weeks!*" He didn't yell when he was angry. He didn't even raise his voice. He just spoke in the same tone of polite disbelief he would use to make a call to his Internet provider to complain about something "unacceptable." His eyes were shiny and slightly bloodshot behind his glasses. She didn't especially like him when he was angry, but maybe everyone disliked their partners when they were angry and it was therefore normal.

"Erika, you've got to get this idea out of your head about there being some objective measure of normality," her psychologist kept telling her. "This 'normal' person of whom you speak doesn't exist!"

"Are you deliberately *sabotaging* this?" Oliver had said, suddenly intense, as if he were on to something like a mistake on a bill, as if he'd just worked out that his Internet provider was double-charging him.

"Of course not!" she'd said, outraged at the suggestion.

Oliver had tried to convince her to go straight next door and tell Vid that they couldn't make it to the barbecue after all. He'd said he'd do it himself. He'd started walking out the door, and she'd grabbed him by his arm to stop him, and for just a few seconds they'd struggled and he'd actually dragged her along the kitchen floor behind him as he tried to walk ahead. It was ungainly and undignified and it was not them. Clementine and Sam sometimes did this mock-wrestling thing in public, which always made Erika and Oliver go rigid with embarrassment. They took pride in *not* behaving like that. That's why Oliver stopped.

He held his hands up high in surrender. "Fine," he said. "Let's just forget all about it. We'll talk to Clementine and Sam another day. We'll just go to the barbecue and have fun."

"No way. We're going ahead. It's going to be better this way," Erika told him. "We ask the question. It's out there. We say, you don't need to give us an answer right now. Then we say, okay, off we go to the barbecue. It gives us an end point. Otherwise we'd just be making awkward conversation."

And now they were due any minute. Everything was ready. The craft table for the kids. The plate of crackers and dips.

But Erika's heart zoomed like a race car around her chest, and her hands trembled uncontrollably.

She swore at the stupid, tiny tablet. It wouldn't break.

The doorbell rang. The sound was like a swift, violent kick to the stomach. The air rushed from her lungs. The tablet fell from her clumsy fingers.

"Doorbell dread," her psychologist called it, almost with satisfaction, because Erika was ticking all the right boxes. "It's very common. Of course you dread the doorbell, because all through your childhood you dreaded discovery."

Erika got down on her knees, the tiles of the bathroom cold and hard against them. The floor was clean. The yellow tablet lay in the center of a tile. She pressed her fingertip to it and looked at it. The doorbell rang again. She put the whole tablet on her tongue and swallowed.

Everything depended on the conversation she was about to have. For God's sake, of course she was anxious. She could feel herself breathing shallowly, taking tiny, rapid sips of air, so she put her hand on her stomach and took a deep breath the way her psychologist had taught her (inflate your belly, not your chest), then she walked out of the bathroom and down the hallway as Clementine, Sam, Holly and Ruby spilled in through the front door, a tumble of noise and movement and different fragrances, as if there were ten of them, not just four.

"I bought a bottle of champagne to take when we go next door." Clementine held up a bottle as Erika kissed her hello. "And I've brought nothing for you. Is that rude? Oh, wait, I've got that book I promised you, Oliver." She rummaged through her big striped bag for the book. "I did spill some hot chocolate on it, I'm sorry, but you can still read through the chocolaty blotches. Are you okay, Erika? You look a bit pale?"

"I'm fine," said Erika stiffly. "Hello, girls."

The girls were dressed in ballet tutus, leggings and hoodies. They had glittery fairy wings attached to their backs by complicated elastic holster-type arrangements. Both girls needed their hair brushed and their faces washed. (Time to put on fairy wings but not to have a quick scrub in the bathroom!) Just looking at them gave Erika that same ache she experienced when she watched Clementine perform.

"Holly, say hello to Erika. Don't mumble," said Clementine. You would think Erika was an elderly aunt who demanded good manners. "Look her in the eye and say hello. Will you give Erika a cuddle, Ruby? Oh, you too, Holly. That's nice."

Erika bent down as the little girls both wound their arms around her neck. They smelled of peanut butter and chocolate.

Ruby, her thumb in her mouth, held up her kitchen whisk expectantly.

"Hello, Whisk," said Erika. "How are you today?"

Ruby smiled around her thumb. Although Erika was always polite to Whisk, she didn't really think Clementine and Sam should encourage the personification of an object, or Ruby's intense attachment to it. Erika would have nipped it in the bud a long time ago. She thought her psychologist agreed with her, although she was annoyingly equivocal about it.

Erika saw that Holly had the little electric blue sequined handbag she'd given her two Christmases ago slung over her shoulder. The ecstasy on Holly's face when she'd opened her present and seen that bag had made Erika's own face contort with such intense feeling she'd had to look away fast.

Holly now used her bag to lug around her growing rock collection. Erika was a little worried about Holly's rock collection, because it was heading toward obsessive and could obviously lead to all sorts of issues, but her psychologist was quite adamant that Holly's rock collection was nothing to be concerned about, it was perfectly normal, and that it was probably not a good idea to tell Clementine to keep an eye on it, but Erika had still told Clementine to keep an eye on it, and Clementine had promised she would, with that patronizing kindly look she sometimes got, as if Erika had dementia.

Oliver squatted down next to Holly. "I found this the other day," he said, holding up a flat oval-shaped blue stone. "It's got these little glittery bits." He pointed with his fingertip. "I thought you might like it."

Erika held her breath. First of all, why was Oliver *encouraging* Holly's rock collecting when she'd shared her concerns with him, and secondly, more important, was Holly about to snub him in the hurtful, honest way of children? Clementine had told Erika that Holly liked to find the stones herself (most of them seemed to be just plain old dirty garden stones) and was apparently completely disinterested when Clementine's lovely father had tried to turn Holly's interest into a learning opportunity and had given her a little gemstone attached to a card with information about its geological properties.

Holly took the stone and examined it through narrowed eyes.

"This is a good stone," she pronounced, opening her bag to add it to her collection.

Erika exhaled.

Oliver straightened, pulling on his trouser legs, exultant.

"What do you say?" said Clementine at the same time as Holly said, "Thank you, Oliver," and then looked up at her mother balefully. "I was *saying* thank you."

Clementine really should have given Holly a chance to speak before she jumped in.

Erika clapped her hands. "I've got a craft table set up for you two," she said.

"That sounds exciting, doesn't it, girls?!" said Clementine in a fake, jolly tone as if Erika had actually suggested something inappropriate and boring for children, like crochet.

"Watch the game last night?" said Sam to Oliver.

"Sure did," said Oliver with the air of a man about to finally take a test for which he'd been studying hard. He had in fact watched "the game" last night specifically so he could answer this question from Sam, as if faking an interest in sports would affect today's outcome.

Sam looked delighted. Normally sports was a conversational dead end with Oliver. "What about that tackle in the first half, eh?"

"Come on now! We don't want to talk about football!" interrupted Clementine. "Put us out of our misery. What's this mysterious thing we need to talk about?"

Erika saw Oliver look panicked. They were still milling about in the hallway. This was not the way it was meant to happen.

"We're not saying a word until everyone is sitting quietly in their designated positions," said Erika. Maybe the pill was working. Her heart rate felt steady.

"Oh, she's a *herrschsüchtige Frau*," said Clementine.

"What's that?" said Holly.

"It means 'bossy woman' in German," said Erika. "I'm surprised your mum remembers such a long word. Shall we ask her to spell it?"

When they were thirteen, Erika and Clementine had studied German at school and developed a love of German insults. They enjoyed the brutal snap of those Germanic syllables. Sometimes they'd shove each other at the same time: just enough to make the other one nearly but not quite lose her balance.

It was one of their few shared passions.

"Just because she got a higher mark than me." Clementine rolled her eyes.

"Oh, only twenty marks or so higher," said Erika. "*Dummkopf.*"

(She got exactly twenty-two marks more than Clementine.)

Clementine laughed, fondly it seemed, and Erika felt herself relax. She had to remember to always be like *this*: sort of flippant and cool, not so intense, or she could be intense but in an amusing, endearing way, not annoyingly so.

In a few minutes they had everyone sorted: the girls were happily using their pink glitter glue sticks on cardboard. Erika saw with vindicated pride that the craft table was a hit. Of course it was. Little girls loved crafts. Clementine's own mother used to have a craft table like this for her when she was little. Erika had adored that craft table: the tidy little jars of gold star stickers, the pots of glue. Surely Clementine had loved that table as much as Erika, so why hadn't she set one up for her own children? Erika had known better than to ever suggest it; too often she saw her interest in the girls misinterpreted as criticism.

"I love these sesame seed crackers," said Clementine as they sat opposite each other in the living room. She shuffled forward in a sitting position to take a cracker, and Erika saw a glimpse of cleavage. White bra. The emerald pendant necklace that Erika had gotten her for her thirtieth birthday dangled from her neck. The coffee table was too far away from the couch, so Clementine just sank gracefully to her knees, like a geisha girl.

She wore a turquoise cardigan over a white T-shirt, a full skirt in a fabric featuring giant white daisies against a yellow background, the skirt spread around her on the floor. She was a splash of color in the middle of Erika's beige living room.

"I remembered you either loved them or hated them," said Erika.

Clementine laughed again. "I'm just so passionate about my crackers."

"She's crackers about crackers," said Sam as Clementine, without asking, cut him a piece of cheese, put it on a cracker and handed it to him.

"Dad joke," said Clementine, rolling her eyes as she sank back on the couch.

"Had a manicure, have you, mate?" said Oliver to Sam, and Erika thought, What's he *talking* about? Is he trying to be all matey and "I'm a straightforward Aussie bloke just like you" but he's getting it all wrong?

But Sam held up his hand to show that his fingernails were painted coral pink. "Yep, Holly's work," he said. "I had to pay for the privilege."

"She doesn't do a bad job," said Clementine. "We just have to remember to take it off before he goes to work tomorrow so no one questions his manhood."

"No one would question my manhood!" Sam thumped his chest, and Oliver laughed, maybe a bit too enthusiastically but really, it was all good. The *tone* felt just right.

"Well," said Oliver. He cleared his throat. Erika could see his knee jiggling. He put a hand on it as if to still it.

"So, to give you some background . . . ," began Erika.

"This must be serious stuff." Clementine raised an eyebrow. "*Background.*"

"We've been trying unsuccessfully to get pregnant for the last two years," said Erika. Just get it out there. Move it along.

Clementine removed the cracker she'd been about to bite from her mouth and held it in front of her. "You've what?"

"We've been through eleven rounds of IVF," said Oliver.

"*What?*" said Clementine.

"I'm sorry to hear that," said Sam quietly.

"But you never . . ." Clementine looked flabbergasted. "I thought you didn't want children. You always said you didn't want children."

"We want children very much," said Oliver. He lifted his chin.

"That was when I was younger," explained Erika. "I changed my mind."

"But I assumed Oliver felt the same way," said Clementine. She looked at Oliver accusingly, as though she expected him to back down, admit she was right and say, "Oh sorry, of course you're right, we don't want children at all. What were we thinking?"

"I always wanted children," said Oliver. "Always." His voice thickened. He cleared his throat.

"But *eleven* rounds of IVF?" said Clementine to Erika. "And you never told me? You went through all that without saying a word? You kept it a secret for the last two years? Why wouldn't you tell me?"

"We just decided to keep it to ourselves," said Erika uncertainly. Clementine sounded hurt. Almost angry. Erika felt everything shift.

Wait . . . was that *wrong*? It had never occurred to her that she had the power to hurt Clementine, but now Erika saw that yet again, she'd gotten it wrong. Clementine was her closest friend and you were meant to share things with your friends: your problems, your secrets. Of course you were. My God, everyone knew that. Women were notorious for sharing everything.

The problem was that Oliver had been so insistent that they tell no one about any of it, and to be fair, Erika hadn't objected. She had no desire to *share*. She didn't want to tell anyone about it. Her fantasy had been calling Clementine with the good news. The good news that never came.

And, after all, she had plenty of experience keeping secrets.

"I'm sorry," she said.

"No, no!" said Clementine. She still hadn't eaten her cracker. Her face was pink. "I'm sorry. Gosh, this isn't about me. Of course, it's fine if you didn't want to talk about it. I respect your privacy. I just wish I could have been there for you. There were probably times when I was complaining about the girls and you were just thinking, Oh for God's sake, shut up, Clementine, don't you know how lucky you are?" She sounded like she was close to tears.

There had been times like that.

"Of course I never thought that," said Erika.

"Anyway, we know now," said Sam. He put his hand over Clementine's. "So, obviously, anything you need . . ."

He looked wary. Maybe he thought they needed money.

There was silence for a moment.

"So the reason we wanted to talk to you today," began Oliver. He looked at Erika. This was her cue. But it was all wrong. She'd messed it up. If she'd just been like a *normal* friend about this the whole way through, if she'd told Clementine, right back at the beginning, when they'd first started IVF, then this conversation would have had a proper, solid foundation. Each disappointment, each failure over the last two years would have been like a deposit of sympathy. They could have called on that deposit. But now, Erika sat opposite a confused, hurt friend and there was nothing in the bank to withdraw.

Self-loathing rose within Erika's stomach like nausea. She never got it quite right. No matter how hard she tried, she always got it just a tiny bit wrong.

"My doctor has said that the only option now for us is to find an egg donor," she said. "Because my eggs are of very poor quality. Useless, in fact." She tried to bring some lightness into the conversation, the way it was in the hallway, but she could tell by everyone's faces that it wasn't working.

Clementine nodded. Erika could see she had no idea what was coming next.

A memory came to her of blond, pretty Diana Dixon marching up to Clementine in the school playground and grimacing at the sight of Erika, the sort of grimace you might give a cockroach. "Why are you playing with *her*?" said Diana, and Erika never forgot either Clementine's lightning-quick flash of humiliation, or the way she lifted her chin and told Diana, "She's my friend."

"So we wondered . . . ," prompted Oliver. He waited for Erika. It was clearly her job to ask the question. Clementine was her friend.

But Erika couldn't speak. Her mouth felt dry and hollowed out. The tablet, maybe. It was probably a side effect. She'd meant to read the little leaflet about side effects. She fixed her eyes on the yellow daisies on Clementine's skirt and began to count them.

Oliver spoke up, like an actor saving the day by taking someone else's line in the script. There was a thin edge of hysteria to his voice. "Clementine," he said. "We're asking . . . the reason we wanted to talk to you today, well, we're wondering if you would consider being our egg donor."

Erika looked up from the daisies at Clementine's face and saw an expression of utter revulsion fly across it as fast as the flash of a camera. It was there and gone so quickly, she could almost choose to believe she'd imagined it, but she hadn't imagined it, because reading faces was one of her skills. It was a legacy of a childhood spent reading her mother's face, monitoring, analyzing, trying to modify her behavior in time, except that her skill rarely allowed her to get things right; it just meant that she always knew when she got things wrong.

It didn't matter what Clementine said or did next; Erika knew how she really felt.

Clementine's face was composed and very still. It was the look of focused concentration she got when she was about to perform, as if she were taking herself to another plane, a transcendent level of consciousness that Erika could never reach. She pushed back a stray lock of hair behind her ear. It was the same long curly lock of hair that fell toward her cello when she played, somehow never quite touching the strings.

"Oh," she said steadily. "I see."

17

The Day of the Barbecue

So, this is a big thing we're asking of you, and it's absolutely not something we'd expect an answer on right away," said Oliver. He leaned forward with his elbows resting on his knees, his hands locked together. He brought to mind a mortgage broker who had just given a lengthy explanation of a complex loan arrangement.

He looked gravely at Clementine and indicated a cream manila folder on the coffee table in front of him.

"We have some literature ready for you." He enunciated the four syllables of the word "literature" with tiny lip-smacks of satisfaction. It was the sort of word that both Oliver and Erika found soothing. Like "documentation." Like "procedure." "It explains exactly what would be involved. Frequently asked questions. The clinic gave it to us to pass on, but if you'd rather not take it now, that's fine, we don't want to overload you, because at this stage we're just, you know, putting it out there, I guess is the right way to describe it."

He sat back against the couch and glanced at Erika, who, bizarrely, had chosen this moment to kneel down beside the coffee table and cut a piece of cheese from the (tiny, Clementine didn't know they made them that small) wheel of Brie.

Oliver looked away from his wife and back at Clementine. "All we're saying today is: Is this something you would possibly consider? But, as I said, we don't need any response at all from you, and by the way, if down the track, you *were* to say you would consider it, there's a mandatory cooling-off period of three months. And you can pull out anytime. *Anytime*. No matter how far we progress. Well, not quite anytime. Not once Erika is pregnant, obviously!" He chuckled nervously, adjusted his glasses and frowned. "Actually, you can pull out right up until when the eggs are inseminated but at that point they legally become our property, um . . ." His voice drifted. "Sorry. That's far too much information at this early stage. I'm nervous. We're both a bit nervous!"

Clementine's heart twisted for him. Oliver generally avoided hazardous topics of conversation—anything political, sexual or overly emotional—but here he was soldiering on his own through this most awkward of conversations because he wanted so badly to be a father. Was there anything more attractive than a man who longed for children?

Sam cleared his throat. He put his hand on Clementine's knee. "So, mate, I'm just getting my head around this. It would be your . . ."

"It would be my sperm," said Oliver. He colored. "I know it all sounds sort of . . ."

"No, no," said Sam. "Of course not. I've got a good friend who went through IVF, so I've got a basic sort of understanding of the, you know, ins and outs."

The ins and outs.

She'd tease him about that unfortunate turn of phrase later on. Clementine knew Sam was talking about his friend Paul, and that in reality Sam had been entirely oblivious to the "process," except for his joy at the outcome: a baby boy for Paul and Emma. Sam loved babies (in Clementine's experience, no man loved babies more; Sam was the first in line for a cuddle of a newborn and would scoop older babies straight from their parents' arms), but he hadn't wanted to hear Paul and Emma talking about "egg retrievals" and "embryo transfers."

Erika lifted a cracker between her fingers. "More cheese, Sam?"

Everyone stared at her.

"No thanks, Erika," said Sam. "I'm good."

It was clearly Clementine's turn to say something, but there was a constricted feeling around her chest that seemed to be preventing from her talking. She wished one of her daughters would yell for her, but predictably, they were being quiet and well behaved the one time she would have liked them to interrupt.

They seemed to love Erika's craft table.

Erika would be an excellent mother, a craft-table, watch-your-manners, hand-sanitizer-in-the-handbag sort of mother. Oliver would be a good father too. Clementine could see him doing something old-fashioned and pains-taking with a dear studious little boy, like making model airplanes.

To their *own* child, thought Clementine despairingly. They'd be good parents to their own child. Not my child.

It wouldn't be your child, Clementine. But it would. Technically, as Holly would say, it would be her child. Her DNA.

People do this for strangers, she told herself. They donate eggs just to be *nice*, to be *kind*. To people they've never met. This was her friend. Her "best friend." So why was the word "No!" so loud in her head?

"Well," she said finally, inadequately. "This is a lot to think about."

"Absolutely," said Oliver. He looked again at Erika but she was still no help to the poor man. She had laid out a line of crackers and was placing a thin sliver of cheese on each one. Who did she think was going to eat them? Oliver blinked once and smiled apologetically at Clementine. "Please don't think this is the end of the road for us if you decide it's not for you. There will be other options. It's just that you were the first person we thought of, being Erika's closest friend, and you're the right age, and you're done having kids—"

"Done having kids?" said Sam. His hand tightened on Clementine's. "We're not necessarily done having kids."

"Oh," said Oliver. "Sorry. Gosh. I thought, that is, Erika was definitely under the impression—"

"You said you'd rather poke your eyes out than have another baby," said Erika to Clementine in that truculent way she had when she could disprove something with facts. "I asked you. It was last September. We had yum cha. I said, 'Are you done with babies?' You said, 'I'd rather poke—'"

"I was joking," interrupted Clementine. "Of course I was joking."

She hadn't been joking. Oh God, but was this her only way out now? Would she have to *give birth* to get herself out of this situation?

"Well, you can certainly still donate eggs if you want to have more children," said Oliver. Three deep, corrugated lines furrowed his forehead, like a cartoon character frowning. "The clinic does prefer known donors to have completed their families, but it's, ah, it's all there in the literature."

"You said that you'd rather poke your eyes out than have another baby?" said Sam to Clementine. "You really said that?"

"I was *joking*!" repeated Clementine. "I'd probably had a bad day with the kids."

Of course she'd always known that this was an issue. Her deluded hope had been that he'd just, well, get over it. Every time the girls were badly behaved, or when the house seemed too small for the four of them and they kept losing things, or when they worried over their financial situation, she secretly hoped that Sam's hopes of another baby were gently, sensibly fading away.

She should never have told Erika she was done with babies. It was a flippant remark. A carefully constructed flippancy was her default position with Erika. She should have confided that Sam didn't feel the same way, because there had always been the risk it could come up in conversation, just as it had today.

She rarely shared information like that with Erika. She deliberately withheld herself. With other friends she didn't think twice, she chatted about whatever came into her head, because she knew they'd probably forget half of what she said. There was no one else in the world, not her mother or her husband, who listened so *ravenously* to what she had to say, as if every word mattered and was worthy of being filed away for future reference.

As a child, whenever Erika had come to play, she would first do a peculiar audit of Clementine's room. She'd open every drawer and silently examine its contents. She'd even get down on her hands and knees to look under Clementine's bed, while Clementine stood, mutely infuriated but, at her mother's request, being *kind* and *polite*. Everyone is different, Clementine.

Erika had obviously learned some social niceties as a grown-up, and didn't go through her cupboards anymore, but Clementine still sensed that avaricious gleam in Erika's eyes whenever they were in conversation. It was as though Erika's desire to look under Clementine's bed was still there and so was Clementine's mute outraged resistance.

But the really ironic thing was that it now appeared Erika had the same policy of not sharing anything important. She'd kept this huge secret for the past two years, and Clementine's first reaction had been to feel hurt by the revelation: Oh yes, it was all fine for *Clementine* to lord it over Erika from up high on her friendship pedestal, graciously bestowing gifts: Why, yes, Erika, you *may* be the godmother of my firstborn!

So, okay, fine then, if their friendship was an illusion and had no substance to it, *on either side*, but now Erika was asking something you asked only of a dearest friend.

She looked down at the cracker in her hand and didn't know what to do with it. The room was silent except for the gentle babble of Holly and Ruby in the next room, doing their crafts like little angels, as if in rebuke to Clementine. *Look how darling we are. Give Daddy another baby. Help your friend have a baby.* Be kind, Clementine, be kind. Why are you so unkind?

A crazy, complicated symphony of feelings rose in her chest. She wanted to throw a tantrum like Ruby, to fling herself to the floor and bang out her frustration with her forehead on the carpet. Ruby always made sure it was carpet before she started banging her head.

Sam moved his hand from her leg and shifted slightly away from her. He'd left a triangle-sized piece of cracker on Erika's spotless white leather couch. Oliver removed his glasses and his eyes looked bruised and tender, like those of a tiny animal emerging from hibernation. He polished them with the edge of his T-shirt. Erika sat immobile and upright, as if at a funeral, her eyes following something past Clementine's head.

"That's Dakota," she said.

"Dakota?" asked Clementine.

"Dakota," said Erika. "The little girl from next door. Vid must be getting impatient. He's sent her over to collect us for the barbecue."

The doorbell rang. Erika jumped violently.

Sam leaped to his feet like a man whose name has finally been called after a tedious wait in a bureaucratic institution. "Let's go have a barbecue."

18

When Sam and Clementine got back from the restaurant and walked in the door, shaking their umbrellas, home from their "date night" less than two hours after they'd left, Clementine's mother was aghast.

"What happened?" She turned off the television and pressed a hand to her throat as if preparing herself for terrible news. "Why are you back already?"

"We're so sorry, Pam," said Sam. "The service at the restaurant was slow, and in the end we just . . . we decided we weren't really in the mood for going out to dinner."

"But the reviews were outstanding," said Pam. The restaurant had been her recommendation. She looked at them expectantly, as if she hoped she could convince them to turn around and go back into the city and give it another go.

Clementine saw that her mother had folded a basket of clean laundry into neat little piles on the couch, and had just now rewarded herself with a cup of tea and a single gingernut biscuit on a saucer, probably to enjoy while she watched *Midsomer Murders*. Clementine felt a stab of regret. It seemed this was her default state now: regretful. It was just the degrees of regret that changed.

"I'm sorry, Mum," she said. "I know you—" I know you thought a romantic dinner could save our marriage. She glanced at Sam, and he returned her look as passively as a stranger on a bus. "We both felt sort of tired, I guess."

Pam's shoulders sagged. "Oh dear," she said. "I'm sorry if I pushed you into it. Maybe it was too soon. I just thought it would be good for you to get out." She visibly rallied. "Well, how about I make you both a cup of tea? I just made myself one. The water is still hot."

"Not for me," said Sam. "I might just—" He looked around the room for inspiration. "I might just . . . go for a drive."

"Go for a drive where?" asked Clementine. She wasn't going to help him. She wasn't going to pretend that going for a "drive" in the pouring rain to escape a cup of tea with your mother-in-law and wife was reasonable.

But of course, her mother was eager to let Sam slip straight off any hook. "Of course you can go for a drive," she said. "Sometimes you need to just drive. It's meditative. Right now you two need to be kind to yourselves."

Sam gave Pam a grateful smile, ignored Clementine and left the house, noiselessly closing the front door behind him.

"You've got the place looking *very* clean and tidy," said Pam, when they were both sitting down with cups of tea and gingernut biscuits. She gave her a quizzical, almost uneasy look. "All I could find to do was fold this tiny bit of laundry. It's like you've got a housekeeper or something!"

"We're just trying to be more organized," said Clementine. She and Sam had both become manic about housework since the barbecue, as if they were being monitored by some unseen presence. "Although we *still* can't find things."

"Well, good, I guess, but there's no need to kill yourselves. You both look exhausted, to be honest." She looked at Clementine over her teacup. "So I take it tonight wasn't a success then?"

"I'm sorry we had you babysitting for no reason," said Clementine.

"Pff!" Pam flicked a hand. "It's my pleasure. You know that. It's good for your father and me to have a night off from each other too. Space is good for a marriage. You have to have your own interests." She frowned. "As long as you don't become obsessive about them, of course."

Pam's father, Clementine's grandfather, had been a schoolteacher who spent every spare moment he had working on the great Australian novel. He worked on it for over fifteen years before he died in his fifties of complications caused by pneumonia. Clementine's grandmother was apparently so angry and grief-stricken and bitter about all the time he'd wasted on that "stupid bloody book," she'd tossed the entire manuscript in the bin without reading a single word. "How could she not read it? What if it *was* the great Australian novel?" Clementine always said, but Pam said Clementine was missing the point. The point was that the book had ruined their marriage! Pam's father loved the book more than he loved her mother. As a consequence, Pam took a keen, possibly fanatical, interest in monitoring the quality of her own marriage. She read books with titles like, *Seven Seven-Second Secrets for Super-Charging Your Marriage.* Clementine's easygoing, laconic father tolerantly endured weekend "marriage retreats." He went along, or gave the appearance of going along, with everything Pam suggested, and it appeared to have worked, because they were undeniably fond of each other.

Pam was just as vigilant about the quality of other people's marriages as she was her own, although she was self-aware enough to know that people didn't always appreciate her vigilance.

"I don't suppose you'd think about seeing a marriage counselor, would you?" she said now to Clementine. "Just to talk things through."

"Oh, well, no, I don't think so," said Clementine. "There's nothing really to say, is there?"

"I suspect there's a lot to say," said Pam. She bit into her biscuit with her strong white teeth. "Well. How was your day? Any, ah, gigs?"

Even after all these years, she still said the word "gig" self-consciously, in the same way that she always said "croissant" with the proper French pronunciation, but with an apologetic, self-deprecating look to make up for her pretentiousness.

"I did one of my talks," said Clementine.

If Sam's face showed a spasm of irritation when she mentioned the talks, her mother's face showed a spasm of delight. "Of course! I forgot you had one scheduled for today. How did it go? I'm *so* proud of your bravery, Clementine, I really am. How was it?"

"Erika came along to watch," said Clementine. "Somewhat bizarrely."

"Not bizarrely at all! She was probably just being supportive."

"I never noticed before that Erika has exactly the same haircut as you," said Clementine.

"I guess it helps that we go to the same hairdresser," said Pam. "Maybe dear old Dee can only do one type of haircut."

"I didn't know you two went to the same hairdresser," said Clementine. "How did that come about?"

"I have no idea," said Pam hurriedly. She was always keen to rush over the details of exactly how much time she spent with Erika, as if it would make Clementine feel envious or usurped. She was too old for that now, although she could still feel the lingering memory of her childhood insecurities. *She's my mother, thank you very much.*

"Speaking of Erika," said Pam. "I actually called her tonight while you were out, just to give her an update on the Sylvia situation, which . . . well, let's just say things aren't improving as she gets older . . . but anyway, Erika told me something a little upsetting." Pam reflected. "Although she didn't seem that upset about it." She used the side of her hand to absentmindedly sweep together some crumbs on the coffee table into a microscopic pile. "Apparently Oliver found a *body*, the poor boy!"

"What do you mean, *he found a body*?" For some reason Clementine felt herself experiencing a flash of anger, directed at her poor mother. It just seemed so outlandish. "He just *stumbled* upon a body, did he? He was just out for a run and he tripped over a *corpse*?"

Pam looked at her steadily. "Yes, Clementine. Oliver found a body. It was one of their neighbors."

Clementine froze. It was Vid she thought of first. Big men like Vid were prone to dropping dead of a heart attack. She didn't want to see Vid again, but she didn't want him to die.

"The old fellow two doors down from them," said Pam.

Clementine felt everything unclench. "Harry," she said.

"That's it. Did you know him?" asked Pam.

"Not really," said Clementine. "From a distance. He didn't like it if you parked on the street anywhere near his house. Once there was a delivery truck in Erika's driveway when we were visiting, and so we had to park on the street near his driveway. He suddenly emerged from behind his azalea bush yelling abuse. Sam told him that his property line didn't extend to the street—he was polite, of course, but you know what the horrible man did? He *spat at us*. Holly and Ruby were thrilled. We lived on that story for days. The spitting man."

"He was probably lonely," said Pam. "Unhappy. Poor old fellow." She tilted her head, listening to the rain. "It's really got a *settled* feeling, that rain, hasn't it? As if it's here to stay."

"It makes everything seem diabolically difficult," said Clementine.

"You know, I'm so happy that Erika is still seeing that lovely psychologist!" said Pam, her eyes brightening at this sudden pleasurable thought. She loved anything to do with mental health. "It means she'll be armed with all the tools she needs to deal with her mother."

"She might not be talking to the psychologist about the hoarding at all," said Clementine "She might be talking about her infertility."

"Infertility?" Pam put down her teacup abruptly. "What are you talking about?"

So Erika hadn't confided in Pam either, even after all this time. What did that signify?

"But she and Oliver don't want children! Erika was always so *vocal* about not wanting children!"

"She wants me to donate my eggs to her," said Clementine blandly. She had been putting off telling her mother about Erika's request, not wanting Pam's forthright opinions further complicating her own already complicated feelings, but now she was conscious of a childish desire for her mother to fully comprehend the continuing cost of being Erika's friend. *Look what you asked of me, Mum, even now all these years later, see how kind I am, Mum, I am still being so* kind.

Although who was she kidding? Donating your eggs was the sort of purely philanthropic act her mother would have killed for the chance to perform. Clementine used to tell her father that if she were ever in a car accident, he needed to double-check that she really was dead before her mother began enthusiastically handing out Clementine's organs.

"Donate your eggs?" said Pam. She gave her head a little shake as if to make things settle back into place. "But how do you feel about this? When did she ask you?"

"The day of the barbecue," said Clementine. "Before we went next door." She thought of Erika and Oliver sitting so straight-backed and tense on their white leather couch. (Only a childless couple would own a white leather couch.) They both had such neat little heads. Oliver's spectacles were so clean. They had seemed so endearing in their earnestness. And then, that instant feeling of distaste at the gynecological word "eggs," and the irrational sensation of violation, as if Erika were proposing she reach right over and help herself to part of Clementine—to some deeply intimate part of her that she'd never get back—followed instantly by that old, familiar shame, because a real friend wouldn't think twice.

She had thought she wouldn't need to feel that awful shame ever again, because Erika was fine now—"in a good place," as people said—and no longer asking for more than Clementine could give.

"Oh my gosh," said Pam. "What did you say?"

"I didn't say anything at the time," said Clementine. "And we haven't talked about it since then. I think Erika is hoping I'll bring it up soon, and obviously, I will, I'm just picking the right moment. Or I'm procrastinating. Maybe I am procrastinating."

She could feel something ascending within her. A rising scale of fury. A melody from her childhood. She looked at her mother's familiar face: the gray fringe cut in that unflinching straight line over her protuberant brown eyes; the big, determined nose; the large, utilitarian ears, for hearing, not earrings. Her mother was all strength and certainty. Never a moment's doubt over a spider or a tight parking spot or a moral dilemma.

"That little girl needs a friend," she'd told Clementine the first time she saw Erika in the school playground. The different kid. The unpleasant-looking kid sitting cross-legged on the asphalt playing with old brown leaves and ants. The kid with the greasy blond hair flat against her head, the pasty dead white skin and the scabby sores dotting her arms. (Fleabites, Clementine learned many years later.) Clementine had looked at the little girl, and looked back at her mother and felt one enormous word caught in her throat: No.

But you didn't say no to Pam, especially not when she used that tone of voice.

So Clementine went and sat down opposite Erika in the playground and said, "What are you doing?" And she'd glanced over at her mother for the nod of approval, because Clementine was being kind, and kindness was *the most important thing of all*, except that Clementine didn't feel kind. She was faking it. She didn't want anything to do with this dirty-looking little girl. Her selfishness was a nasty secret she had to hide at all cost because Clementine was privileged.

Pam was a woman ahead of her time in her use of the word "privilege." Clementine learned to feel bad about her white middle-class privilege long before it became fashionable. Her mother was a social worker, and unlike many of her exhausted, jaded, bitter-jokes coworkers, Pam never lost her passion for her vocation. She worked part-time while bringing up three children and she loved to share unflinching accounts of what really went on in the world.

Clementine's family wasn't particularly wealthy, but privilege was measured on a different scale when you saw what Pam did. Life was a lottery, and Clementine knew from a very early age that she had apparently won it.

"What are you going to say to Erika?" said Pam.

"What choice do I have?" said Clementine.

"Of course you have a choice, Clementine; it will be your biological child. It's a big thing to ask. You don't—"

"Mum," said Clementine. "Think about it." For once she was the unequivocal one. Her mother hadn't been there at the barbecue. Her mother didn't have those ghastly images burned forever across her memory.

She watched her mother think about it, and come to the same conclusion.

"I see what you mean," she said uneasily.

"I'm going to do it," said Clementine fast, before her mother could speak. "I'm going to say yes. I have to say yes."

19

"Are you okay? You're not still upset about our friend Harry?" said Vid, lying next to Tiffany in their dark bedroom while the rain continued its incessant soundtrack.

Thanks to their red velvet "absolute blackout" curtains, Tiffany could see absolutely nothing but black. Normally the darkness felt luxurious, like a hotel room, but tonight it felt suffocating. Like death. There was too much death on her mind these days.

Although she couldn't see Vid in their king-sized bed, she knew he would be lying flat on his back, his hands crossed behind his head like a sunbather. He slept the entire night like that, without changing position. It still made Tiffany laugh after all these years. It was such a casual, confident, aristocratic approach to sleep. *You may approach, sleep.* So very Vid.

"He wasn't our friend, was he?" said Tiffany. "That's the point. He was our neighbor but he wasn't our friend."

"He didn't *want* to be our friend, you know," Vid reminded her.

It was true that if Harry had been at all interested in friendship with them, he would have gotten it. Vid was open to friendship with anyone he encountered in his daily life: baristas and barristers, service station attendants and cellists.

Definitely cellists.

If Harry had been a different sort of old man, they would have had him over all the time and they would have noticed his absence so much sooner.

Soon enough to have saved his life? Today, the police had told Oliver and Tiffany that it seemed most likely that Harry had either fallen down the stairs, or had a stroke or heart attack and perhaps fallen as a result. There would be a coroner's inquest. It seemed like a formality. The police were going through a process; ticking off the boxes.

"He probably died instantly," the policeman told Tiffany, but how would he know? He had no medical expertise. He was just saying it to make her feel better.

Anyway, let's be practical—even if they had been Harry's friends, they wouldn't have been over there every five minutes. He'd probably still be dead; he just wouldn't be quite *so* dead as he was today. He'd gotten deader and deader over the weeks it took before they noticed. She gagged at the sickly sweet sensory memory. A smell had never made her vomit before. Well, she'd never smelled death before.

Oliver was an accountant. He probably hadn't smelled death either, but while she'd been sick in Harry's sandstone pot (Harry would have been *furious*), white-faced Oliver calmly made the necessary phone calls, rubbed her back and offered her a clean, precisely folded white tissue from his pocket. "Unused," he promised. Oliver was the man to have around in a crisis. A man with a tissue and a conscience. The guy was a freaking hero.

"Oliver is a freaking hero," she said out loud, even though she knew Vid probably didn't need to hear any more about Oliver's freaking heroism.

"He is a good man," said Vid patiently. He yawned. "We should have them over." He said it automatically, and now he must surely be lying there thinking of the last time they'd had them over.

"Hey, I know! Let's have them over for a barbecue!" said Tiffany. "Great idea! Wait, haven't they got some really nice friends? Isn't one of them a cellist?"

"That's not funny," said Vid, and he sounded profoundly sad. "That's not even a little bit funny."

"Sorry," said Tiffany. "Sick joke."

"For coffee?" said Vid sadly. "We can have Erika and Oliver over for coffee, can't we?"

"Go to sleep," said Tiffany.

"Yes, boss," said Vid, and within seconds she heard his breathing slow. He could go to sleep in an instant, even on those nights when she knew he was upset or angry or worried about something. Nothing ever affected that man's sleep or his appetite.

"Wake up," she whispered, but if she woke him, he would keep talking and he'd been up since five that morning with the aquatic center project. One of his boys had gotten sick and he was worried he'd underquoted. The man needed his sleep.

She turned on her side and tried to calmly sort her way through all the things that were churning through her mind.

Number one. Finding Harry's body today. Not a nice experience, but get over it. Harry was probably happy to be dead. He seemed like a man who was done with living. So move right along.

Number two. Dakota. Everyone—Vid, Dakota's teacher, Tiffany's sisters—all said that Dakota was fine. It was all in Tiffany's head. Maybe it was. She would continue to monitor.

Number three. The Information Morning at Dakota's new school tomorrow. Feelings of resentment (don't you send me emails reminding me that ATTENDANCE IS COMPULSORY, how dare you talk to me in capital letters) probably related to subconscious feelings of inferiority over snooty school and other parents. Get over yourself. It's not about you. It's about Dakota.

Number four, but perhaps overriding everything else, her feelings of guilt and horror over what had happened at the barbecue. Like the memory of a nightmare you can't quite get out of your head. Well, yes, Tiffany, we get it, all very distressing, over and over it we go, not achieving anything, just stop thinking about it, you can't change what you did or didn't do, what you should and shouldn't have done.

The problem was that every item on her list was so nebulous. Impossible to pin down. She remembered the days when her worries were always related to money and solutions could be calculated.

To comfort and distract herself, she worked her way through a conservative estimate of her current net present value: Property. Shares. Self-managed superannuation fund. Family trust. Term deposits. Checking account. Doing this always calmed her. It was like imagining the protective walls of an impenetrable fortress. She was safe. No matter what happened. If her marriage fell apart (her marriage wouldn't fall apart), if the stock market or property market crashed, if Vid died or she died or if one of them got a rare disease requiring endless medical bills, the family was safe. She'd constructed this fortress herself—with Vid's help, of course, but it was mainly her fortress—and she was proud of it.

Go to sleep then, safe in the financial fortress you built on a transgression and yet still it stands.

She closed her eyes and opened them again instantly. She was tired but wide awake. She felt all pop-eyed like she was on coke. So this was insomnia. She'd always thought she wasn't the type for it.

She felt a sudden need to go check on Dakota. She wasn't the type for that either. She hadn't been one of those mothers who go in to check that her sleeping baby is still breathing. (She'd caught Vid doing it a few times. He'd been a little shamefaced. Mr. I'm So Cool and Casual and This Is My Fourth Kid.)

She got out of bed with her arms outstretched and expertly shuffled her way to the doorjamb, which always turned up sooner than she expected. It was much easier to see once she got out on the landing because they always left a light on, turned down low, in case Dakota got up in the night. She pushed Dakota's bedroom door open and stood there for a moment letting her eyes adjust.

Tiffany couldn't hear anything over the rain. She wanted to hear the even sound of Dakota breathing. She tiptoed forward, past the crammed bookshelf, and stood next to the bed looking down at Dakota, trying to make out the form of her body. Dakota appeared to be lying flat on her back just like her father, although usually she slept curled up on her side.

At the same moment she registered the twin shimmers of Dakota's eyes staring up at her, she heard Dakota say in a perfectly clear, wide-awake voice, "What's the matter, Mum?"

Tiffany jumped and yelped. "I thought you were asleep," she said, pressing her hand to her chest. "You gave me the fright of my life."

"I'm not asleep," said Dakota.

"Can't you sleep? Why are you lying there awake like that? What's the matter?"

"Nothing," said Dakota. "I'm just awake."

"Is something worrying you? Move over." Dakota moved over and Tiffany got into bed with her, feeling an immediate comfort she hadn't known she craved.

"Are you upset about Harry?" said Tiffany. Dakota had responded to the news of Harry's death in the same impassive way she now responded to everything.

"Not really," said Dakota flatly. "Not that much."

"No. Well. We didn't know him very well and he wasn't . . ."

"Very nice," finished Dakota.

"No. He wasn't. But is there something else?" said Tiffany. "Something on your mind?"

"There's nothing on my mind," said Dakota. "Nothing at all." She sounded absolutely certain of this, and Dakota had never been able to lie.

"You're not worried about going to Saint Anastasias tomorrow?" said Tiffany.

"No," said Dakota.

"It should be interesting," said Tiffany vaguely. She could feel sleep tugging at her consciousness like a drug. Maybe it was nothing. Prepubescent stuff. Hormones. Growing up.

"Shall I just lie here until you fall asleep?" said Tiffany.

"If you want," said Dakota frostily.

Dakota's mother lay sound asleep next to her, not snoring exactly but making a long, thin whistling sound each time she breathed out.

Long strands of her mum's hair floated across Dakota's face and tickled her nose. She had hooked one leg over Dakota's leg, locking her close, like she had her in a leg-cuff.

Holding her breath, Dakota inched her leg free. She pulled back the covers and got up on her knees and flattened herself against the bedroom wall like Spider-Man. She slid her way down the wall to the end of the bed. It was a covert operation. She was escaping her captor. Yes! She'd done it! She tiptoed across her bedroom, avoiding the land mines in the carpet.

Stupid stuff. Don't think stupid, little-kid thoughts like that, Dakota, when there are real wars happening right now and real refugees in tiny boats in the middle of the ocean and real people stepping on land mines. Would you like to step on a land mine? She sat on her cushioned window seat and hugged her knees to her chest. She tried to feel gratitude for her window seat, but she felt nothing about her window seat. Instead, she actually thought the terribly rude, ungrateful thought: I don't give a shit about this window seat.

Dakota had not properly understood until recently how her brain was a private space with only her in it. Yesterday she'd looked at her teacher and screamed the F-word in her head. Nothing happened. Nobody knew she'd done that. Nobody would ever know.

Everybody else probably worked this out when they were, like, three years old, but it was a revelation to Dakota. Thinking about it made her feel as if she were all alone in a circle-shaped room: circle-shaped because her head was circle-shaped, with two little round windows, which were her eyes, and people tried to look in, to understand her, by looking through her eyes, but they couldn't see in. Not really. She was there in her circle-shaped room all on her own.

She could say to her mum, "I love my window seat," and if she just said it the right way, not so enthusiastically that she made her suspicious, her mum would think she meant it and she'd never know the truth.

So if Dakota could do that, if Dakota could think shocking, kind of angry, hard thoughts like, I don't give a shit about window seats, then probably grown-ups had shocking, angry, hard thoughts too, which were probably much worse because they could watch R-rated movies.

For example, her mum might say, "Good night, Dakota, I love you, Dakota," but inside the circle-shaped room of her brain, her real self was thinking: I can't believe you are my daughter, Dakota, I can't believe I have a daughter who would do what you did.

Her mother probably thought the reason Dakota had turned out to be such a disappointment was because she was "growing up with money," although funnily enough, she didn't actually *have* any money, except for some birthday money in a bank account she wasn't allowed to touch.

Dakota's mum did *not* "grow up with money." (Neither did Dakota's dad, but he didn't go on about that; he just really loved spending it.)

When Dakota's mum was Dakota's age, she'd gone to a "rich kid's" party and fallen in love with her house. It was like a castle, she said. She could still describe everything about that house in pretty boring detail. She'd especially loved the window seats. She was obsessed with window seats. They were "the height of luxury." For years and years, her mum had dreamed of a two-story house with marble bathrooms and bay windows and window seats. It was a really architecturally specific dream. She had even drawn pictures of it. So when she and Dakota's dad had talked to the builders about this house, they'd said: Window seats, please. The more the better.

The funny thing was that Dakota had once said something to her auntie Louise, who was one of her mum's big sisters, about how their family had grown up "poor," and her auntie burst out laughing. "We weren't *poor*," she said, "we just weren't rich. We had holidays, we had toys, we had a great life. Your mum just thought she didn't belong out here in the lower-class suburbs." Then she'd gone and told the other aunties, who'd all teased her mum, but her mum didn't give a shit, she just laughed and said, "*Whatevah*," like she was an American girl on a TV show.

Anyway, Dakota still tried her best to love and appreciate her window seats, but she wasn't very good at it. She got, like, one out of ten for appreciation.

The blind was down and she didn't want to risk opening it and waking up her mum, so she pulled it over her head like a tent.

It was raining outside, so she couldn't see much. Harry's house was just a blurred, spooky shape. She wondered if Harry's ghost was in there, muttering angrily, kicking stuff with the toe of his foot and occasionally turning his head to one side and spitting in disgust: Why did it take you people so long to find my body? Are you stupid or what?

She wasn't *glad* he was dead, but she wasn't sad either. She didn't feel anything. There was just a big nothing feeling in her head about Harry.

She'd told her mum the truth when she'd said there was nothing on her mind. She was trying to make her brain like a blank piece of paper.

The only thing allowed on her piece of paper was school stuff.

Nothing else. Not sad thoughts, not happy thoughts, not scary thoughts. Just facts about Australia's indigenous culture and global warming and fractions.

It was good that she was going to the new school next year. They had a good "academic record." So hopefully they would stuff her brain full of more facts so there wouldn't be any room to think about it, to remember what she'd done. Before, she'd felt a bit nervous about starting somewhere new, but now that didn't matter. Remembering her old worries about making friends was like remembering something from when she was only a really little kid, even though the barbecue had only happened back at the end of term two.

Her parents still loved her. She was sure of this. They probably weren't thinking secret angry thoughts.

She remembered her dad the day after, standing in the backyard, swinging that big iron bar over and over like a baseball bat, his face bright red. It had been terrifying. Then he'd come inside and had a shower without saying a single word, and her dad liked to talk. Things had to be serious for her dad not to talk.

But then, after that, slowly, her mum and dad had returned to their normal selves. They loved her too much not to forgive her. They knew she knew the hugeness of what she'd done. There had been no punishment. That's how big this thing was. It wasn't kid stuff. Not like, "No TV until you tidy your room." Actually, Dakota had never gotten many punishments, or "consequences." Other kids did heaps of little wrong things every single day of their lives. Dakota just saved it all up and did one giant wrong thing.

It was up to her to punish herself.

She had thought about cutting herself. She'd read about cutting in a YA book that the librarian said was too old for her, but she got'd her mum to buy it for her. (Her mum bought her any book she wanted.) Teenagers did it. It was called "self-harm." She'd thought she'd try out self-harm, even though she really, really hated blood. When her parents were busy on their computers, she'd gone into their bathroom and found a razor blade and sat on the edge of the bath for ages trying to get up the courage to press it into her skin, but she couldn't do it. She was too weak. Too cowardly. Instead she hit herself as hard as she could on the top of her thighs with closed fists. Later, there were bruises, so that was good. But then she had come up with a better punishment: something that hurt more than cutting. Something that affected her every day, and no one even noticed the difference.

It made her feel less guilty but at the same time it made her feel desolate. "Desolate" was the most perfectly beautiful word for how she felt. Sometimes she repeated it over and over to herself like a song: desolate, desolate, desolate.

She wondered for a moment if Harry had felt desolate and that's why he'd been so angry with everyone. She remembered how that afternoon she'd sat on this window seat, reading, and she'd looked up and seen a light on in a room on the second floor of Harry's house and she'd wondered what Harry was doing up there, and what did he do with all those rooms in that house anyway, when he lived there all alone?

Now Harry was dead and Dakota felt nothing about that, nothing at all.

20

The Day of the Barbecue

Here they come," Tiffany called out to Vid in the kitchen as she stood at the front door and watched Dakota walk up the driveway, hand in hand with Clementine's pink tutu–clad daughters who were skipping by her side. As Tiffany watched, the littler one toppled over in that slow-motion toddler way and Dakota tried to carry her. The child was about half Dakota's height, so her legs dragged on the ground and Dakota tilted to one side, staggering under the little girl's weight.

"Dakota is being such a good sister!" said Tiffany as Vid appeared at the front door wearing his striped apron, smelling strongly of garlic and lemon from the prawns he was marinating.

"Don't even think about it," said Vid.

Fifteen years ago, when he proposed, while Tiffany was still admiring her engagement ring (Tiffany for Tiffany, naturally), Vid had said, "Before you put it on, we need to talk about children, okay?" With three volatile, angry teenage daughters, Vid had no desire for more children, but Tiffany was a young woman, so of course she would want children, it was only natural, he understood this, so Vid's compromise, in order to close the deal, was this: Just one baby. A one-child policy. Like China. He couldn't take any more than that. His heart and his bank account couldn't handle it. He said he would understand if one baby was not enough, but for him it was not negotiable. Take it or leave it, and by the way, if she walked away, the ring was still hers and he would always love her.

Tiffany took the deal. Babies were the last thing on her mind back then, and she really did not fancy stretch marks.

She had never regretted it, except sometimes, like right now, she felt a kind of twinge. Dakota would have been a loving, responsible older sister, just like Tiffany's own older sisters had been. It seemed wrong to deny her that, especially as Dakota never demanded anything except more library books.

"Maybe we should renegotiate our deal," said Tiffany.

"Don't even joke about it," said Vid. "I am not laughing. Look at this face." He pulled a mournful face. "Serious face. Four weddings will bankrupt me. It will be the death of me. It will be like that movie, you know, *Four Weddings and a Funeral*. My funeral." Vid chuckled, delighted with himself. "Four weddings and my funeral. You get it? Four daughters' weddings and Vid's funeral."

"I get it, Vid," said Tiffany, knowing that she'd be hearing this joke for months, possibly years to come.

She watched Erika and Oliver, Clementine and Sam, approach the house behind the children. There was something odd about their formation, there was too much space around them, as if they weren't two couples who knew each other well but four individual guests who hadn't met before this day and had happened to arrive at the same time.

"Hi!" called out Erika, timing it just a bit wrong, she was too far away. Their driveway was very long.

"Hi!" called back Tiffany, walking down the steps to meet them.

As they got closer, she saw they all had identical glazed smiles, like people who have recently gotten into drugs or religion, or a new pyramid sales scheme. Tiffany felt a hint of trepidation. How was this afternoon going to pan out?

Vid walked straight past her, toward the guests, his arms outstretched. Jeez Louise, Vid, you peanut, you would think they were beloved relatives returning from a long trip overseas.

Barney thought the guests were his beloved relatives too, and rushed to ecstatically sniff everyone's shoes as though it were a race to get them all sniffed in record time.

"Welcome, welcome!" cried Vid. "And look at these beautiful little girls! Hello! I hope you don't mind me sending Dakota over to fetch you. I didn't want the meat to be overcooked. Barney, calm down, you crazy dog."

He kissed Clementine on both cheeks. "Because I remember you're a foodie, like me, right? We like good food! Last time we met at Erika's place, I remember we talked food, you know."

"Did you?" said Erika suspiciously, as if all conversational topics should have been first cleared with her. "I don't remember that." She handed Tiffany a jar of chocolate nuts. "I hope you don't have allergies, because these are nuts. Chocolate nuts."

"No allergies," said Tiffany. "Actually, I love these." She wasn't just being polite. They made her feel nostalgic. Her grandfather used to buy them every Christmas.

"Really?" said Erika doubtfully. "Well, that's good."

She was a real odd bod, that girl, as Tiffany's sister Karen would say.

Clementine had lost her glazed expression and she was looking at Vid as if he were the answer to all her problems.

"Mum, this one is Ruby and this one is Holly. Can I take them up to my room?" said Dakota to Tiffany. Her eyes shone as she presented the tangle-haired little pixie girls, who wore fairy wings and appeared to have recently upended bottles of glitter all over themselves.

"If it's okay with their mum and dad," said Tiffany.

"Dakota is very responsible, you know," said Vid. "She'll look after them."

"Of course it's okay with us," said Sam as he kissed Tiffany on the cheek, with a well-brought-up Aussie boy flick of his eyes at her body: up, down and, quick, *away*!

"It's great to see you again, Tiffany," he said with a slight exhalation, as if he were relieved to be here too. He and Clementine were like people arriving at a wake after a funeral, ready to unloosen ties and let the tension drain from their shoulders, desperate to eat and drink and remind themselves that they were alive. He hunkered down at the knees and fondled Barney's ears, and Barney reacted with no dignity whatsoever, throwing himself on the ground and offering up his stomach for a rub, as if no one had ever paid him any attention before.

"We appreciate your hospitality." Oliver shook Vid's hand and then awkwardly kissed Tiffany too, as if he'd been issued a challenge not to let any part of his body touch hers.

"Come in, come in!" Vid shepherded the group inside. "Let's have a drink before we go out to the barbecue."

"I'm sorry the little girls are dropping glitter everywhere," said Erika, watching Dakota lead the girls upstairs, followed by Barney, who was now in a state of manic excitement.

Tiffany saw an irritated spasm cross Clementine's face, presumably because another woman was apologizing for her children.

"Oh, it's fine," she said.

"I set up a craft table for them," said Erika. "We thought they were doing crafts, but they were really just—"

"Making a terrible mess," finished Clementine, but she and Erika were both smiling now, as if it were funny.

Tiffany considered herself a pretty good judge of character and situations, her instincts were normally spot-on, but right now these four had her bamboozled. Were they friends or enemies?

"We brought champagne." Clementine held a bottle of Moët aloft, with the sparkly pride of someone who doesn't buy Moët very often. (Vid had three cases in the cellar.)

"Thank you! You didn't need to do that!" Vid grabbed the champagne bottle in one meaty hand like it was a petrol pump. "But the important question is, Clementine, did you bring your cello?"

"Of course," said Clementine. She patted her handbag. "I never go anywhere without it. It's right here. I've got a fancy new collapsible one."

Vid stared blankly at her handbag for a fraction of a second and then he roared with delighted laughter. It wasn't *that* funny, thought Tiffany. Vid pointed the bottle of champagne at Clementine like a gun. "You got me! You got me!"

Yes, she's got you, all right, thought Tiffany as she went quick-smart to the cupboard for champagne glasses, because Vid was about to open that bottle in his normal jubilant fashion.

It was fine that Vid had the hots for Clementine. Tiffany understood that, she kind of liked it, and judging by the way Clementine was touching her hair right now, she kind of liked it too. That was just sex. Sex was easy.

What Tiffany didn't understand was the other three people in the room, because as Vid uncorked the bottle with predictable "Whoa!" results, and Clementine grabbed two glasses from Tiffany and danced about, laughing, trying to catch the spilling, frothing champagne, Oliver, Erika and Sam all watched Clementine, and Tiffany couldn't tell, with any of them, if it was with deep affection or utter contempt.

21

Clementine placed her book facedown on her lap in the circle of lamp-light reflected on the duvet. She listened to the rain and looked at the dark empty side of their double bed.

When Sam had come back from his "drive," after her mother had gone home ("Another time," she'd said robustly. "We'll try again another time."), they hadn't said a word about their disastrous night out. They'd been polite and cool to each other like not especially friendly flatmates. "There is some leftover pasta in the fridge." "Good, I might have some." "I'm off to bed." "Good night." "Good night."

Sam had gone off to the study to sleep on the sofa bed that gave whoever slept on it a sore lower back. ("It was fine, *fine!*" guests would always assure them the next morning, discreetly massaging their lower backs.)

It appeared the study was Sam's bedroom now. They didn't even go through the pretense of starting out in the same bed, and then one of them creeping off in the middle of the night, pillow under the arm. We sleep in separate rooms now. It gave her a shocked, sick feeling when she actually let the thought crystallize like that.

The last time she and Sam had slept a proper full ordinary night together

in this bed, a night without twisted-sheet dreams or teeth grinding or toss-
ing and turning, was the night before the barbecue.

It seemed extraordinary now to imagine them going to bed, sleeping
through the night and waking up together in the morning. What had that
last night of extraordinary ordinariness been like? She couldn't remember a
single thing about it, except that she knew they'd been so different from the
people they were now, just eight weeks later.

Did they have sex? Probably not. They so rarely got around to it. That's
why they were so susceptible that night. To the sex.

Her mother would have been hoping that tonight's dinner at the fancy
restaurant would have resulted in them coming home and "making love." If
they hadn't come home early, if they'd walked in the door holding hands,
Pam would have slipped off quickly with a "wink, wink, nudge, nudge" smile,
and then she would have called the next day and said something horrifically
inappropriate like: "I do hope you weren't too tired to make love, darling, a
healthy sex life is crucial for a healthy marriage."

It would have made Clementine want to put her fingers in her ears
and chant "la la la" as she used to do when her mother delivered sex education lectures while she drove Clementine and Erika to parties. Erika, who
practically took notes every time Clementine's mother opened her mouth,
used to listen attentively to the lectures and ask very specific procedural
questions. "When exactly does the condom go on?" "When the boy's
penis . . ." "LA LA LA!" Clementine would yell.

Her mother had always been far too open and jolly about sex, as if it were
something good for you, like water aerobics. She used to have *The Joy of Sex*
sitting unabashedly on her bedside table as if it were a nice novel. Clementine chiefly remembered the *hairiness* of that book.

Clementine wanted sex to be something subtle and secret. Lights off.
Mysterious. Hairless. An image came to her of Tiffany in that crazy backyard, before all the fairy lights came on: Tiffany's T-shirt bright white in the
hazy light. A sweet taste filled Clementine's mouth. It was the taste of Vid's
dessert. Now it was the taste of shame.

Two or three nights after the barbecue, Clementine had dreamed she
was having sex onstage at the Opera House concert hall with someone who
was not Sam. Holly and Ruby were in the audience watching their mother
have sex with some other man. Right there in the front row, legs swinging,

while Clementine moaned and groaned in the most depraved way, and at first they just watched with blank concentration, like they were watching *Dora the Explorer*, but then they started to cry, and Clementine called out "Just a minute!" as if she were finishing the washing up, not her orgasm, and then her parents and Sam's parents, all four of them, came running down the aisle of the concert hall with disgusted faces, and Clementine's mother screamed, "How could you, Clementine, how could you?"

It wasn't a hard dream to interpret. In Clementine's mind what happened would forever be tied up with sex. Skanky, sleazy sex.

Fragments of that revolting dream had lingered for days, as if it had been an actual memory. She had to keep reassuring herself: It's okay, Clementine. You never actually performed a sex show at the Opera House with your kids in the audience.

It still felt more like a memory than a dream.

They'd both had bad dreams that first week after the barbecue. Their sheets got tangled, their pillows stank of sweat. Sam's shouts would violently wrench her awake, as though someone had grabbed her by her shirtfront and yanked her upward to a sitting position, her heart hammering. Sam would be sitting up next to her, confused and gibbering, and her first instinctive reaction would always be pure rage, never sympathy.

Sam had begun grinding his teeth while he slept. An unbearable melody in perfect three-quarter time. *Click*-two-three, *click*-two-three. She would lie there, eyes open in the darkness, counting along for what seemed like hours at a time.

Apparently Clementine had started talking in her sleep. Once she'd woken up to find Sam leaning over her, shouting (he said he wasn't shouting, but he was), "Shut up, shut up, shut up!"

Whoever got the most frustrated would leave to sleep or read in the study. That's when the sofa bed got made up and stayed made up. Eventually they'd have to talk about it. It couldn't go on forever, could it?

Don't think about it now. It would sort itself out. She had other more important things to worry about. For example, tomorrow she needed to call Erika and arrange to see her for a drink after work. Then she would tell her that *of course* she would donate her eggs. It would be her pleasure, her honor.

For some reason, a memory came to her of the first and only time she'd seen inside Erika's childhood home.

They'd been friends for about six months and Clementine was always (mostly at her mother's insistence) inviting Erika over to play, but the invitation was never returned, and Clementine, with a child's well-developed sense of fairness, was getting sick of it. It was fun going to other people's places. You often got treats you weren't allowed at your own place. So why was Erika being so strange and secretive and frankly, selfish?

Then one day Clementine's mother was driving them both to some school picnic, and they'd stopped at Erika's place to quickly pick up something she'd forgotten. A hat? Clementine couldn't remember. What she did remember was jumping out of the car and running after her, to tell Erika Mum said to bring a warm top as well because it was getting chilly, and how she'd stopped in the hallway of the house, bewildered. The front door wouldn't swing all the way open. Erika must have turned sideways to get through. The door was blocked by a ceiling-high tower of overflowing cardboard boxes.

"Get out of here! What are you doing here?" Erika had screamed, suddenly appearing in the hallway, her face a frightening grotesque mask of fury, and Clementine had leaped back, but she'd never forgotten that glimpse of Erika's hallway.

It was like coming upon a slum in a suburban home. The *stuff*: skyscrapers of old newspapers, tangles of coat hangers and winter coats and shoes, a fry pan filled with bead necklaces, and piles of bulging, knotted plastic bags. It was like someone's life had exploded.

And the smell. The smell of rot and mold and decay.

Erika's mother, Sylvia, was a *nurse*, supposedly a perfectly capable one. She held down a job at a nursing home for years before she retired. It seemed so extraordinary to Clementine that someone who lived like that could work in health care, where things like cleanliness and hygiene and order mattered so much. According to Erika, who was now able to freely discuss her mother's hoarding, it wasn't that unusual; in fact, it was quite common for hoarders to work in the health care industry. "They say it has something to do with them focusing on taking care of others, so they don't take care of themselves," Erika said. Then she added, "Or their children."

For years, Erika's mother's problems had been something they all referred to obliquely and delicately, even when those shows started appearing on TV and they suddenly had a word for the horror: "hoarding." Erika's mum was a "hoarder." It was a thing. A condition. But it wasn't until Erika had started with her "lovely psychologist" about a year ago that Erika herself had begun saying the word "hoarding" out loud and discussing the psychology behind it in this strange, new clipped way, as if it had never been a deep, dark secret at all.

How could Clementine begrudge sharing her home and her life with Erika after she'd seen her home? She couldn't and yet she did.

It was the same now. She hadn't become a good person. She still didn't feel pleasure at the thought of helping her friend achieve her deepest desire. In truth, she still felt the same overwhelming aversion as when they'd first asked her to donate her eggs, but the difference was that now she *relished* her aversion. She wanted the doctors to cut her open. She wanted them to remove a piece of herself and hand it over to Erika. Here you go. Let's balance the scales.

She turned out her lamp and rolled over to the middle of the bed and tried to think about anything, anything at all, other than that day. That so-called ordinary day.

22

The Day of the Barbecue

Erika watched Clementine try to rescue the Moët that was foaming and frothing from the bottle, while Vid stood in the middle of his gigantic kitchen, the champagne held aloft in both hands, grinning idiotically like a Formula One winner posing for a photo.

Clementine laughed as if it were all a great hoot, as if it didn't matter that expensive champagne was being wasted. She shouldn't have spent that much. It wasn't necessary to turn up to a backyard barbecue with French champagne. She and Sam always lived beyond their means. The *mortgage* on their damp little trendy place! Erika and Oliver couldn't believe it when they heard how much they'd borrowed, and *then* they'd taken the little girls off for a holiday in Italy last year! Fiscal madness. They'd put the trip on their credit card even though the children would have been just as happy with a one-hour drive to the Central Coast, but only Tuscany would do for Sam and Clementine.

That's why Clementine really needed to get the full-time orchestra job. She always got herself worked up over auditions, suddenly doubting herself. Erika couldn't imagine having a job where you doubted your ability to perform it. In Erika's world, you were either qualified for a job or you weren't.

Perhaps Erika had misinterpreted the expression on Clementine's face. It wasn't that she didn't want to help them by donating her eggs; it was just that she had so much on her mind at the moment. They should have waited until after the audition to ask her. But that was months away. If she got it, she'd be starting a new job. If she didn't get it, she'd be devastated. It was now or never.

Maybe it was never.

Was that tablet she'd taken affecting her balance? No, of course it wasn't. She was fine.

"Here you go!" Clementine handed Erika a glass, not quite meeting her eyes.

"I'll have one of those too," said Oliver. His disappointment with the way their "meeting" had turned out tugged at the corners of his mouth, so he looked like a sad clown. He'd been so hopeful about today. "Do you think she'll say yes?" he'd said suddenly last night as they watched TV, and Erika could hardly bear the yearning in his voice, and her fear made her snap, "How would I know?"

"Yeah, I'll have a drink too," said Sam. It was like everyone was dying of thirst. Erika *had* served sparkling mineral water at her place, with lemon. She took a big mouthful of champagne. She wasn't that fond of it. Did everyone just pretend to like champagne?

"Well, I know it's not very classy of me, but I'm having a beer." Tiffany went to the giant stainless-steel refrigerator and stood with her hip jutted at an angle. She wore denim jeans faded to almost white with rips at the knees (they were plausible rips; Erika could almost forgive her for them) and a plain white T-shirt, and her long blond hair had that just-off-the beach look that movie stars favored. Just looking at Tiffany made Erika think about sex, so God knew what she was doing to the men, although when she looked at her own husband, she saw that Oliver was looking out the window, staring at nothing, dreaming of babies. The perfect husband. Just in need of a perfect wife.

"Actually, I'll have a beer"—Sam put down his champagne glass on the island bench—"if one is going."

"I've got some struklji in the oven, just five more minutes," said Vid. He opened the oven and peered in. "It's a savory cheese strudel, very good, Slovenian, an old family recipe—no, not really, I got it from the Internet!" He roared with laughter. "My auntie used to make it, and I asked my mother for the recipe, and she said, 'How would I know!' My mother, she's no cook. Me, I'm a great cook."

"He *is* a great cook. Very humble too." Tiffany tipped back her head and took a long swig of her beer, her back arched, her chest thrust out, like a girl on a sexist football commercial. Erika couldn't look away. Did she do it on *purpose?* It was extraordinary. Erika caught Clementine's eye, and Clementine raised one eyebrow back at her, and Erika tried not to laugh, and everything Erika cherished about their friendship was encapsulated in that secret, just-for-her raised eyebrow.

"I'd love a husband who cooked," said Clementine to Tiffany. "Where did you pick him up?"

"That would be telling," said Tiffany sparkily.

See, this was the sort of conversation Erika didn't get. Wasn't that kind of inappropriate? Flirtatious? And Clementine and Tiffany were being so familiar with each other, as if Erika were the outsider and Clementine and Tiffany were the old friends.

"Hey, I cook!" Sam flicked Clementine's shoulder.

"Ow," said Clementine. She said to Tiffany and Vid, "The truth is, we share the cooking, but neither of us is very good at it."

"What?" said Sam with mock outrage. "What about my signature dish?"

"Your shepherd's pie. It's amazing. Exquisite. You follow the instructions on that packet mix to the letter." Clementine put her arm around his waist.

And also this. She didn't get this. How could they be teasing each other so fondly after all the tension at Erika's place? Tension caused by Erika, but really, Clementine and Sam should have been on the same page about something as significant as whether or not they were going to have a third child. It should have been clarified, discussed. Clementine should not have been going around telling people she'd rather poke her eyes out so that people thought they could *rely* on that information, thank you very much.

Was all this lovable banter for the benefit of Vid and Tiffany? She and Oliver didn't do married-couple banter. Oliver spoke fondly but politely to Erika in public, as if she were a beloved aunt, perhaps, not his wife. People probably thought they had a terrible marriage.

"Let me top you off there," said Tiffany to Erika, holding up the champagne bottle.

"Oh gosh, that went down fast." Erika looked at her empty glass, mystified.

"I wonder if I should go check on the kids," said Sam. He looked up at the ceiling. "It sounds suspiciously quiet up there."

"Ah, relax, don't worry, they're fine with Dakota," said Vid.

"Sam is the worrier," said Clementine.

"Yes, Clementine prefers the free-range-parenting approach," said Sam. "No need to watch them at the shopping center, a security guard will take care of them."

"Sam, that happened *once*," protested Clementine. "I turned my back on Holly for one second in JB Hi-Fi," she said to Vid and Tiffany, although Erika didn't remember hearing this story before. "And she'd run off to find a Barbie DVD or something, and got disoriented and wandered out of the shop. It was terrifying."

"Yes, see, so that's why you *can't* turn your back," said Sam.

"Yes, Mr. Never-Made-a-Mistake-in-Your-Life." Clementine rolled her eyes.

"Never made that sort of mistake," said Sam.

"That's nothing. I lost Dakota at the beach once," said Vid.

Erika and Oliver exchanged looks. Were these parents trying to outdo each other with just how incompetent and irresponsible they were? When Oliver and Erika had a child, it would never be out of their sight. Never. They would risk-assess every situation. They would give their child all the attention they hadn't gotten from their own parents. They would do everything right that their parents had gotten wrong.

"I have never been so scared in my life as that day at the beach," said Tiffany. "I wanted to kill him. I thought to myself, if something has happened to Dakota, I will kill him, I will literally *kill* him, I will never forgive him."

"But look, I'm still alive! We found her. It all worked out fine," said Vid. "Kids get lost. It's part of life."

No, it's not, thought Erika.

"Ah, no, it's not," said Tiffany, echoing Erika's thoughts. "It's not inevitable."

"Agreed." Sam clinked his beer bottle against Tiffany's. "Jeez. These feckless partners of ours."

"You and me, we are the *feckless* ones," said Vid to Clementine, and he made "feckless" sound like a delicious way to be.

"We're *relaxed*," said Clementine. "Anyway, it happened once, and now I watch them like a hawk."

"What about you two, eh?" said Vid to Erika and Oliver, perhaps noticing that his neighbors were being left out of the conversation.

"I watch Erika like a hawk," said Oliver unexpectedly. "I haven't lost her once."

Everyone laughed and Oliver looked triumphant. He couldn't normally pull off a clever comeback. Don't ruin it, my love, thought Erika as she saw Oliver's mouth move in preparation to speak again. Stop there. Don't try to say the same thing again a different way to get a bigger laugh.

"But what about kids, eh?" said Vid. "Are you two planning to have children?"

There was a brief pause. A tightening, a constriction of the atmosphere, as if people had stopped breathing.

"Vid," said Tiffany. "You can't ask people that. It's personal."

"What? Why not? What's personal about children?" Vid looked nonplussed.

"We're hoping to have children," said Oliver. His face collapsed inward, like a popped balloon. Poor Oliver. So soon after his tiny social triumph.

"One day," said Erika. Everyone seemed to be deliberately not looking at her, the way people did when you had food in your teeth and they didn't want to tell you, so they kept trying not to see. She used her fingernail to check her teeth for sesame seeds from the crackers. She'd meant to sound upbeat and positive. "One day soon."

"Yes, but you can't wait too long," said Vid.

"For God's sake, *Vid*!" said Tiffany.

There was a piercing yell from upstairs.

23

I t's Clementine."

The rain was so loud right now, Erika could only just distinguish Clementine's voice on the phone.

"Speak up," she said.

"Sorry. It's Clementine. Good morning! How are you?"

"Yeah, hi, how are you?" Erika moved her mobile phone to the other ear and tucked it against her shoulder, so she could continue taking things from the house through to the garage to pack in the car.

"I wondered if you wanted to meet up for a drink after work," said Clementine. "Today. Or another day."

"I'm not going to work," said Erika. "I'm taking the day off. I have to go to my mother's house."

When she'd called the office, she had told her secretary to tell anyone who asked that she'd taken the day off because her mother was ill, which was technically true.

There was a pause. "Oh," said Clementine, and her tone changed as it always did when they talked about Erika's mother. She became tentative and gentle, as if she were talking to someone with a terminal disease. "Mum did mention that she called you last night."

"Yes," said Erika. She felt a tiny eruption of fury at the thought of Clementine and her mother talking cozily about her—poor, poor Erika—as they must have done since she was a child.

She said to Clementine, "How was dinner?"

"Great," said Clementine, which meant that it wasn't, because otherwise she would have rhapsodized about the amazing flavors of the such and such.

Don't tell me about it then, Clementine. I don't care if your marriage is falling apart, if your perfect life is not so perfect these days. See how the rest of us live.

"So you're going to your mother's place," said Clementine. "To, uh, help her clean."

"As much as I can." Erika picked up the three-liter container of disinfectant and put it down again. It was too hard to carry while she tried to talk on the phone. She picked up the two mops instead and walked through the connecting door to the garage, switching on the light as she did. Their garage was spotless. Like a showroom for their spotless blue Statesman.

"Has Oliver taken the day off work too?" Clementine knew that Oliver always came with her. Erika remembered when she'd told Clementine about the first time Oliver had helped with her mother's house and how wonderful he'd been, just getting the job done, never a word of complaint, and how Clementine had gotten such a soft, teary look on her face when she heard this, and for some reason that soft, teary look made Erika feel angry, because she already *knew* how lucky she was to have Oliver's help, she already felt grateful and cherished, but Clementine's reaction made her feel ashamed, as if Erika didn't deserve it, as if he were doing more than anyone could expect of a husband.

"Oliver is home from work, but he's sick," said Erika. She opened the boot of her car and slid in the mops.

"Oh. Well, do you want me to come with you today?" said Clementine. "I could come. I'm playing at a wedding this morning, but then I'm free until school pickup time."

Erika closed her eyes. She could hear notes of both hope and fear in Clementine's voice. She remembered Clementine as a child, the day she'd discovered the way Erika lived: sweet little Clementine, with her porcelain skin, her clear blue eyes and her clean, lovely life, standing at Erika's front door, her round eyes even rounder still.

"You'd get bitten," Erika told her bluntly. "There are fleas." Clementine's porcelain skin always got the first mosquito bite. She looked so juicy.

"I'd wear repellent!" said Clementine enthusiastically. It was almost like she wanted to come.

"No," said Erika. "No. I'm fine. Thank you. You should be practicing for your audition."

"Yes," said Clementine with a sound like a sigh. "You're right, I guess."

"Who has a wedding on a Wednesday morning?" said Erika, mostly to change the subject but also because part of her didn't want to hear what she could sense was coming. "Don't all the guests have to take time off work?"

"People who want to save money," said Clementine vaguely. "And it's outdoors, and they didn't have a wet-weather plan, of course. Anyway, listen, I didn't want to do this over the phone, but . . ."

Here it came. The offer. It had only been a matter of time. Erika walked back inside and studied the huge bottle of disinfectant.

"I know you probably haven't wanted to bring it up again since the barbecue," said Clementine. "I'm sorry it's taken me so long to get back to you."

She sounded incongruously formal.

"But I didn't want you to think it was just because . . ." Her voice wavered. "And obviously, Sam and I, we haven't been thinking straight . . ."

"Clementine," said Erika. "You don't have—"

"So I want to do it," said Clementine. "Donate my eggs, that is. I want to help you have a baby. I'd love to help. I'm ready to, you know, get the ball rolling." She cleared her throat self-consciously, as if the words "get the ball rolling" were in a foreign language she was only just learning. "I feel good about it."

Erika didn't say anything. She managed to heft the bottle of disinfectant up onto her hip, like an obese toddler. She staggered back out to the garage.

"I want you to know that my decision has got nothing to do with what happened," said Clementine. "I would have said yes anyway."

Erika grunted as she opened the passenger door of her car and dropped the disinfectant onto the seat.

"Oh, Clementine," she said, and she was conscious of the sudden candidness of her tone, as if she'd been speaking falsely up until now. This was her true voice. It echoed around the garage. This was the voice she used with Oliver in the middle of the night when they shared the most shameful secrets of their shameful childhoods. "We both know that's a lie."

24

The Day of the Barbecue

That sounds like Holly," said Sam. He put down his beer bottle. "I'll go."

"Oh dear," said Tiffany. "I'll show you where they are."

"Mummy!" Holly shrieked from upstairs. "Mummy, Mummy, Mummy!"

"Looks like I'm needed too," said Clementine with obvious relief.

Erika wanted to go too, to check if Holly was okay, but with both parents there, it was clearly not appropriate, and would be the sort of overstepping behavior that would earn Erika an exasperated sigh from Clementine. Now it was just Erika, Oliver and Vid in the room, and it was immediately obvious that this particular social combination didn't work, even though Vid, of course, would give it his ebullient best shot.

Oliver stared glumly into his champagne glass while Vid opened the oven door to check on his baking and closed it again.

Erika looked around for inspiration. There was a large glass bowl in the middle of the island bench, filled with different-sized, different-colored pieces of glass.

"This is pretty," she said, pulling it toward her to examine the contents.

"It's Tiffany's," said Vid. "She calls it sea glass. I call it rubbish." He picked up a long oval-shaped piece of dark green glass. "Look at this! I said to her, babe, this is from a broken Heineken bottle! Some drunk leaves it at the beach, and then you bring home his rubbish! She goes on about it being polished by the sea or whatever."

"I guess it makes a nice decoration," said Erika, although she agreed with him. It was a bowl of rubbish.

"She's a hoarder, my wife," continued Vid. "If it wasn't for me, she'd be like one of those people you see on TV, you know, those ones who have so much crap, they can't get out their front door."

"Tiffany isn't a hoarder," said Erika.

Oliver cleared his throat. A little warning bell.

"She is, she really is!" said Vid. "You should see her wardrobe. Her shoes. That woman is Imelda Marcos."

"She's not a hoarder, though," said Erika. She avoided looking in Oliver's direction. "My mother is a real hoarder."

Oliver held out his hand, palm down, in front of Erika, as if to stop a waiter refilling his glass, except instead of "no more wine," he meant, "no more sharing." In Oliver's world, you told no one anything. Family was private. Family was shameful. They had that in common, except that Erika no longer wanted to be ashamed.

"Like for real?" said Vid, interested. "Like on the TV shows?"

The TV shows. Erika remembered the first time she'd turned on the TV and seen her mother's hallway, there for the world to see in all its disgusting glory, and how she'd leaped back, both hands pressed to her chest as if she'd been shot. It was like something from a nightmare; an enemy had filmed her dirty secret and broadcast it. Her rational mind had worked it out in the next instant. Of *course* it wasn't her mother's hallway, it belonged to an elderly Welsh man on the other side of the world, but even then Erika still couldn't shake that feeling of exposure, of public humiliation, and she'd turned it off with an angry swipe of the remote, as if she were slapping someone's face. She'd never watched one of those shows the whole way through; she couldn't bear that glib, pseudo-sympathetic tone.

"Yes, for real," said Erika. "Like on the TV shows."

"Wow," said Vid.

"She has a pathological attachment to inanimate objects," Erika heard herself say. Oliver sighed.

"She accumulates stuff to insulate herself from the world," continued Erika. She couldn't stop.

For most of her life, she had avoided analyzing her mother's "habit" or even thinking about it much, except when absolutely necessary. It was as though her mother had a socially unacceptable fetish. When she had left home, she was able to detach herself further still, but then, one night about a year ago, Erika had typed the word "hoarder" into Google, and just like that, she had developed a voracious appetite for information. She read textbooks, journal articles and case studies, initially with a racing heart, as if she were doing something illegal, but as she accumulated facts and statistics and terms like "pathological attachment to inanimate objects," her heart slowed. She wasn't alone. She wasn't that special. There was even a Children of Hoarders website where people like Erika shared story after story of identical frustrations. Erika's entire childhood, which had once seemed so unique in its secret dirty shame, was nothing more than a category, a type, a box to be ticked.

It was all that research that had led to her decision to get counseling. "My mother is a hoarder," she'd said to the psychologist at her very first session, the moment she sat down, as dispassionately as if she were saying "I have a bad cough" to her GP. It had been exhilarating, as if she'd once had a fear of heights and now she was skydiving. She was talking about it. She was going to learn tips and *techniques*. She was going to repair herself like a broken appliance. She'd be as good as new. No more anxiety over visiting her mother. No more waves of panic when some smell or word or passing thought reminded her of her childhood. She'd get this sorted.

The exhilaration had diminished a little when it had turned out the repair process wasn't quite as speedy or systematic as she'd hoped, but she was still optimistic and she still felt it was a sign of her good mental health that she could discuss her mother's problem so freely now. "It's not a sign of mental health," Oliver had said once, with unusual irritability, after Erika had begun telling an old lady in a supermarket checkout queue exactly why she needed to buy so many heavy-duty garbage bags. "It makes you look *unstable*." Oliver didn't understand that Erika experienced a strange, wondrous pleasure in *telling on her mother*. I'm not keeping your secrets any longer, Mum. I'm reporting you to this nice little old lady in the shopping center, I'm reporting you to whoever cares to listen.

Vid seemed fascinated, intrigued.

"Wow," he said. "So she just can't throw anything out, eh? I remember on one of those shows I watched, this old fella, he kept newspapers, right? Piles of them, and I just thought, mate, what are you *doing*, you'll *never* read them, chuck them in the bin!"

"Well," said Erika.

"Chuck what in the bin?" Tiffany reappeared with Dakota (who appeared so colorless and ordinary, standing next to her vibrant mother) and Holly, who seemed to be bright-eyed and bushy-tailed after all that yelling. She could be a drama queen.

"Everything okay?" said Erika.

"Oh yes, all good," said Tiffany. "Holly just had a bump playing tennis on the Wii."

"Did a tennis ball hit your nose?" Oliver asked Holly. It was like the whole shape and texture of his face changed when he spoke to children, as if he stopped clenching his teeth or something.

"Uh, Oliver, the tennis balls are not technically *real*," said Holly. She held up two fingers on each hand to place quotation marks around the word "real."

Oliver slapped the side of his head. "Silly me."

"Ruby's head went 'wham!' against my nose." Holly rubbed her nose resentfully, remembering. "She has a super-hard head."

"Ouch," said Oliver.

"Dakota is going to take Holly to show her the little house where Barney sleeps," said Tiffany.

"I want a puppy for my birthday," said Holly. "Exactly like Barney."

"We'll give you Barney!" said Vid. "He is very naughty."

"Really?" said Holly. "Can I have him?"

"No," said Dakota. "That's just my dad being silly."

"Oh," said Holly, and she threw Vid a baleful look.

Maybe I'll get her a puppy for her birthday, thought Erika. She'd tie a red ribbon around its collar and Holly would throw her arms around her, and Clementine would smile indulgently and fondly. (Was she drunk? Her thoughts seemed to keep skidding off in all kinds of hysterical directions.)

"Oh dear, oh well, I'll let your mum and dad deal with that!" said Tiffany. She lifted her T-shirt and scratched her flat, tan stomach. "And then we should all move out to the cabana, don't you think, Vid? It's too nice to be inside. Is that strudel finally ready?"

"What are Clementine and Sam doing?" asked Erika.

"Ruby wanted them to try to play tennis with her on the Wii," said Tiffany. "She's too little for it really, and then I think they forgot Ruby and started to get competitive with each other."

"Ruby needs her nappy changed," confided Holly to Erika. She waved a hand in front of her nose.

"They'll need the bag then," said Erika, picking up Clementine's nappy bag. It was so typical of Clementine and Sam to start playing some computer game while their child needed changing, and they were visiting people they barely knew. They were like teenagers sometimes. "I'll take it up."

"It's the room at the end of the hallway." Tiffany's tone became abruptly sharp. "Not on the marble!" She spun Vid back toward the stove just before he dumped a hot baking dish on the island bench.

Erika put the bag over her shoulder and walked up the softly carpeted curved staircase. At the top of the stairs there was a huge landing without any furniture, like an empty carpeted field. Erika stopped to allow her five-year-old self to relish the feeling of space. She let her arms float from her sides. There was an enormous painting of an eye on one wall, with a four-poster bed reflected in the pupil of the eye (nonsensical!), illuminated by a single low-hanging light fitting, like an upside-down milk bottle. It was like a room in a gallery of modern art. How long would it take her mother to ruin a "space" like this with her crap?

Erika walked down the hallway toward the murmur of voices in the end room. The carpet was so plush, she bounced along like an astronaut. Whoops. She swayed a little and her shoulder brushed the wall.

"She should have asked me in private." It was Clementine, speaking quietly but perfectly clearly. "Not with all four of us there. With cheese and crackers, for God's sake. That stingy little piece of cheese. It was so weird. Wasn't it weird?"

Erika froze. She was close enough to the room to see their shadows. She stood back against the hallway wall away from the door.

"She probably thought it involved all four of us," said Sam.

"I guess," said Clementine.

"Do you want to do it?" said Sam.

"No. I don't want to do it. I mean that's my first instinctive response. Just, no. I don't want to do it. This sounds so awful, but I just . . . *hate* the thought of it. It's almost . . . repulsive to me. Oh God, I don't mean that, I just really *don't want to do it.*"

Repulsive.

Erika closed her eyes. No amount of therapy or long hot showers would ever get her clean enough. She was still that dirty, flea-bitten kid.

"Well, you don't *have* to do it," said Sam. "It's just something they're asking you to consider, you don't need to get all worked up about it."

"But there's no one else in her life! There's only me. It's always only me. She hasn't got any other friends. It's like she always wants another *piece* of me." Clementine's voice rose.

"Shh," said Sam.

"They can't hear us." But Clementine lowered her voice again and Erika had to strain to hear. "I think I'd feel like it was my baby. I'd feel like they had my baby. What if it looked like Holly and Ruby?"

"That shouldn't worry you too much, seeing as you'd rather poke your eyes—"

"That was a joke. Erika shouldn't have passed that on, I didn't actually mean—" Clementine's voice rose again.

"Yes, I know, sure, look, let's just get through this thing and we'll talk about it when we get home."

"Daddy!" Ruby's little voice piped up. "Play again! Right now. Now, now, now."

"That's enough, Ruby, we need to go back downstairs," said Clementine.

"We need to change her, that's what we need to do," said Sam. "Where's the nappy bag?"

"It's downstairs, of course, it's not attached to my wrist."

"Jeez, don't get snippy on me, I'll get it." Sam came out of the room and stopped short.

"Erika!" he said, and it was almost funny the way he took a step back, his eyes wide with fear, as if she were an intruder.

25

Tiffany was searching through the bottom drawer of Dakota's chest of drawers for an Alannah Hill white cardigan with a scattering of tiny white pearls on the shoulders that suddenly seemed like exactly the right sort of thing for a private school mother to wear to a "compulsory" Information Morning.

She was sure this was the cardigan she'd pulled from her bag and made Dakota wear when they'd gone to Vid's cousin's baby's christening a few weeks back and it had suddenly gotten cold. It had hung around Dakota's wrists, but Dakota never cared much what she was wearing. Knowing Dakota, she'd come home and jammed it in one of her drawers. It probably needed cleaning, but Tiffany was obsessed with finding it, as if it were the only solution to a far more complex problem.

She pulled out everything from the bottom drawer and placed it on the floor next to her. There was a book jammed right at the back of the drawer. She went to put it on the floor and saw that it was only half a book. The cover was missing. It had been torn in half. Almost every page had been scribbled upon in angry black marker, in some cases so violently, there were holes through the paper.

She sat back on her haunches, staring at it, breathing rapidly. The title at the top of the page said, THE HUNGER GAMES. Wasn't that the book that her sister Karen had told her was too grown-up for Dakota? "You've got to take responsibility for what she reads," Karen had said bossily. "Don't you know how violent that book is?" But Tiffany had believed she shouldn't censor Dakota's reading. It wasn't pornography, after all. It was a young adult book. Tiffany knew what the book was about (she'd watched the movie trailer on YouTube) and even fairy tales were violent. What about "Hansel and Gretel"?! Dakota had always loved the most gruesome fairy tales.

Had the book had such a profoundly terrible impact on Dakota that she'd felt the need to destroy it? It was like it had been brutally vandalized. Tiffany pulled more clothes out and found the remainder of the book.

Dakota loved her books, and she always took such care of them. Her bookshelf was in beautiful order. She didn't even freaking well dog-ear pages. She used a bookmark! And now she was tearing up a book and hiding it? It didn't make sense. Reading was her greatest pleasure.

Tiffany looked at the ceiling. Although, was Dakota reading as much as she once had? She had to read for homework, of course, and Dakota diligently sat down at her desk and did all her homework without ever being asked, without Tiffany having to monitor her at all. But what about reading for pleasure?

When was the last time Tiffany had come across her reading in bed or on the window seat? She couldn't remember. Jeez Louise, had this book distressed her so much that *she couldn't even read anymore?* Tiffany's negligence was breathtaking. Terrible mother. Terrible neighbor. Terrible woman.

"Have you finished polishing those shoes yet, Vid?" she called out. "We don't want to leave late! The traffic will be bad in the rain!"

Tiffany shoved everything including the book back into the drawer. Obviously she wouldn't say anything to Dakota now, not when they were just about to leave for the Information Morning.

She put it out of her mind for later.

26

The Day of the Barbecue

Sam said "Erika!" and Clementine clapped her hand over her mouth as if to grab back her words and then quickly dropped it as evidence of her guilt. Her stupidity and thoughtlessness were beyond belief.

"Oh! Hi! Thanks!" she said as Erika came into the room and handed her the nappy bag. "How did you guess we needed that? Is Holly okay?"

As she babbled, she frantically rewound the conversation. What could Erika have overheard? Anything? All of it? Oh God, not the part about being "repulsed." It was her *tone* that was the worst. The tone of contempt.

She kept talking, talking as if she could somehow conceal what she'd said with layers of new conversation. "Dakota took her to see the dog kennel or something. She wants a puppy for her birthday. Don't you dare give her one, will you, only joking, I know you wouldn't. Isn't this house amazing? I bet even the dog kennel is five-star!"

From behind Erika, Sam widened his eyes and ran his finger across his throat.

"Tiffany wants us all to go outside to the cabana," said Erika. She sounded dry and cool as usual. Maybe she hadn't heard anything.

"I'll go back down, check on Holly," said Sam. "You all right with Ruby?"

"Of course I'm all right with Ruby," said Clementine. He always did that when he left her with one or both of the girls, as if he needed to confirm that she would indeed remember to take care of her own children.

"Where are you going to change her?" Erika looked around her.

This was what rich people called a "media room." There were leather couches facing the laughably gigantic screen on the wall. Sam had just about lost his mind with envy when he saw it.

"Oh God," said Clementine. "I don't know. The floor, I guess." She started laying out the change mat and wipes. "Everything looks so expensive, doesn't it?"

"I'm stinky," said Ruby. She tilted her head seductively, as if being stinky were something to be prized.

"Yes, you are," said Clementine.

"Wasn't Holly toilet-trained by this age?" asked Erika as Clementine changed Ruby.

"We've been putting it off," admitted Clementine. Normally she would have been annoyed by the implied criticism in Erika's question, but now she was anxious to humbly admit her failure, as if that would somehow acquit her of the nasty things she'd said. (My God, she'd complained about the size of the *cheese*.)

"Once you start, you've got to commit, and you're sort of stuck at home, you can't go anywhere—well, you can, but it's tricky . . . and, um, but we're all set, we've got her big-girl undies ready, haven't we, Ruby? And we thought, after we get my audition and Holly's birthday party and Sam's parents' ruby wedding anniversary out of the way, we'd commit."

Shut up, shut up, shut up. She couldn't stop talking.

"Right," said Erika blankly. Normally she would have had an aggravating counter-opinion. Ever since Ruby and Holly were babies, Erika had been reading parenting articles relevant to their ages and passing on tips about "milestones." Clementine had always believed this was evidence of Erika's obsessive, bordering on strange, interest in Clementine's life, not her interest in having children of her own. How self-obsessed she'd been.

"Up!" demanded Ruby as soon as Clementine had finished changing her. She held out her arms to Erika, and Erika lifted her onto her hip. "Over there!" Ruby thrust her body to one side to indicate which direction Erika should head, as if she were astride a recalcitrant horse.

"You're a bossy little thing," said Erika as she took Ruby closer to the bookshelf, where Clementine could see a porcelain doll that Ruby was hoping she could get her hands on.

"Oh, that's what you want! I don't think we can let you touch that," said Erika, and she twisted her body away so that Ruby's outstretched hands couldn't grab the doll.

Erika's eyes met Clementine's over the top of Ruby's head. There was something a little unfocused and strange about the way she looked at Clementine, but she didn't seem hurt or angry. She mustn't have heard. She wouldn't have just lurked outside the door listening. That wasn't Erika's style. She would have barged right in to hand over the nappy bag, to show up their incompetence, to prove how much better she'd be at this than them.

Clementine watched Erika bend her forehead tenderly toward Ruby's, and she felt choked with guilt for her lack of generosity.

But she still couldn't, she wouldn't, do what her friend had asked.

I don't want to do it. I don't want to do it. She bent down to put the change mat back in the nappy bag, and she realized it wasn't Erika she was mentally addressing but her mother: *I've been kind, I've been good, but that's enough now, don't make me do this too.*

27

O liver?" said Erika quietly, just in case he was still asleep. She stood at the end of their bed, looking at him. One arm was outside the covers, bent at an attractive angle to show his very excellent triceps. He was lean, verging on skinny, but well built. (Early in their relationship, they'd gone to the beach with Clementine and Sam and Holly, who was a baby at the time, and Clementine had whispered in Erika's ear, "Your new boyfriend is unexpectedly buff, isn't he?" It had pleased Erika more than she liked to admit.)

"Mmmm?" Oliver rolled over onto his back and opened his eyes.

"I'm ready to go over to Mum's place," she said.

Oliver yawned, rubbed his eyes and retrieved his glasses from the bedside table. He glanced out the window at the pouring rain. "Maybe you should wait till the deluge eases."

"I'd be waiting all day," said Erika. She looked at her bed, made up with snowy white, crisp bed linen. Oliver made the bed each day with taut hospital corners. She was surprised by how badly she wanted to take off her clothes and get back into bed with him and just forget everything. She wasn't normally a napper.

"How are you feeling?" she said.

"I think I might be feeling better," said Oliver worriedly. He sat upright in bed and tapped under his eyes, checking his sinuses. "Oh no. I feel good! I should have gone into work." Whenever he took a sick day, the poor man obsessively monitored his health the whole time in case he was misusing his sick leave benefits. "Or I could help you at your mother's place." He sat up and swung his feet onto the floor. "I could change it to a day of personal time."

"You need one more day of rest," said Erika. "And you're not going near my mother's place when you're sick."

"Actually, I do feel a bit dizzy," said Oliver with relief. "Yes, I am now experiencing indisputable dizziness. I could not run the audit clearance meeting. No way."

"You could not run the audit clearance meeting. Lie back down. I'll make you some tea and toast before I go."

"You're wonderful," he said. He was always so pathetically grateful for any nurturing he got when he was sick. He had been making his own doctor's appointments by the time he was ten. No wonder he was a hypochondriac. Not that Erika had gotten much nurturing from having a nurse for a mother, certainly not for sniffles (no warm chicken soup on a tray like Clementine got from Pam), although the few times in her life that Erika had gotten properly sick, her mother had nursed her, and nursed her extremely well, as if she'd finally gotten interesting.

"Did I hear you talking to someone on the phone before?" said Oliver as she was about to leave the room.

"Clementine," said Erika. She hesitated. She didn't want to tell him she'd said yes. She didn't want to see him sit bolt upright in bed, the color back in his cheeks.

Oliver didn't open his eyes. "Any news?"

"No," said Erika. "Not yet."

She just needed to think about it. Today she had that "emergency" session with her psychologist. Maybe that would get things clearer in her mind. So much to cover at today's session! She might need to bring along an agenda. That wouldn't make her look like a type A personality at all. Not that Erika had a problem with being type A. Why would you want to be any other personality type?

As she made Oliver's tea and toast, she thought about the first time their doctor had said it was time to give up on Erika's eggs.

"We can pay someone to donate to us, right?" Erika had said. She didn't care. She was almost relieved, because she could forget now about her secret fear of passing on her various genetic stains. There had never been any particular pleasure for her in imagining a child with her own eyes or hair or personality traits. Who would want her thin lifeless hair? Her skinny knock-kneed legs? And what if the child hoarded? It was fine that the child would not be biologically hers. She was ready to move on almost instantly.

It was Oliver who had seemed to genuinely *grieve*. It was odd. Touching but baffling. She knew he loved her. It was one of the most wonderful surprises of her life. But to actually want a child who looked like Erika, who behaved like Erika, who shared her physical and mental attributes? Come on, now. That was going a step too far.

Anyway, they had money. They could pay for someone's eggs. They would get this job done, finally, once and for all.

But apparently not.

"Well, no," said their doctor. "That's illegal here." Their doctor was American. "You're allowed to pay your donor for her time and medical costs but that's it. It's not like back home, where young college students donate their eggs for money. So Australia does have a real shortage of egg donors." She looked at them sadly, resignedly. She'd obviously given this spiel so many times before. "What you're looking for is an altruistic donor. There *are* women who are prepared to donate to strangers, but they're difficult to find. The easiest, least complicated option, which I would suggest you consider first, is finding a good friend or a relative to help you."

"Oh, that's fine. We wouldn't want a stranger's eggs anyway," said Oliver immediately, and Erika thought, Wouldn't we? Why not? "We don't want to just build a baby from spare parts," he said. Their doctor's face went blank and professional as she listened to Oliver. After all, that was her trade: building babies. "We want this child to come from a place of love," Oliver said with a tremble of emotion, and Erika blushed, she literally blushed, because what in the world was he going on about? She had no problem talking about ovulation and menstrual cycles and follicles in front of her IVF doctor, but not *love*. That was so personal.

Oliver was the one who had suggested Clementine, in the car on the way home, and Erika had instantly, instinctively balked. No. No way. Clementine didn't like needles. Clementine was so busy trying to balance her family and career. Erika didn't like to ask Clementine for favors; she preferred doing favors for Clementine.

But then she thought of Holly and Ruby, and suddenly she'd been overwhelmed by the most extraordinary desire. Her own Holly or Ruby. Suddenly this abstract idea she'd been working toward for so long became real. Ruby's beautiful green cat's eyes with Oliver's dark hair. Holly's rosebud lips with Oliver's nose. For the first time since she'd begun the IVF process she felt true desperation for a baby. For *that* baby. She wanted it as much as Oliver did. It almost seemed like she wanted Clementine's baby far more than she'd ever wanted her own baby.

The kettle boiled and she remembered how she had walked down that bouncy, soft-carpeted hallway at Tiffany and Vid's house, encased in that strange bubble where nothing seemed quite real, except that she'd overheard Clementine's voice perfectly: "It's almost . . . repulsive to me. Oh God, I don't mean that, I just really don't want to do it."

Why did she remember that part of the night so clearly? It would be better if Clementine's words had vanished from her memory, but her memory of that part of the afternoon was crystalline, more distinct even than a regular memory, as if the tablet and the first glass of champagne had produced a chemical reaction that had at first heightened her memory before turning it murky.

She heard Clementine say, "What if it looked like Holly or Ruby?"

Even after all these weeks, her cheeks burned at the memory. Clementine had spoken Erika's secret, most precious hopes out loud in a tone of disdain.

She remembered walking into that room and seeing Clementine's horrified face. She was so clearly terrified that Erika had overheard.

She remembered how she'd carried Ruby downstairs on her hip while rage and pain raced like bacteria through her bloodstream. Rage and pain for Oliver, who had so blissfully, innocently assumed that if they asked Clementine to donate her eggs, his little baby would come from "a place of love." A place of love. What a joke.

They'd gone out into that preposterous backyard and Tiffany had offered her wine, that very good wine, and she'd drunk it faster than she'd ever drunk a glass of wine before, and every time Erika had looked at Clementine, laughing, chatting, having the time of her life, she had silently screamed, *You can keep your damned eggs!*

And it was at that point her memories of exactly what happened that afternoon began to loosen, fragment and crumble.

28

The Day of the Barbecue

This is some backyard," said Sam.

"It's . . . amazing," said Clementine.

Vid and Tiffany's house had been impressive, especially the artwork, but this lavishly landscaped backyard, with its tinkling water features, its fountains and urns, its white marble statues and its scented candle–lit, luxuriously fitted-out cabana, was another level of extravagance altogether. The fragrance of roasting meat filled the air, and Clementine wanted to laugh out loud with delight, like a child walking into Disneyland. She was enchanted by the opulence of it all. There was something so hedonistic and generous about it, especially after poor Erika's rigidly minimalist home.

Of course, she *understood* the reasons for Erika's obsession with minimalism, she wasn't completely insensitive.

"Yeah, the backyard is all Vid's. He goes for the understated look," said Tiffany as she indicated a seat for Clementine, refilled her glass with champagne and offered the plate of Vid's freshly baked strudels.

Clementine wondered if Tiffany had some experience in the hospitality field. She almost had one arm folded behind her back as she bent at the waist and poured drinks.

From where Clementine sat in the long, low cabana, she could see her daughters playing on a large rectangle of grass next to a gazebo with ornate columns and a wrought-iron dome. They were throwing a tennis ball for the little dog. Ruby had the ball at the moment and she was holding it up high above her head, while the dog, taut and trembling with anticipation, sat in front of her, poised to spring.

"You must tell Dakota to let us know when she gets sick of looking after the girls," said Clementine to Tiffany, although she hoped it wouldn't be anytime soon.

"She's having a great time with them," said Tiffany. "You just relax and enjoy the view of the Trevi Fountain there." She nodded at the largest, most extravagant fountain, a monolithic creation built like a wedding cake with winged angels holding uplifted hands as if to sing, except instead they spurted great crisscrossing arcs of water from their mouths. "That's what my sisters call it."

"Her sisters have the wrong country," said Vid. "The Gardens of Versailles was my inspiration, in France, you know! I got books, pictures, I studied up. This is all my own design, you know, I sketched it out: the gazebo, the fountain, everything! Then I got friends in to build it all for me. I know a lot of tradies. But her sisters!" He pointed his thumb at Tiffany. "When they saw this backyard, they laughed and laughed, they just about wet their pants." He shrugged, unbothered. "I said to them, it's no problem that my art has given you joy!"

"I think it's incredible," said Clementine.

"No pool?" asked Sam, who had grown up splashing about in a backyard above-ground pool with his brothers and sister. "You've got enough room for one."

He looked about the backyard as if planning a redesign, and Clementine could tell exactly where his mind was heading. Sometimes he talked wistfully about selling up and moving out to a good old-fashioned quarter-acre block in the suburbs, where there would be room for a pool and a trampoline, a cubby house and a chook shed and a vegetable garden, a house where his children could have the sort of childhood he'd had, even though nobody had childhoods like that anymore, and even though Sam was more urban than her, and loved being able to walk to restaurants and bars and catch the ferry into the city.

Clementine shuddered at the thought of the third child in that suburban dream of his, now at the front of his mind thanks to Erika's request. God, there might even be a *fourth* child romping about in his imaginary backyard.

"No pool! I'm not a fan of chlorine. Unnatural," said Vid, as if there were anything natural about all this glossy marble and concrete.

"It's incredible," said Clementine again, in case Sam's comment could be interpreted as criticism. "Is that a maze over there in the corner? For lovers' trysts?"

She didn't know why she'd said "lovers' trysts." What a thing to say. Had she ever said the word "tryst" out loud in her life before? Was that even how you pronounced it?

"Yes, and for Easter egg hunts with all of Dakota's cousins," said Tiffany.

"Taking care of that topiary must take up a bit of your time," commented Oliver, looking at the sculptured hedges.

"I have a good friend, you know, he takes care of it." Vid made giant snip-snip movements with his hands to indicate someone else doing his hedge clipping.

The late afternoon sun streamed into the cabana and created a rainbow effect in the mist of water billowing from the wonderfully absurd fountain. Clementine felt a sudden burst of optimism. Surely Erika hadn't overheard what she'd said, and even if she had, Clementine would make it right, as she had so many times before, and then she'd find a nice, gentle way to explain why she couldn't donate her eggs. An anonymous egg donor would be more suitable for all concerned. They existed! Didn't they? People were always getting pregnant using donated eggs. Or celebrities were, anyway.

And Sam didn't *really* want another baby, any more than he really wanted to be a tradesman like his dad. He sometimes said he should have done something with his hands. After a frustrating day at work he'd go on about how he wasn't really cut out for the corporate world, but then next thing he was all excited about a TV commercial he was shooting. Everyone had another sort of life up their sleeve that might have made them happy. Yes, Sam could have been a plumber married to a stay-at-home domestically minded wife who kept the house in perfect order, with five strapping football-playing sons, but then he probably would have dreamed of having a fun office job and living in a cool, funky suburb by the harbor with a cellist and two gorgeous little girls, thank you very much.

She took a bite of Vid's strudel. Sam, who was already halfway through eating one, laughed at her. "I *knew* your eyes would roll back into your head when you tasted that."

"It's spectacular," said Clementine.

"Yeah, not bad, hey," said Vid. "Tell me, do you taste a little hint of something, like the *idea* of a flavor, you know, the dream of a flavor, and you just can't quite put your finger on it?"

"It's sage," said Clementine.

"It *is* sage!" cried Vid.

"My wife is so sage," said Sam. Tiffany chuckled and Clementine saw the pleasure on her husband's face that he'd made the hot chick laugh.

She said, "Don't encourage the bad dad humor, Tiffany."

"Sorry." Tiffany grinned at her.

Clementine smiled back and found her eyes drawn irresistibly to Tiffany's cleavage. It was like something from a Wonderbra ad. Were those breasts real? Tiffany could probably afford the best. Clementine's friend Emmeline would know. Emmeline had perfect pitch and an unerring eye for a fake boob. That glorious cleavage had to be as unnatural as this backyard. Tiffany adjusted her T-shirt. Oh God, she'd been staring for too long now. Clementine looked away fast and back at the children.

"This strudel is very good," said Oliver in his careful, polite way, wiping a fragment of pastry off the side of his mouth.

"Yes, it's excellent," said Erika.

Clementine turned her head. Erika had slurred the word "excellent," just a little. In fact, if it were anyone else, Clementine wouldn't have used the word "slur," but Erika had a very precise way of speaking. Each vowel was always enunciated just so. Was Erika a little tipsy? If so, it would be a first. She'd always hated the idea of losing control. So did Oliver. Presumably that was part of the reason why they were attracted to each other.

"So now you've passed that test," said Vid. "I've got another one."

"I'll win this one," said Sam. "Bring it on. Sporting trivia? Limbo? I'm great at limbo."

"He is surprisingly good at limbo," said Clementine.

"Oh, me too," said Tiffany. "Or I used to be. I'm not as flexible as I once was."

She put down her drink, bent her body back at an extraordinary angle so that her T-shirt rode up, and thrust out her pelvis. Was that a tattoo just below the waistband of her jeans? Clementine strained to see. Tiffany took a couple of steps forward and hummed limbo music as she ducked under an invisible pole.

She straightened and pressed her hand to her lower back. "Ow. Getting old."

"Jeez," said Sam a little hoarsely. "You might give me a run for my money."

Clementine stifled a giggle. Yes, my darling, I think she would give you a run for your money.

"Where are the kids?" he asked suddenly, as if coming back to reality.

"They're right there," said Clementine. She pointed at the gazebo, where Dakota and the girls were still playing with the dog. "I'm watching them."

"Do you do yoga?" Oliver asked Tiffany. "You've got great flexibility."

"*Great* flexibility," agreed Sam. Clementine reached over and discreetly pinched the flesh above his knee as hard as she could.

"Ah-ya." Sam grabbed her hand to stop her.

"What's that, mate?" asked Oliver.

"Bah! It's not a limbo competition!" said Vid. "It's a *music* competition. It's my favorite piece of classical music. Now, look, I will be honest with you. I don't know anything about classical music. I know nothing. I'm an electrician! A simple electrician! What would I know about classical music? I come from peasant stock. My family—we were peasants! Simple peasants!"

"Here we go with the simple peasants." Tiffany rolled her eyes.

"But I like classical music," continued Vid, ignoring her. "I like it. I buy CDs all the time! Don't know what I'm buying! Just pick them at random off the shelf! Nobody else buys CDs anymore, I know, but I do, and I got this one day, at the shopping center, you know, and on the way home, I played it in the car, and when this came on, I had to pull over, I had to stop on the side of the road because it was like . . . it was like I was drowning. I was drowning in feeling. I cried, you know, I cried like a baby."

He pointed at Clementine. "I bet the cellist knows what I mean."

"Sure," said Clementine.

"So let's see if you can name it, hey? Maybe it's not even good music! What do I know?"

He fiddled with his phone. Naturally the cabana had a built-in sound system that was linked to his mobile phone.

"Who says only the cellist can enter this competition?" said Sam. Clementine could hear him imitating Vid's speech cadences without realizing he was doing it. It was so embarrassing the way he did that, picking up waiters' accents in restaurants and coming over all Indian or Chinese. "What about the marketing manager, eh?"

"What about the accountant?" Oliver followed the joke with heavy-handed jolliness.

Erika said nothing. She sat with her forearms perfectly still on the armrests of her chair staring off into the distance. It was unusual too for Erika to disengage from a conversation like this. Normally she listened to social chit-chat as if she'd be sitting for a quiz later.

"You can *all* enter!" cried Vid. "Silence."

He lifted his phone as though it were a conductor's baton and then dropped it in a dramatic swooping motion. Nothing happened.

He swore, jabbing at the screen.

"Give it here." Tiffany took the phone and pressed some keys. Immediately, the lush opening notes of Fauré's "After a Dream" cascaded through the cabana with perfect clarity.

Clementine straightened. It almost felt like a trick that out of all the pieces of music he could have picked, he'd chosen this one. She knew exactly what he meant when he'd described "drowning in feeling." She'd felt it too, when she was fifteen, sitting with her bored parents (her father's head kept snapping forward as he dropped off to sleep) at the Opera House: that extraordinary feeling of submersion, as if she'd been drenched in something exquisite.

"Louder!" cried Vid. "It needs to be loud."

Tiffany turned up the volume.

Next to her, Sam automatically adjusted his posture and assumed his stoic, polite, I'm-listening-to-classical-music-and-hoping-it-will-be-over-soon face. Tiffany refilled glasses with no discernible reaction to the music, while Erika continued to stare into the distance and Oliver wrinkled his brow, concentrating. Oliver could possibly name the composer. He was one of those well-educated private school boys who knew a lot about a lot of things, but he couldn't *feel* the music. Clementine and Vid were the only ones feeling it.

Vid met her eyes, lifted his glass in a secret salute and winked as if to say, *Yeah, I know.*

29

Vid sat at the wrought-iron table on his front veranda with sheets of newspaper laid out, polishing Dakota's school shoes so that she would look smart for the Information Morning at Saint Anastasias. He remembered how he used to polish his elder daughters' shoes when they were all at school. Three little pairs of black shoes going down in size. Now his daughters all wobbled about on stilettos with pointy heels.

Something was making him feel especially mournful today, and he was not exactly sure what it was and it made him feel angry. Perhaps it was related to the weather. He had heard an interview on the radio about how the lack of sunshine was having a detrimental psychological effect on the people of Sydney. Serotonin levels were dipping, causing depression rates to rise. An Englishman had rung up and said, "What a load of rubbish! This is nothing, you Aussies are so soft! Come to England and we'll show you rain."

Vid didn't think he was so soft that he'd let a little bad weather worry him.

There was the sound of a car in the cul-de-sac and Vid looked up to see Erika from next door driving off down the street in her blue Statesman.

He wondered if Erika had seen Clementine lately.

He dipped the brush in the black polish and swirled it around.

He had told not one single person that he had seen Clementine perform the other night, as if it were a secret when there was no reason for it to be a secret. Yes, *possibly* it was a little strange that he had gone to see her perform—but come on, now, why was it so strange? It was a free country. Anyone could go see her perform.

"Isn't that right, Barney?" he said to the dog, which sat at his feet, very upright and alert, as if guarding him from something. "It's a free country?"

Barney shot him a concerned look and then suddenly trotted off, as if a decision had been reached that nothing could be done with Vid and he might as well go and check in with some other members of the family.

Vid carefully polished the side of the shoe. Women could not polish shoes. They were too impatient and quick. They never did a good job of it.

Could Clementine polish a shoe? He wished he could ask her. He would like to hear her answer. Clementine was still their friend, surely? Why would she not return his calls? He only wanted to say hello, to check in with her. He had even left messages, and he didn't like leaving messages. He preferred people to see there was a missed call from him and call straight back. She must have had his number programmed into her phone by now, surely? It was hurtful to him. He'd never had anyone not return his calls before. Even his ex-wife returned his calls.

He held the shoe up and examined it, remembering the music. It had been extraordinary. Breathtaking.

It had been a spur-of-the-moment decision. He was at the Quay. He'd been going to meet a good friend at the Opera Bar, but his friend's elderly mother had gotten sick and he'd had to cancel at the last minute, so Vid had wandered up into the Opera House, where he'd had a very nice, long discussion with a girl at the ticket counter. He'd said he wanted to go to the symphony and it turned out that was no problem, there were plenty of seats available to *Thus Spake Zarathustra*. Vid had no idea what that meant, but the girl said he would recognize some of the music from *2001: A Space Odyssey*, and she was right, of course he did.

He had not had his hopes up that Clementine would be playing. He knew she wasn't a full-time employee of the orchestra. She filled in for them when they needed her. She was a subbie. He also knew she had an audition coming up for a full-time position that she very much wanted, and he'd confirmed with Erika that the audition hadn't happened yet.

So he knew there was only a very small chance she would be playing, but then again, he'd always been lucky. He was a very lucky person. Some people had the luck, some people did not, but he had the luck, he'd always had the luck (except, of course, for what happened at the barbecue, but that was just a deviation in the path of his lucky life). But the other night he'd been lucky, because there she was, right there on the stage, wearing a long black dress, chatting with the musician sitting next to her, as calm as if they were waiting for a bus, with that beautiful, gleaming instrument leaning back against her shoulder the same way a small tired child does.

When he found his seat he got into conversation with the man sitting next to him, who was Croatian, his name was Ezra, and he was there with his wife and they were both "subscribers." (Vid was now a subscriber too.) Vid told him he'd never been to the symphony before but he loved classical music, and he knew that cellist, sitting right there, and so he was going to be clapping very loudly for her, and Ezra told him that the audience didn't normally clap in between movements, so maybe to wait until other people clapped first, and Ezra's wife, Ursula, leaned forward and said, "You clap when you want to clap." (Vid was going to have Ezra and Ursula over for dinner as soon as he could arrange it. He had Ezra's number in his phone. Good people. Very good people.)

He'd assumed the symphony would be like a show or a movie, where all the lights went out, but the lights stayed on, and so he could see Clementine the whole time. At one point he even thought she'd looked right at him, but he couldn't be sure.

She was clearly the best player in the whole orchestra. Any fool could see that. He was transfixed by the way her hand quivered rapidly on the neck of the cello, by the way her bow moved in tandem with the other musicians' bows, by the way she tilted back her head, exposing her neck.

He was transfixed by the whole experience really.

(Ezra was right, nobody clapped when Vid thought they should clap. They *coughed*. Every time the orchestra stopped playing, there was a little symphony of coughing and throat-clearing. It reminded Vid of church.)

He had to leave at the intermission because Tiffany was expecting him, but Ezra and Ursula said that the first half was always the best half anyway.

As he drove home from the city he could still feel the music, as if he'd taken some hallucinogenic drug. He had so much feeling trapped within his chest, he had to take shallow breaths while he waited for it to subside.

He wanted to call her, to tell her that she was the best player on that stage, by a *long shot*, but then he kept remembering her face the last time he'd seen her in this backyard, and he understood that she didn't want to be reminded of that day. He didn't want to be reminded of it either, but still he *longed*, not for her exactly, he didn't *want* Clementine, not really, not in a sexual way, but he longed for something, and it felt like she was the only one who could give it to him.

A police car was pulling into Harry's driveway as Vid, Tiffany and Dakota left for the Information Morning.

"Maybe we should stop," said Tiffany. Face the music. I let my young daughter read *The Hunger Games*, Officer. I didn't notice my neighbor was dead. I may have behaved in despicable ways.

Vid put his foot on the accelerator. "What? No." The Lexus purred forward obediently onto the street. "You've already spoken to the police. You've told them everything you know. There's nothing more to say. They're just finishing their report, you know, wasting taxpayers' money."

"I should have taken Harry meals," fretted Tiffany. "That's what a good neighbor would have done. Why didn't I ever take him a meal?"

"Is that what you think the police want to ask you? 'Why didn't you take him meals, you lousy neighbor?' You could say, 'Well, Officer, I'll tell you why! Because he would have thrown those meals in my face, you know! Like a cream pie!'"

"You shouldn't only be nice to nice people," said Tiffany, observing the large homes they were passing, nice comfy double-brick homes with well-maintained lawns beneath towering canopies of trees. Had she become one of those entitled types? A little pleased with herself? Too busy to care?

"Of course you should only be nice to nice people!" Vid looked at Dakota in the rearview mirror. "You hear that, Dakota? Don't waste your time on people who are not nice!"

Tiffany looked over her shoulder at Dakota, who sat upright and pale in her current school uniform (they'd be dropping her off at school afterwards), her body pressed right up against the side of the car, as if she were making room for other passengers. Why did you rip up that book, Dakota?

"Once Mum took Harry over a quiche," said Dakota without looking at her mother. "I remember. It was a mushroom quiche."

"Did I? Wait, I did, didn't I?" said Tiffany, thrilled by the memory. It had been after a Christmas party they'd had catered. "He said he hated mushrooms."

Vid chuckled. "There you go."

"It wasn't his fault he didn't like mushrooms!" she said. "I should have tried again."

"He was rude about it, though, right?" said Vid.

Harry had been rude about the quiche. He had slammed the door so fast, she'd had to jump back to make sure her fingers weren't jammed. Still, she knew that his wife and child had died years ago. He was a sad and lonely old man. She should have tried harder.

"Don't you feel bad?" she said to Vid. "At all?"

Vid shrugged his big shoulders. He steered with his fingers barely touching the bottom of the wheel. "I feel sad that he died alone, but you know, what's done is done, and the man spat at our beautiful Dakota!"

"He didn't spit *at* me," said Dakota. "He just spat on the ground when he saw me. I made him feel like spitting."

"That makes me feel like killing the man," said Vid. His fingers flexed on the wheel.

"He's already very, very dead," said Tiffany. She thought of the stench that had hit her when Oliver opened the door. She'd known straightaway. "I just feel . . ."

"You feel *regret*," said Dakota in a flat voice, from the backseat.

Tiffany turned again quickly. It was the sort of remark that Dakota used to make all the time, testing her vocabulary, testing out ideas, trying to work out exactly how the world worked.

"I do feel regret," said Tiffany, eager to chat, to have one of those conversations she used to have all the time with Dakota, where she was always left amazed and delighted by her daughter's quirky, clever observations, but Dakota just kept staring out the window, her jaw set, almost as if she were angry, and after a moment Tiffany gave up and faced the other way.

Vid talked for the rest of the drive about a new Japanese restaurant some clients of his had been talking about, which served the best tempura in Sydney, possibly the world, possibly the universe.

"Here we are!" said Vid as they approached a giant set of iron gates. "Look at your new school, Dakota!"

Tiffany turned to smile at Dakota, but now Dakota had her eyes closed, and she was letting her forehead bump quite hard against the window, as if she'd passed out.

"Dakota!" said Tiffany sharply.

"What?" Dakota opened her eyes.

"Look!" said Tiffany. She made a gesture at the surroundings. "What do you think?"

"It's nice," said Dakota.

"Nice?!" said Tiffany. "*Nice?*" She looked at the lush, green fields. The imposing buildings. There was a massive sports arena in the distance that looked like the freaking Colosseum. "It's like *Downton* friggin' *Abbey*."

Vid wound down his window a fraction. "Smell that?"

"What?" Tiffany sniffed. Some sort of fertilizer? Damp earth?

"The smell of money." He rubbed his fingertips together. He had the same look of satisfaction as when he walked into an opulent hotel foyer. It was all just fun to him. He had the money. He could afford the best. So he'd buy the best and take pleasure in it. His relationship with money was completely uncomplicated.

Tiffany thought of her own high school: a cheerful, graffitied concrete jungle out in the western suburbs. Did the girls here smoke ciggies in the toilets? Maybe they did lines of excellent-grade coke in marble bathrooms.

Vid parked in a lot rapidly filling with shimmering luxury cars. Tiffany automatically curled her lip at the sight of all those cars. It was a habit left over from her childhood, when her family had sniffed at wealthy people as if there were something unsavory and immoral about them. She still did it, even though her car was just as luxurious, even though she'd been the one to *buy* this car, with money she'd freaking well earned.

The feeling didn't abate as the parents and their daughters were led into a magnificent hall. The smell of good perfume and cologne filled the air as dads in their suits and ties, and mums in effortlessly casually chic spring outfits, who obviously had older daughters at the school because they all knew one another, traded cozy, chummy, entitled rich-people remarks. "How was Japan?" "Great! How was Aspen?" "Well, you know the children had never been to Athens before, so . . ."

"Snap!" A middle-aged woman with dark curly hair sat down next to Tiffany and pointed at their matching Stella McCartney silk skirts. She was wearing a white cardigan exactly like the one Tiffany had been looking for in Dakota's drawer.

"Got mine on sale." The woman leaned forward and put her hand over her mouth. "Forty percent off."

"Fifty percent off," whispered back Tiffany. An outright lie. She'd paid full price, but life was a competition, and she knew the non-working wives of wealthy men loved to talk about how they'd saved by bargain-shopping for designer clothes. It was their contribution to the household finances.

"Dammit!" The woman laughed nicely, which made Tiffany wish she'd told the truth. "I'm Lisa," she said. "Are you new to the school?"

"My stepdaughters went here," said Tiffany, thinking that her stepdaughters would rather die than be described as her stepdaughters. They, as was their right, had many years ago decided the best way to show loyalty to their mother was by doing their level best to pretend that Tiffany didn't really exist. They tended to give a little start when she spoke, as if the potted plant had tried to join in the conversation. They loved Dakota, though, so that was all that mattered.

"My two older daughters are here at the school," said Lisa. "Cara here is our baby." Lisa gestured to a little girl sitting next to her, swinging her legs and chewing gum. "Oh God, Cara, I told you to throw that out before we came in! How embarrassing. And my husband, Andrew."

The husband leaned forward to give a little wave. He was in his late fifties with lots of gray hair (he'd be proud of his hair, like Vid was of his) and that distinguished, statesmanlike confidence that comes with professional success in a career like medicine or law.

He had distinctive pale hazel eyes, with dark rings around the irises. Tiffany's heart lurched as if she'd tripped in a dream.

"Hi, Andrew," said Tiffany.

30

The Day of the Barbecue

So. Our stomachs are full," said Vid, patting his.

Tiffany knew he meant: My stomach is full, so I need a cigarette, like people once did in the civilized world.

"Anyone for seconds?" asked Tiffany. "Or thirds?" She scanned the long table as people pushed away their plates with satisfied sighs and complimentary murmurs.

Vid, at the head of the table, leaned back in his chair and tapped his fingers on his armrests like a king benevolently regarding his loyal subjects, except that in this case, the king had cooked dinner and his subjects had praised him up big-time: the *tenderness* of the meat and so on and so forth. Clementine in particular had laid it on thick.

Vid and Clementine were getting on like a house on fire. Earlier, they'd spoken for ten minutes straight about caramelized onions. Tiffany had just got her own back by talking to Clementine's husband about the footie.

"You're really into your sports, aren't you, Tiffany?" said Sam now. "You're not just faking it to be polite."

"Oh, I never fake it," said Tiffany.

"Why would she?" said Vid. He lifted his hands as if to indicate his mar-velous physique.

Everyone laughed, except for Oliver and Erika, who gave pained smiles. Tiffany decided she'd better try to curb the risqué jokes as she saw her neighbors give pointed looks at the children, who were out of earshot any-way. Dakota had the two little girls on either side of her in the hanging egg chair in the back corner of the cabana, and she was showing them some-thing on her iPad. The girls were happily snuggled up to Dakota's sides like the dream little sisters she'd never have (a deal was a deal, but how could you not have a pang of regret watching that?) and were enthralled by what-ever Dakota was showing them. Hopefully it didn't involve people's heads exploding. Barney was over in a far corner of the backyard contentedly in-volved with some sort of illicit hole-digging operation, which Tiffany was pretending not to notice. Every now and then, he'd look over his shoulder to make sure he wasn't about to be caught.

"Poor Oliver pretends to be interested in sports whenever we're around," said Clementine. "Sam says, 'Did you catch the game last night?' and you can see Oliver thinking, 'What game?'"

"I don't mind watching a bit of the tennis," said Oliver.

"Oliver *plays* sports," said Sam. "That's the difference between him and me. I get my heart rate up yelling at the screen."

"Oliver and Erika actually met on the squash court," said Clementine. "They're very athletic people."

There was something a bit over-eager about the way Clementine spoke, as if she felt the need to champion the couple, like she was their newly appointed publicist.

"Were you playing against each other?" asked Tiffany as she refilled Erika's wineglass yet again. Tiffany wouldn't have picked her to be a heavy drinker, not that it was her business. Anyway, it wasn't like Erika had to drive home; she only had to walk next door.

"We worked for the same accounting firm," said Erika. "Some of the staff started a squash comp on Thursday nights. Oliver and I volunteered to do the draw."

"We have a shared love of spreadsheets," said Oliver, and he smiled at Erika, as if over some secret memory involving spreadsheets.

"I love a good spreadsheet myself," said Tiffany.

"Do you?" Clementine spun her head. "What do you use spreadsheets for?" There was just the faintest emphasis on the word "you."

"For my work," said Tiffany, with just the faintest emphasis on the word "work."

"Oh!" said Clementine. "I didn't . . . what do you do?"

"I buy unrenovated properties, fix them up, sell them," said Tiffany.

"You flip them," said Sam.

"Yep," said Tiffany. "I flip them. Like pancakes."

"She doesn't just flip!" said Vid. "She's a big-time property developer!"

"I'm not," said Tiffany. "I've only just gone a bit bigger. I'm doing a small apartment block. Six two-bedroom apartments."

"Yep, she's like Donald Trump! My wife earns the big bucks. You think this big motherfucking house, excuse my French, comes from my money?! You think all that artwork inside, all those masterpieces, comes from my money?"

Oh God, Vid. Next he was going to say, "I'm just a simple electrician."

"I'm just a simple electrician!" said Vid. "I married up."

A simple electrician with thirty employees, thought Tiffany. But go for your life, Vid. I'll take full credit for our money.

"They're not masterpieces, by the way," said Tiffany.

"So how did you two meet?" asked Oliver in his courteous, proper way. He reminded Tiffany of a priest making conversation with his parishioners after Sunday Mass.

"We met at a property auction," said Tiffany before Vid got a chance to answer. "It was a studio apartment in the city. My first ever investment."

"Ah. But that wasn't the first time I met her," said Vid, with the anticipatory tone of someone sharing his favorite dirty joke.

"Vid," warned Tiffany. She met his eyes across the table. Jesus. He was hopeless. It was because he liked Clementine and Sam, and whenever he really liked people, he felt compelled to share the story. He was like a big kid desperate to show off to his new friends by saying the naughtiest word he knew. If it were just the neighbors there, he would never have said it.

Vid looked back at Tiffany, disappointed. He gave a little shrug and lifted his hands in defeat. "But maybe that's a story for another day."

"This is all very mysterious," said Clementine.

"So were you bidding against each other at the auction?" asked Sam.

"I stopped bidding," said Vid, "when I saw how badly she wanted it."

"A lie," said Tiffany. "I outbid him fair and square."

She'd made two hundred thousand dollars on that place, in just under six months. It was her first hit. Her first moneymaking high.

Or maybe not quite. Her second.

"But you can't tell us how you already knew each other?" said Clementine.

"My wife has an inquiring mind," said Sam, "which is a nice way of saying she's nosy."

"Oh, don't pretend you don't want to know," said Clementine. "He's a bigger gossip than me." She looked over at Tiffany. "But I'll stop asking. Sorry. I was just intrigued."

To hell with it. Tiffany lowered her voice. "It was like this," she said. Everyone leaned forward.

31

Erika stood in the pouring rain on the sidewalk outside her childhood home, an umbrella in one hand, a bucketful of cleaning supplies in the other. She didn't move, only her eyes moved, expertly tracking the amount of time and work and arguing and begging and pleading and tug-of-warring required.

Clementine's mother hadn't been exaggerating when she'd said on the phone that it was "pretty bad." When Erika was a child, her mother's belongings had never spread beyond the front door. The house always had a sullen, furtive look to it with its closed blinds and its thirsty wilted garden. But it wasn't a house that would make a passerby turn their head and stare. All their secrets were kept inside, behind the front door that could never open the whole way. Their worst fear was a knock on the door. Erika's mother would react instantly, as if to a sniper attack. You had to drop down low so you couldn't be seen by spying eyes through a window. You had to be still and silent and wait, your heart thudding in your ears, until that nosy, rude person who *dared* to knock finally saw sense and slunk away, never seeing, never knowing the disgusting truth about the way Erika and her mother lived.

It was only over recent years that her mother's belongings had finally burst through the front door, proliferating like the mushroom cells of a killer virus.

Today she could see: a pallet of bricks, a pedestal fan standing companionably next to a mangy artificial Christmas tree of the same height, a mountain of bulging rubbish bags, a city of unopened delivery boxes that had gotten wet in the recent rain so the cardboard had turned to soft pulp, a stack of framed prints that looked like they'd come from a teenager's room (they weren't Erika's) and dozens of pieces of women's clothing with the arms and legs flung out at panicky angles, as if there had been a recent massacre.

The problem was that her mother now had too much time and too much money. When Erika was growing up, her mother had had her full-time nursing job as well as the occasional checks Erika's father sent from his new home in the UK, where he lived with his replacement, upgraded family, so they'd had money, but there was still a ceiling to how much new stuff she could accumulate, although Sylvia had given it a red-hot go. However, when Erika's grandmother had died, leaving a considerable sum of money to Sylvia, her mother's hoarding had been given a whole new financial boost. Thanks, Grandma.

And of course, now there was online shopping too. Her mother had learned how to use a computer, and she managed to keep it plugged in and accessible, and because Erika had arranged for all her bills to be paid by direct debit, the electricity never got turned off, as it had when Erika was growing up and the paper bills used to vanish into the abyss.

If the front lawn looked like this, the inside of the house would be monstrous. Her heart galloped. It was as though she had the sole responsibility of rescuing someone by lifting something impossibly, incomprehensibly heavy: a train, a building. Of *course* it couldn't be done. Not on her own. Not in this rain. And not without Oliver by her side: methodical and unemotional, looking for solutions, speaking to her mother in his reasonable let's-work-our-way-through-this voice.

Oliver didn't take every object personally, the way Erika did. To Erika, every piece of junk represented a choice her mother had made of an object over Erika. She loved random, crappy objects more than she loved Erika. She must, because she fought for them, she screamed for them, and she was fully prepared to bury her only daughter in them, and so each time Erika picked up an object, it was with a wordless cry of despair: You choose *this* over me! She should have waited until he was better. Or she should have at least taken her anxiety medication—that's why she'd been prescribed the tablets, to help her get through exactly this sort of moment—but she hadn't taken one since the day of the barbecue. She hadn't even looked at the box. She couldn't risk more of those terrifying memory gaps.

"Erika! I'm so happy to see you! Oh! Sorry to startle you like that!"

It was the woman who had been living next door to her mother for the last five years. Erika's mother had adored this woman for quite a long time, long for her, anyway, maybe six months, before, predictably, she'd committed some sin, and gone from a "really quite extraordinary person" to "*that* woman."

"Hi," said Erika. She couldn't remember her name. She didn't want to remember her name. It would only increase her sense of responsibility.

"Isn't the weather terrible," said the woman. "It's just torrential!"

Why did people feel the need to comment on the rain, when they had absolutely nothing of value to add to the conversation?

"Torrential," agreed Erika. "A veritable downpour of cats and dogs!"

"Um, yes. So I was pleased to see you here, actually," said the woman. She held a child's tiny transparent umbrella tightly over her head. The rest of her was getting wet. She shot a pained look at Erika's mother's front yard. "I, ah, just wanted to let you know that we're putting our house on the market."

"Ah," said Erika. Her jaw clicked as her back teeth began to grind. It would be so much easier if this were one of the horrible neighbors, like the couple with the JESUS LOVES YOU sign in their window, who made regular complaints about the state of Sylvia's house to the department of Community Services, or the snooty ones across the road, who made aggressive legal threats. But this woman was so nice and non-confrontational. Michelle. Dammit. She'd accidentally remembered her name.

Michelle clasped her hands together as if to beg. "So, I know your mother has . . . um, difficulties, please know I do understand, I have a close family member with mental health issues, oh gosh, I hope this isn't offending you, it's just that—"

Erika took a breath. "It's fine," she said. "I understand. You're saying the state of my mother's house will affect the value of your property."

"By maybe a hundred thousand dollars," said Michelle pleadingly. "According to the agent."

The agent was being conservative. By Erika's calculations, the loss could be much higher. No one wants to buy a house in a nice middle-class suburb next door to a junkyard.

"I'll get it fixed," said Erika.

You are not responsible for your parents' living conditions. That's what the children of hoarders were told, but how could she not feel responsible when she was this poor woman's only hope? Someone's financial outcome depended on Erika stepping up, and she took financial outcomes seriously. Of course she was responsible. She saw one of the blinds at her mother's window twitch. She'd be inside, peering out, muttering to herself.

"I know it's hard," said Michelle. "I know it's an illness. I've seen the TV shows."

Oh, for God's sake. The TV shows. Always with the TV shows. Everyone was an expert after half an hour of neatly packaged television: the drama of the disgusting rubbish, the clever counsellor, the cleanup, the happy hoarder seeing her floor for the first time in years . . . and *fixed*! They all lived happily ever after, when in fact, cleaning away the rubbish was only alleviating the symptoms, not curing the illness.

Years ago, Erika had still had hopes of a cure. If she could get her mother to see a professional. There was medication. There was cognitive behavioral therapy. Talk therapy. If only Sylvia could talk to someone about the day Erika's dad had left and how it had triggered some latent madness. Sylvia had always been a compulsive shopper, a bright, beautiful, nutty personality, a real character, a party girl, that Sylvia, but she'd stayed on the right side of crazy until she'd read that little two-word note he left on the fridge: *Sorry, Sylvia*. No mention of Erika. He'd never found her particularly relevant. And that's when it had begun. That very day Sylvia had gone out shopping and came home laden with bags. By Christmas, the purple-flowered carpet in the living room had vanished beneath the first layer of stuff, and Erika had never seen it again. Sometimes she caught a glimpse of the outline of a petal, and it was like coming across an ancient relic. To think that she had once lived in a normal house.

She accepted now that there would be no cure. There would be no end until the day Sylvia died. In the meantime, Erika would keep battling the symptoms.

"So I'd better—" Erika gestured with her mops toward the house.

"I got on well with your mum when we first moved in," said Michelle. "But then it was like I offended her. I was never sure exactly what I did."

"You did nothing," said Erika. "That's just what my mother does. It's part of the illness."

"Right," said Michelle. "Well . . . thank you." She smiled apologetically and fluttered her fingers in a bye-bye way at Erika. Far too nice for her own good.

As soon as Erika reached her mother's front porch, the front door opened.

"Quick! Get inside!" Her mother was wild-eyed, as if they were under attack. "What were you talking to *her* for?"

Erika turned sideways to come in. Sometimes when she went to other people's places, she automatically turned sideways to enter the front door, forgetting that most people had doors that opened the full way.

She inched her way past the towers of magazines and books and newspapers, the open cardboard boxes containing random junk, the bookshelf filled with kitchen crockery, the unplugged washing machine with the lid up, the ubiquitous bulging plastic rubbish bags, the knickknacks, the vases, the shoes, the brooms. It was always ironic to see the brooms, because there was never any floor free to sweep.

"What are you doing here?" said her mother. "I thought this was against the 'rules.'" She made quotation marks with her fingers around the word "rules." It made Erika think of Holly.

"Mum, what are you wearing?" sighed Erika. She didn't know whether to laugh or cry.

Her mother wore what appeared to be a brand-new blue-sequined flapper-style dress that was too big for her thin frame and a feathered headband that sat low on her forehead, so that she had to peer up to keep it from slipping into her eyes. She posed like a star on the red carpet, one hand on her thrust-forward hip. "Isn't it beautiful? I got it online, you'd be proud of me, it was on special! I've been invited to a party. A *Great Gatsby* party!"

"What party?" Erika walked down the hallway toward the living room, studying the house. No worse than usual. The normal fire hazards everywhere, but she couldn't smell anything rotten or decaying. Perhaps if she concentrated on the front yard today? If the rain slowed to a drizzle?

"It's a sixtieth birthday party," said her mother. "I'm so looking forward to it! How are you, darling? You look a bit washed out. I wish you wouldn't turn up with *equipment,* as if I were a job you had to do."

"You are a job I have to do," said Erika.

"Well, that's just silly. I'd rather just have a chat with you and hear what you've been up to. If only I'd known you were coming I would have baked something from that new recipe book, the one I was telling you about when you got so grumpy the other day—"

"Yes, but *who* is turning sixty?" asked Erika. It seemed unlikely that her mother would be invited to a party. Since she'd retired from her job at the nursing home, she'd lost touch with her friends, even the most determined, patient ones, or else she'd discarded them. Her mother didn't hoard friends.

Erika walked into the kitchen, and her heart sank. The front yard would have to wait. It had to be the kitchen today. There were paper plates sitting on top of the hot plates. Half-empty food containers with green mold. She wasn't meant to be here for another two weeks, and if it wasn't for the problem with the front yard, she wouldn't be seeing this, but now that she had seen it, it was impossible to walk away. It was a health hazard. It was an affront to human decency. She put down her buckets and pulled out the packet of disposable gloves.

"Felicity Hogan is turning sixty," sighed her mother with a little flare of the nostrils on the word "Felicity," as though Erika was spoiling her pleasure in the party by reminding her who was hosting it. "Oh, look at you, now you're putting on *gloves* as if you're about to do an operation."

"Mum," said Erika. "Felicity turned sixty last year. No, actually, it was the year before. You didn't go to the party. I remember you said it was tacky having a *Great Gatsby* party."

"What?" Her mother's face fell, and she pushed the headband farther up her forehead so that her hair stuck up around it, making her look like an unhinged tennis player. "You think you're always so clever and right, but you're wrong, Erika!" The disappointment turned her voice strident. Those jagged edges were always there beneath the fluffy blanket of her maternal love. "Let me get the invitation for you! Why would I have an invitation for a party that happened two years ago, answer me that, Miss Smarty-Pants?"

Erika laughed bitterly. "Are you joking? Are you serious? Because, Mum, *you don't throw anything out!*"

Her mother tore off her headband and dropped it. Her tone changed. "I am aware that I have a problem, Erika, do you think I'm not aware of it? I'm not stupid. Do you think I wouldn't like a bigger, nicer house with enough storage and linen cupboards and things so I could get on top of things? If your father hadn't left us, I could have stayed at home all day and kept house, like your precious Clementine's mother, like Pam, oh-I'm-such-a-perfect-mother Pam, with my rich husband and my perfect house."

"Pam worked," said Erika shortly. She tore a rubbish bag off the roll and began to dump plastic food containers inside it. "She was a social worker, remember?"

"A *part-time* social worker. And of course I remember. How could I forget? You were her little social work project on the side. She *made* Clementine be your friend. She probably gave her a little gold star sticker each time you came to play."

It didn't even hurt. Did her mother think it was an earth-shattering revelation?

"Yep," said Erika. "Pam knew my home situation was not ideal."

"Your home situation wasn't 'ideal.' How melodramatic. I tried my best! I put food on the table! Clothes on your back!"

"We didn't have hot water for a year," said Erika. "Not because we couldn't afford it but because you were too ashamed to let anyone in to repair the water heater."

"I was not ashamed!" her mother yelled with such force, the tendons on her neck stood out and her face turned blood red.

"You should have been," said Erika evenly. At times like this, she felt herself become eerily calm; it would be hours or even days later, when she was alone, in the car or the shower, that she'd find herself screaming back something in response.

"I will admit that I sometimes got a teeny bit paranoid that they might take you away," said her mother. She blinked pitifully at Erika. "I always thought that Pam might get it into that do-gooder, lefty head of hers to complain to the Department of Community Services that I wasn't polishing my skirting boards or whatever."

"Skirting boards! When have you even seen the skirting boards in this house?" said Erika.

Her mother laughed merrily as if it were all in good fun. Erika's mother had such a pretty laugh, like a girl at a ball. ("Could she be bipolar?" Oliver asked when he first witnessed his mother-in-law's extraordinary ability to flip her temper on and off like a switch, but Erika told him that she suspected people with bipolar disorder didn't *decide* on their behavior; her mother was mad, of course she was mad, but she chose exactly when and how to be mad.)

"We had rats," said Erika. "No one was concerned about the skirting boards being clean."

"Rats?" said her mother. "Come on. We never had rats. Maybe a mouse. A dear little mouse."

They did have rats. Or rodents of some sort, anyway. They'd die, and the stink would be terrible, unbearable, but they wouldn't be able to find them in the cities of *stuff* that filled each room. They just had to wait it out. The stink would reach its peak and then finally fade. Except it never really faded. The stink leached into Erika.

"Also, Clementine's father wasn't rich," she told her mother. "He was just an ordinary father with an ordinary job."

"Something to do with construction, wasn't it?" said her mother with the chatty charm of a guest at a cocktail party.

"He worked for an engineering firm," said Erika. She didn't really know what Clementine's father's job had involved. He was retired now, and had apparently taken up French cooking, and was very good at it.

Once, when Erika was fourteen and her mother was at work, Clementine's father drove over and installed a lock on her bedroom door for her so that she could keep her room free of her mother's junk. It was his idea. He hadn't said a single word about the state of Erika's home. When he'd finished the job, he'd picked up his toolbox, handed her the precious key, and put one hand briefly on her shoulder. His silence had been a revelation to Erika, who had grown up surrounded not just by physical items, but by words: a swirling deluge of cruel, kind, soft, shrill words.

That was Erika's experience of fatherhood: the solid, silent weight of someone else's dad's hand on her shoulder. That was the sort of father Oliver would be. He'd give his love with simple, practical actions, not words.

"Well, he might not have been rich, but Pam wasn't a single mother, was she? She had support! I had no support. I was on my own. You have no idea. You wait until you have children of your own!"

Erika continued to mechanically fill her bag of rubbish, but she felt an alert stillness come over her, as though she were an animal sensing a predator. Years ago, when Erika had told her mother that she never wanted to have children, her mother had said with flippant cruelty: "Yes, I really can't see you as a mother."

Of course, she hadn't told her about her attempts to become pregnant. The thought had never crossed her mind.

"Oh, but wait, you're not going to have children of your own, are you?" Her mother shot her a triumphant look. "You don't want children because you're too busy with your important career! So bad luck to me. I don't *get to be a grandmother.*" It was like the thought had just occurred to her, and now that it had, she needed to wallow in the terrible injustice of it. "I just have to put up with that, don't I? Everyone else gets grandchildren, but not me, my daughter is such an important career woman with her important job in the city and her—hey!" Her mother grabbed her arm. "What are you doing? Don't throw that out!"

"What?" Erika looked at the rubbish in her gloved hand: a banana skin, a half-eaten tuna sandwich, a soggy paper towel.

Her mother extracted a tiny grease-stained piece of notepaper from her hand. "There! That! I'd written down something important on that! It was the name of a book, I think, or a DVD maybe, I was listening to the radio and I thought, I must write that down!" She held it up to the light and peered at it. "Now look what you've gone and done, I can't even read it!"

Erika said nothing.

She had a policy of passive resistance now. She never argued back. Not since the day she'd found herself engaged in a ludicrous ten-minute tug-of-war over a broken-stringed tennis racquet, while her mother screamed, "But I'm selling it on the eBay!" She lost in the end, of course. The tennis racquet stayed and it never got sold on eBay. Her mother didn't know how to sell something on eBay.

Her mother brandished the slip of paper at her. "You march on in here, Miss Know-It-All, and start messing around with my things, thinking you're doing me some great favor, and all you do is make things worse! It's lucky you don't want children! You'd just throw away their toys, wouldn't you? Take their precious little things and toss them in the bin! What a wonderful mother you'd be!"

Erika turned away. She lifted the swollen rubbish bag up by the ends and banged it against the floor. She double-knotted the ends and carried it to the back door.

She thought of Clementine's phone call: "I want to help you have a baby." The strange pitch of her voice. The thing was, Clementine really *did* want to help her have a baby now. That's what accounted for the strange pitch of her voice. She wanted to do this badly. This was her opportunity for instant redemption. She thought of how Oliver's face would be transformed by hope when she told him. Should she take Clementine's charity even if it was given for the wrong reason? End justifies the means and all that?

Did she even want a baby anymore?

She shifted the rubbish bag into her left hand so she could open the back door, and at that moment the rubbish bag split and oozed its contents: a thick, endless, inexorable discharge.

Her mother slapped her knee and laughed her pretty laugh.

32

The Day of the Barbecue

Dakota looked over at where the grown-ups were sitting around the table and saw her mother slide her eyes toward her before leaning forward as if she was about to share a secret.

Holly and Ruby were squashed into the swinging egg chair on either side of her, and she was showing them the Duck Song Game app. They both loved it. The girls were pretty cute and she liked them a lot, but she'd kind of had enough of them now. She felt like going back inside to her bedroom and reading her book.

The grown-ups were all giggling excitedly now and lowering their voices as though they were teenagers telling rude jokes, and Dakota felt irritated.

They did this sometimes. She'd overheard enough bits and pieces to know that the rude, silly thing was something to do with how her mum and dad had met, but when she asked them, they always said they'd met when they were both bidding for the same house, and then they shot each other glinting looks that they thought she was too stupid to catch.

Her older half sisters said they knew the secret, and the secret was that her dad had had a love affair with her mum when he was still married to Angelina. Angelina was her dad's first wife, and it was very hard, almost impossible, for Dakota to imagine this, even though she had an excellent imagination.

But her mother said there was absolutely no love affair while her dad was still married to someone else, and Dakota believed her.

It was frustrating that she didn't just come out and say the secret, because Dakota was old enough to handle whatever it was. Okay, so it was true, she'd never seen an R-rated movie, but she watched the news and she knew about sex and murder and ISIS and pedophiles. What else could there possibly *be* to know?

Also, as a matter of fact, she was more mature than her parents when it came to sex. There had been a sex education talk at her school where the parents had had to come too, and the lady giving the talk had said, "Now, some of this is going to make you feel like giggling, and that's natural, you can have a little giggle, but then we'll just move along."

She'd said this to the *kids*, but it was the *grown-ups* who couldn't keep it together. Her dad, who wasn't used to keeping quiet for such a long period of time (the only times he stopped talking were when he went to sleep and sometimes when he listened to his classical music; you couldn't see a movie with him), had kept saying things under his breath to her friend Ashok's dad, and in the end they were both snorting so hard, they'd had to leave the room, and even then you could still hear them laughing outside.

This secret they were keeping from her was probably nothing. "Is that all?" Dakota would say, and she'd roll her eyes and feel embarrassed for them.

Holly and Ruby squabbled over Dakota's iPad.

"My turn!"

"No, my turn!"

"Play nicely," said Dakota, and she heard the way she sounded, and you would have thought she was, like, forty years old. Seriously.

33

The lines around Andrew's eyes had deepened, but apart from that, he looked exactly the same. Tiffany saw the unmistakable glimmer of recognition in his pale eyes even as he gave her the appropriate, courteous smile for a fellow parent at a school event.

Did she see fear too? Or laughter? Confusion? He was probably trying to place her. She was out of context. She was way, way out of context.

Tiffany didn't have a chance to introduce herself, because at that moment a silver-haired, elegantly suited woman glided onto the stage and instantly quieted the room with her presence. The school principal. Robyn Byrne. She wrote a weekly column in the local paper about educating girls.

"Good *morning*, ladies and gentlemen, girls," the principal said, in a way that made it clear she expected to be answered, and so everyone did, automatically, with that preprogrammed singsong rhythm: Good morn-ing, Ms. Byrne, followed by a faint ripple of chuckles as CEOs, barristers and ear, nose and throat specialists realized they'd been tricked into school yard subservience.

Tiffany looked to her left, at Vid, who was smiling goofily down at Dakota, as if she were a toddler at a Wiggles concert. Dakota sat motionless, that awful catatonic look on her face.

"A very warm welcome to Saint Anastasias," said the school principal.

A very warm welcome to crippling school fees.

"Thank you for venturing out today in this truly dreadful weather!" Ms. Byrne lifted both arms ballerina-style to indicate the heavens above, and everyone glanced up at the soaring ceilings protecting them from the rain.

Tiffany chanced another quick look sideways at Andrew. He wasn't looking up but was instead staring straight ahead at the school principal, his legs crossed, a Rolex-watched wrist draped languidly over one knee in an almost feminine pose.

A nice man. The creepy eyes were misleading. She could remember them filled with laughter.

"Your daughters will leave this school as confident, resilient young women." Ms. Byrne was off, delivering the private school party line. Resilience. What crap. No kid was going to go to school in a place that looked like freaking Buckingham Palace and come out of it *resilient*. She should be honest: "Your daughter will leave this school with a grand sense of entitlement that will serve her well in life; she'll find it especially useful on Sydney roads."

Tiffany looked again at Dakota, who continued to stare unseeingly at the stage, while next to her, Vid pulled his mobile phone from his pocket and nonchalantly checked text messages, his chunky thumb swiping the screen back and forth. Manners! What would people think? Yes, Tiffany, what would people think? What would people think if Andrew told his wife about his connection to Tiffany? But why would he? Oh darling, the funniest thing, but that woman sitting next to you this morning was actually an old friend!

She *was* an old friend.

What if he did tell his wife, and what if his wife told all the other mothers, or just one mother, who couldn't resist telling one other mother? Until finally word got out to the daughters? What would that mean for Dakota's social standing at this school? Would that help her become a "resilient young woman"? Yeah, well, it probably would. Nothing like a bit of social ostracism to toughen you up.

Tiffany closed her eyes briefly.

She had to keep her footing. She thought of her sisters, all those years ago, saying, "How *could* you, Tiffany?" But she'd felt no shame, she'd never felt shame, so why was she sitting here drenched in it now?

She knew why. She knew exactly why. It was because everything felt out of balance since the barbecue. They had been the hosts. It was their home. It had happened in their home, and it was more than that—their behavior had contributed. Contributory negligence. She could not claim innocence. Neither could Vid.

So what if she took responsibility for all of it?

For Harry lying on the floor of his home, calling weakly for help that never came.

For Clementine's eyes gleaming in the twilight, and it had all been in good fun, no harm intended. Just because they were parents didn't mean they weren't people.

For the lines she'd once crossed. Only once.

The school principal's voice rose as she tapped closed fingertips together in her refined version of applause, to welcome three girls in school uniform onto the stage, each carrying a musical instrument.

Tiffany looked at the lustrous gold wood of the instruments, the red school ribbons encircling perfect ponytails, the elegant cut and quality of their school blazers, and she saw with absolute clarity what would happen if Andrew told his wife how he knew Tiffany. Nothing nasty or cruel would ever be said out loud, but green-coated, red-ribboned girls would destroy Dakota with stifled giggles and low whispers, with fake smiles and cryptic, cutting comments on social media. Dakota would pay.

The girls lifted their bows in unison. Music filled the hall. The music of another world. Clementine's world. Not the bass beat of Tiffany's world.

Tiffany looked sideways at Dakota's beautiful, young profile in time to catch an expression of immense sadness cross her face. It was as though Tiffany's little girl was being struck down by some terrible grief. It was as though everything Tiffany had just foreseen had already come to be.

"Mum." Dakota suddenly turned to face Tiffany and whispered, "I think I'm going to be sick."

Tiffany felt a surge of gratitude and maternal love. It was not grief, it was nausea. She could fix this. Easy. "Let's go," she whispered back, and she stood, urgently gesturing at Vid. She walked out past her new friend in the Stella McCartney skirt, her daughter and Andrew, who nodded politely, with maybe a little tightness around his mouth, but she could have been imagining it. Once they were outside, Dakota said she didn't want to find a bathroom, she just needed to go home, please, right away. Her face was white.

Vid, in his inimitable way, found a woman wearing a name badge, explained the situation, and was given an information folder and sent on his way with an understanding smile. He was comfortable in any social situation: garden party or cage fighting contest, it was all the same to Vid, it was all *interesting*.

Would he find her connection to Andrew interesting?

Dakota climbed into the back of the car.

"Do you want the front seat?" babbled Tiffany.

Dakota shook her head dumbly.

"Sit in the middle, at least," said Tiffany. "So you can see the road ahead. Better for your tummy."

Dakota slid over to the middle, and Vid and Tiffany got in the front and they drove out of the school grounds and toward home. After a while, when it seemed clear that Dakota wasn't going to be sick, Vid lit up a cigarette and began to speak.

"So, pretty good school, right? What do you think? The girls playing their instruments were good, eh? Maybe you could play the cello, Dakota! Like Clementine. We could get Clementine to give you lessons."

"Vid," said Tiffany. For God's sake. Was he completely deluded? Did he really believe Clementine would want to have anything to do with them ever again after what had happened? She would find every excuse in the world not to teach Dakota. And her location wasn't exactly convenient. If Dakota really did want to learn a musical instrument, they'd find someone local. "Clementine won't want to give Dakota lessons."

There was a strange sound in the backseat.

"Are you going to be sick, honey?" Tiffany whipped her head around.

Dakota's eyes locked on to Tiffany's. It was as though she were trapped within her own body, pleading desperately with Tiffany to help.

"Can you breathe?" said Tiffany. "Dakota, can you breathe? Are you choking?"

"Dakota?" Vid chucked his cigarette from the window and wrenched the steering wheel to the left, coming to a stop on the side of the road with a squeal of brakes and the outraged shriek of a horn from behind him.

Tiffany and Vid opened their car doors and flung themselves out into the pouring rain. They opened the back doors and climbed in on either side of Dakota.

"What is it? What is it?" said Tiffany.

"It . . . it . . ." Dakota's chest heaved. Tears spilled from her eyes and rolled down her face. Her chest heaved some more.

Tiffany's heart thudded. What could have happened to her? What could be so awful? It had to be sexual abuse. Someone had touched her. Someone had hurt her.

"Dakota," said Vid. "Dakota, my angel, take a very deep breath, okay?" There was a quiver of terror in his voice, as if his mind was following a similar path. "And then you need to tell us what the matter is."

Dakota took a deep, shaky breath.

At last she whispered, "Clementine."

"Clementine?" repeated Tiffany.

"She hates me," sobbed Dakota.

"She does not!" responded Tiffany immediately, instinctively to the banned word "hate." "I only meant she wouldn't want to give lessons because I got the impression she doesn't especially like teaching, she's going for a full-time job with—"

"Yes, she does so hate me!" snapped Dakota, and it was a relief to hear ordinary, ten-year-old petulance.

"Why would you think Clementine hates you?" said Vid.

Dakota threw herself at her father. He wrapped her in his arms, and his mystified eyes met Tiffany's over her head.

"Oh, Dakota," said Tiffany. "Sweetheart. No. No." She leaned forward and rested her cheek against Dakota's narrow, hunched back and put her hand on her knobbly spine, her heart breaking for her, because she knew exactly what Dakota was going to say.

34

This morning's wedding was only a ten-minute drive from Clementine's house, thankfully, and she knew exactly where she was going, so she wouldn't get lost. That was the worst part of being a freelancer, the driving to unknown locations.

She'd never been late for a gig, touch wood, because she always allowed time for the inevitable mistakes.

The wedding was at a sheltered little harbor inlet park with huge native figs and an old bandstand. Clementine didn't enjoy playing outdoors: lugging her cello and music stand around parks trying to find the right place, sheet music flapping about in the wind in spite of the clothes pegs she used to keep it secure, cold days when you couldn't feel your fingers, hot days where your makeup ran down your face, no acoustics so the sound dissipated pointlessly into the atmosphere. But for some reason this particular spot was always kind to them; the sound of their music floated across the blue sparkle of the harbor and punctual brides posted glowing online tributes after their honeymoons.

Not today, though. Today was going to be awful. There was no point to a harbor view you couldn't see. Clementine looked at the heavy gray band of cloud pressing down on Sydney's skyline. The world felt narrower. People walked around sort of hunkered down, ducking beneath the sky. It had been raining steadily all morning, and although it had slowed to a soft drizzle now, it could make a comeback at any moment.

"They're still going ahead with it outside then?" Clementine had said on the phone this morning to Kim, first violinist and manager of Passing Notes.

"They've hired a pop-up tent for us," said Kim. "The guests will have to make do with umbrellas. The bride was in tears this morning. She thought there was no way the rain would last this long. I remember when she first booked and I said to her, 'What's your wet-weather plan?' and she said, 'It won't rain.' Why do they always say that? Why are brides so deluded?"

Kim was in the middle of a nasty divorce.

Clementine wondered if she was at the beginning of a nasty divorce. Today, as Sam left for the ferry, she'd said, "Have a good day at work," and she was sure she'd caught him rolling his eyes, as if he'd never heard anything so inane, or as if she were the last person in the world he wanted to wish him a good day at work. It had hurt, a sudden sharp sting, like a reprimand, like when her C string snapped this morning just as she'd bent her head and pinged her cheek. That had never happened to her before. She didn't even know it was possible. There was too much tension in her playing. Too much tension in her body. Too much tension in her home. The sting of the string had felt personal, and she'd sat there in the dark early morning and refused to let herself press her fingertips to her cheek.

She parked her car right near the entrance to the park. She was twenty minutes early because she'd still allowed a twenty-minute "getting lost" buffer just in case. She yawned and studied the weather. The rain *might* hold off just long enough for the ceremony. If the bride was lucky.

She put her head back against the seat and closed her eyes.

Today she had gotten up at 5 A.M. and worked with the metronome on the Beethoven excerpt. "Feel the inner pulse," Marianne used to say, although then she'd suddenly cry, "Too choppy! Too choppy!"

Clementine massaged her aching shoulder. Her first cello teacher, Mr. Winterbottom (her older brothers and her father all called him Mr. Winter-Bum), used to say, "Nobody plays pain-free," if Clementine ever complained that something hurt. Clementine's mother hadn't liked that at all. Pam had researched the Alexander technique and in fact the exercises still helped when Clementine remembered to do them.

Mr. Winterbottom used to tap her knee with his bow and say, "More practice, missy, you can't coast on your talent, because I can assure you, you don't have enough to spare," and, "It's hard for you to put the emotionality in your music because you're too young, you've never actually felt anything. You need to have your heart broken." When she was sixteen, he'd sent her to audition for the Sydney Youth Orchestra but told her that she had no hope of getting in, she simply wasn't good enough, though it would be good experience. There was no screen, just the audition panel, all smiling supportively, but after she sat down with her cello, she couldn't even put her bow to her strings because she was so stricken by unexpected terror. It was like a terrible illness had befallen her. She stood up and walked off the stage without playing a note. There just didn't seem to be any other option. Mr. Winterbottom said he'd never been so ashamed of a student in all his teaching days, and he had a *lot* of students. Kids lugging cello cases came and went from his house all day long: a production line of cellists learning to self-loathe.

After the audition debacle her mother had found her a new teacher, and her beloved Marianne had said on the first day that auditions were unnatural and frightening and she herself had always hated them and that she would never send Clementine for an audition for which she wasn't properly prepared.

Why had cancer pointed its cruel, random finger at beautiful Marianne and not Mr. Awful Winter-Bum, who was still alive and well and churning out neurotic musicians?

Clementine opened her eyes and sighed as a tiny spatter of raindrops fell upon the windshield. It was the rain warming up before its big entrance. She turned on the radio and heard an announcer say: "As Sydney's 'Big Wet' continues, people have been warned to stay away from storm water drains and creeks."

Her phone rang on the seat next to her, and she snatched it up to look at the screen. There was no name but she recognized that particular configuration of numbers.

Vid.

He'd called so many times since the barbecue, she'd learned to recognize his number, but she never bothered to program his details into her phone, because he wasn't a friend, he was an acquaintance, a friend's neighbor, whom she never wanted to see again. Erika had no right to give him her number. Vid and Tiffany should have passed on any messages through her. What did he *want* from her?

She held up the phone in front of her, staring at the screen, trying to imagine him holding the phone in his big hand. She remembered him saying, "You and me, we are the feckless ones." The feckless ones. She closed her eyes, and her stomach cramped on cue. She wondered if she would eventually pay with a stomach ulcer. Was that what caused stomach ulcers? Regret-filled bile?

The phone stopped ringing and she waited for the text message to tell her that Vid had once again not left her a message. There had been only two occasions when he had given in and left a clearly reluctant message: "Clementine? This is Vid. How are you? I will call again." He was one of those people who avoided leaving messages and just wanted you to pick up the damned phone. Her dad was the same.

Her phone rang again instantly. It would be Vid again, she thought, but it wasn't; she didn't recognize the number. He wouldn't try to trick her into answering by calling from a different number, would he? It wasn't Vid. It was Erika's IVF clinic. They were returning Clementine's call about setting up an appointment with the counselor to discuss egg donation.

Erika had given her the number for the clinic this morning, irritably and impatiently, as if she hadn't really expected Clementine to go ahead and make the call.

Clementine took out her diary from her handbag and held it on her lap while she made the appointment for the day before her audition. The clinic was in the city. She would only just make it back in time for her lesson with the scarily talented little Wendy Chang (grade five at age nine). The lady making the appointment was lovely, she was being so nice to Clementine as she explained about an initial blood test she might like to do now or later, it was completely up to her, and it occurred to Clementine that the lady probably thought Clementine was a kind, altruistic person, doing this out of the goodness of her heart, not doing it to slither out from under the weight of an obligation.

She heard Erika's resigned voice on the phone that morning: "Oh, Clementine, we both know that's a lie." But then she'd immediately gotten down to business, giving her the number of the clinic, as if she didn't care that it was a lie. She didn't care about Clementine's motivations, she just wanted the eggs.

What had Clementine been expecting? Gratitude and joy? "Oh, thank you, Clementine, what a wonderful friend you are!"

She jumped as someone thumped on the driver's window. It was Kim, her violin case in hand, standing under a giant umbrella and looking miserable.

Clementine wound down her window.

"Isn't this fun," said Kim flatly.

The pop-up tent didn't inspire confidence. It looked cheap, like they'd gotten it from a two-dollar shop.

"I don't think it's going to hold," said Nancy, their viola player, scrutinizing the flimsy-looking white fabric. It was already sagging in places with puddles of water. Clementine could see the dark shapes of leaves floating in the little ponds above their heads.

"It's completely dry so far," said Kim worriedly. Their booking contract specified that they be fed and had to be able to keep their instruments dry. They had the right to pack up and leave in the case of wet weather, but they'd never yet had to do it.

"I'm sure it will be fine," said their second violinist, Indira, who always took on the role of optimist, as well as the role of making sure they were fed. She had been known to put down her violin in the middle of a piece to waylay a passing waiter if she saw something delicious, which was very embarrassing.

"How's the practice going?" asked Nancy as they tuned.

Clementine sighed inwardly. Here we go. "Pretty good," she said.

"How will poor Sam cope with school pickups and all that when you're away on tour?" said Nancy.

"Nancy. I'm not going to get it," said Clementine.

"I think you've got a great chance of getting it!" said Nancy.

Nancy didn't want her to get the job. She pretended it was because she didn't want Clementine to leave the quartet, but Nancy always made Clementine think of that Gore Vidal quote: "Every time a friend succeeds, I die a little."

Nancy was the sort of friend who was always pointing out slim-figured women to Clementine: "Look at her tiny waist / long legs / tight butt. Wouldn't you just *love* to look like that? Don't you just *hate* her? It makes you feel *so* depressed, doesn't it?" (Because if it doesn't, it damn well should!)

"Oh well, if you don't get it, you won't have to deal with all the orchestra politics," said Nancy. "It's like being part of a big corporation. Meetings. Policies. Personally, I couldn't stand it, but that's just me."

"You'll love it, Clementine, the camaraderie, the travel, the money!" said Indira.

"Would Sam mind socializing with all the musicians, do you think?" said Nancy. Nancy liked to mention the fact that Sam wasn't a musician at every opportunity. It was like she sensed a possible weak spot there, so she kept pushing her thumb against it. She'd once said to Clementine, "I could never marry a non-musician, but that's just me."

"He gets on with most people," said Clementine shortly.

"I just thought it wouldn't be his scene," said Nancy. "He's more the rugged, outdoorsy type, isn't he?"

"Sam isn't outdoorsy," snorted Clementine. Shut up, Nancy. Nancy was your quintessential entitled eastern suburbs princess. Her father was a judge.

"Didn't you once say he was tone-deaf?" said Nancy.

"He *pretends* to be tone-deaf," said Clementine. "He thinks it's funny to say that."

"He likes eighties rock," said Kim fondly.

"Gosh, your legs look amazing in those pants, Kim," said Nancy. "Don't you just hate her, Clementine?"

"I'm actually quite fond of her," said Clementine.

"Oh! By the way! Nearly forgot to tell you. I heard that Remi Beauchamp is auditioning." Nancy threw down her trump card.

"I thought he was in Chicago," said Clementine. She felt a numb sort of acceptance. She'd known Remi for years and had always been in awe of his flawless intonation. Even if she got through the first round, the orchestra would ultimately choose him.

"He's back," said Nancy, and tried to pull her lips down in a sad face. The result was kind of terrifying. She looked like the Joker from *Batman*. "But I'm sure you've still got a good chance."

"First guests are arriving," said Kim. "Shall we start with the Vivaldi?"

They all turned to the right page on their sheet music and positioned their instruments.

Kim tucked her violin under her chin, gave them a nod and began to play. Her eyes met Clementine's and she stepped back on one foot just enough so that she could give Nancy the finger behind her head, a quick, subtle movement that anyone else would think was just her fingers moving on the strings.

As they played, Clementine let her mind drift. She didn't need to think. They had been playing together since before Holly was a baby, and they had all gotten used to each other. Nancy had a tendency to rush, although she disputed this, and believed the others dragged. Now they just went with her.

They moved on to *Air on* G and Clementine watched the poor wedding guests milling about, umbrellas held aloft over rueful faces, high heels sinking into the wet grass, desperate for it to be over.

"The bride is here!" A woman wearing a tiny hat suddenly approached. She reminded Clementine of a Mr. Potato Head. "Start the bridal march, go, go, go!" She waved both her hands in her version of a conductor. It seemed like she might have already gotten into the champagne.

Kim always arranged for one person to have the official job of signaling them when to start the bridal entrance music, but for some reason random guests (women, it was always women) took the job on themselves, and were often responsible for making them start too early. Once they'd played the entrance song ten times before they finally saw the bride.

"Oops! Sorry, false alarm!" The potato-head lady made an exaggerated face of apology.

Brides were rarely early. They'd played at one wedding where the bride was an hour late and they'd had to pack up and go because they had another booking.

Erika had been early to her own wedding. "We can't be early," said Clementine, her only bridesmaid. "Your guests will still be arriving."

"Oliver will be there," said Erika. She had her hair pushed back off her forehead, and a lot of smoky eyeshadow. She looked like an entirely different person. "He's the only one I care about." It was one of the few times when Erika had been the one prepared to break a rule of etiquette.

Clementine had felt not quite envy but maybe something like it, because she saw that Erika was truly only thinking about her marriage, not her wedding. She didn't especially care about her dress or her hair or the music or even her guests; all she cared about was Oliver. Whereas when Clementine got married she *had* cared about all that peripheral stuff. (The hairdresser mucked up her hair, for example, and Clementine had looked like Morticia on her wedding day.) She and Sam had barely seen each other at their wedding because they were too busy catching up with friends and relatives who had come from overseas and interstate, whereas Erika and Oliver saw *only* each other. It was kind of sickening. Kind of lovely.

She wondered now if the signs had always been there. Sure, she and Sam made each other laugh, they had passion (or they did before kids), they had fun, but their relationship wasn't strong enough to withstand their first true test. It was a feeble marriage. A shoddy marriage. A marriage from the two-dollar shop.

The tent swayed. Clementine felt something wet on her face. Was she crying? Or was it rain?

"It's leaking," said Nancy, looking up. "It's totally leaking."

The rain suddenly intensified.

"This is bad," said Indira, who had the most expensive instrument at the moment. It was on loan from a retired violinist.

"We're out of here." Kim lowered her violin. "Pack it up."

Clementine was back in her car, her hand on the keys in the ignition, when her phone rang. She grabbed for it when she saw the single word on the screen: SCHOOL.

"Helen?" she said, to save time on the niceties, because it was generally Helen, the school secretary, who made phone calls from the school.

Her heart thumped. Disasters loomed now at every corner.

"Everything is fine, Clementine," said Helen quickly. "It's just Holly is insisting her tummy is hurting again. We tried everything to distract her, but to no avail, I'm afraid. We're at a loss and she's disrupting the class and well . . . she seems so genuine. We don't want it to be a case of the boy who cried wolf."

Clementine sighed. This had happened last week too, and by the time she'd gotten Holly home, her stomach had been magically fixed.

"Do you know how her behavior has been today?" Clementine asked Helen.

According to Holly's adorable, kind of dippy kindergarten teacher, Miss

Trent, Holly had been having "occasional difficulties with her self-regulation" at school, and as a result wasn't always making "the right choices." Certainly her behavior at home hadn't been wonderful. She was going through a naughty, whiny stage, and had recently perfected a brand-new seagull-like squawk that she used instead of saying no. It set Clementine's teeth on edge.

"Not *too* bad, apparently," said Helen cautiously. "The rain isn't helping. All the children have turned feral. So have we, actually. They say we've got at least another week of this weather, can you believe it?"

Clementine looked at the wedding ceremony taking place in the park. The bride and the groom were facing each other, holding hands, while other people held umbrellas over their heads. The bride was laughing so hard, she could barely stand, and the groom was supporting her, laughing too. They didn't seem to care that their string quartet had vanished.

She and Sam had laughed a lot during their wedding ceremony. "I've never seen a bride and groom laugh so much," their celebrant had said acerbically, as though they weren't taking their wedding seriously enough. Sam couldn't stop laughing at Clementine's Morticia hair, which had made her laugh too, and made it not matter.

But you couldn't laugh your way out of everything. They'd had eight years of laughter; a good run. They'd vowed to be true to each other in good times and bad, but they'd laughed as they said it, because everything was just so, so funny to them. They thought a bad hairstyle was as bad as life got. The celebrant was right to be annoyed. She should have grabbed them by their shirtfronts and cried, "This is serious! Life gets serious, and you two aren't concentrating!"

"I'm minutes away," she said to Helen.

35

The Day of the Barbecue

V id already knew me because he'd seen me perform," said Tiffany to Clementine.

"Mummy!" called out Holly from the egg chair. "Come and see this!"

"Just a minute!" called back Clementine, without taking her eyes off Tiffany. "So you were a performer . . . ?"

"A performer like you, Clementine!" said Vid delightedly.

"Not quite like Clementine," corrected Tiffany with a snort.

"Mummy!" shouted Ruby.

"Just a *minute*," called back Clementine. She looked at Tiffany. "Are you a musician?"

"No, no, no." Tiffany began stacking plates. "I was a dancer."

"She was a *famous* dancer," said Vid.

"I wasn't *famous*," said Tiffany, although she had been kind of famous in certain circles.

"Were you a famous limbo dancer?" asked Sam, with a glint in his eye.

"No, but there was sometimes a pole involved." Tiffany glinted right back at him.

There was silence around the table. Vid beamed.

"Do you mean you were a pole dancer?" Clementine lowered her voice. "Like a . . . like a stripper?"

"Clementine, of course she wasn't a *stripper*," said Erika.

"Well," said Tiffany.

There was a pause.

"Oh," said Erika. "Sorry, I didn't mean—"

"You've certainly got the body for it," said Clementine.

"Well," said Tiffany again. This was where it got tricky. She couldn't say, Yeah, too right I do, girlfriend. You weren't allowed to be proud of your body. Women expected humility on this topic. "When I was nineteen, I did."

"Did you enjoy it?" Sam asked Tiffany.

Clementine gave him a look. "What?" Sam lifted his hands. "I'm just asking if she enjoyed a previous occupation. That's a valid question."

"I loved it," said Tiffany. "For the most part. It was like any job. Good parts and bad parts, but I mostly enjoyed it."

"Good money?" continued Sam.

"Great money," said Tiffany. "That's why I did it. I was doing my degree, and I could earn so much more money doing that than being a checkout chick."

"*I* was a checkout chick," said Clementine. "I didn't especially love it, by the way, if anyone is interested."

"Such a pity. You would have made a wonderful stripper, darling," said Sam.

"Thank you, sweetheart," said Clementine evenly.

"You could have made your cello faces as you spun around the pole. That would have got you some good tips." Sam threw back his head, closed his eyes and made his eyebrows go up and down, presumably in imitation of Clementine's face as she played the cello.

Clementine looked down at the table and pressed her fingertips to her forehead. Her whole body shook. Tiffany stared. Was she crying?

"She's laughing," said Erika dismissively. "You won't be able to get any sense out of her for the next few minutes."

Oliver cleared his throat. "I read an article recently about a move to make pole dancing an Olympic sport," he said. "Apparently it's very athletic. You need good core strength."

Tiffany had to smile at the poor fellow doing his level best to maneuver the conversation back into safe middle-class-dinner-party-conversation territory.

"Oh yes, Oliver, it's *very* athletic," said Vid meaningfully, one eyebrow lifted, and Clementine dissolved again.

Tiffany thought how much simpler the world would be if everyone shared Vid's almost childlike approach to all things sexual. Vid liked sex in the same way he like classical music and blue cheese and fast cars. To him, it was all the same. The good stuff of life. It was just naked pretty dancing girls in a club. What was the big deal?

Erika turned pointedly in her seat to look over her shoulder toward the kids. "So does your daughter—?" she said to Tiffany.

"Dakota knows I was a dancer." Tiffany lifted her chin. *Don't you freaking well question my parenting choices.* "I'll wait till she's older to give her more details than that."

Vid's older daughters and ex-wife didn't know either. Oh God, the *judgment* that would come her way from his daughters, who dressed like Kardashians but behaved around Tiffany as if they had the moral high ground normally reserved for nuns. If they ever found out, they would leap on that secret like rabid dogs.

"Right," said Erika. "Of course. Right."

Clementine lifted her head and ran her fingertips beneath her eyes. Her voice still trembled with laughter. "So, forgive me, because I guess I've led a very, you know, *vanilla* life," she said.

"I don't know about that," said Sam. "What are you implying? I read *Fifty Shades of Grey*. I studied it. I tried to set up the study as the Red Room of Pain."

Clementine elbowed him. "I'm just fascinated. Did you find it . . . well, I don't know, where to start! Weren't the men watching you kind of . . . sleazy?"

"Of course, some of them were, but most of them were just ordinary blokes."

"*I* wasn't sleazy," said Vid. "Ah, well, maybe I was a little bit sleazy. In a good way sleazy!"

"So did you go to those places often?" Clementine asked him, and Tiffany could hear the effort she was making to keep her tone clear of judgment.

This was what Vid never understood and Tiffany always forgot: people had such *complicated* feelings when they heard that she'd been a dancer. It was all mixed up with their feelings about sex, which sadly for most people were always inextricably linked with shame and class and morality (some people thought she was confessing to an illegal act), and for the women there were issues relating to body image and jealousy and insecurity, and the men didn't want to look too interested, even though they were generally very interested, and some men got that angry, defensive look as if she were trying to trick them into revealing a weakness, and most people, men and women, wanted to giggle like teenagers but didn't know if they should. It was a freaking minefield. Never again, Vid, never again.

"Sure, I went lots!" said Vid easily. "When my marriage broke up, my friends wanted to take me out, and, you know, my friends didn't go to symphonies or whatever, you know, they went to clubs. And when I saw this woman dance, well, she blew my mind. She just blew my mind." He put a pretend gun to his head, pulled a pretend trigger and made his fingertips explode. "That's why I recognized her straightaway at that auction. Even though she had her clothes on."

Vid slapped his knee and roared with laughter. Clementine and Sam chuckled in a kind of horrified way, while Erika frowned and poor Oliver blushed.

"Anyway," said Tiffany. "That's probably enough of that."

There was a sudden discordant shriek: *"Mummy!"*

36

It was raining so hard, Clementine didn't hear the front door open. She jumped when she saw Sam materialize in the doorway to Holly's room, his blue and white pin-striped shirt so wet it was transparent.

"You scared the life out of me!" she said, her hand to her chest. "Why are you home so early?" She knew it sounded like an accusation. She should have said, maybe, "This is a nice surprise!" and *then* said, conversationally, gently: "Why so early, honey?"

She'd never called him "honey" in her life.

Sam plucked at the saturated fabric of his shirt.

"What are you doing?" he said.

"Looking for something," she said. "As usual." She was sitting on Holly's bed with a pile of clothes in front of her, searching for Holly's "strawberry top," a white long-sleeved top with a giant strawberry on the front that Holly needed right now if she was to ever feel happiness again, and which, of course, was nowhere to be found.

She felt strangely self-conscious. Would she normally have jumped to her feet at the sight of Sam, and kissed him hello? She couldn't remember. It was so strange that she would even consider this: the correct etiquette for greeting her husband.

She didn't particularly want to hug him when he was once again soaked. Nobody in Sydney could be surprised by rain anymore. You were an idiot if you found yourself caught in the rain. It was all anyone could talk about. Umbrella sales had gone up by 40 percent. But ever since the rain had started, Sam left every day for the ferry without an umbrella or raincoat. She watched him each morning from the kitchen window, bolting along the footpath through the rain, his briefcase held over his head, and the sight of his bobbing body disappearing into the distance made her want to laugh and cry. Maybe it was a form of masochism. He thought he didn't deserve an umbrella. He probably thought she didn't deserve one either.

"Why are you home so early?" she said again.

"Well, I got your message." Sam's face was a mask of anxiety with a hint of aggressive defensiveness. "So I left work early."

"My message that said Holly was perfectly fine?" said Clementine. "My message that said there was nothing to worry about?"

"This is the second time she's had this stomach thing," said Sam.

"I assume you saw her in the living room," said Clementine. "Happily playing on the iPad without a care in the world."

"I think we need to get her checked out. It could be her appendix or something. It could come and go."

"Yeah, it comes when she's at school and it goes when she's playing on the iPad. She's playing *us*," said Clementine. "As soon as I got her in the car, she was fine. She talked the whole way home about her party. She wants to invite Dakota, by the way." She said the last part quickly, without looking at him.

"Dakota," said Sam. He straightened as if sensing danger. "*That* Dakota?"

"Yes, *that* Dakota."

"She can't invite her," said Sam. "Obviously. Jesus."

"I told her that Dakota was probably too big for a sixth birthday party. And she had a meltdown. She said that we told her she could invite whoever she wanted, and we *did* say that. We made kind of a big deal of it."

"Yeah, well, we meant anyone except Dakota," said Sam.

"She was inconsolable."

"She doesn't even *know* Dakota," said Sam. He pulled his shirt out of the waistband of his trousers, and went to wring it with his hands and then reconsidered. "She met her one time. Like you said, she's too old. She wouldn't want to come to Holly's party!"

"Well, anyway, I gave in," said Clementine. "She was becoming hysteri-cal. It was kind of frightening."

"You just said yourself that she was putting it on about the stomach thing," said Sam. "So she's putting it on about Dakota too. She *played* you, Clementine."

He said this mockingly. Before, he'd always teased, but he'd never mocked.

"I don't think so," said Clementine. "Look. Holly wants to invite her, and it's her party, and she's obviously going through a bad stage at the moment, which is maybe not unexpected, so if she wants to have Dakota at her party, she's having Dakota at her party. It's not that big a deal!"

Sam clenched his jaw. "She's not coming."

Clementine threw her hands up. "She *is* coming."

They stared at each other.

How did they get out of this? How did a couple resolve something like this, where there was no possibility of compromise, where one person had to give in? What happened if *no one* gave in?

"I called Erika today," she said, to change the subject. "I told her that I'd donate my eggs."

"Right," said Sam.

He began to take his shirt off. Clementine found herself not quite but almost averting her eyes in the polite way you did when someone else's hus-band took off their shirt.

"She was funny about it," said Clementine. "I think she definitely over-heard what I said that day, when we were upstairs? Those horrible things I said."

"I need to get changed," said Sam distractedly, as if she were boring him.

"So you're fine with me donating my eggs?" asked Clementine, without making eye contact, as if it were an inconsequential question.

"It's your decision," said Sam. "She's your friend. Nothing to do with me."

His disinterest felt almost exquisitely painful, as if it were a pain she needed, a boil she needed lanced.

"So you definitely don't want another baby?" she said. There it was again. Like at dinner the other night at the restaurant. That desire to push him, to *shove* him off this ledge where they were stranded.

"Another baby?" said Sam. He hung his wet shirt on the handle of Holly's door. "*Us?* Have another baby? You're not serious."

"Oh. Right," said Clementine. She piled clothes on top of each other. "You haven't seen Holly's strawberry top, have you? It's vanished." She looked around her in frustration and tried not to cry. "Oh, I can't stand it, why do things keep *vanishing*?"

37

The Day of the Barbecue

M*ummy!*" It was only Holly calling for her mother's attention.
"Holly!" sighed Clementine. "You gave me a fright! You don't need
to call out as if it's a matter of life or death each time."

She stood up and left the table, carefully avoiding Sam's eyes. She
couldn't wait to be alone with him in the car to go over the night's events.
They'd be dining out on the story of this night forever. It was getting curiouser and curiouser. They'd gone down the rabbit hole. Erika, who had
never wanted children, now wanted babies. Oliver wanted Clementine's
eggs. Their hostess used to be a stripper.

"Have you ever heard of the boy who called wolf?" she said to Holly.

"I don't know anyone called Wolf. I've been calling you a million, tril-
lion times." Holly looked up at her accusingly from her spot in the swinging
chair next to Dakota.

"Sorry," said Clementine. "What is it?"

"Why is your face all red?" asked Holly.

"I don't know," said Clementine. She pressed cold fingertips to her hot
face. The air was getting cooler. "Are you girls warm enough?"

"Yes," said Holly. "Look at this game Dakota showed us! It's so awesome."

She pointed at some colorful animated game on the screen of the iPad in Dakota's hand.

"Wow!" said Clementine, staring at the game without seeing it. "Awesome.

"Thank you for taking care of them like this," said Clementine to Dakota. "You let me know when you've had enough, okay? When you get bored?"

"Ruby and I are not boring!" protested Holly.

Dakota smiled conspiratorially up at Clementine. She seemed like such a serious, good little girl. It was hard to believe she was the daughter of such colorful people as Vid and Tiffany.

"All okay here? You girls being good?" Sam stood next to her.

Clementine glanced up and met his eyes. There was a spark there. A spark she hadn't seen for a while. Maybe they'd have good sex tonight, proper good sex, the kind that used to be a given, not that weirdly uncomfortable let's-get-this-over-with sex they'd been having for the last couple of years. Something had gone wrong with their sex life after Ruby was born, or it had for Clementine; sometimes she felt a sense of loss, of actual grief over the loss of their sex life, and other times she wondered if it was all in her head, if she was being typically melodramatic about something natural and inevitable. It happened to everyone, it was called getting "stale," it was called marriage.

She sometimes felt a terrible sense of *inappropriateness* during sex, almost an incestuous feeling. It was like she and Sam were old, beloved friends who for some reason—a religious or legal or medical reason—were obligated to have sex every few weeks in front of a small panel of impartial observers, and it wasn't exactly unpleasant to have sex with an attractive old friend, but it was awkward, and a relief for all concerned when it was done.

She'd never spoken about it to Sam. How could she put that into words? "Sometimes our sex life feels incestuous and religious and ever so slightly yucky, Sam, don't you think? Any suggestions?"

There were no words available to her, and besides, she loathed talking about sex. It made her think of her mother, and strangely enough, of Erika. All that "open" talk in the car about contraception and self-respect.

She knew that part of the problem was that the girls were such unsettled sleepers. It meant that both Clementine and Sam were on edge the whole time, listening for that inevitable cry that could break the spell at any moment. With limited time, you couldn't linger. They had to get down to business, to the old tried-and-tested moves and positions, because otherwise it would be yet another case of "mission abort." It meant there was always a certain "move it along" tension to the proceedings. (Sometimes she even caught herself thinking, "Hurry, hurry!") It also meant that they never stopped being "Mummy" and "Daddy," and there was something so frumpy and ordinary and unglamorous about Mummy and Daddy having quick, furtive sex while their children slept. These days, Sam wasn't suggesting sex that often, which made Clementine feel kind of hurt: She *assumed* he still found her attractive; it would be all too easy to let herself fall into the body-loathing abyss—the world was so eager to give her a shove—but she was standing firm for now. At the same time, she'd often feel relieved when they both rolled over to face different directions, because honestly, who could be bothered? She suspected that he felt exactly the same mixture of hurt and relief, and the thought of *him* feeling relief about not having to have sex with her hurt her further, even though she felt the same way, and so it went on.

But now there was a spark, and she felt a great sense of exhilaration and relief. So *this* was all they needed! A barbecue with a friendly ex-stripper and a music-appreciating electrician who looked like Tony Soprano. She'd always fancied Tony Soprano.

"Why are you laughing, Mummy?" said Holly.

"I'm not laughing," said Clementine. "I'm smiling. I'm just happy."

She caught Dakota giving her a dubious look, and she tried to pull herself together.

"Daddy is all red too," said Holly.

"Pink." Ruby removed her thumb from her mouth to comment. "Daddy is pink."

"Pink," agreed Holly.

"I expect he's a bit *hot* and *bothered*," said Clementine.

"Why?" said Holly.

"Maybe I need a cold shower," said Sam, discreetly pinching the flesh of Clementine's upper arm. "I should stand in the fountain, eh?"

"Silly Daddy," said Ruby.

38

The Day of the Barbecue

Y ou okay?" said Oliver quietly, his hand on Erika's arm.

Erika felt a surge of irritability. "Yes. Why? Do I not look okay?"

Was she squinting? It wasn't her fault. The hazy afternoon light was making everything blur. The lack of visibility was affecting her balance too. She kept finding herself tipping forward or backward and having to anchor herself by grabbing the side of the table.

The music in the cabana was up quite loud now, making her head thump. Tiffany was playing "November Rain," which was significant in some way, something to do with her sordid past; Erika didn't want to know.

"You just seem like you're drinking more than usual," said Oliver, and for a moment Erika felt outraged, because she was always, always, the most sober person at any party. Often she didn't bother to drink at all—she didn't like the taste of it that much—although the wine tonight seemed very good, very smooth and delicious, probably prohibitively expensive.

"Well, I'm not!" she said.

"Sorry," said Oliver.

Her outrage melted away, because it wasn't Oliver's fault that his parents were alcoholics.

"I'm fine," she said, and she inclined her body toward him with the vague idea that she might hug him, even though they were both sitting in separate chairs. She wanted to hug him for his childhood, for the time when he was seven and he couldn't wake up his drunk parents to get out of bed to drive him to school, and he had a maths test that morning, and he sat on the end of their bed and cried with frustration, and now his parents told it as a hilarious story: *The time Oliver cried because he missed a maths test. Our little accountant in the making!* And each time they told it, Oliver obligingly chuckled, except with the saddest eyes you'd ever seen. But as she leaned toward him, Oliver held out his hands as if to catch her from falling, an appalled expression on his face, as if she were about to make a spectacle of herself, and Erika sat back with a little *tch* sound. She couldn't give her husband a hug, but it was fine for Tiffany, at a family barbecue, to casually mention that she used to be a pole dancer, a *stripper*, no less.

Clementine and Sam were giddy over it. Clementine's face was *luminous* right now. Clementine had always been susceptible to excitement. As a teenager, she used to get herself worked up when they went to parties together. Certain types of music sent her mad with happiness, as did certain types of cocktails—you could never tell whether the music or the alcohol was making her drunker. More than once, Erika, always the designated driver, had had to peel her off some guy, and sometimes those guys had gotten aggressive, and the next morning Clementine would thank her, and say thank God I didn't sleep with him, and Erika would feel a warm glow of satisfaction, like a best friend in a movie, but of course they weren't like best friends in a movie, were they? What were the precise words she'd overheard? "It's like she always wants another piece of me."

The shame rose like bile, and Erika put down her empty wineglass too hard on the table. Tiffany, predictably, picked up the wine bottle to refill it. She must have done waitressing as well as stripping. Maybe she'd been one of those topless waitresses. Why not? Marvelous. How interesting. What fun!

"That's your phone ringing, Vid," said Tiffany as she poured the wine.

Vid picked up his phone, and his face turned sour when he saw the name. "It is our friend Harry," he said. "From next door. It will be the music, you know, offending him. It offends him when anyone is happy."

"You'd better answer," said Tiffany.

"He kicked my dog today!" said Vid. "I don't have to answer him. He's always been on the nasty side, but harming an innocent animal! That was my final straw, you know."

"Harry didn't really kick the dog, did he?" said Oliver.

"We only suspect it," said Tiffany. "No proof." She picked up the phone. "Hello, Harry," she said. "Are we too loud?"

"Not loud at all," grumbled Vid. "It's *daytime*."

"Yes," said Tiffany into the phone. "No, that's fine. We'll turn it down. Sorry to disturb you."

She gave Vid his phone back and turned down the volume on the music.

"Hmmph," said Vid. "You should have turned it *up*."

"We probably had it a bit too loud," said Tiffany. "He's an old man. We have to be respectful."

"He's not respectful to us," grumbled Vid. He turned to Clementine. It was obvious he was developing quite the crush on her. "So, listen, tell me, do you play your cello at weddings? Because my eldest daughter is getting married this spring, you know."

"I play in a string quartet," said Clementine. "We're called Passing Notes. You could book us if you like. Will the food be good?"

"*Will the food be good?*" repeated Vid with extravagant emphasis. "Of *course* the food will be good, the food will be magnificent!"

"That's how Clementine and I met," said Sam. "She was playing at my friend's wedding."

"Ah! Of course!" said Vid, as if he'd been there. "And you thought: Who is that beautiful cellist!"

Clementine pretended to smooth her hair. "Yes, that's right."

"What was your pickup line?" Tiffany asked Sam.

Bet you wish you chose the flute, thought Erika gloomily as she drained her glass. She and Oliver might as well go back home and leave these four to it. They were all so busy flirting and finding each other fascinating.

"I waited until they'd finished playing and they were packing away their instruments and, you know, Clementine's not tall, the cello is nearly as big as her, so I said, which I thought was pretty brilliant: 'Bet you wish you chose the flute.'"

"Genius!" Vid slapped his leg.

"Not really," said Sam. "People say it to cellists all the time. It's like the worst possible cliché I could have chosen."

"Of course it was!" said Vid. "I would *never* have said that!"

"But she took pity on me anyway," said Sam.

"Mummy, I'm cold." Ruby appeared at Clementine's side, Whisk under her arm like a teddy bear.

"Do you want to wear your special new coat Grandma got you?" said Clementine.

Clementine's mother had bought the girls beautiful little winter coats she'd seen on special in David Jones. Erika knew this because she'd been shopping with Pam when she found them. Erika liked going shopping with Pam because she rarely, if ever, actually bought anything. This drove Clementine nuts, whereas Erika loved watching Pam frown while she turned a garment inside out to study the quality of the lining, then slowly take her reading glasses out of her handbag so she could confirm the price tag, then hem and haw and finally say, "Nope!"

The cute little woolen coats, with their black toggles and hoods, however, had been impossible for Pam to resist, and Erika had agreed, even though they probably wouldn't get that much wear in Sydney's climate.

As Clementine removed Ruby's fairy wings and helped her into her pink coat (Holly's was green) Erika didn't say anything about being there when the coats were purchased. She had learned over the years that although Clementine didn't want to go shopping with her mother, she didn't seem especially pleased to hear that Erika had gone shopping with her. She never said anything. It was just a flicker. A Clementine flicker that said, "Stop stealing my mother. You've got your own."

The pink coat, Erika saw with satisfaction, fit Ruby perfectly. She'd told Pam to get the bigger size.

"You look like Little Pink Riding Hood," said Oliver, as Ruby twirled around in her coat.

Ruby chuckled. She got the joke, the clever little thing. She climbed onto her mother's lap and snuggled up contentedly as if Clementine were a favorite couch, and stuck her thumb in her mouth.

"So does Whisk ever actually . . . whisk?" Tiffany asked Clementine.

"No, when Whisk became Whisk, she wasn't allowed to do anything so menial," said Clementine. "Her whisking days were over."

Ruby took her thumb out of her mouth. "Shh. Whisk is sleepy." She caressed Whisk as if it were a baby, and everyone laughed, as she knew they would. Ruby stuck her thumb back in her mouth with a satisfied smirk.

"I think Ruby *and* Whisk must be getting tired," said Clementine. "We should be going soon."

"But first you must have dessert," said Vid firmly. "I made *cremeschnitte*. It's another old family recipe I got off the Internet."

"It's a vanilla and custard cream cake," said Tiffany. "To die for."

"Well, then," said Clementine. "We'd better not miss that."

"We've got those nice chocolate almonds you brought too, Erika," said Tiffany. "I love them. My grandfather used to have them every Christmas. Brings back memories."

Erika smiled thinly back at her. Yeah, sure they bring back memories. Chocolate nuts were really going to stand up well against to-die-for *creme-bloody-schnitte*.

"Hey, look!" said Oliver, suddenly animated. "Kids!" He pointed up at a tree toward the back of the garden. "Is that a possum I spy?"

39

The freaking rain had gotten louder again. It was starting to do Tiffany's head in. Vid and Tiffany, who had both canceled appointments so they could stay home for the rest of the day, were having coffee in the kitchen while Dakota watched TV in the adjoining room with Barney curled up on the couch next to her. They were keeping her home from school, of course. "Give the other kids a chance to catch up," said Vid.

Tiffany was still reeling from Dakota's sobbing confession in the back of the car on the side of the road.

It was tiny. It was huge. Blind Freddy could have seen it, and yet Tiffany might have missed it forever. If Vid hadn't made his remark about Clementine teaching her the cello, Dakota might never have broken down, and they might never have learned the truth.

Tiffany and Vid had both been prepared to sit on either side of Dakota for the whole day, letting her talk, or just being there for her, but Dakota had finally said, "Uh, guys? Don't take this the wrong way, but can I get a bit of space?" And she'd made a circular motion with her hands to indicate the space she required around her. She already seemed more like herself, as if that glass bubble she'd encased herself in was already thinning and cracking.

It was time to be thinking about dinner, but Tiffany had suddenly developed a craving for chocolate to go with her coffee, and she'd remembered the jar of chocolate almonds sitting in the back of the pantry.

Vid grunted as he tried to loosen the lid. "What the . . . ?" His face was red. He'd never been defeated by a lid before. He held it up and examined the label. "Where did we get these from anyway?"

"Erika brought them to the barbecue," said Tiffany.

Vid's face shuttered instantly, and Tiffany saw with startled clarity just how affected he still was, even after all these weeks, by what had happened, even though he said he didn't think about it anymore. What a fool she was to have taken his words at face value. Vid was all smoke and mirrors. The more distressed he was, the more he joked.

"I think this lid is super-glued on," said Vid with a final twist. "I really do."

"Dammit," said Tiffany. "I had a real craving for one."

She took the jar from him and began tapping the lid around the edges with a butter knife, as her mother always did.

"That won't work," scoffed Vid. "Give it back. Let me try again."

"Has Clementine called you back yet?" said Tiffany.

"No," said Vid.

"Do you leave actual messages?" said Tiffany. "Or do you just hang up?"

"Hang up," admitted Vid. "Why won't she answer? I thought she liked me."

They wanted Clementine to talk to Dakota, to set the record straight.

"She did like you," said Tiffany. "She liked you a lot. That's part of the problem."

Vid took the jar from Tiffany and began twisting the lid again, grunting and swearing. "Fuck it. Open, you fucker. We should all . . . just . . . see each other again. That would make us all feel better, I think. This . . . *silence*, it makes everything . . . bigger, worse . . . Oh, to hell with this thing!"

He gave the lid such a violent wrench, the jar flew from his hands and onto the floor, where it shattered instantly, sending chocolate nuts and glass shards cascading across the tiles.

"There you go," said Vid morosely. "It's open now."

40

The Day of the Barbecue

D o you see it? Look closely!" Oliver stood beneath a tree just outside the cabana, holding Holly up high, his hands gripping her calves as though she were a little circus performer.

There was a rustle of leaves and a flash of surprised bright round eyes as the possum suddenly emerged.

"I *see* it!" shrieked Holly.

"It's a ringtail possum," said Oliver. "See how he's got the white tip on his tail? Little factoid for you: he's got two thumbs on each front foot to help him climb. Two thumbs! Imagine that!"

Good Lord, Oliver would be a wonderful father, thought Clementine, pressing her lips to Ruby's scalp. Maybe she could do it. Give them her eggs. She donated her blood, why not her eggs? And then she could just *forget* that the child was biologically hers. It was a state-of-mind thing.

Be generous, Clementine, be kind. Not everyone has your good fortune. Clementine thought of the time her mother invited Erika to come away on a beach holiday with them when they were thirteen, a holiday Clementine had been desperately anticipating because it would be two weeks without that shameful prickly sensation she'd been experiencing every day at school, when Erika would hurry up to her each lunchtime and stand far too close, her voice low and intimate, "Let's eat lunch over there. Somewhere private." Clementine was only a kid. The necessary negotiations, all conducted within the parameters of her mother's all-important code of kindness, felt amazingly complex. Sometimes she'd promise Erika she'd spend just half of lunchtime with her. Sometimes she'd convince Erika to join her with other kids, but Erika was happiest when it was just the two of them. Clementine had other friendships she wanted to cultivate: normal, easy friendships. It felt like Clementine had to make a daily choice: my happiness or her happiness?

She'd wanted a holiday with just her big brothers, where she would have been included in their adventures, but instead it had been a holiday where the boys had gone one way and the girls another, and every single day Clementine had had to forcibly suppress her rage and disguise her selfishness because poor Erika had never had a family holiday like this, and you had to share what you had.

She looked over at Erika, who had sunk down in her chair and was scowling into her wineglass. There was no doubt about it. Erika was tipsy.

Was she drinking more than usual because of the awful things she'd overheard? Clementine stretched her arm around Ruby's curved little body to pick up her own wineglass again.

Vid and Tiffany stacked plates to take inside.

"Let me do it," said Sam to Tiffany. He stood and held out his hands for the plates. "You relax for a bit."

"All right," said Tiffany, handing over the plates and sinking back into her chair. "You won't have to ask me twice."

"You got the girls?" called Sam to Clementine over his shoulder as he went to follow Vid out of the yard.

"Yes, I've got the girls," said Clementine, indicating Ruby on her lap and Holly still with Oliver, checking out the possum.

"I think Dakota has gone inside to read a book," said Tiffany, looking around. "Sorry. She does that sometimes, disappears, and you find her lying on her bed reading."

"That's no problem," said Clementine. "It was great to have her playing with them for as long as we did."

"Dakota is obsessed with reading at the moment," said Tiffany, and

Clementine could see by the way she pulled her lips down at the corners that she was trying to conceal her pride. "When I was her age, I was obsessed with makeup and clothes and boys."

Yeah, and I bet the boys were obsessed with you, thought Clementine.

"Were you obsessed with music?" Tiffany pulled at a strand of hair that had gotten caught on her lip. Literally everything she did was sensual. What would she be like as an old lady? It was impossible to imagine Tiffany elderly, whereas Clementine only had to glance at Erika frowning ferociously off into the distance to see the old lady she would one day be, the lines between her eyes that would become deep furrows, the slight stoop in her back that would become a hunch.

Imagining Erika as a grumpy old lady, full of complaints and refutations, made Clementine feel fondly toward her. Somehow she knew there would be an unspoken truce on their unspoken battle over God knew what when they were old. They could both surrender to their innate grumpiness. It was going to be a lovely relief.

"I guess it was important to me," said Clementine. Music wasn't her obsession so much as her escape. She didn't have to share that world with Erika, except for when she came to watch her perform, but there was enough space between them then—both literally and figuratively.

"Were your parents musical?" asked Tiffany.

"Not in the slightest," said Clementine. She laughed a little. "I'm surrounded by the unmusical. Mum and Dad. Sam. My kids!"

"Is that tricky?" asked Tiffany.

"Tricky?" repeated Clementine.

What a funny choice of word. Was it tricky being surrounded by the unmusical?

Nobody could accuse Clementine's parents of being unsupportive. They'd helped her with the money to buy her beautiful Viennese cello (she'd paid back a little over half, and after Ruby was born, her dad told her not to worry about the rest, he'd "take it off her inheritance"), an instrument that aroused so many conflicting emotions in Clementine, it sometimes felt like a marriage. Her dad was proud of Clementine in a distant, awestruck way. She'd been so touched that time she'd discovered him watching the tennis with a copy of *Classical Music for Dummies* facedown on the couch next to him. But Clementine knew that nothing she played would ever come close to a Johnny Cash song for her dad.

Clementine's mother was supportive too, of course she was—after all, she'd been the one to drive Clementine to lessons and auditions and performances without ever a word of complaint—but over the years, Clementine had come to feel that her mother had complicated feelings about her music. It wasn't disapproval—why would it be?—but it often *felt* like disapproval. She sometimes wondered if Pam saw Clementine's career as flighty or self-indulgent, more like a hobby, especially when compared to Erika's solid, sensible job. When Pam talked to Erika about her work, she nodded along respectfully, whereas Pam seemed to find Clementine's job amusing, a little outlandish. "You're imagining it," Sam always said. He thought it said more about Clementine's resentment toward her mother for making Erika part of her family and thereby forcing a friendship upon her.

"You probably felt supplanted by Erika," he'd once said.

"No," said Clementine. "I just wanted her to go home."

"Exactly," said Sam, as if he'd made his point.

And what about Sam? Was it "tricky" that he wasn't a musician? Sometimes, after a performance, he'd ask her how it had gone and she'd say "Good" and he'd say "That's good" and that would be it, and she'd feel a little wistful because if he were a fellow musician, she would have had so much more to share with him. She knew lots of couples who worked together in orchestras and talked constantly about work. Ainsley and Hu, for example, had a pact that they were only allowed to talk about work up until when they crossed the Anzac Bridge because otherwise it just got "too intense." Clementine couldn't imagine that. She and Sam talked about other things. The children. *Game of Thrones*. Their families. They didn't need to talk about music. It didn't matter.

Now Erika sat up straight, as though rousing herself. "I was there when Clementine heard the cello for the first time," she said to Tiffany. There was an unmistakable sloppiness to her speech. "One of the boys in our class had a mother who played the cello, and she came in one day and played it for us. I thought it was nice enough, but then I looked over at Clementine, and she looked like she'd found nirvana."

Clementine remembered when she'd first heard that luscious sound. She hadn't known a sound like that was possible, and the fact that an ordinary-looking mother had the ability to make it! It was Erika who'd told Clementine she should ask her parents if she could have cello lessons, and Clementine often wondered if it would have occurred to her to have asked. She thought perhaps not; she would have tried to find a way to *listen* to the cello again, but no one in even her extended family played a stringed instrument.

Erika must not remember that she was the one who suggested it or else she would have found ways to mention it at every opportunity, to take ownership of Clementine's career.

"So you two have known each other since you were kids," said Tiffany. "That's great to have a friendship last all these years."

"Clementine's mother kind of adopted me," said Erika. "Because I didn't have a great home environment." She made air quotes around the words "home environment." "It wasn't really *Clementine's* choice, was it, Clementine?"

41

"Thank you for fitting me in today." Erika sat in the blue leather recliner across from her psychologist, who sat in a matching lounge chair angled toward her, as though Erika were a guest on a talk show. There was a large round ottoman in between them, with a box of tissues on it, as if the ottoman were a coffee table. (A tiny annoyance. Why not get a coffee table?)

"No problem at all. I've had a lot of cancellations because of the rain. They're advising people to stay off the roads if possible." Erika's psychologist's name was apparently Merilyn. That's how she'd introduced herself, and that's the name that appeared on her stationery, but as far as Erika was concerned, it was a real error of judgment. Merilyn was entirely the wrong name for her. She looked nothing like a Merilyn. She looked like a Pat.

Merilyn bore a startling resemblance to a secretary who had worked for Erika for many years, and was correctly, appropriately, called Pat. That particular type of (round, rosy) face and the name Pat were therefore linked together forever in Erika's subconscious, and every time she looked at her psychologist, she had to remind herself: "Not-Pat."

"This rain really is extraordinary, isn't it?" said Not-Pat, looking out the window.

There was no way Erika was going to waste a minute of paid time discussing the weather, so she ignored that fatuous remark and launched straight in.

"So whenever I get invited to someone's place, I always take a jar of chocolate nuts," she said. "Chocolate almonds."

"Yum," said Not-Pat cheerily.

"I'm not that keen on them myself," said Erika.

Not-Pat tilted her head. "Why do you take them then?"

"Clementine's mother used to take chocolate nuts whenever she went to someone's place," said Erika. "I think she bought them in bulk. She was quite thrifty like that."

"She was like a role model for you," suggested Not-Pat.

"They used to invite me to come with them," said Erika. "To barbecues and . . . things. I always said yes. I was always so happy to get out of my house."

"That's understandable," said Not-Pat. She was looking at Erika curiously.

"I'm doing that thing my mum does when she tells a story," said Erika. "She rambles. She can't stick to the point. I read that it's quite common with hoarders. They can't keep their conversation in order any better than their homes."

"Rambling is good," said Not-Pat. "Actually, I think you're circling. I think you're coming to something."

"Well, you know, chocolate nuts aren't really an appropriate hostess gift anymore," said Erika. "Because of allergies. Everyone has allergies these days. Once Clementine looked at my jar of nuts and said, 'You can tell you don't have kids, Erika.'"

"Did that offend you?"

"Not especially," said Erika, considering. "You would think it would have because we'd just that day found out that we'd failed another round of IVF. Clementine didn't know that, of course. She would have felt terrible for saying that if she'd known."

Not-Pat tilted her head even farther, like a cute little Disney chipmunk listening out for something in the woods. "You went through IVF? Or you're going through IVF?"

"I know it's strange that I haven't mentioned it up until now," said Erika defensively.

"Not strange," said Not-Pat. "But I do find it interesting."

"About eight weeks ago," said Erika, "we had a barbecue at our next-door neighbor's place."

"Okay," said Not-Pat.

Watch me circle, Not-Pat.

"Yesterday," said Erika, "my husband found our neighbor's body." She wondered if she was doing this on purpose. This was what her mother did. She threw people off balance for the pleasure of watching them wobble. It was fun.

Not-Pat definitely wobbled. She was probably regretting right now that she'd agreed to this emergency appointment. "Um. The neighbor who had the barbecue?"

"No," said Erika. "He was on the other side of them. He was an old man. Not an especially nice man. He didn't have friends or family. Everyone is feeling terrible because his body was there for weeks. Except I'm not feeling terrible."

"Why is that, do you think?"

"I don't *want* to feel terrible," said Erika impatiently. "I don't have *time* to feel terrible. I don't have the . . . space in my head. Look, I don't even know why I mentioned that. It's not relevant. Anyway, we've given up on the IVF because my eggs are rotten, and before the barbecue, we asked Clementine if she would donate eggs to me. To us."

Not-Pat nodded bravely. "How did she react?"

"Something happened at the barbecue," said Erika.

"What happened?" Poor Not-Pat looked like she was about to break out in a sweat.

"The thing is, beforehand, I took one of those tablets you prescribed," said Erika. "A whole one. I know you said I should start out with a half, or even a quarter, but I took a whole one, because I couldn't break it, and then, at the barbecue, I think maybe I drank more than I would normally drink." She saw Clementine running about, trying to catch the frothing champagne.

"Oh dear," said Not-Pat with a grimace so exaggerated it was almost comical.

"As you may know, there's a big warning label on the front of the packet," said Erika. "It says the tablets can increase the effects of alcohol, but I just thought: Well, *I* never drink much, I'll be fine, but I had a glass of champagne and maybe I drank it too fast. I was feeling a certain level of stress. Anyway. I think I actually got drunk, which is not something I've ever done, and I have gaps in my memory about that night. Black spots. Like blackouts?"

"They're probably more like brownouts," said Not-Pat. "Alcohol affects your ability to transfer your memories from your short-term memory to your long-term memory."

"So you think they're gone forever?"

Not-Pat shrugged. Erika glared at her. She didn't pay for *shrugging*.

"Something might trigger a memory for you," said Not-Pat. "A taste. A smell. Something someone might say that makes you remember. Or sometimes being back in the same place might help. You could 'return to the scene of the crime,' so to speak!" She laughed a little at the words "scene of the crime," but Erika didn't smile back. Not-Pat's smile vanished.

"Right," said Erika.

She would think about that later.

"So anyway, I took chocolate nuts to the barbecue. Like I always do."

Not-Pat waited.

"I guess I was just thinking about all those times that Clementine's mother asked me along to family events," said Erika. "Her dad would be driving, her mum would have the jar of nuts on her lap, and I'd be in the backseat with Clementine. Her older brothers were mostly off doing their own thing by then, so it was often just the two of us. I'd be looking out the window, feeling so pleased with myself, so blissful, pretending Clementine and I were sisters, and that her parents were my parents."

She looked up at Not-Pat, surprised to find that *this* was what she'd been circling, this not-exactly-shocking little factoid, as Oliver would say. "Clementine wasn't blissfully pretending she was my sister. Clementine didn't want me there at all."

"Ah," said Not-Pat.

"I always knew that, of course. Deep down, I knew it. But lately I've been trying to put myself in *her* place, to be the one looking out the other window, the *real* daughter, with this imposter always hanging about." Erika looked unseeingly at the plush, padded surface of Not-Pat's ottoman. "I wonder how that felt."

42

The Day of the Barbecue

Erika had the dangerous, truculent look of a drunk about to reveal secrets.

Clementine's stomach tightened. "We're still friends now, aren't we?" she said lightly.

Erika made a sound that was almost a guffaw.

Dear God, revealing the painful complexities of her friendship with Erika felt like a more intimate, socially unacceptable revelation than the news that Tiffany used to be a stripper.

Tiffany cleared her throat, and Clementine watched her make a marginal adjustment of the wine bottle so that it was farther away from Erika.

"Excuse me," said Erika. She stood. She didn't sway, but she had the careful stance of an inexperienced passenger on a boat, someone very aware that the ground could move at any moment. "I'll just go inside to the bathroom." She blinked rapidly. "For a moment."

"Oh, there's one right here," said Tiffany, pointing at a door at the back of the cabana. Of course there was. Clementine's whole family could quite happily have moved into that cabana.

But Erika was already heading back into the house.

"She's a bit tipsy, I think," said Clementine apologetically, because Erika's strange behavior was clearly her responsibility. She thought of their younger years when Erika would take charge, hailing cabs and making coffee when Clementine drank too much. It was strange to be apologizing for Erika.

"Probably my fault for refilling her glass too often," said Tiffany. "I'll lose my responsible service of liquor license."

"Oh, have you got one?" said Clementine. Maybe that was a requirement for strippers.

Tiffany smiled faintly. "No," she said. "Just joking."

Clementine's arm ached, so she shifted Ruby's body, trying to get her into a more comfortable position. Judging by how noisily she was sucking her thumb, she was about to fall asleep, but the movement of her arm was enough to stir Ruby, and she suddenly jerked her head.

"Holly," she said indistinctly, speaking around her thumb.

"Over there." Clementine pointed at Oliver and Holly, who were still possum hunting.

Ruby slid off Clementine's lap. "Bye," she said with a wave of her whisk, and toddled over to them.

"That little pink coat is adorable on her," said Tiffany as they both watched Oliver bend down to pick up Ruby.

"She's probably going to complain she's too hot in a minute," said Clementine. "It weighs a ton."

Clementine looked back at Tiffany, who was scratching something on the side of her neck but somehow making even that look erotic. What was it like to have a body like that? Did it automatically make you more sexually adventurous, because you just looked in the mirror and felt hot? So you were therefore destined to be a stripper? Or were there librarians with bodies like that? Of course, there were librarians *exactly* like that in porn movies.

She was so intrigued, so titillated by this woman. She had another mouthful of wine and leaned across the table. "Can I ask you a question?" she said.

"Sure," said Tiffany.

"Obviously a lot of men who watched you dance would have been married, right?"

"We didn't get them to do surveys at the door," said Tiffany. "But yes, probably."

"Do you think they were betraying their middle-aged wives at home with the children by, you know, sitting there lusting over a gorgeous nineteen-year-old? Isn't it effectively infidelity?"

"Their middle-aged wives were probably at home reading *Fifty Shades of Grey*," said Tiffany. "Or lusting after the lead in a chick flick."

"But that's fiction," said Clementine.

"I was fiction," said Tiffany.

"Right," said Clementine uncertainly. No, you weren't. "But do you—oh!" Hundreds of tiny lights suddenly flickered to life, transforming the backyard into a twinkling, magical fairyland. It was like the setting for a stage play.

"That's what happens when you're married to a crazy electrician. They're preset to go on at half past five at this time of year," explained Tiffany. "We could probably make it even earlier. Hey, look at your kids."

Holly and Ruby had lost their minds. They ran in delirious circles around the backyard, laughing and pointing, their bright little faces transfixed, their hands reaching out, clasping and unclasping, as if to catch the lights like bubbles. Barney ran with them, tail wagging, yapping delightedly. Oliver looked on, his hands shoved in his pockets, smiling fiercely at them.

Vid and Sam reappeared in the cabana, laden with trays of food. Tiffany and Clementine both stood to help them.

"And then there was light," said Sam. "We should get Vid to come over and do something with our sad old backyard. The girls look like they've never seen electricity before."

Oliver came over to the table. "So is this the dish you mentioned earlier, Vid?" he said in his awkward, earnest way. "What did you say it was called?"

"*Cremeschnitte*," said Vid. "You wait. You just wait."

"Have you got plates?" Tiffany asked him.

"Erika is bringing out your good blue plates," said Vid. "She's just behind us. And if the little girls don't like my dessert we have ice creams in the freezer, although, of course, they will like it."

"Tiffany, did I hear you say there was a bathroom through there?" asked Oliver, pointing at the back of the cabana.

"Yes, that's it," said Tiffany. Oliver hurried off. It was just the four of them standing around the end of the table.

"Also I have chosen music to go with my dessert," said Vid. He picked up his phone again. "No more of this head-banging stuff my wife likes. Clementine, have you heard of someone called Yo-Yo Ma?" He enunciated the name clearly. "He's pretty good, I think."

Clementine smiled at him. He was too adorable. "Yes, Vid. I've heard of Yo-Yo Ma. He is pretty good."

"Okay, well, this is him, right? And let me tell you, this is the *sound* of the taste of my *cremeschnitte*."

The ineffable sound of Yo-Yo Ma playing the opening movement of Elgar's Cello Concerto filled the cabana. Clementine shivered. It was glorious.

Sam said, "Shall I open these chocolate nuts Erika brought?"

"Oh yes, please," said Tiffany. "Just what I feel like."

"Like your nuts then?" said Sam.

"I just love sweet-tasting nuts," said Tiffany.

"Is that so?" said Sam, his hand on the lid.

"Oh stop it, you two are so rude," said Clementine, and felt a burst of warmth because she could see already how a fun, flirty friendship between them all was about to unfurl. It would be a friendship involving good food, wine and music, and there would be a sexual frisson to everything they did, and God knows her life could do with a bit of sexual frisson.

(When was the last time she and Sam had even *had* sex? A week ago? No, two weeks ago. Had they crossed the finish line? No, they had not. Holly had called out for "a glass of water, pleeeease!" Her timing was uncannily and hilariously precise.)

Instead of the painful little foursome with Erika and Oliver, they'd become an easygoing group of six. It would be so much easier to like Erika and Oliver with Vid and Tiffany around as a buffer. Vid and Tiffany were edgier and rawer (and richer) than all their other nice, normal, middle-class friends. Vid and Tiffany opened up possibilities. Possibilities of exactly what? She didn't know. It didn't matter. It was like that non-specific anticipatory feeling of being a teenager.

"So I don't see how this *cremeschnitte* could be any better than your strudel," said Clementine to Vid as the music billowed and blossomed around her.

He raised an eyebrow. "Ah, Clementine, you know I am not one to blow my own trumpet, as the saying goes. Ha ha! Yes, I am! I love to blow my own trumpet. Ha ha! I'd be a good trumpet player because I have outstanding lung capacity." He banged his chest King Kong style.

"You've got the right personality for a trumpeter," said Clementine.

"You mean he's full of himself?" said Tiffany.

"How many trumpeters does it take to change a lightbulb?" said Clementine.

"How many?"

"Five. One to change it, and four to stand around and say, I could do it better."

"How many electricians does it take to change a lightbulb?" said Vid.

"How many?"

"One," said Vid.

"One?"

"Yeah, one," said Vid. He shrugged. "I'm an *electrician*."

Clementine laughed. "That's not funny."

"But you're laughing, you know. Anyway, listen, Clementine, you be the judge," said Vid. He dug a spoon into the decadent dessert and held it close to Clementine's mouth. "Try it."

She took a mouthful. It *was* good. The man cooked like a dream. Clementine pretended to swoon, her hand against her forehead. She let herself fall against his arm, and he steadied her. Vid smelled deliciously of cigarette smoke and alcohol. He smelled like an expensive bar.

"Jesus, this lid is on tight," said Sam with gritted teeth, the jar of nuts under one arm like a football.

"Come on, Muscles," said Tiffany.

"Listen!" said Vid, his head on one side as the second movement began.

"You can't exactly *dance* to this, though, can you?" said Tiffany.

Clementine tried to imagine Tiffany dancing in some dark, smoky club, mirrored disco balls hanging from the ceiling. Where did she get that idea from? She'd never actually been in a strip club. All her knowledge came from TV shows. She looked around. Erika and Oliver weren't there to look disapproving. This was her chance to find out more. She was a tiny bit tipsy, she knew it, but this was fascinating, amusing, and she wanted some fun lowbrow tidbits to share with her highbrow friends. She lowered her voice and leaned toward Tiffany. "Did you used to do . . . you know, what are they called?" She knew perfectly well what they were called. "Lap dances?"

Tiffany looked back at her speculatively.

"Sure," she said. "Why? Do you want one?"

43

We can't find stuff because we keep too much stuff," said Sam. "We need to have regular throw-outs. We need to de-clutter."

He went to Holly's chest of drawers, pulled out an entire drawer, dumped the contents on her bed and picked up a T-shirt at random. "See! She never wears this. She says it's all scratchy."

"This isn't helping me find her strawberry top," said Clementine, looking at the mound of clothes. It made her think of Erika's mother. You could almost understand how you could lose control of your possessions until it was just so overwhelming you didn't even know where to start. "This is just making a mess."

Sam tried to pull out another drawer, but it jammed. He pulled harder and swore. The chest of drawers rattled. There was something disturbing about seeing him there in his business pants but no shirt, pulling violently on the little white drawer, his jaw clenched, his muscles flexed. For heaven's sake!

"Leave it!" said Clementine. "You're going to break it!"

He ignored her and yanked again, and this time the drawer finally came free and he dumped another pile of clothes on the bed.

"You know what I was doing," he said suddenly, standing there with the empty drawer hanging from his hands. "Just before it happened?"

Oh God.

"You were trying to open a jar of nuts," said Clementine dully. She knew this. He'd told her this before. She didn't know why he kept bringing up the jar of nuts. It had nothing to do with anything.

"I was so *desperate* to open that fucking jar," said Sam. "I had beads of sweat popping on my forehead, because I knew Vid would take it off me and he'd just open it with one twist of a meaty hand, and you couldn't take your eyes off him."

"*What?*" said Clementine. This was new. "Don't pretend you were doing it for *me*. It was for her. It was to impress Tiffany!"

"Yeah, and what were you doing? Tell me that! What were *you* doing?" He slammed the empty drawer on Holly's bed, stepped toward her and loomed over her. She felt little flecks of spit land on her face.

Hit me, she thought. She lifted her face. It would feel so right. It would begin something. It would end something. Please, please hit me. But he took a sudden step back, hands lifted, like a guy in a pub brawl making it clear he isn't getting involved.

"We were *all* doing it!" shouted Clementine. "All four of us!"

44

The Day of the Barbecue

W hy? Do you want one?" Tiffany couldn't resist. These people were so freaking cute, so easily shockable.

"A *lap dance?*" Clementine's eyes shone. Tiffany knew she was just drunk enough and, yes, vanilla enough, to be the perfect target. "No!"

"Sure. A lap dance."

Oh God, Tiffany had forgotten how much she enjoyed this. It had been so long since she'd felt that rush of sexual power straight to the head like a line of cocaine.

"Do we get a discount?" said Sam.

"No charge," said Tiffany. "On the house."

"Enjoy my wife's lap dance," said Vid to Clementine. He pulled out a chair. "I insist."

"Oh, stop it," giggled Clementine. "Anyway, the music is wrong. She can't do a lap dance to a *cello concerto.*"

"I could give it a shot," said Tiffany. She had no intention of giving her next-door neighbor's friend a lap dance. It was a joke. It was all in good fun.

"She is very adaptable," said Vid.

"It's very kind of you, but I really don't want a lap dance," said Clementine.

"Thank you anyway." Her voice sounded husky. She cleared her throat self-consciously.

"I think you do," said Sam.

"*Sam*," said Clementine.

Tiffany watched Sam and Clementine look at each other, their faces flushed, their pupils dilated. It would be a kindness. A public service. She could see exactly where their sex life was at. They were tired parents of young kids. They thought it was all over, and it wasn't, they didn't need an affair or a midlife crisis, it was all still in them, they were still attracted to each other, they just needed a little electric shock to the system, a little stimulus, maybe some sex toys, some good-quality soft porn. She could be their good-quality soft porn.

Tiffany caught Vid's eye. He raised an eyebrow. He was *loving* this, of course he was. He moved his chin just subtly. It meant: *Go on. Blow their nice little suburban minds.*

Sam stood behind Clementine and pushed her shoulders so she sat. His eyes locked on to Tiffany's. He was her favorite sort of customer. Appreciative, friendly, he wasn't taking it too seriously but he was taking it seriously enough. He'd tip generously and gratefully.

He really wanted to see his wife get a lap dance. Of course he did. The man was only human. Tiffany looked at Clementine, who was so weak with laughter (and desire, Tiffany knew it, even if Clementine didn't), she could barely sit up straight in her chair.

Tiffany wasn't going to do it, not properly, not in the backyard with kids around, but as a joke, for the fun of it, she moved, slowly, in time to the freaking *concerto* (oh yes, you can do a lap dance to a cello concerto, no problem at all), almost in parody of herself, except not quite, because she still had her professional pride, and she'd been one of the best in the business, it was never just about the money, it was about making a connection, a human connection, and playing it with just the right amount of theatricality, reality, *poetry*.

Vid wolf-whistled.

Clementine smacked her hand over her eyes and peeked between her fingers.

There was a tremendous crash of crockery and an extraordinary scream that tore straight through the night: *"Clementine!"*

45

H ope you feel better soon," said the police officer as Oliver stood at the front door to wave her and her partner off.

"*Thank you*," said Oliver with maybe excessive gratitude, because the police officer flicked him a look as if she'd missed something. It was just that he was genuinely touched by her taking the time to comment upon his health. Did his gratitude seem suspicious? Guilty? He'd never been one of those people who felt guilty when they saw a police car drive by. His conscience was generally clear. Most people drove ten kilometers over the speed limit while he made a practice of driving five kilometers under.

The police had been there following up on Harry's death. They were having trouble tracking down his next of kin. Oliver wished he could be more helpful. He admitted that his conversations with Harry had never crossed over into the personal. They'd chatted about the weather and the garden and that abandoned car in the street. He'd felt, rightly or wrongly, that Harry wouldn't have appreciated personal questions.

The police wanted to confirm again when he had last seen Harry, and he was able to give them an exact date: the day before the barbecue. He said that Harry had seemed in good health. He didn't mention anything about

Harry complaining about Vid's dog. It didn't seem relevant. He didn't want to paint Harry in a bad light.

"You seem very sure about that date," said the nice policewoman.

"Well, yes," said Oliver. "It's because the day after that there was . . . an incident. Next door."

She raised her eyebrows and he gave her the details, briefly, because to his surprise, he found he got strangely breathless as he talked about it. The policewoman made no comment. Perhaps she already knew. There was a police report on file, after all.

Of course, the police would see no connection, no cross-reference between Harry's death and the barbecue, but as Oliver closed the door and went back into the kitchen to boil the jug to make himself a hot lemon and honey drink, he found himself thinking of those two minutes.

He estimated it had been about two minutes. Two minutes of self-pity. Two minutes that might have changed everything, because if he'd been out there, he would have seen what was going on. He reckoned there was a good chance he would have seen.

Come on now. That was a stretch. Melodramatic. Putting himself center stage. "You're not responsible for the whole world, Oliver," his mother had once said to him, in a moment of sobriety or drunkenness, it had always been hard to tell the difference.

Oliver switched on the electric kettle.

But it was not a stretch, because what had happened at the barbecue had crashed like a meteorite through their lives, and if he hadn't been so distracted, if life had continued in its normal, predictable way, surely he would have noticed much sooner that Harry hadn't been around, and he might have banged on his door weeks earlier.

Harry would probably still be dead, but he wouldn't have been dead for quite so unforgivably, tragically long.

Or he might even have saved him.

The kettle bubbled and hissed, and Oliver remembered how he'd stood in that luxurious little bathroom at the back of the cabana, letting the hot water run and run pointlessly over his hands while he stared at his own sad stupid face.

46

The Day of the Barbecue

Oliver stood in the cabana bathroom washing his hands. It was a fancy, soft-lit, scented bathroom. The light fixture was an imitation chandelier, all glittery glimmer. If his mother were here at this barbecue and at the nasty stage of her inexorable progress toward inebriation, she would whisper, "So tacky!" loudly in Oliver's ear, loud enough that he'd be terrified someone would overhear.

He let the water run needlessly over his hands. He was delaying the moment when he'd have to go back outside again. Frankly, he'd had enough. He liked everyone here well enough, it was just that socializing was a mental and physical effort that left him exhausted and drained, and it wasn't a good sort of tiredness, like when the lactic acid built up in his muscles after a solid workout.

He heard laughing outside. Vid's big booming laugh. Oliver pasted a smile on his face in preparation, ready to share the joke. Ha ha. Good one. Whatever it was. He probably wouldn't really find it funny.

Erika was drunk. He wanted to take Erika home and put her to bed like a child, and wait for the morning, when she would be his beloved wife again. He'd never seen her slur her words before or look at him with glassy, unfocused eyes. It was nothing to get himself worked up about. She wasn't falling over or dropping things or vomiting in the garden. It was just regular drunkenness. Some people did it every weekend. Clementine was a "little merry" too, hectic spots of color on each cheek, but he didn't care what Clementine did.

When he was a kid, it used to feel like his parents disappeared when they got drunk. As the levels of their glasses went down, he could sense them pulling away from him, as if they were together on the same boat, slowly pulling away from the shore where Oliver was left stranded, still himself, still boring, sensible Oliver, and he'd think, Please don't go, stay here with me, because his real mother was funny and his real father was smart, but they always went. First his dad got stupid and his mum got giggly, and then his mum got nasty and his dad got angry, and so it went until there was no point staying and Oliver went to watch movies in his bedroom. He'd had his own VCR in his bedroom. He'd had a privileged upbringing, had never wanted for anything.

He met his own eyes in the mirror. Come on. Pull yourself together. Go back out.

Today was not meant to have been the day when Erika got drunk for the first time in their marriage. Today was the day when they were meant to have put their proposal to Clementine, and Oliver had hoped—he knew it was unrealistic—but he had really hoped that she might—

He heard Erika scream, "Clementine!"

He didn't stop to turn off the tap.

47

The Day of the Barbecue

The air rushed from Clementine's lungs. Afterwards, everyone would say, "It happened so fast," and it did happen fast, but at the same time it slowed down, every second a freeze-frame in unforgettable full color, lit by golden fairy lights.

Clementine leaped to her feet so fast her chair fell over. What? Where? Who?

Her first thought was that one of the girls had hurt themselves. Very badly. Blood. There would be blood. She couldn't stand blood. Maybe they'd need stiches. Or a broken bone sticking out of the skin. Teeth. Chipped teeth. Holly or Ruby? Probably Holly. The backyard spun around her in a whirl of color. She couldn't hear crying. Where was the crying? They both had such loud cries. Holly was enraged when she hurt herself. Ruby wanted to ensure she communicated the need for an urgent parental response.

She saw Holly first, standing in the gazebo with her little blue sequined bag, perfectly fine, looking impassively at . . . what?

Erika running. She was looking at Erika running.

Erika was running toward the fountain. Vid's "Trevi Fountain." What was she *doing*? She looked like she was going to dive in.

Erika had lost her mind. She was having a nervous breakdown, some sort of psychotic episode. Clementine knew she wasn't right tonight. She never got drunk, and she'd been behaving so strangely. It was Clementine's fault.

Erika leaped up and over the side of the fountain in one swift, athletic move. She was waist-deep in water. She slipped, almost fell, righted herself and waded toward the middle. What in the world was she doing? Clementine was mortified for her.

And now Oliver was running from the cabana toward the fountain to drag Erika away. To stop her embarrassing herself. He didn't even stop when he reached the side of the fountain, he crashed straight over the side.

He and Erika waded, slipped and slid, from opposite sides of the fountain together, like two lovers in a movie rushing to embrace after a long absence.

But they didn't embrace. They lifted Ruby's tiny lifeless body high up between them.

48

The Day of the Barbecue

Ruby's head sagged sideways. Water streamed from her. Her little pink coat was heavy and sodden with water. Her arms dangled uselessly like a rag doll's.

Clementine thought: Cold. She'll be so cold.

Ruby hated the cold. Her teeth chattered like a windup toy when she got too cold. The water at swimming lessons was never warm enough for her, even in the middle of summer. "Cold, cold!" she'd cry.

Clementine ran to snatch Ruby from Oliver, to snuggle her close to her chest and warm her up. She could already feel how her wet body would soak her clothes. She got to the side of the fountain and held out her hands, but Oliver ignored Clementine as he climbed out of the fountain with Ruby cradled in his arms.

"Me," said Clementine stupidly. She meant: Give her to *me*.

Oliver placed Ruby flat on her back on the hard, uncomfortable terracotta tiles next to the fountain.

"Ruby!" said Oliver loudly, as if Ruby were in trouble. He shook Ruby's little shoulder. Much too roughly. "Ruby! Wake up, Ruby!" He sounded angry. He never sounded angry.

234 | Liane Moriarty

Clementine fell hard on her knees on the tiles next to them. "Give her to me," she said desperately, but she couldn't get close to her. Oliver and Erika were taking up the space.

Ruby's skin was white. Her lips were violet. Her head lolled. Her eyes were open but stared straight ahead. Her teeth weren't chattering. Oliver put one hand under Ruby's neck and the other hand on her forehead and tipped back her head as if to stare at the sky. He put his thumb on her chin, pulled open her mouth and then he stuck in two fingers as if he were trying to fish something out.

"Oliver, give her to me," demanded Clementine. She just needed to get her into her arms so she could fix her.

Oliver bent his head down close to Ruby's face and turned his ear to her mouth, as if to listen to her whisper something. He looked at Erika and shook his head. A tiny shake that said: No. He unbuttoned the black toggles of her pink coat.

Understanding exploded through Clementine's body at the same moment as the music stopped abruptly. There was a moment of complete, eerie silence in the backyard before Sam began to shout, as if he were in a violent argument with someone. "We need an ambulance!" He ran back and forth, idiotically, dementedly, patting his pockets. "I can't find my phone. Where's my phone? My *phone!*"

Vid said calmly, "I'm calling an ambulance, Sam." He lifted his phone from his ear to prove it. "It's ringing. It's ringing right now."

"Tell them she's not breathing," said Erika. She and Oliver were moving themselves into position side by side next to Ruby. "It's important they know she's not breathing."

"What's wrong with Ruby?" said Holly. She came and stood next to Clementine and plucked at her sleeve. Clementine tried to answer, but her chest was so tightly constricted, she couldn't speak.

"Does she want Whisk?" said Holly. "Here's Whisk. Mummy, quickly, give Ruby Whisk. That will make her feel better."

Clementine took Whisk. She curled her fingers around the cold wires.

"Come here with me, Holly." Tiffany took Holly by the hand and pulled her back.

Oliver said to Erika, "Fifteen and two, right?" His face was dead white. There were droplets of water on his glasses like rain and beads of water sliding down his face like sweat. His eyes were fixed on Erika, as if they were the only two people there.

"Yes. Fifteen and two," said Erika. She pushed her wet hair out of her eyes.

Oliver laced his fingers, locked his elbows and put his big hands over Ruby's chest.

"Oh God," said Sam. He clutched his hands behind the back of his neck and dropped his head as if he were protecting himself from a blow, and walked around in circles. "Oh dear God."

Oliver began to rock back and forth, counting out loud as he rhythmically compressed Ruby's chest. "One and two and three and four and five."

"Oliver is hurting Ruby!" wailed Holly.

"No," said Tiffany. "He's not hurting her. He's helping her. He and Erika are doing exactly the right thing. They're helping her." Her voice trembled.

"Twelve and thirteen and fourteen and fifteen and one and two."

On the count of fifteen, Erika pinched Ruby's nose and bent her face toward Ruby's, her mouth open, as if to kiss her like a lover, in a move so sensual and intimate, so terrifying and wrong, so familiar and shocking. This is what you do. Everyone knew this is what you did to save a life, but you didn't see it happen, not in real life, not in someone's backyard, not with your *own* child, who had just moments before been running about trying to catch the lights.

Nothing happened.

Erika breathed once more into Ruby's mouth, while Oliver continued to rock and chant: "One and two and three and four and five."

Clementine felt herself rocking in time with him, muttering over and over: pleasepleasepleasepleasepleaseplease.

So this is how it happens, a part of her thought as she rocked and begged. This is what it feels like. You don't change. There is no special protection when you cross that invisible line from your ordinary life to that parallel world where tragedies happen. It happens just like this. You don't become someone else. You're still exactly the same. Everything around you still smells and looks and feels exactly the same. She could still taste Vid's dessert. She could still smell the roast meat from the barbecue. She could hear the dog yapping endlessly and she could feel a thin line of blood trickling down her shin from where her knees had smacked hard against the pavers.

"Oh dear God, please, *God*," Sam moaned, and he sounded so weak and desperate, and he didn't believe in God, he was an atheist, and his horror was her horror but she didn't want to know about it, and Clementine thought savagely, Shut up, Sam, just shut up.

She could hear Vid saying, "We have a very little girl here who is not breathing. Do you understand me? She is not breathing. We need you right now. Please send an ambulance *right now*." Clementine felt an immense animosity toward him for saying that, as if he were saying something awful about Ruby, as if by saying she wasn't breathing, he was making it so. "We must be at the top of your list, we must be top priority, if we need to pay extra, that is no problem, we will pay anything."

Did he honestly think he could *pay* for a faster ambulance? That rich people could arrange for a VIP ambulance service?

"And nine and ten and eleven and twelve and thirteen and fourteen and fifteen."

Erika bent her head once more.

Sam crouched down next to Clementine and took her hand. She grabbed on to it as if he could pull her back to before, as if he could pull her back to just minutes earlier.

Hadn't that only just happened? Just then? Just that moment before this moment? Surely she'd only looked away for a minute. It couldn't have been more than a minute.

"The ambulance is on its way," said Vid. "I'll go wait on the street so they know where to go."

"We'll come too," said Tiffany. "You come and help us look out for the ambulance, Holly."

Holly went, without resisting, without looking back, her hand trustingly held in Tiffany's as if they were going to see another pet.

Of course, a minute was enough.

Never take your eyes off them. Never look away. It happens so fast. It happens without a sound. All those stories in the news. All those parents. All those mistakes she'd read about. Backyard drownings. Unfenced pools. Children unsupervised in the bath. Children with stupid, foolish, neglectful parents. Children who died surrounded by so-called responsible adults. And each time she would pretend to be non-judgmental, but really, deep down she was thinking: Not me. That could never really happen to me.

Erika lifted her head from her second breath and her eyes met Clementine's with a look of unutterable despair. Tiny beads of water clung to her eyelashes. Her lips, the lips that had been pressed against Ruby's, were chapped.

Oliver's voice didn't change. "One and two and three and four and five."

49

The Day of the Barbecue

. . . and six and seven and eight and nine and ten."

Erika listened to Oliver count, waiting for her cue. The number fifteen.

Her shirt stuck to her. Her jeans were so cold and clammy against her thighs.

Clementine's face looked like a skull. It was like the skin was pulled back too tight. She was an alien version of Clementine, staring at Erika as if she were begging for clemency.

Ruby wasn't responding.

It wasn't working even though they were doing it exactly right. Two rescue breaths after every fifteen compressions but *do not stop the compressions*, they'd changed the rules since the last time they'd done a first aid course, now you did non-stop compressions. She knew that was right.

She and Oliver had done a refresher first aid course back in March. It was a free course offered through Oliver's work. The managing partner at Oliver's new accounting firm was a passionate advocate for first aid education. He liked to interrupt meetings by pointing at someone and saying, "Sanjeev is having a heart attack!" and then, while Sanjeev obligingly pretended to grab his chest, the managing partner would spin in his chair to point out someone else, often an unsuspecting intern, "You there! What do you do? Save Sanjeev!" And then he'd count down the time before Sanjeev was dead and it was too late.

The course had been fun. Oliver and Erika were the star students. They'd both done first aid courses before this. Of course they had. They had their bronze medallions, their rescue diving certificates. They were the sort of people who believed in first aid courses, and anyway, no matter the subject, Oliver and Erika had always been star students. Even when the subject wasn't a matter of life and death, they took it as seriously as if it were.

Erika could see their teacher now. Paul was a ruddy-faced, heavy-breathing man who looked like a potential heart attack victim himself. "Got it in one," Paul kept saying to Erika and Oliver with an approving click of his fingers each time they got something right.

Fifteen compressions and two rescue breaths. They were doing it right. They were doing it exactly right. They were following the rules, *Paul*, so why was Ruby just lying there, why wasn't she responding, Paul, you *hateful, stupid, red-faced, finger-clicking man*?

"... thirteen and fourteen and fifteen and one ..."

"Where is the ambulance?" said Sam. "I can't hear a siren. Why can't I hear a siren?"

Erika pinched Ruby's nostrils together again, bent her head and exhaled a silent scream of fury into Ruby's body. *YOU DO AS I SAY, RUBY. YOU BREATHE.* It was her mother's voice, her mother at her most manic and vicious and terrifying, her mother when she caught Erika trying to throw something out. *YOU BREATHE RIGHT THIS INSTANT, RUBY, HOW DARE YOU IGNORE ME, YOU BREATHE, NOW, RIGHT NOW.*

Erika lifted her head.

Ruby's chest jolted. Water spewed up from her mouth. Oliver made a high, startled sound of surprise like a dog's whimper and lifted his hands.

Got it in one, said Paul in Erika's head, with a click of his fingers, and Erika turned Ruby's head to the side, just like they'd done with the rubbery-tasting plastic mannequin, and Ruby vomited more water, over and over, while Clementine sobbed and heaved as if she were being sick too. The long, thin wail of an ambulance pierced Erika's consciousness as if it had been there all along, and together she and Oliver turned Ruby onto her side, into the recovery position as they'd been taught.

Good girl, thought Erika, and she ran her hand gently over Ruby's head, brushing the wet strands of hair from her eyes as she continued to vomit water. Good girl.

50

"Erika?"

"Mmmm," Erika fidgeted and focused on the rain falling outside Not-Pat's window. Was it easing perhaps?

For the first time ever, she was longing for her session with Not-Pat to end. Normally, she found therapy such a soothing process, like getting a massage, a lovely self-validating massage of her ego, but today Not-Pat was just annoying her. She'd latched on to the subject of Erika's friendship with Clementine like a little rat terrier with a bone.

Each time Not-Pat said Clementine's name, Erika felt like she was being pinched, very hard.

Look, she was paying for this. She didn't have to put up with it.

"I don't want to talk about Clementine anymore!" she snapped.

"All righty," said Not-Pat in her folksy way, and she wrote something down on her notepad. Erika had to restrain herself from reaching over and grabbing the notebook from her lap. Did she have a legal right to demand access to Not-Pat's notes? She would find out.

In the meantime, she distracted Not-Pat by telling her the story of Ruby's accident.

"Oh my goodness me!" Not-Pat's hand rushed to her mouth.

When Erika had finished, Not-Pat said, "You know, Erika, it's perfectly understandable if your memory of that afternoon feels disjointed. You suffered a shock. It would have been a traumatic event."

"I would think that would have made my memory clearer," said Erika, and in fact, there were some parts of her memory that were frighteningly vivid. She could feel the shock of the water around her legs as she leaped into the fountain, the plumes of water drenching her like rain.

"Why do you think you're so concerned about your memory of that afternoon?" asked Not-Pat.

"I have this feeling there's something important I've forgotten," said Erika. "It almost feels like there's something I've forgotten to *do*. Like when people talk about how they start to get this niggling worry they've left the iron on when they leave the house."

"I know that feeling," said Not-Pat with a wry smile.

"But that's my point, I *do not know that feeling!*" said Erika. "I'm not that sort of person. I have perfect recall! I never forget anything like that."

She never worried that she'd left the iron on, because she knew she'd never do such a thing. Once, Clementine had left her house with two hot plates on at full strength. "The house didn't burn down!" she'd said happily, as if it had been a fascinating experiment. "Nothing burned at all!" Another time she'd gone out with the front door wide open. "An open invitation to the neighborhood burglars," said Sam. "Come on in, boys, and help yourself to my three-hundred-thousand-dollar cello. It's just lying here on the bed for you. Great place for it!"

Clementine's excuse had been that she was "deep in thought."

"About your music?" asked Oliver, respectful of her talent, and Clementine had said, "No, I was trying to work out why Caramello Koalas don't taste as good as they once did. I was thinking: Has the chocolate changed or have I changed?" Then she and Sam had got into a discussion about Caramello Koalas, as if it mattered. There had been no consequences for Clementine's negligence. There never had been a consequence for Clementine's negligence until that Sunday afternoon, and Erika had never wished for that.

Just a financial penalty maybe. Sunburn. A hangover. Clementine never even got hangovers.

"I just need to get it clear in my head," she said to Not-Pat.

"Well, as I said earlier, you could try going back to your next-door neighbor's backyard, if you haven't already done so, and some relaxation exercises might help. You could try some of those self-meditation exercises I've given you in the past. But honestly, Erika, you might be fighting a losing battle when you consider the medication you took that afternoon combined with the alcohol. It's possible you've remembered as much as you ever will remember. It may even be that you're subconsciously protecting yourself; that part of you doesn't want to remember."

"You mean I'm repressing it?" Erika had said disdainfully. "There are actually no empirical studies on the validity of memory repression! In fact I can send you some links to articles about false memory syndrome if you like—"

But at that point, the little timer on Not-Pat's desk gave its smug little click to indicate the session was over. Not-Pat jumped up like a jack-in-the-box. She wasn't normally so fast to get to her feet. Maybe she hadn't enjoyed this session much either.

Erika hurried out to her car parked in the quiet street outside Not-Pat's home office and sat for a few minutes with the ignition on, listening to the thunderous rain on her roof and watching her windshield wipers work feverishly.

"Calm down," she said to the windshield wipers. Their manic rhythm reminded her of her mother when she got herself into a state over something inconsequential. She didn't want to go back to her mother's house. She'd taken the whole day off work to help her mother, but she didn't think she had the fortitude to manage going there *twice in one day*. That was too much. Like asking someone to get back into a freezing-cold swimming pool and swim one hundred laps after they'd already done one hundred laps that morning, and now that they'd had a shower and were all warm and dry again.

She closed her eyes and tried some of the breathing exercises that Not-Pat had taught her in a previous session. Inhale. Hold. Exhale. Inhale. Hold. Exhale. She let the memories spin through her head: The fairy lights in the trees. The smell of cooked marinated meat. The sour taste of too much wine.

She saw that face again. That ghastly, featureless face she'd seen in her office yesterday. Like a ghoul.

She thought suddenly: *Harry*. It's Harry's face. Grumpy old Harry. Was there something important she needed to do *for* Harry? No. *Because* of Harry. Something to do with Harry. Don't chase the memory, or it will disappear. She'd learned this. Relax, *breathe*. Harry's neatly combed white hair. No, that wasn't a memory. That was an image Oliver had put in her mind: Harry's hair, still neatly combed in death.

Harry at the letter box, muttering to himself as he studied an envelope. Barney streaking across the yard. Vid coming out his front door.

An obligation. A request. A responsibility. Something that Harry needed from her.

Shards of broken blue crockery on terra-cotta tiles.

Look up. Look *up*.

She opened her eyes in the fogged-up car and looked up. Nothing to see except rain.

For heaven's sake, she was only thinking about Harry because he'd died. It was a casebook example of false memory syndrome. If Erika had a weaker personality, a more malleable mind, then an over-eager therapist could help her fabricate an entire memory about the barbecue and Harry. Next thing she'd be convinced that Harry had been there at the barbecue molesting Ruby or some such nonsense.

She turned the keys in the ignition, indicated and looked over her shoulder at the traffic. She would try Not-Pat's idea of "returning to the scene of the crime." When she got home, she would ask Vid and Tiffany if she could stand alone in their backyard in the rain for a while. That wouldn't sound odd at all. Ha ha. No, the best thing would be if she went over when she knew they were out.

It probably wouldn't help, but it couldn't hurt.

51

The Day of the Barbecue

The two blue-uniformed paramedics came into the backyard with the absolute authority of conductors walking onto a stage. They didn't run, but they moved fast, with a rigid calmness.

It was as though the rest of them weren't grown-ups anymore. It was as though they'd all been playing a game, a game where they'd pretended to be in control of their lives, a game where they'd pretended they had interesting professions and healthy bank accounts and families and backyard barbecues, but now a curtain had been pulled briskly aside and the grown-ups had marched in because rules had been broken.

Rules had been very badly broken. The circle of people surrounding Ruby parted automatically so the paramedics could get to her. Ruby mumbled incoherently, terrifyingly. She seemed drowsy and drugged, as if she were coming out of anesthesia.

The paramedics moved as if in a choreographed dance they'd done many times before. As they examined Ruby with plastic-gloved hands, the older man asked rapid questions without looking up, confident that the answers would be provided. He spoke in a voice that was fractionally louder and slower than a normal speaking voice, as if he were speaking to children.

"What happened here?"

"What's her name?"

"And how old is Ruby?"

"When was Ruby last seen?"

"So no one saw her fall? You don't know if she hit her head?"

"Did she have a pulse when she was pulled from the fountain?"

"Are you the parents?"

He looked briefly up as he asked the last question at Erika and Oliver. A reasonable assumption. They were the ones in wet clothes.

"No," said Sam. "We are." He indicated Clementine.

"They rescued her," said Clementine. It seemed important to get this on the record. "Our friends. They did CPR. They got her breathing."

"How long did you perform CPR for?" said the paramedic.

"It would have been about five minutes," said Oliver. He looked at Erika to confirm.

"At the most," said Erika.

"We did two rescue breaths for every fifteen compressions," said Oliver anxiously.

Five minutes? It wasn't possible, thought Clementine. It had been an unbearably long stretch of time.

There was something in Ruby's mouth, a tube in her nose, a mask over her face. She'd been turned into a generic patient. Not their wicked, funny little Ruby.

"Have you got any towels?" asked the younger paramedic. He was using a pair of large, serrated scissors to cut a straight line through Ruby's clothes: her tutu, her long-sleeved T-shirt, unpeeling the layers of clothing to reveal Ruby's tiny white chest.

"Of course." Vid hurried inside and returned with a stack of beautifully folded white fluffy towels.

"What are you doing?" asked Sam sharply as the paramedic dried Ruby's body firmly and pressed two sticky pads to her chest.

"These are defibrillator pads," said the paramedic. "In case she arrests again. We're just preparing for the worst-case scenario. It can also give us useful information."

Ruby's little arms flailed about.

"We're going to sedate her," said the older paramedic. "Are there any allergies I need to know about?"

"None," said Sam.

"Is she on any medication? What's her medical history?"

"She's never even had antibiotics," said Clementine.

The paramedic tapped the side of a needle. Clementine saw white dots in front of her eyes.

"Watch her," said the paramedic sharply, and Clementine realized he meant her only when Sam took her arm.

Sam had always been the one to take the girls for their injections. Clementine couldn't bear needles.

"Head between your knees," said the paramedic.

"I'm okay," said Clementine, breathing deeply.

"Why are the police here?" asked Sam. Clementine looked up and saw Vid talking to a very young-looking policewoman with a pert ponytail. She took notes as Vid spoke. What was he saying? The mother wasn't watching. She was talking to me. She was telling jokes.

Clementine saw that Erika had gotten up from her position by the fountain next to Ruby without Clementine noticing and moved inside the cabana. She had two white towels draped over her shoulders and another on her lap, where Holly now sat, her back to Clementine, her head resting on Erika's shoulder.

"It's standard for an event like this," said the paramedic as he continued to treat Ruby. "They'll just ask some questions to clarify what happened. We'll also need them to help block off the street for the rescue helicopter."

"A helicopter?" said Sam. "They're sending a helicopter? Where are they going to land it?"

"Basically outside the front door," said the paramedic. He bent over Ruby's arm. Clementine looked away.

"You're kidding," said Sam.

"They land on highways, backyards, tennis courts. This place is perfect. Nice wide cul-de-sac. Underground power lines. They do it all the time."

"Huh," said Sam.

"Yeah, the blades are shorter than on a normal helicopter."

For God's sake, were they having a chatty, masculine conversation about helicopters?

Except that Clementine could see that even though Sam sounded like himself, he wasn't really, because he was opening and shutting his fists, rapidly and obsessively, over and over, as if he were freezing cold or mad.

"But why do they need a helicopter?" said Clementine. The panic, which had receded a little when she'd seen Ruby's chest move and even more so when the paramedics arrived, skyrocketed again. "She's okay now, isn't she? She's going to be okay? She's breathing now. Isn't she breathing?"

She looked at Sam and saw the dread in his eyes. He was always a step ahead of her when it came to recognizing danger ahead. Glass half empty, she called it. Alert, he called it. Two crass, ugly words came into her head for the first time: brain damage.

"It's pretty standard procedure for a serious pediatric event. There will be a doctor on board. I expect they'll intubate her and make sure she has stabilized before she goes on the helicopter," said the paramedic. He looked up at her. His skin had the roughened look of someone who spends a lot of time outdoors. There was a kind of professional weariness in his eyes, like a war veteran who has seen things a civilian could never understand. "Your friends did everything right."

52

We were all doing it. Clementine's words hung in the air while she and Sam looked at each other over the mound of Holly's clothes, breathing heavily.

Clementine heard the rain lashing Holly's window and wondered if their little house could withstand this weather for much longer. Perhaps the walls would finally soften and sag and collapse.

"I know we were all doing it," said Sam. "All four of us. Acting like idiots. Like teenagers. Our behavior was disgusting. It makes me want to vomit when I think of it."

The extreme violence of his words made Clementine want to leap to their defense. They'd been people at a barbecue having a laugh, flirting, being silly. It had meant nothing. If the girls had kept chasing the fairy lights then nothing more would have come of it. They would have looked back on that day with laughter, not shame.

"It was bad luck," she said. "It was very bad luck."

"It was not!" exploded Sam. "It was negligence! Our negligence. I should have been watching the girls. I should have known that I couldn't depend on you."

"*What?*" Clementine felt a crazy, almost exhilarated feeling of rage and injustice blow straight through her body like a white-hot flame, making her feel as if she could lift off the ground. Finally, after all these weeks, they were going to fight.

"It was the one time," he said coldly. "The *one* time I let my attention slip."

"Yes, maybe I thought I could sit back and relax," said Clementine. Her voice shook with fury. "Because the *better* parent was there, because Mr. Fucking Perfect was on duty!"

Sam gave a bitter half laugh. "Fine then, it was all my fault."

"Oh, for God's sake, don't be such a martyr," said Clementine. "We were both there, we were both equally responsible. This is silly."

They looked at each other with flat dislike. Their different parenting styles had always been a teasing point of contention, a hairline fracture in an otherwise solid marriage, but now that tiny fracture had become a chasm.

"I think I'm done," said Sam.

"It's a pointless conversation," agreed Clementine.

"No," said Sam. "I think maybe I'm done with us."

"Done with us," repeated Clementine slowly. Was this what gunshot victims meant when they said they initially felt no pain? "You're 'done with us.'"

"I think we should consider separating," said Sam. "Possibly. I don't know. Don't you think?"

53

The Day of the Barbecue

Tiffany stood in her backyard being interviewed by a young police officer. She looked over her shoulder at the paramedics next to the tiny form of Ruby. Sam and Clementine were talking to the paramedics, and they looked like entirely different people from the ones who had been sitting around the table only minutes earlier. Their faces had collapsed, like popped balloons.

"What happened here?" the policewoman said to Tiffany. She pointed with her foot at the broken crockery on the pathway leading from the back door. There were dangerous-looking shards and chunks of broken blue china everywhere. Tiffany had loved those blue plates.

"Oh," said Tiffany. She tried to imagine this scene through the policewoman's eyes. Did it look like a crime scene? Did she think there had been a fight? Or that they had all been drunk? The policewoman had already spoken to Vid, so presumably she already knew exactly what had happened. She was double-checking their stories, making sure everything matched up. It made Tiffany nervous.

"Our guest, Erika, our next-door neighbor—she was carrying plates from inside, and I think that's when she realized that Ruby was in the fountain . . ." Tiffany's voice broke. She thought of Ruby's squat little toddler body, her blond curls. "And then I think she dropped them, because she ran to pull her out."

What had Tiffany been doing? She'd been distracting Ruby's parents. She'd made them forget they were parents.

"It happened so fast," she told the policewoman.

"Unfortunately, it's not an unusual scenario," said the policewoman. "Children drown in plain sight surrounded by people. It's silent. It's fast. Lack of parental supervision is the most common cause of drownings."

"Yes," said Tiffany. She wanted to say: No, you don't understand. We're not those kind of people. We *were* supervising them. Just not then. Just not at that moment. It was silent. It was fast. For one moment, they all looked away.

Tiffany thought of her older sisters. She could never tell them about this. "For fuck's sake, Tiffany," they would say, because the Collins girls took pride in their down-to-earth practicality. Their common sense. They were from the western suburbs and proud of it. They didn't make mistakes like that. They'd be distressed that something like this could happen at their own little sister's house. They'd relate it to money. To her bloated bank account. They wouldn't pull their punches.

If they ever learned that she'd been pretending to give the child's mother a lap dance at the time it happened, they would be united in their horror. Tiffany's dancing career still mystified and shamed them. "Just thinking about you in that trashy club makes me sick to my stomach," her sister Emma, the dramatic one of the family, liked to say, all these years later, and she wasn't actually being dramatic, she meant it, it really did make her sick to her stomach. "She was a disgrace to the sisterhood," agreed Louise, who had recently discovered feminism, and she meant it too, but their words had slid straight off Tiffany as if she were made of Teflon. Their words would stick now, even if her intentions had never been more innocent, because the safety of a child trumped everything, as it should.

Tiffany looked up as the frantic, dramatic sound of chopping helicopter blades suddenly filled the air. "Is that helicopter . . . for us?"

"Yep, that's for us." The policewoman looked up too, and took a radio out of her trouser pocket. "Excuse me."

She hurried off.

"Where's it going to land?" said Tiffany to herself. The helicopter hovered over them like a giant bird, and the sound intensified. Out of the corner of her eye she saw poor Barney streak across the yard to escape the loud noise.

"Mum!" Dakota appeared by her side in the backyard, her eyes big and wide. She held her book in her hand, her finger still marking the page. "What happened? Why is there a helicopter here? I heard the ambulance before but I didn't think it was for *us*."

Tiffany put her arm around her and pulled her close, wanting to feel her skinny little body for a moment. She had forgotten all about her up until now. "Ruby fell in the fountain. She nearly drowned."

Dakota immediately pulled away from her hug and grabbed Tiffany's arm. She said something, but Tiffany couldn't hear her over the increasing volume of the helicopter.

She saw Vid at the end of the path that led down to the side of the house, gesturing for her to come out the front. He had yet another policeman with him. He wouldn't like that. Vid had a police phobia. One of his greatest, genuine but amusing fears was going to jail for a crime he didn't commit. "Innocent people go to jail every day," he often told Tiffany, completely straight-faced, as if it were more likely than not that this could happen to him. It made him excessively law abiding. He'd paid far too much tax until Tiffany had taken over his financial affairs. He still wanted to throw extra money at the tax man just in case.

"Daddy needs me. Go and wait in the house!" she yelled at Dakota. "Everything is fine."

Dakota grabbed at Tiffany's arm again, pinching the flesh too hard. Tiffany shook her off. "Later!" she yelled. "Go!"

Dakota ran off, shoulders rounded, her face in her hands, and Tiffany thought impatiently, jeez Louise, Dakota, I don't have time for this, it's not about you.

54

Tiffany and Vid listened to the rain and stared dully at the crash site on the kitchen floor created by the dropped jar of chocolate nuts.

"You wouldn't think there'd have been that much glass in that jar," said Vid.

"Or that many nuts," agreed Tiffany. "We're okay, Dakota!" she called out. "Just in case you're wondering! Your dad dropped a jar!"

There was silence. Tiffany could just make out the hum of the television beneath the rain.

"Nobody is hurt!" called out Vid. "We don't need any help!"

There was a pause. "*Okay!*" called back Dakota in a magnificently dismissive tone.

Tiffany and Vid smiled at each other.

"I should have guessed why she was behaving so strangely," said Tiffany. "It's so obvious to me now that she would blame herself."

"You kept telling me there was something wrong," said Vid. "But why didn't she just tell us how she felt before today?" He lowered his voice, although there was no chance that Dakota could overhear. "Why keep it all bottled up like that? That's not good."

"It sounds like she was worried that we blamed her too. She seemed to think we were angry with her."

"Crazy!" said Vid angrily.

"I know. Well, we were upset, obviously, and distracted, and that's what children do. They assume they're to blame for everything. So everything we did she misinterpreted."

"But she wasn't even there when it happened!"

"That's the point." Tiffany tried not to show her impatience. Vid had been there too when Dakota had sobbingly explained exactly why she thought everyone blamed her for Ruby's accident, but he was so busy throwing up his hands in disbelief, he hadn't listened properly to a word she'd said. "She got it into her head that Clementine believed Dakota was in charge of the kids. I mean, we did keep telling her she was such a good babysitter."

"Yes, but—"

"I know," said Tiffany. "Of course Clementine and Sam wouldn't blame her. No one blames her. She's ten years old, for God's sake. We all knew she'd gone inside to read her book. If anyone was to blame in this family, it was me. I was the one offering lap dances to our guests."

"Stop that," said Vid quickly, predictably. He'd shut down every conversation like this since the barbecue. "It was a terrible *accident.*"

Yeah, talk about keeping things bottled up. No wonder Dakota thought that what had happened at the barbecue was a shameful secret. *They'd never said a word to her about it!* That must have seemed so strange and freaky to the poor kid. Of course she thought it was about her.

She remembered how the week directly after the barbecue she'd been so preoccupied with work. That bloody town house that had been nothing but trouble from the start had gotten passed in at auction, and the Land and Environment Court decision hadn't gone her way. It had been a shit week all round, and beneath all that stress was the absolute horror of what had happened. She hadn't given Dakota a thought. Not a single thought. Dakota had just been another job to cross off her list. As long as she had her uniform and lunch and was safely deposited at school, then the job was done. Vid had been the same. It had been a shit week for him too. He'd lost that government contract, which had turned out to be a blessing in disguise, but he hadn't known that then. By the time Vid and Tiffany had emerged from their fogs and started talking properly to Dakota again, the damage was done. The poor kid interpreted their reemergence as *her parents forgiving her.*

Forgiving her!

"I'll get the dustpan," said Vid. "Don't move. You have bare feet."

He went to get the dustpan and broom.

Tiffany watched Vid's massive shoulders as he crouched down, carefully sweeping up the glass and nuts. She thought about secrets and the damage they did.

"I recognized one of the parents at the school today," she said.

"Oh yeah, who was it?" Vid kept sweeping.

"From my dancing days," said Tiffany.

Vid looked up. "Is that right, eh?"

"One of my regulars," said Tiffany. "Sort of a friend really. A nice guy."

"Good tipper?" asked Vid.

"Great tipper," said Tiffany.

"Excellent," said Vid.

"He booked a lot of private shows," said Tiffany carefully.

"Good for him," said Vid. "The man had great taste." He studied the floor carefully and continued sweeping up the tiny fragments of glass.

"Vid," said Tiffany. "Come on. It's a bit . . . uncomfortable, isn't it? Standing on the netball courts next to a guy who saw your wife strip?"

"Why should I be uncomfortable?" He looked up at her from the floor. "I'm proud of you. I probably wouldn't want to see his wife strip. Did you sleep with him?"

"I never slept with any of them," said Tiffany. "You know that."

Vid studied her thoughtfully. "Well then, so what is the big deal?" he finally said. "You weren't a hooker."

"But it's a prestigious private school. To some of those women there's probably not much difference between a dancer and a hooker. If word gets out, if he tells his wife—"

"He's not going to tell his wife," said Vid. He stood up and moved to another corner of the floor where the nuts had rolled.

"He might tell his wife, and then all the girls will find out, and Dakota will get bullied and that will lead to depression and that will lead to drug addiction."

"That drug, ice—now that's a terrible drug," said Vid. "Let's tell her to stick to the nice drugs, the ones that make you feel mellow, not like you want to claw off your skin."

"Vid."

"He's not going to tell his wife," said Vid. "I would bet you a million dollars he doesn't tell his wife. And so what if he does? All the girls will say is, 'Oh, Dakota, you're so lucky, your mum is very talented, very beautiful, very flexible.'"

"*Vid.*"

"You did nothing wrong. Did you rob a bank? No, you did not. And if this thing you're worried about happens, and it won't happen, but if it does happen that Dakota is unhappy, we pull her out of that school! Easy. We send her somewhere else. Come on now. Not every man in Sydney saw you dance. We'll find another school where no one knows you."

"Things aren't that simple," said Tiffany.

"They are if we want them to be," said Vid. He swept up the final shards of glass and stood. "You're getting yourself all worked up over nothing. You're finding catastrophes. It's like with grumpy old Harry next door. . . ."

"That's not nothing," said Tiffany. "Our next-door neighbor dies and we don't even know. That's not nothing."

Vid shrugged. "Okay, so what did Dakota say in the car today? We feel *regret.* Yes, we do. Sure we do. We feel regret over Harry. We should have visited him more, even when he slammed the door in our face. And if you want, you can feel regret over your dancing, even though you were good at it and you liked it and you didn't hurt anyone, and you made a lot of money, you know, so I think, good for you, but okay, if you want, you feel regret. Just like we feel regret over little Ruby, you know, of course we do. We all feel terrible. We all wish that things had been different. We wish that very much. We wish—I wish—I'd never invited those people in the first place and I wish I'd kept a better eye on those little girls, so that every time I walk into my own backyard I don't have to remember—"

He stopped. His mouth worked as if he were chewing on a tough piece of steak.

"I'll never forget her little white face," said Vid finally. He'd gotten control of his voice but his eyes were very bright. He held the blue dustpan full of chocolate nuts and glass tightly in his hand. "Her blue lips. The whole time I was calling the ambulance, I was thinking to myself: It's too late. It's too late. She's gone."

He turned away and Tiffany closed her eyes briefly.

A speeding ticket had arrived last week and she'd recognized the date immediately. A camera must have picked her up going over the limit when she'd driven Clementine to the hospital. She would never forget that drive. It was like a nightmare that stayed with you forever. She and Clementine had experienced that *together*. It was not right that Tiffany and her family be cut cleanly from Clementine's life.

She thought of Dakota and how she'd buried her groundless remorse so deep, she'd become an eerie ghost of herself.

"Right," she said. She felt suddenly very, very angry. "Where are the keys? We're going out."

55

The Day of the Barbecue

Tiffany registered the sudden eerie whisper-quietness of her neighborhood. The police and the paramedics and the helicopter had all left. Sunday night in the suburbs. Time for homework and ironing and *60 Minutes*.

It was dark now. The streetlights were on. They stood in the front yard. Tiffany was about to drive Clementine to the hospital. She had her car keys ready in the palm of her hand. Only one parent had been allowed to go in the helicopter with Ruby and Sam had gone, which meant Clementine had to get to the hospital on her own.

"I'll drive myself," said Clementine now. She must have been running fingers through her hair, because it stood out in a mad halo around her head, like she'd had an electric shock.

"No, you won't. You're probably over the limit anyway," said Tiffany.

"Haven't you been drinking?" said Clementine.

"I only had one light beer," said Tiffany.

"Oh," said Clementine. She chewed her lip and Tiffany saw that she'd drawn blood. "Right."

The plan was for Oliver and Erika to take care of Holly, just Oliver really, because Erika was clearly not quite right, although she'd finally stopped shaking.

"I'll get these two ladies onto the couch with a DVD and some popcorn," said Oliver. The poor man was still in wet clothes himself.

Clementine suddenly threw her arms so violently around Oliver she nearly knocked him off balance. "I haven't even said thank you," she said into his chest. "I haven't even thanked you both." Her voice was so full of raw emotion it was almost painful to hear.

She reached an arm out to Erika, to hug her too, but Erika stepped away. "Fix your hair, Clementine," she said. She smoothed down the strands of hair around Clementine's face with both hands. "You'll scare Ruby. You look like a witch."

"Thanks," said Clementine with a shaky breath. "Right."

She bent down to Holly's height. "You be a good girl for Erika and Oliver, okay? And, um, you might get to stay with Grandma tonight!"

"Hooray!" said Holly. She stopped. "And Ruby too?"

"I think it will be just you tonight, Holly," said Clementine. She looked up at the sky where the helicopter had just disappeared and pulled her cardigan tighter around her. Holly stared up at her mother and her lower lip trembled.

"Let's go, Holly," said Oliver, taking her hand. He looked at Tiffany. "Er. Thank you for your hospitality, Tiffany. Vid."

Vid slapped him on the shoulder. "Mate."

Oliver hurried Holly off down the driveway, telling her about the movie they were about to see.

"You'll call us?" Erika put her hand on Clementine's arm, and Tiffany could see that this was her version of a hug. Her sister Karen was exactly the same.

"I can't believe she's in that helicopter right now." Clementine stared at the sky. "I should have been the one to go with her, not Sam. I don't know why I let him go, what if, what if—"

"Snap out of it," said Erika. "Who cares who went in the helicopter? She's sedated. She won't even remember it. Off you go. Do I need to slap you across the face?"

"What?" Clementine blinked. "No!"

"So call us, okay?" said Erika.

"Of course I'll call you," said Clementine snippily.

They really were like sisters.

As Erika followed Oliver and Holly down the driveway, in bare feet, her wet shoes in her hand, Vid came from inside with Tiffany's car keys, followed by Dakota.

"Well. So. We hope little Ruby is all good, back to her little monkey self in no time. I'm sure she will be," said Vid to Clementine. "You have private health coverage, right? Tell them you want the best doctors. No trainees."

Poor Vid. He didn't shine at times like these. Tiffany could see the tension in his shoulders, as if he were squaring up for a fight. It was like his entire body resisted negative emotion.

Clementine studied Vid. Her face twisted with some unreadable emotion. "Yes," she said formally. "Thank you." She looked at Tiffany. "Can we—?"

"Of course," said Tiffany. She pointed the remote on her key ring at the garage door to open it, and as she did she saw Dakota bravely open her mouth and start to say something to Clementine, but Clementine walked straight past Dakota, her eyes on the car, clearly desperate to get to the hospital as fast as she could.

56

I'm just going to pop over next door for a moment," said Erika to Oliver when she got home. "My psychologist thinks the best way to get my memory back is to 'return to the scene of the crime,' so to speak."

"There was no crime," said Oliver thickly. He was up and dressed and sucking on a cough lolly.

"It's a figure of speech," said Erika. "That's why I said, 'so to speak.'"

"I don't think Vid and Tiffany are home at the moment," said Oliver. "I saw their car leave as you were coming in."

"I know. I saw it too. I'd actually rather go over when they're not there," said Erika. "Less distracting."

"What? You can't go over while they're not home," said Oliver. "That's trespassing."

"Oh, for heaven's sake, Vid and Tiffany wouldn't care," said Erika. "I'd just explain . . . well, I'd just explain what I was doing." It would be awkward, but it would be worth it. She wanted to get some return on the money she'd invested in Not-Pat's session.

"And it's raining," pointed out Oliver. Now he was crunching the cough lolly between his teeth. "There's no point going over in the rain. It wasn't raining that day." He suddenly swallowed the lolly in one gulp and gave her a hard look. "You're not going to remember anything by standing in their backyard. You were drunk, that's all. I've told you before. Drunk people forget stuff. It's perfectly normal."

"And I've told you before, I got drunk because of the *medication*," said Erika. Don't take your childhood issues out on me.

"It's not relevant how or why you got drunk, I'm just saying," said Oliver. "It's not going to help. Come on. It's a crazy idea. Stay here. Tell me about your mother's place. How bad was it?"

"This won't take a minute," said Erika as she walked to the front door. "I'll be back in a moment. I'll tell you about Mum then."

"I've made a chicken curry for dinner." Oliver kept talking as he walked behind her. He held the door as she opened it. "I started to feel a bit better this afternoon, and I wasn't sure if we had any coconut milk but we did. Oh, and I nearly forgot, the police came today! About Harry. They're having trouble finding—"

"Hold all those thoughts!" Erika picked up her umbrella. Oliver wasn't normally so loquacious, but a sick day at home alone always left him banked up with conversation. Also, she had a feeling those cold and flu tablets he took made him a little hyper, not that she would ever tell him that due to his horror of ever being affected by drugs and alcohol. It was cute how chatty he got.

She hurried out in the rain over the front yard and up Vid and Tiffany's driveway. She rang the doorbell first, for form's sake, just in case someone was home, or someone, somewhere was secretly observing her, although the only neighbor who could possibly have done that was Harry and he was dead. She waited a good minute, and then she headed around into the backyard. As she went down the path at the side of the house, security lights switched on automatically, turning the rain to gold. She hoped she wouldn't trip some alarm.

All the fairy lights in the backyard were on, and she remembered how Tiffany had said they were on some sort of automatic timer. Just the sight of the fairy lights created a deluge of sensory memory from that afternoon. She could smell Vid's caramelized onions that Clementine had fussed over. She could feel the way the ground had gently rocked beneath her feet. The woolly sensation in her head. This was *working*. Not-Pat was a genius, worth every cent.

Don't get distracted, she reminded herself. Focus, except don't focus too much. Relax and remember.

She had walked down this footpath from the back door. She was carrying the blue and white plates. She was looking at the plates. She liked the plates. She *coveted* the plates. My God, she hadn't taken the plates, had she? No. She'd dropped the plates. She remembered that.

The music. There was music, and beneath the music, or above the music, there was a sound, an urgent sound, and the sound was related in some way to . . . Harry. Oh, why did she keep coming back to Harry? What did that mean? Just because of his phone call earlier about turning down the music?

She walked a little farther down the footpath. She couldn't see the fountain from here. She needed to see the fountain. Her heart thudded in rhythm with the rain pelleting her umbrella.

She stopped, confused. Where was the fountain? She turned to the left. She turned to the right. She let the umbrella fall back behind her head and squinted through the rain.

The fountain was gone. There was nothing but an ugly slab of empty concrete where it had once stood, and Erika's memories were dissolving, disappearing, being washed away like a chalk drawing on pavement in the rain, and all she felt right now was cold and wet and foolish.

57

Clementine followed Sam into their bedroom, where he pulled a T-shirt from a drawer and shrugged it on. He took off his work pants and pulled on a pair of jeans. His movements were jerky, like a twitchy junkie in need of a fix. He avoided meeting her eye.

She said, "Do you mean it? Are you serious? About separating?"

"Probably not," he said with a lift of his shoulders, as if the state of their marriage was neither here nor there to him.

She was so agitated she couldn't sort out her breathing. It was like she couldn't remember the process. She kept holding her breath and then taking sudden gasps of air.

She said, "For God's sake, you can't just say things like that! You've never, we've never . . ."

She meant that they'd never used words like "separation" and "divorce" even in their worst screaming matches. They yelled things like, "You're infuriating!" "You don't think!" "You are the most annoying woman in the history of annoying women!" "I hate you!" "I hate you more!" and they always, always used the word "always," even though Clementine's mother had said you should never use that word in an argument with your spouse, as in, for example, "You always forget to refill the water jug!" (But Sam did always forget. It was accurate.)

But they'd never allowed for the possibility of their marriage ending. They could stomp and yell and sulk, safe in the knowledge that the scaffolding of their lives was rock solid. Paradoxically, it gave them permission to yell louder, to scream stupider, sillier, more irrational things, to just let their feelings swirl freely through them, because it was going to be fine in the morning.

"Sorry," said Sam. "I shouldn't have said that." He looked at her, and an expression of pure exhaustion crossed his face, and for a moment, it was him again, not that cold, peculiar stranger. "I was just upset about the idea of Dakota coming to Holly's party. I don't want Holly having anything to do with that family."

"They're not bad people," said Clementine, momentarily distracted from the point at hand by the loathing in Sam's tone. Clementine didn't want to see Vid and Tiffany, because they were a reminder of the worst day of her life. Just thinking about them made her shudder, the way you shuddered at the thought of some food or drink in which you had over-indulged until it made you sick. But she didn't loathe them.

"Look, they're just not our type of people," said Sam. "To be frank, I don't want my child associating with people like them."

"What? Because she used to be a dancer?" said Clementine.

"She used to be a *stripper*," said Sam, with such disgust, it made Clementine feel instantly defensive on Tiffany's behalf.

It would be too easy to put Tiffany into a particular box for a "certain kind of person" and to decide that the powerful shot of desire Clementine had felt when Tiffany offered her a lap dance was merely a cheap trick of her body, an involuntary response, like using a vibrator. It would be easy to decide that Clementine's behavior was disgusting and Tiffany was disgusting and what had happened was all just so disgusting. But that was a cop-out. That was like saying that what had happened to Ruby could never have happened if they'd been at a barbecue with "the right sort of people." Of course it could still have happened if they'd been distracted by a conversation about philosophy or politics or prize-winning literature.

"Tiffany is nice. Really nice! They're nice people!" she said. She thought about Vid and Tiffany and the warmth and friendliness they'd showed them that night. They were both so unabashedly themselves. There was no sub-terfuge, no obfuscation. "They're kind of sweet people really."

"Sweet!" exploded Sam. "Are you out of your mind? You've got no idea what you're talking about. I've *been* to those strip clubs. Have you ever been to one?"

"No, but so what?"

"They're revolting, depressing places. They're not glamorous. They're not sexy. You've got no grip on reality. Seriously." It was just another version of the ongoing argument of their marriage. Sam had reality gripped. Apparently Clementine did not. Sam wanted to get to the airport early. Clementine wanted to be the last one to board. Sam wanted to book ahead. Clementine wanted to wing it. It used to balance out. It used to be a joke.

"*Seriously.*" She imitated his tone mockingly under her breath.

"Seriously," he said. "No one wants to be there at those places. Not the girls. Not the punters."

"Oh, right, *no one* wants to be there," repeated Clementine. The word "punters" irked her (conservative old-man word), or was it just that every-thing about him irked her now? "So I guess you and the other *punters* were just forced to go along."

"In most cases, it's a drunk group of blokes and someone says, let's do this for a lark, and you go along and it's funny, but then you see all those hard-faced women gyrating about and you realize it's seedy, it's disgusting—"

"Yeah, that's right, Sam, because you seemed really *disgusted* by Tiffany that night," said Clementine. This was insane. This was historical revision-ism at its best, and hadn't Sam *always* specialized in that, hadn't she always said she wished she had a permanent film rolling of their life so she could go back and prove that, yes, he did so say that thing he now denied? "You were laughing. You were encouraging her. You liked her, don't pretend you didn't like her, I know you did."

She regretted it as soon as she said it because she knew him so well, she could see how her words flayed him.

"You're right. And that's what I have to live with," he said. "I have to live with that forever, but it doesn't mean I want to socialize with her. You know she was probably a hooker, right?"

"She wasn't! Dancing was just a job. It was just a fun job."

"How would you know?" said Sam.

"We talked about it. When she drove me to the hospital."

Sam stopped. "So you had a fun chat about Tiffany's stripping days on the way to the hospital, while Ruby . . . while Ruby . . ." His voice cracked. He took a breath, and when he spoke again, he had regained control of his voice. "How nice. How very *sweet*."

The rage felt as powerful and unconsenting and extraordinary as a contraction. It took her a moment to catch her breath. He was questioning her love for Ruby. He was implying she'd somehow betrayed Ruby, that she didn't care, that her love was inferior to his, and in fact, now that she thought about it, hadn't that always been his implication, that he loved the children more than she did because he worried more, he hovered more?

"You have no idea what that drive to the hospital was like," she said carefully. She could hear the anger she was trying to contain rippling through her speech, so that each word sounded offbeat. "It was the worst—"

Sam held up his hand like a stop sign. "I have no interest in hearing about this."

Clementine lifted both her own hands in frustration and then let them drop. Their relationship was becoming so twisted and tangled, it was like they were lost in the overgrown forest of a fairy tale and she couldn't see how to hack their way back through to the place she knew was still there, the place where surely they still loved each other.

58

The Day of the Barbecue

Tiffany drove toward Westmead Children's Hospital as fast as she dared, while Clementine phoned her parents and in-laws. They were brief but terrible phone calls to hear. As soon as Clementine heard her mother's voice, she burst into tears. Tiffany could hear the poor woman shouting through the phone, "What is it? What happened? For the love of God, Clementine, stop crying and *tell* me!"

After the phone calls they drove in silence, while Clementine sniffed noisily, her phone in her lap and her face turned toward the window.

Finally Tiffany spoke. "I'm so sorry," she began.

"It's not your fault," said Clementine. "It's our fault. My fault."

Tiffany was silent, her eyes on the road ahead. What if a little girl died because Tiffany still liked to be admired? Because she knew Vid liked it? Because she thought she was so freaking *edgy*?

"I was distracting you," she said. She wanted it on the record before someone accused her.

"I started it," said Clementine dully. She turned and looked out the window. "My child. My responsibility."

Tiffany didn't know what to say. It wasn't like arguing over a dinner bill. No, I insist! Let me take this one.

"I was watching both girls all afternoon," said Clementine. "I knew exactly where they both were all the time. Except for then. Sam thinks I'm not as careful as him, but I was watching them. I was."

"Of course you were. I know you were," said Tiffany.

"She must have been so scared," said Clementine. "When the water . . ." Tiffany looked over and saw Clementine rocking, the seat belt pulling tight against her chest, her fist pressed to her mouth. "She would have been swallowing all that water and panicking and . . ."

Tiffany strained to make out the words as she pulled up at a traffic light.

Clementine bent forward and rested her arms against the dashboard as if she were in the brace position for an airplane accident. Then she sat back again and pressed her hands hard against her lower abdomen and moaned, making Tiffany think of a woman in labor.

"Deep breaths," said Tiffany. "In through the nose, out the mouth. Make a 'whoosh' sound, like this: *Ha*."

Clementine obeyed.

"I do yoga sometimes," said Tiffany. Distract her. That's all she could do. "Do you do yoga?"

"I keep meaning to," said Clementine.

"I took Vid once," said Tiffany. "It was the funniest thing I'd ever seen."

"What's that ahead?" said Clementine. "Please tell me that's not a traffic jam."

"I'm sure it's not," said Tiffany. She looked at the line of twinkling red brake lights in front of her, and her heart sank. "Not at this time of night. Surely not."

Clementine couldn't believe what she was seeing. It was like the universe was playing with her, laughing at her, punishing her.

"You're kidding," she said as they pulled up behind a stopped car. She twisted around in her seat. There were cars pulling up behind them, one after another, all of them coming to a complete stop. The lane next to them came to a standstill too. They were trapped in a sea of metal.

"If there's a side street coming up"—Tiffany jabbed her finger at the car's built-in satellite navigator—"we could duck down and find a back way, but I can't seem to see—"

"I should have gone with Ruby," said Clementine.

She and Sam hadn't even discussed it when the doctor had said only one parent could go in the helicopter. "I'll go," Sam had said without even looking at Clementine. Surely it was normally the mother who went. Children needed their mothers when they were sick. Just because Sam took the girls for their injections didn't give him first place in line during medical emergencies. They called out "Mummy!" if they were sick in the night, and Clementine was the one who would go and sit and cuddle them while Sam went to measure out the medicine. Why had she just passively stood aside and let him go? She was the *mother*. Clementine should have gone. She loathed herself for not insisting. She loathed Sam for not giving her the option.

"Oh God," she said out loud. Her stomach cramped violently. "We're not moving at all."

The brake lights on the car in front went off and Tiffany hunched hopefully over the steering wheel. They inched forward and stopped immediately. From behind them a car horn tooted and another one responded with a furious, ludicrous scream.

"Oh, fuck it," moaned Clementine. "Fuck it, fuck it, fuck it."

She couldn't sit still. She plucked at the diagonal strap of her seat belt. It felt like she was being physically restrained from seeing Ruby. The need to be there with her right now was overwhelming. She wanted to scream with it. She could feel her arms straining with the desire to hold her.

"She's in good hands," said Tiffany. "My niece was in intensive care once at Westmead, and my sister said they were amazing. She was so . . . um, impressed, and . . ." She fell silent.

Clementine looked out the window and then opened it to let in some air. She imagined herself throwing open the door and running. No footpath. She'd just run along the highway, past all those stupid horrible metal cars, screaming, "Get out of my way!"

"I'll see if we can find a traffic report." Tiffany switched on the radio.

She pushed buttons, flicking past fragments of sound before finally settling on what sounded like a news report.

"Come on," said Tiffany to the radio.

Finally they heard it. "A three car pile-up," said Vince "the roving traffic reporter" cheerily from his viewpoint in a helicopter. Someone else in a helicopter. "Traffic at a *standstill*. It's unbelievable! This is not your average Sunday evening! It looks like a peak-hour gridlock on a Monday morning."

Tiffany switched off the radio.

"So that confirms we're in a traffic jam," she said.

They sat in silence.

The car in front of them moved and then stopped almost immediately.

"I can't . . . I have to . . ." Clementine undid her seat belt. The roof of the car was so close to her head. "I have to get out of here, I can't just sit here."

"There's nowhere to go." Tiffany looked panicky. "We're moving. Look! We're moving. It will clear."

"Did you see how white she was?" said Clementine. "Her face was so white. She normally has these pink little cheeks." She could feel her self-control slipping, like a foot sliding on gravel. She looked at Tiffany. "Talk to me about something else. Anything else."

"Okay," said Tiffany. "Um."

Clementine couldn't bear it.

"I've got an audition coming up. A very important audition. It was the biggest thing in my life this morning. Did you have to audition to be a dancer?" She pressed her hands over her face and spoke through her fingers. "What if she stops breathing again?"

"I don't think she can stop breathing, because she's intubated," said Tiffany. "To help her breathe."

The line of traffic moved again. Stopped.

"Fuuuuuck this!" Clementine slammed her closed fist on the dashboard.

"I did have to audition," said Tiffany quickly. "For my job at the club. I went with my friend Erin. Otherwise I might have chickened out."

She stopped.

"Go on," said Clementine. "Keep talking. Please keep talking."

"So we turned up at the club, and I thought we might have trouble taking it seriously, but there was this woman in charge of the auditions. Her name was Emerald Blaze. I know. It sounds comical, but honestly, she was formidable. As soon as we saw her we took it dead seriously. She was an amazing dancer. She moved in slow motion. It made me think of silk. Slippery silk. Almost too sexy. Like you were seeing something you shouldn't see. She said, 'Girls, it's not about fancy pole tricks. It's about the tease.' That advice earned me a lot of money. So the first thing we had to do was just walk up onstage, walk around the pole and walk off. It doesn't sound like much but it was terrifying, knowing all the girls were watching and judging you, and of course we weren't used to the high heels yet—I thought I was going to fall—and what else? I remember Emerald had this whole thing about not being yourself. You had to come up with a stage name and invent your own backstory. Should I stop?"

"What?" Clementine kneaded her stomach with her fists. The traffic inched forward. "No. Please don't stop. Keep talking. What was your stage name?"

"Barbie. Kind of embarrassing. I used to love my Barbie dolls."

"Please keep talking," she said.

And so Tiffany talked.

She talked about the deep bass beat of the music and the haze of cigarette smoke and the drugs and the girls and the rules and how she got pretty good on the pole, she could do lots of spinning tricks, and hold herself out perpendicular to the pole, although it hurt her shoulders afterwards, but she'd done gymnastics at a competitive level as a kid, so . . .

Clementine thought of Holly's gymnastic classes. Maybe it was time for her to learn the violin instead.

The car inched forward.

"Go on," she said.

Tiffany went on.

She talked about the one time she had to push the panic button doing a private show, but that was honestly the only time she didn't feel safe, and the barrister who wanted to just sit there and tenderly hold her feet, and how she saw him a few weeks later, being interviewed about a case on TV, and the scruffy-looking guy in a faded polo shirt who turned out to be mega-rich and handed over stacks of tipping dollars, not like the bankers in expensive suits who teased you with a single token, it was worth two dollars, for God's sake, and the young country boys who kept on going back to the ATM for more cash and booking her again until finally she said, "Fellas, this is it. I've got nothing more to show you," and the B-grade celebrity who used to book her and Erin for shower shows and say "Bravo! Bravo!" as if he were at the opera.

"Or the symphony." Tiffany looked sideways at Clementine.

"Shower shows?" said Clementine.

"Yes, so you'd have a shower while your customer sat on a couch and watched you loofah up—or soap each other up, if there were two of you. I liked the shower shows. The club got really hot and sticky. It was a relief to cool off."

"Right," said Clementine. God Almighty. Shower shows. She wondered if she was going to be sick. There was a very good chance she was going to be sick.

"Should I stop talking now?" said Tiffany.

"No," said Clementine. She closed her eyes, saw Ruby and opened them again. "Keep talking!" she said in a louder voice.

And so for the next twenty surreal minutes, while Clementine fixed her eyes on the brake lights of the car in front and willed them to vanish, Tiffany talked and talked, and the words flowed over Clementine and she kept losing track, hearing only fragments: *the podiums in the private rooms were really hard so you carried this small fluffy rug . . . some girls needed to drink to work but I . . . competitive, this one night I thought to hell with it . . .*

Until finally they came to the traffic cones, and the bright white flashing lights, and a tow truck slowly lifting a small mangled red car up by its bumper bar at an unnatural angle and a policeman waving them on and Tiffany said, in a suddenly very different tone of voice, "Right then," and put her foot down hard on the accelerator and neither of them said another word until they drove into the hospital parking lot.

59

So did it work? Did you remember anything more?" said Oliver. They were sitting at the dining room table, eating the chicken curry he'd made. Outside, the rain eased to a drizzle as if it were thinking about stopping, but Erika wasn't falling for that. There was nothing else on the polished expanse of mahogany except what they needed: shining cutlery, place mats, un-smudged glasses of iced water on coasters. Sitting down to eat at a table like this was something neither of them ever took for granted. Before they ate, their eyes always met in brief acknowledgment, an unspoken moment of gratitude for space and order.

"No," said Erika. "The fountain is gone. It's all concreted over. The backyard looks scarred. It was kind of sad."

"I guess they didn't want the memory," said Oliver.

"Whereas I did want the memory," said Erika. She carefully put down her knife and fork. ("Stop waving your cutlery about!" Pam used to tell Clementine and her brothers; Erika was the only one who listened. Clementine still liked to emphasize a point with her fork.)

"Yes," said Oliver. "I know."

"I've written it down, you know, everything I do and don't remember."

In fact, she'd typed it up in a Word document (saved as "Memory.doc") in the hope that treating it like a professional problem would bring about a professional solution.

"Good idea," said Oliver. He was listening to her, but she could tell he was also listening to the gurgling sound of rainwater cascading from their overflowing gutters onto their back deck. He was worried about the timber starting to rot.

"I remember coming out of the house, holding the plates," said Erika. Her memories were like the rapid flashes of a strobe light: on, off, on, off. "And then next thing I'm in the fountain, and you're there, and together we're lifting up Ruby between us, but I can't remember anything in between. It's completely blank. I don't remember seeing Ruby, or getting to the fountain. Suddenly I'm just *in* there."

"You dropped the plates and you ran," said Oliver. "You screamed for Clementine and then you ran. I saw you running."

"Yes, but why can't I remember that?" said Erika. "Why can't I remember thinking: 'Oh my God, Ruby is in the fountain'? How could I forget that?"

"The shock, the alcohol, the medication—all those things," said Oliver. "Honestly, I think you have to let it go."

"Yes," sighed Erika. She picked up her cutlery again. "I know. You're right."

She should tell him now that Clementine had agreed to be their egg donor. It was cruel to withhold information that would make him so happy.

"How bad was your mother's place today?" asked Oliver.

"The worst it's been in a while."

"I'm sorry," said Oliver. "And I'm sorry you had to go on your own."

"It's fine. I didn't do much. I kind of gave up. The bad news is that the woman next door is selling."

"Okay," said Oliver, carefully chewing. "So that's a problem." She watched him weighing it all up.

"She was nice about it," said Erika.

"We'll just have to work with her," said Oliver. "Find out exactly when she's listing, the open-for-inspection times."

"I feel like Mum might deliberately sabotage her," said Erika. "Just to be malicious."

"Possibly," said Oliver. He'd grown up with purposeless malice too, but he accepted it like the weather, whereas Erika still resisted it, resented it, tried to find meaning behind it. She thought of her mother's laugh when the rubbish bag had split. Why would she laugh? How was that funny?

"We'll work it out," said Oliver. "We forget about the inside and focus on the outside. That's all that matters until the neighbor sells."

He'd always been so gloriously calm when it came to the problem of Sylvia.

When he realized how distressed Erika got whenever she visited her mother's house, which used to be a couple of times a week, he had initially insisted that she simply refuse to ever go there, but Erika's sense of responsibility for her mother couldn't let her do that. She needed to ensure her mother's living conditions hadn't become a fire or health hazard. So Oliver developed a plan, with a spreadsheet, of course, setting out a schedule of visits. The idea was that Erika would go to her mother's place only six times a year, together with Oliver, and each time they went they would have at least six hours blocked out, and they would be armed and ready for battle, with gloves and masks and rubbish bags. There would be no more going over for "dinner," as if Sylvia were a normal mother. What a sick joke those dinner invitations had always been. Sylvia would promise to make some meal from Erika's childhood—long, long ago, before the kitchen disappeared, she'd been a good cook—but the meal had never, ever materialized, and yet each time, part of Erika had believed that it would happen, even though she knew perfectly well that Sylvia's kitchen was no longer usable. "I was a little tired," Sylvia would say. "Shall we just get takeaway?" Those nights had always ended in a screaming match over the state of the house. Now Erika no longer begged her mother to seek professional help. Oliver had helped her see that Sylvia was never going to change. She would never be cured. Oliver said to Erika, "*You* get professional help. You can't change her, but you can change how you react to her." So that's what she'd done.

He would be the most wonderful, calm, wise father. She imagined him explaining the world to a son, a little boy with Ruby and Holly's startling blue eyes, sitting at the table with them, with his own place mat and his own glass of water. Their child would never have to eat a meal sitting on his or her bed because the dining room table had disappeared beneath piles of junk. Their child's friends could come over to play anytime. Anytime! Even for dinner. They would have extra place mats.

That was the plan. That was the dream. To give a child the precious gift of an ordinary childhood. It was just that she could see Oliver in the dream so much more clearly than she could see herself.

Tell him, she told herself. Just tell him. He deserves it.

"Clementine called again today," she said. A tiny white lie. "While I was at Mum's place."

Oliver lifted his head and she saw the hope, so naked and raw, it made her feel sick.

"She's happy to do it," she said. "To donate her eggs."

Let her do it. They'd saved Ruby's life. A life for a life. Clementine owed them. Let her do it.

Oliver carefully put down his knife and fork on either side of his plate. His eyes were shining. "Do you think—?" he began. "Are you worried she's offering for the wrong reasons? Because of Ruby?"

Erika shrugged. The movement of her shoulders felt unnatural. She wasn't going to tell him what she'd overheard. It would only upset him. And it shamed her. She didn't want Oliver to know that her closest friend didn't really care for her. "She says it's nothing to do with that, but I guess we'll never really know, will we? Anyway, it's a fair exchange. We saved Ruby, she gives us a baby."

"Um . . . are you joking?" said Oliver.

"I don't know if I'm joking," said Erika reflectively. "I might be serious. We *did* save Ruby's life. That's a fact. Why shouldn't they repay us by doing something in return? And what does it matter what her motivations are?"

Oliver considered. "Yes, it matters," he said. "Doesn't it? If she doesn't really feel comfortable with it? If she wouldn't have done it otherwise?"

"Well, she has to see the counselor at the clinic anyway," said Erika. "Before it all goes ahead. Surely it's up to the counselor to talk to her about all that sort of thing. Her motivations. Her . . . psychological state."

Oliver's brow cleared. There was a procedure to follow. Experts who would decide.

"You're right," he said happily. He picked up his cutlery. "That's great news. Amazing news. A step in the right direction. We'll get there. We'll be parents. One way or another."

"Yes," said Erika. "Yes, we will."

He put down his knife and fork again and wiped the side of his mouth. "Can I ask you something that might sound strange?"

Erika stiffened. "Sure."

"The day of the barbecue, Clementine said that you'd always told her you didn't want children. You're not just doing all of this for me, are you?" His glasses slipped forward a fraction as he frowned. "All that you've had to go through over the last few years . . ."

"It hasn't been that bad," said Erika.

IVF had been a well-ordered process. She appreciated the rigor of it, the rules and the science. She especially enjoyed the sterility: the gowns that went straight into a basket after you wore them only once, the booties you put on over your shoes, the blue paper hair nets. And it had been nice, spending time with Oliver, working on this important secret project together. She remembered each retrieval and transfer, breathing in that beautiful antiseptic fragrance, holding Oliver's hand, nothing to do except submit to the process. Oliver had taken on the responsibility of all the medication. He had done all her injections, tenderly, professionally. Never left a single bruise. She didn't mind the early-morning blood tests. The dizzy rush to the head. "Yes, that is correct, that is my name," she'd say as the nurse held up the neatly labeled test tube of blood in a blue-gloved hand for her to check.

Clementine would hate those needles. Clementine's terror in return for Oliver's joy. It was an equitable deal, wasn't it?

"Yes, but *you* do want a baby too, don't you?" said Oliver. "For yourself? Not just for me?"

"Of course I do," said Erika. It had always been for him. Always. That acquisitive desire she'd felt for a little Holly or Ruby of her own was gone now. She wasn't sure exactly why. Probably because of what she'd overheard and maybe because of something else: murky feelings related to those lost moments from her memory.

But none of that mattered. She ate her chicken curry and let her eyes roam around their beautiful uncluttered room.

"What's that?" she said suddenly.

She stood up and went to the bookshelf. There was a sparkle of blue in between the spines of two books. Oliver turned to watch her.

"Oh," he said as she pulled out Holly's little blue sequined bag. "That."

Erika opened the bag full of Holly's rocks.

"She must have left it here," she said, lifting out a small white polished pebble.

"The night of the barbecue," said Oliver.

"I'll give it back to Clementine," said Erika.

"Holly doesn't want it back," said Oliver. He opened his mouth as if he were about to say something else, but then he changed his mind and instead took a sip of water and replaced the glass carefully on the coaster.

"Really? I thought she loved—"

"We might be pregnant by Christmas," said Oliver dreamily. "Imagine that."

"Imagine that," agreed Erika, and she dropped the stone back into the bag.

60

The Day of the Barbecue

Is Ruby dead?" asked Holly, playing with the handle of her little blue sequined handbag full of rocks, which she held with both hands on her lap.

"No," said Erika. "She's not dead. She went in the helicopter with your daddy to the hospital. She'll be there by now, and the doctors will make her better."

They were sitting under a duvet on the couch while Oliver made them hot chocolate. *Madagascar* was on TV. Erika had taken out her contact lenses, so all she could see were flashes of color on the television.

She had a feeling of impending sleep, like a huge black wave about to crash over her. Except she couldn't fall sleep. Not while Holly was here. And it was only . . . what? Around 6 or 7 P.M. It felt much later. It felt like the middle of the night.

"She *might* die." Holly stared at the television.

"I don't think she will, but she's very sick. It's very serious. Yes. She might."

"*Erika*," said Oliver as he walked into the room carrying the tray with the hot chocolates.

"What?" Weren't you meant to be as truthful as possible with children?

No one knew how long Ruby had been submerged before they'd pulled her out. There were no guarantees. She could have significant brain damage. Hypothermia. She might not make it through the night. Why did Erika feel as if she should know exactly how long Ruby had been under the water for? Why did she feel strangely responsible, as if she'd failed in some way? She'd gotten to Ruby first. She'd been the first one to act. She wasn't Ruby's parent. But there was something. Something she'd done or not done.

"There you go," said Oliver. He was still in his wet clothes. He'd get sick. He handed Holly the mug of hot chocolate. "I didn't make it too hot, but just take a little sip in case, okay?"

"Thank you," said Holly loudly.

"Good manners, Holly," said Oliver.

"Get changed," said Erika as she took the hot chocolate from him. "You'll catch a cold."

"Are you okay?" asked Oliver.

"Why? Do I not look okay?" She took a sip of her hot chocolate, and somehow missed her mouth. She wiped her finger across her chin.

"No," said Oliver. "You don't."

"Manners," said Holly to Erika.

"What are you talking about?" snapped Erika. The child wasn't making sense. It occurred to her that she'd just snapped at Holly in exactly the same way that Sylvia used to do when Erika was a child. The moment Erika started telling her mother something she would snap, "What are you talking about?" And Erika would think: Let me finish and then you'll *know* what I'm talking about!

"You forgot to say thank you," said Holly. She looked frightened. "To Oliver."

"Oh," said Erika. "Of course. You're right. I'm sorry, Holly, I didn't mean to snap at you."

Erika watched two giant teardrops quiver on the bottom eyelashes of Holly's big blue eyes. It was more than just her snapping. Holly wasn't that sensitive.

"Holly," she said. "Holly. Sweetie. It's fine, everything is fine, give me a cuddle, there, although I actually think . . . I might . . . I'm sorry." She couldn't hold on. Holly needed her comfort right now, but she couldn't give it to her. She handed back the cup to Oliver, and he reached out with surprise to take it just in time before it slipped from her hands. "I'm just so sleepy."

She let that big black pool of nothingness take her, drag her under. She could hear a phone ringing, but it was too late, she couldn't get back now, it was much too big and powerful to resist.

Oliver looked at his comatose wife with a dull, sick sense of recognition. She'd passed out, drunk. It meant she'd effectively left. Gone. Not back until the morning. He'd never ever looked at his wife with dislike before, but as he studied her drooping head and gaping mouth he felt his face distort with resentment. They didn't even know yet if Ruby was going to be okay. How could she sleep? But of course, drunks could always sleep.

She's not *a* drunk, he reminded himself. She's just drunk. For the first time since you've known her.

"She must be exhausted," said Holly, looking at Erika with fascination.

Oliver smiled at Holly's use of the word "exhausted." "I think you're right," he said. "She's exhausted. How's your drink? Not too hot."

"No, it's not too hot," said Holly. She took a very careful, tentative sip. There was a little mustache of milk on her upper lip.

"Oliver," said Holly quietly. She held up her little blue handbag, and her eyes filled with more tears.

"Did you want me to put that somewhere safe?" Oliver held out his hand.

"Oliver," she said again, but much more quietly this time.

"What is it, darling?" Oliver crouched down in front of her. His clothes were still wet and filthy from the fountain.

Holly leaned forward and began to whisper urgently in his ear.

61

The Day of the Barbecue

The four grandparents arrived at the hospital at the same time.

Clementine had come out of the ICU to make a quick phone call to Erika, to update her on Ruby's progress and to make sure that Holly could stay with them for a little longer until they sorted out where she would spend the night.

To her surprise, Oliver had answered Erika's phone. Holly was fine, he said. She was on the couch under a blanket with Erika watching a DVD. He said that Erika was asleep, and he sounded embarrassed about that, or bewildered, but apart from that, he spoke exactly as Oliver always did, with polite, throat-clearing reticence, as if it had been an ordinary night, as if he and Erika hadn't just saved Ruby's life.

From where Clementine stood on the first-floor landing, she could see the ground floor of the hospital, and the sliding doors at the entrance. She recognized Sam's parents first as they hurried in, their agitation clear in the way they half-ran, half-walked. They would have been caught in the same traffic jam as she and Tiffany had, and they would have felt that same demented frustration. Sam's dad had grown up in the country and abhorred traffic lights.

She watched as the four of them grabbed at each other, like the survivors of a natural disaster running into each other at a refugee camp. Her father, dressed in his "around the house" clothes, jeans and a misshapen jumper that would never normally be seen in public, hugged Sam's tiny mother, and she put her arms up and clung to his back in a way that was almost frightening to see because it was so out of character. Clementine saw Sam's dad put his hand on Clementine's mother's arm, and they both turned around, their faces lifted, studying the hospital signs for clues about where to go.

Clementine's mother caught sight of Clementine first, and she pointed at the same time as Clementine raised her hand, and then they all hurried up the long wide walkway toward her.

Clementine walked down to meet them halfway. Her mother was first, followed by Sam's parents, with her dad at the back; he'd had a knee operation after a skiing accident a few months back. The expressions on their faces were painful to see. They each looked terrified, and sick, and as if they were laboring to breathe, as if the walkway were a mountain Clementine had forced them to climb. These were four fit, trim grandparents enjoying their retirement, but now they appeared much older. For the first time, they looked elderly.

Ruby and Holly were the only grandchildren on both sides of the family. They were adored and spoiled, and Sam and Clementine lapped up the adoration with such casual *vanity*, for hadn't they created these exquisite little angels? Why yes, they had, so they deserved their pick of free babysitters and they deserved to sit back and be fed homemade treats when they went to visit, for look what they offered in return: these glorious grandchildren!

"She's okay," she said. By okay, she meant "alive"; she wanted them to know that Ruby was still alive. But she spoke too soon, before they could properly hear, and she could see all four of them straining to understand, in a panic to get to her faster, and Sam's mother grabbed for the banister, as if it were bad news.

"Ruby is okay!" she called again, louder, and then they were all around her, asking questions, creating a roadblock for people trying to get up the walkway.

"They have her sedated," said Clementine. "And she's still . . . intubated."

She tripped on the terrifying word and thought of Ruby's white little face and the huge tube extending from her mouth. It looked like it was choking her, not helping her breathe.

"They've done a CT scan and there is no sign of swelling or brain injury, everything looks fine," said Clementine. *Swelling or brain injury.* She tried to make the medical words feel meaningless, like a foreign language, just sounds coming out of her mouth, because she couldn't risk letting herself feel their full significance. "They've done a chest X-ray and there is some fluid in the lungs, but that's to be expected, they're not too concerned, they've started her on a course of antibiotics. Her ribs are okay. No fractures."

"Why wouldn't her ribs be okay?" asked her father.

Clementine cursed herself. She was trying to tell them anything positive she could, but there was no need to tell them all the things that could have gone wrong but didn't.

"Sometimes the force of the compressions, the CPR—but it's fine, it didn't." She heard Oliver counting out loud and for a moment she couldn't speak. "In the morning they'll reduce the medication, wake her up, and get her breathing on her own."

"Can we see her?" said Clementine's mother.

"I don't know," said Clementine. "I'll ask." She shouldn't have let them come to the hospital. It would have been more sensible to tell them to wait at home, better for their elderly hearts. She hadn't thought. She'd just expected them to come, as though she were still a child and she needed the grown-ups.

Once she and Sam had been out at dinner with Erika and Oliver and they'd gotten into a conversation about whether they felt like grown-ups. She and Sam had said they didn't. Not really. Erika and Oliver had looked perplexed and kind of appalled.

"Of course I feel like a grown-up," said Erika. "I'm free. I'm in charge."

Oliver had said, "I couldn't *wait* to be a grown-up."

"So then," said Clementine's mother, breathing heavily. Was she having a heart attack? Suddenly she lunged at Clementine. "Why weren't you watching her?" She was so close, Clementine could smell the spicy scent on her breath of whatever she'd been eating for dinner. "You shouldn't have taken your eyes off her. Not for a single second. Not around water, for God's sake."

"Pam," said Clementine's father. He went to take his wife's arm, and she shook it off. A young pregnant woman squeezed her way past them and stared curiously.

"You're smarter than that. You know better!" continued Pam, her eyes fixed on Clementine with such intensity it was as though Clementine were a stranger to her, as though she were trying to work out who this person was who had harmed her granddaughter. "Were you drunk? How *could* you? How could you be so stupid?" Her face crumpled into a million lines before she covered it with both hands.

Clementine hadn't even told her yet that it was Erika who had saved Ruby. Erika. The better daughter. The grateful daughter. The daughter who would never have made a mistake like this.

Clementine's father put his arm around his wife. "It's okay," he mouthed over her head. He led her up the walkway. "Let's go and sit down."

"It's the shock," said Sam's mother, Joy. She was a woman who never left the house without "her face," but tonight it was bare of makeup. Clementine had never seen her without lipstick before, maybe no one had. It looked like her lips were missing. She must have been having her nightly read in the bath when she got the call. Clementine imagined her panic. The throwing on of clothes before she was even properly dry.

"Come on, darling," said Joy. "Chin up."

Clementine could barely stand for shame.

62

The Morning After the Barbecue

"Clementine."

"What?"

She must have dozed off. She didn't think she'd closed her eyes all night, but Sam was leaning over her, shaking her shoulder where she sat in the green leather chair next to Ruby's bed.

There were purple shadows under Sam's red-rimmed eyes, black stubble along his jaw and a thin line of white spittle around his lips. He had refused to sit at all. "Darl, you're not helping your daughter by standing for the whole night," the nurse had told him, but Sam seemed psychopathically determined to stand, as if Ruby's life depended on it, as if he were guarding her from harm, and eventually the nurse gave up, although every now and then she shot Sam a look as if she were just itching to stick a needle in his arm and knock him out.

The nurse's name was Kylie. She was a New Zealander, and she spoke slowly and simply to them, saying everything twice, as if English were their second language. Probably all parents were dull-witted with shock. Kylie explained that in intensive care, every patient got their own nurse: "I've only got one job tonight and that's Ruby." She told them there was a room available on the same floor where they could sleep, and she gave them little toiletry bags with toothbrushes and combs, of the style you might receive on an overnight premium economy flight. She advised them to try to get some sleep because Ruby was sedated and she wasn't going to know if they were there or not, but they'd already let Ruby down once, they weren't leaving her again.

Sam spent the night watching Ruby and the screens monitoring Ruby's heart rhythm, her temperature, her breathing rate and her oxygen levels, as if he knew what they meant, and indeed he had asked Kylie to explain, so maybe he really did understand. Clementine hadn't listened to the explanations. She spent the night with her eyes traveling back and forth between Ruby and Kylie's face. She felt that Kylie's face would tell her if there was anything to be concerned about, although she was wrong, because during the night Ruby's oxygen levels dropped, and Kylie's face remained exactly the same, while the doctor on duty was called and Sam moved quietly to the corner of the room with a clenched fist pressed hard against his cheek, as if he were poised to knock himself out. Ruby's oxygen levels went back up to an acceptable level again, but the adrenaline buzzed through Clementine for the next few hours. It was a reminder that they could not, should not relax, even for a moment.

"The doctor is here," said Sam now as Clementine rubbed her eyes and swallowed, her mouth dry and sour. "They're going to extubate, wake her up."

"Good morning!" said a pale-haired, pale-skinned doctor. "Let's see if we can wake up this little sleeping beauty, shall we?"

It was fast. The tubes came out. The mask was removed.

After twenty minutes, Ruby frowned heavily. Her eyelids twitched.

"Ruby?" said Sam, as if he were begging for his life.

Ruby's eyes finally fluttered opened. She stared at the cannula in her arm with an expression of pure disgust. Thankfully, her thumb-sucking hand was free, and she jammed her thumb in her mouth. She looked up, found her parents, and looked angrier still.

"Whisk," she demanded hoarsely.

The relief Clementine experienced as she rushed to deliver Whisk was exquisite, glorious, like the cessation of an agonizing pain, like a gasp of air when you'd been forced to hold your breath.

She looked for Sam with the vague expectation that something would now happen between them, something important and climactic. They would grab hands, for example, their fingers would lock together in mutual joy and they would smile down at Ruby while tears rained down their faces.

But it didn't happen. They looked at each other and yes, they *did* smile and yes, their eyes *were* full of tears, but something wasn't quite right. She didn't know who looked away first, she didn't know if it was her coldness or his coldness, if she was blaming him or he was blaming her, but then Ruby began to cry, distressed by her sore throat from the tube, and the doctor started talking and it was all too late. It was another moment they'd never get back to do right.

63

Dinner is ready!" called Sam, and he sounded perfectly normal, not at all like the stranger who, less than one hour ago, had discussed separating. "I think I'm done with us." Now he sounded just like Daddy, like Sam, like himself.

The smell of Sam's signature dish, shepherd's pie, filled the house. Clementine loved his shepherd's pie, but the girls hated it, which was annoying because it seemed like the sort of nutritious, kid-friendly food they should like, so every week they kept deluding themselves and trying again.

"When will it *ever* stop *raining*?" asked Holly as she turned off her iPad with all the technological insouciance of a millennium kid. "It is actually driving me *crazy*."

"Me too," said Clementine. "Ruby! Come on! Dinnertime."

Ruby looked up from where she was sitting in the middle of a circle of dolls and plush toys. She had placed them around her in imitation of "story circle" at day care, and had been pretending to read them a *Curious George* book, holding it up in the same way that her teacher obviously did at day care, and carefully licking her finger each time she turned the page.

"It's nap time!" said Ruby cheerfully, and knocked the toys into sleeping positions with a casual backhand. Hopefully she hadn't learned that at day care too.

"What's for dinner?" Holly ran to the table and sat herself up. She grabbed her knife and fork with ominous enthusiasm. "Pasta? It's pasta, right?"

"It's shepherd's pie," said Sam as Clementine strapped Ruby into the "big girl" booster seat she now used instead of a high chair.

"*What?*" Holly slumped as if to news of a great injustice. "Shepherd's pie? *Again?* We had it *last night.*"

"You did not have it last night," said Sam evenly, putting the plate in front of her. "You had pasta with Grandma last night while Mummy and Daddy went out to dinner."

"There's some still in the fridge!" said Holly excitedly. "I remember! We didn't eat it all! And Grandma said that—"

"There's none left in the fridge," said Clementine. "I ate it last night."

"*What?*" cried Holly. Life was a series of travesties. "But you went to a restaurant!"

"It wasn't a very good restaurant, so we came home early," said Clementine. Mummy and Daddy can no longer stand to go out to dinner together. Mummy and Daddy no longer like each other very much. Mummy and Daddy might be "separating."

"*What?*"

"Sit up straight, Holly," said Clementine mechanically.

Holly squawked.

"Please don't make that sound," said Clementine. "Please."

Holly made the sound again but softer.

"*Holly.*"

"Yuck," said Ruby. She picked up her spoon and held it limply between her fingertips over the plate. She let it swing back and forth. "No fank you."

"I'll give you 'no fank you,'" said Sam. "Come on, girls. Just a little bit."

"Mmmm, delicious," said Clementine, taking a mouthful. "Good work, Daddy."

"Well, I'm *not* eating any of it," said Holly. She folded her arms and pressed her lips together. "I have too many taste buds."

"What do you mean you have too many taste buds?" said Sam as he determinedly shoveled food into his own mouth.

"Kids have more taste buds than grown-ups, that's why it tastes yucky," said Holly.

"She saw it on that TV show," said Clementine. "Remember? The one with the—"

"I don't care how many taste buds you've got," said Sam. "You can try a mouthful."

"Blerk," said Holly.

"Let's see some good manners," said Clementine.

Sam didn't look at her.

It was as though he'd just been waiting all these years for the perfect excuse to hate her and finally he'd gotten it. Her throat filled. The shepherd's pie wasn't as good as it normally was. Too heavy on the Worcestershire sauce.

She put down her fork and had a mouthful of water.

"I've got a sore tummy," moaned Holly.

"No, you don't," said Clementine.

Clementine's mother thought their marriage was a problem that could be fixed with a good dose of common sense and elbow grease. Marriages were hard work! But what could they say to a counselor? They weren't fighting over money or sex or housework. There were no knotty issues to untangle. Everything was the same as before the barbecue. It was just that nothing felt the same.

She looked at Ruby, who sat in front of her in perfect, pink-cheeked, giggling, naughty health, and remembered how strange it had felt when Ruby was transferred out of the hushed, important environment of ICU and into an ordinary ward with ordinary patients and busy, distracted nurses. No lovely Kylie just for them. It was like going from a five-star hotel to a youth hostel. Then, after two nights in the ordinary ward, an extraordinarily young, tired doctor flipped through Ruby's paperwork and said, "You should be able to take her home tomorrow." Her chest was clear. She hadn't needed physio. The antibiotics had successfully fought off the chest infection before it took hold of her. Of course, there would be neurological checkups, outpatient care, she'd be monitored, but she was fine.

First-world medical care meant they didn't have to pay for their first-world negligence. They'd brought her home to a stack of presents and an overly loving big sister, who at intervals would try to pick her up and cuddle her, something she'd never done much of before, and would inevitably squeeze too hard and Ruby would shriek and Holly would get yelled at.

No one behaved normally except for Ruby, who clearly wanted the fuss over. She did not want to sleep in the big bed with either of her parents. She wanted her own cot. And she did not want a parent sleeping on the floor of her bedroom. She would stagger to her feet on the cot, her thumb in her mouth, and point Whisk at the offending parent: "Go away!" she would say. So they went. Ruby seemed to sense if anyone became too clingy or sappy. Clementine sometimes sat holding her, quietly crying, and if Ruby noticed, she would look up angrily and say, "Stop dat." She did not want to be cherished, thank you very much, unless it involved an extra biscuit.

They should have been like lottery winners. They'd gotten a reprieve, a last-minute pardon. They were allowed to return to their ordinary lives and their ordinary worries, to arguments over shepherd's pie. So why were they not living their lives in a permanent state of joy and relief?

"I am not going to eat one single bit of this," said Holly. She folded her arms dramatically. "Not. One. Single. Bit."

"Well, in that case, I'm not going to let you have one single minute on my iPad," said Sam. "Not. One. Single. Minute."

"What?" cried Holly, predictably shocked and enraged, as if this were a brand-new threat, not one she heard virtually every day of her life. "No fair!"

"Just one mouthful," said Sam to Holly. "You too, Ruby."

"Did you play with Isabel at Honey Bees today?" said Clementine to Ruby.

"Ummmm . . . yes," said Ruby. She lifted her eyes and tapped her fingers to her mouth, trying to remember. "I mean no."

They said she was fine at day care. Not traumatized or affected in any way as far as they could see, just happy to be back. In that first month after the accident, Clementine had decided, and she truly meant it at the time, that she would give up her career and become a stay-at-home mother. (She had even allowed for the fact that they wouldn't be able to afford the mortgage repayments, they would sell the house, sell the cello and rent a modest flat, where Clementine would spend her days grating vegetables, doing crafts and never removing her eyes from her children.) She had said to Ruby, "Would you like to give up Honey Bees and stay home with Mummy every day?" Ruby had looked at her as if she'd asked for a treat and been offered a raw carrot. "No fank you," she enunciated very clearly. So that was the end of that as a means of atonement.

"*Fine* then, I'll have one mouthful." Holly picked up her fork and took the teeniest tiniest possible mouthful. Her face contorted into a paroxysm of disgust.

"Oh, for God's sake!" Sam thumped the palm of his hand flat on the tabletop so hard all their plates rattled and everyone jumped. He stood, grabbed both the girls' plates and walked into the kitchen, where he dropped them into the sink with a loud clatter.

There was silence. Holly and Ruby looked flabbergasted. This was never part of the shepherd's pie routine. It wasn't meant to be serious. They weren't a family who yelled and thumped tables.

Ruby's lip trembled. Her eyes swam with tears.

"It's okay, Ruby," said Clementine.

Ruby ducked her head and covered her face with her hands as if she were trying to hide.

"Oh God, Ruby, I'm so sorry, sweetheart," said Sam from the kitchen. He sounded close to tears. "I just got frustrated. I'm very sorry. Very, very sorry."

Ruby lifted her tearstained face and sucked noisily and deliberately on her thumb.

"That was actually a very loud voice, Daddy," said Holly shakily. "It hurt my ears."

"I know, I'm sorry. What wants ice cream?" said Sam. "Lots of ice cream!"

"What? They can't have ice cream for dinner." Clementine, whose chair faced away from the kitchen, turned around to look at him.

"Sure they can," said Sam feverishly. "Why not?" He went to the freezer.

"They should at least have a bread roll first," said Clementine.

"I want ice cream!" howled Ruby, suddenly recovered and furious, waving her pink, waterlogged thumb in the air for emphasis.

"Me too!" said Holly.

"Bloody hell, Sam," said Clementine. "They're not having ice cream for dinner."

Their parenting these days was all over the place. They veered from excessive leniency to excessive strictness and back again.

"They're having ice cream," said Sam. He put the tub of ice cream on the counter and pulled off the lid. He was frenzied, agitated. It was like he was on drugs. "Who cares if they have ice cream for dinner? Seize the day. Live for the moment. Life is short. Dance like no one is watching or whatever that crap is."

Clementine stared at him. "Why are you being so—?"

"Where's the ice cream scoop?" said Sam, his head down as he looked through the cutlery drawer. "The one with the polar bear—"

"It's *lost!*" shouted Clementine. "Like everything else!"

64

The Morning After the Barbecue

Dakota felt her unhappiness before she opened her eyes. It was like her whole body felt different, flatter, heavier and yet emptier, as if something had been sucked out of her. Yesterday, she had done something terrible, disgusting and irresponsible. She had played with a beautiful little girl like she was a doll and then she'd just tossed her aside when she'd gotten bored with her and gone to play with something else and *the little girl had nearly drowned.* She thought about the lady on the corner who was having a baby. Dakota and her mum had run into her at the shops just last week, and Dakota's mum had suggested that Dakota could babysit one day when she was older and the lady had been all, "That would be great!" and everyone had been all smiley, smiley, not knowing that Dakota was so irresponsible she could never ever be a babysitter, she would let the baby electrocute itself or get burned by an iron or pull a saucepan of hot, bubbling soup over itself or—

BANG!

Dakota jumped. There was an awful banging, crashing, smashing sound coming from the backyard. She threw off her covers and ran to her bedroom window. She got up on her knees on the window seat and pulled back the blind.

Her dad was standing in the fountain, except all the water was gone so there was nothing but ugly muddy ground. He was swinging a big metal bar like a baseball bat at the giant monument in the middle of the fountain. Dakota was reminded of some old footage she'd seen on TV once from a war or a revolution or something where hundreds of people were using ropes to pull down a giant statue of a man, and they all cheered as it slowly toppled.

Except in this case, it was just one person: her dad. And she'd never seen him look or act like this: angry and silent and violent, as if he wanted to kill someone or something. She watched the marble head of an angel baby go flying through the air, and then she couldn't stand to watch anymore. She ran back to her bed and hid under the covers like a little kid trying to hide from a thunderstorm.

65

"Where are we going, Mum?" said Dakota for the third time from the back of the car.

"Maybe that new Japanese restaurant I was telling you about this morning?" said Vid hopefully from the passenger seat. "That's over this way, isn't it? Best tempura in Sydney, apparently. Did you make a reservation? I bet you made a reservation, hey? As a surprise?"

"We're not going to a restaurant," said Tiffany as she drove through a roundabout, keeping an eye out for road signs.

She knew exactly where she was going because she'd renovated a few properties around here. She'd done nicely with them too. It was so easy to give the hipsters what they wanted: their little hipster hearts reliably exploded over an original (looking) decorative ceiling.

"We're just going to make a quick visit," said Tiffany. "We're going to just *drop by*."

"People don't really do that anymore," said Vid gloomily. He'd love it if people still dropped by. He sighed. "You know, if we're going where I think we're going, it's not a good idea. Are we going where I think we're going?"

"Yep," said Tiffany. She glanced at him and he shrugged. He avoided confrontation. He just wanted everyone to be happy. The conflicted expression on Vid's face at a wake (he had a big extended family; people died regularly) was always priceless: I'm not allowed to look happy even though I'm at a party with all these great people!

"Where are we going, Dad?" Dakota leaned forward and pushed her face in between the two seats.

"We're going out to dinner." Vid pulled out his phone. "I'm going to make us a reservation right now."

"This is it," said Tiffany triumphantly. She drove slowly down a narrow, car-lined street. That was the problem with these cool, inner-city locations, it was all very funky, but you could never get a freaking parking spot.

"You'll never get a park," said Vid to her. He had his phone to his ear. "Forget it. It's not a good idea. Yes, hello! I hear you have the best tempura in Sydney, is that right? It is right?! Great! Well, can we try some tonight? No! Come on, now, are you sure you can't squeeze us in a corner somewhere? We are only three small people!"

"Where are we?" said Dakota.

"We're going to drop by at Clementine and Sam's place!" said Tiffany with cheery bravado. The earlier conviction she'd felt suddenly wavered. She had their address only because Erika had given it to her so they could send Ruby a get-well present, for which they'd received a polite but standoffish thank-you card by return mail. The thank-you card had made it clear: We don't want to see you ever again.

"What?" said Dakota. "Why?"

"Is that a spot? Can I do it?" said Tiffany as she reverse-parked the Lexus in between two hybrids. "Of course I can do it, I am the champion!"

"Got us a reservation!" Vid waved his mobile triumphantly. He looked around. "So you found a spot."

"I'll just go knock on the door," said Tiffany. "Make sure they're home."

"Yeah, we'll stay here," said Vid. "You check if they're . . . in the mood."

"Do they know we're coming?" said Dakota.

"No," said Tiffany. "It's a surprise visit. I'll tell them we were in the area." Vid snorted.

Tiffany got out of the car, popped her umbrella open and slung her bag over her shoulder. She'd put one of Vid's strudels from the freezer into her bag before they left.

She stopped. The rain fell softly, in a resigned, bored fashion, like it was sick of itself too. Tiffany paused. Was this the right thing to do? Eventually they would all forget. Move on with their lives.

"Mum?" Tiffany turned. Dakota had wound down her window and was poking her head out. She looked flushed and breathless. "If Holly and Ruby are there, and if they, like, do *want* to see me, um, I'll, like, come inside."

"Me too." Vid leaned over the seat. "I'll, like, come inside too."

It was the right thing to do.

She drew herself upright and walked toward the house. She thought, randomly, of the night she'd auditioned for the job at the club, the terror of walking that catwalk in those high platform shoes. She remembered telling Clementine about it. Yeah, it really compared to an audition for the Sydney Royal Chamber Orchestra, but Clementine had needed distraction, so Tiffany just told her whatever crap came into her head, and afterwards she'd felt embarrassed, as if she'd *made* Clementine listen to sleazy, sordid stories from her past.

Number 9 was a cute, charming, narrow little two-story sandstone house. It was jammed in between two other almost identical-looking terraces. Tiffany studied them and wondered whether they were heritage-listed. She imagined a demolition ball smashing through all that charmingness and a three-level apartment block going up in its place. Wrong! Oh so very wrong and evil! But oh so profitable.

As she rapped the lion's head doorknocker, she wondered if she might hear cello music, but instead she heard a man's voice shouting. Sam? Surely not. He was too genial. Now she could hear a woman yelling. Oh, jeez Louise. Great timing. She'd "dropped by" when they were in the middle of a fight. She turned indecisively back toward the street. Mission abort? Go eat Sydney's best freaking tempura.

The door swung open.

It was Holly. She wore a blue and white checked school uniform, long fluffy purple socks and strands of colored beads around her neck.

"Hello." Tiffany smiled. "Remember me?"

"You're Dakota's mum," said Holly. "I'm going to invite Dakota to my birthday party. My daddy said she wouldn't want to come."

"I think she'd love to come," said Tiffany.

Holly got a look of pure vindication on her face. She turned on her heel and ran. "Da-ad!"

"Tiffany!" Clementine appeared in the hallway. She looked aghast. "Hi. How—I didn't even hear the knock on the door . . . um, how are you?"

"I'm fine," said Tiffany.

Clementine looked thinner than when Tiffany had seen her last, and drabber, older.

"We're going out to dinner," said Tiffany. "And I knew you lived nearby, so I thought I'd drop off some of Vid's strudel, I remember you liked it. Dakota and Vid are in the car."

She took the container with the frozen strudel from her handbag and handed it over to Clementine, who took it warily, as if it were radioactive.

"Thank you," she said. "And thank you again for the lovely doll you sent for Ruby."

"You're welcome," said Tiffany. "We got your thank-you card. I think Vid has been trying to call you. . . ."

Clementine winced. "I'm sorry, yes, I know, I've been meaning to give you a call, it's just . . ."

"It's just that you don't really want to have any contact with us because you don't want to think about that day and because you didn't really know us that well in the first place," said Tiffany. She was sick of the bullshit. "I get it. I do get it."

Clementine flinched.

"But the thing is, Dakota blames herself for what happened to Ruby that day. She's been making herself sick with guilt over it."

Clementine's mouth dropped. She looked like she might cry. "Really? Seriously? I'm so sorry. I'll talk to her. I'll tell her it was nothing to do with her."

"Dakota needs to see Ruby," said Tiffany. "She needs to see she's okay. And actually, I think *Vid* needs to see her too. Just for a minute. I know we don't know your family that well, but it happened at our *home* and you've got to realize, this affected us too, and . . . and . . ."

She stopped, because Ruby had suddenly come running down the hallway, carrying her whisk. When she saw the unexpected guest at the front door she wrapped her arm around her mother's leg, put her thumb in her mouth and considered Tiffany.

"Hello, Ruby." Tiffany squatted down to Ruby's height and put the back of her hand on her pink, velvety cheek. Ruby gazed back at her with big blue disinterested eyes. Some random grown-up who didn't appear to be carrying gifts.

Tiffany smiled up at Clementine. It turned out that she'd needed to see Ruby too. "She looks great," she said.

Clementine pushed open the front door a little wider. "Why don't you go and get Vid and Dakota?" she said.

66

Another rainy morning. Another talk to a group of elderly people. Clementine's eyes felt hot and dry as she drove into the parking lot of the community hall where the Hills District Retirees Association held their monthly meeting. She'd been up most of the night with the word "separate" going round and round in her head, until finally she'd sat up, found a notepad and a pen, and wrote: *I'm worried that my marriage is over.* Because wasn't there some research that suggested the act of writing down your worries reduced stress? In fact, it was shocking to see it written down so baldly like that. It hadn't helped her stress levels at all. She had torn out the sheet of paper and ripped it up into tiny pieces.

When Vid, Tiffany and Dakota had left last night after their unexpected visit, Clementine had felt almost cheerful. There had been a definite sense of relief: the slip-sliding feeling of release after a fearfully anticipated event had finally taken place. The *idea* of seeing Vid and Tiffany had been so much more traumatic than the reality. All their qualities had become exaggerated in her memories of that night when in fact they were just ordinary, friendly people. Tiffany wasn't quite as sexy as Clementine remembered. Vid wasn't quite as charismatic. They didn't have special hypnotic sexual powers. And poor little Dakota was just a kid who had been carrying around a terrible burden of guilt that had not been hers to bear.

But it was immediately clear that Sam didn't feel the same way. As soon as they'd left, he'd turned on his heel and gone straight into the kitchen to pack the dishwasher. He'd refused to talk about anything except the ongoing administration of their lives: he was taking Holly for her taekwondo class before school, she would transfer some money onto the credit card, they didn't need to worry about dinner tomorrow night because they were going to Clementine's parents' house. Then off they'd gone to their separate beds. It had occurred to her during the long night that she and Sam already *were* separated. People could legally separate and live under the same roof. That's exactly what they were doing.

It was a relief when her alarm had gone off and she could give up trying to sleep. She'd gotten up and done her audition practice, and then she'd had an early-morning lesson with thirteen-year-old Logan, who she had been teaching for the past two years and who didn't want to be there but smiled so politely at her as if he did. Logan's music teacher had told his mother that he had talent, and that "it would be a crime not to foster it." Logan *was* technically proficient but his heart was with the electric guitar. That was his passion. As Logan had played that morning, dutifully following every one of Clementine's instructions, she'd found herself wondering if that was how she sounded to Ainsley when she practiced her audition pieces. What was that awful word she'd used? "Robotic." Should she tell poor little Logan he sounded robotic? But what would be the point? She bet he didn't sound robotic on his electric guitar.

Now it was only 10:30 A.M. and she felt like she'd been up for hours.

Because she had in fact been up for hours, she reminded herself as she put up her umbrella to walk through the crowded parking lot.

"Where's your violin, dear?" asked the head of the Hills District Retirees Association when Clementine introduced herself.

"My violin?" said Clementine. "I'm actually a cellist but, um—"

"Your cello then," said the woman with a little roll of her eyes to indicate Clementine's unnecessary attention to petty detail: a cello was just a big violin, after all! "Where's your cello, dear?"

"But I'm not playing the cello," said Clementine uneasily. "I'm a guest speaker. I'm doing a talk."

She had a moment of sudden terror. She was doing a talk, wasn't she? This wasn't a gig? Of course it wasn't. She was doing a talk.

"Oh, are you?" said the woman disappointedly. She studied the piece of paper in her hand. "It says here you're a *cellist*. We thought you'd be playing for us."

She looked at Clementine expectantly, as if a solution might present itself. Clementine lifted her hands. "I'm sorry," she said. "I'm doing a talk. It's called 'One Ordinary Day.'"

For God's sake.

She felt exhausted. Was there really any point to all this? Was she actually helping or was she just doing it to make herself feel better, to pay her penance, her dues, to even things up on the universal scale of right and wrong?

The community talks had all come about because she'd been trying to redeem herself in her mother's eyes. A few days after they'd brought Ruby home from hospital, Clementine had been having a cup of tea with her mother and she'd said (she could still hear the reedy, self-conscious tone with which she'd spoken) that she felt she should do something to raise awareness of how easily an accident like this could happen and make sure no one else made the same mistake she had made. She felt she should "tell her story."

She'd meant she should write one of those touching "please share" Facebook posts that would go viral. (She probably would never have gotten around to doing even that.)

But her mother had been thrilled. "What a wonderful idea!" Clementine could do talks to community groups, mothers' groups, associations—they were always looking for guest speakers. She could "partner" with a first aid course provider like St. John Ambulance, hand out leaflets at the end, maybe offering a discount on a course. Pam would set it all up. She had all the contacts. She had a wide circle of friends who belonged to caring community groups across Sydney. They were always desperate for guest speakers. She'd be like Clementine's "agent." "This could save lives, Clementine," Pam had said, with that familiar evangelical look in her eyes. Oh God, Clementine had thought. But it was too late. As her father would say, "The Pam train has left the station. Nothing can stop it now."

She *did* feel it was the right thing to do. It was just that it was hard to fit the talks into an already crammed life, especially when she was driving all over Sydney to do them in between gigs and teaching and school pickups and audition practice.

And then there was the fact that she had to relive the worst, most shameful day of her life.

"This is a story that begins with a barbecue," she said today to the members of the Hills District Retirees Association, who were eating lamb with gravy and roast potatoes and peas for lunch as she spoke. "An ordinary neighborhood barbecue in an ordinary backyard."

You need to make it a story, her mother had told her. A story has power.

"We can't hear you!" called out someone from the back of the room. "Can you hear her? I can't hear a word she's saying."

Clementine leaned in closer to the microphone.

She heard someone at the table nearest the lectern say, "I thought we had a violinist coming today."

Beads of sweat ran all the way down her back.

She kept talking. She told her story as cutlery scraped against plates. She gave them facts and figures. A child can be submerged in ten seconds, lose consciousness in two minutes and sustain permanent brain damage in four to six minutes. Nine out of ten children who have died in the water were being watched by adults. A child can drown in as little as one inch of water. She talked about the importance of first aid training and how thirty thousand Australians died of cardiac arrest every year because there was no one around with the basic CPR knowledge to save their lives. She talked about the wonderful work that CareFlight did and how they were always grateful for donations.

When she'd finished, the president of the association gave her a box of chocolates and asked her fellow members to join her in a round of applause for their very interesting guest speaker today. Very informative, and thank goodness her daughter was all recovered and maybe next time Clementine could come and play her cello for them!

Afterwards, as she was heading for the door, her dress damp against her back, a man approached her, wiping his mouth with his napkin. She steeled herself. Sometimes people couldn't resist coming up afterwards to tell her off, to inform her that she should never have taken her eyes off her toddler.

But as soon as she saw the man's face she knew he wasn't one of those.

He was the other sort. He had the relaxed authority of someone who had once been the boss, but the bruised eyes of someone who had suffered a devastating loss. It was a look around the eyes like fruit that has gone soft and is close to rotting.

He had a story he needed to share. It was her job to listen. This was her real penance.

He would probably cry. The women didn't cry. Elderly women were as tough as nails but it seemed that men got softer as they aged; their emotions caught them off guard, as if some protective barrier had been worn away by time.

She braced herself.

"My grandson would have been thirty-two this weekend," he said.

"Ah," said Clementine.

She waited for the story. There was always a chain of events that had to be explained: if this *hadn't* happened, if this *had* happened. In this case, it had all started with a broken phone. His daughter's downstairs phone was broken, so she ran upstairs to answer it, and at that moment the next-door neighbor knocked on the front door and got talking to his son-in-law, and in the meantime, the little fella got outside. He dragged a chair over to the pool gate. There was a tennis ball floating in the pool. He was trying to get to the ball. He liked playing cricket. Was pretty good at it too. He was a little pocket rocket. Couldn't sit still. You wouldn't have thought he'd be big enough to drag that chair but he did it. Determined.

"I'm so sorry," said Clementine.

"Well, I just wanted to tell you that you are doing a good thing," said the man. He hadn't cried, thank God. "Raising awareness. It's a good thing. Makes people think twice. Families don't get over it when something like this happens. My daughter's marriage broke up. My wife was never the same again. She was the one on the phone, you see. Never forgave herself for ringing at that time. Not her fault, of course, or the neighbor's fault, just bad luck, bad timing, but there you go. Accidents happen. Anyhow. You did a good job today, pet. Spoke very well."

"Thank you," said Clementine.

"You sure you don't want to stay and join us for dessert? They do a very tasty pavlova here."

"That's nice of you," said Clementine. "But I have to go."

"No worries, off you go, I'm sure you're busy," said the man. He patted her on the arm.

She headed toward the door, released.

"Tom," he said suddenly.

She turned back, steeled herself. Here it came.

His eyes filled with tears. Overflowed. "The little fella's name. In case you wondered. His name was Tom."

All the way home she cried: for the little fella, for the grandmother who'd made the phone call, for the grandfather who'd shared his story, and for the parents, because their marriage hadn't survived, and because it seemed like Clementine's marriage wasn't going to survive either.

67

It was early Thursday evening when Tiffany walked into the living area and saw Dakota sitting cross-legged on the window seat. She was reading a book in a little circle of lamplight, the blue fluffy blanket over her legs, while raindrops slid down the window behind her. Barney was curled up in her lap. Dakota was absentmindedly caressing one of his ears as she read.

Tiffany caught herself just in time from exclaiming, "You're reading!" and said instead, "You're . . . there!"

Dakota looked up from her book quizzically.

"I didn't know where you were," said Tiffany.

"I'm here," said Dakota. Her eyes returned to her book.

"Yes, you are." Tiffany backed away. "Yes, you are definitely here . . . there."

She found Vid sitting at the kitchen table with his laptop watching a "master class" on making the perfect tempura batter. He was officially obsessed after last night's dinner, which had sent him into rhapsodies.

"She's reading again," whispered Tiffany, pointing over her shoulder.

Vid gave a cursory thumbs-up and kept looking at the screen.

"You fry by sound, not by sight," he said. "Interesting, eh? I have to listen." He put his hand to his ear to demonstrate.

Tiffany sat down next to him and watched the chef demonstrate how to "gently stretch" a shrimp.

"It was good we went last night," she said.

Vid shrugged. "They were strange. They didn't say anything. Silent."

"That's because you didn't give them a chance to speak," said Tiffany. When Vid got nervous he talked. Last night he hadn't appeared to draw breath for the entire ten-minute duration of their strange little visit.

It was only the three children who had behaved normally. Holly and Ruby had been thrilled to see Dakota, and had dragged her off to see bedrooms and toys and everything else in their house. "This is our fridge," Holly had said. "This is our television. That's my mum's cello. Don't touch it! You're not allowed to touch it under any circ-an-chance."

In the meantime, the four grown-ups had stood in a strange, awkward foursome in the living room. Sam avoided all eye contact with Tiffany, as if it were illegal to look at her. Everything about him seemed clenched.

"They never even offered us a drink!" said Vid. He couldn't get over that. He'd be offering drinks during an earthquake.

"Yeah, well," said Tiffany. "They didn't want us there."

"Hmmph," said Vid. "The little girl looks good. Very healthy. Rosy cheeks. We should have all been happy. Celebrating."

"I think they blame themselves," said Tiffany.

"But she's fine, she's perfect, she's beautiful!" said Vid robustly. "Thanks to Erika and Oliver. All good. No need for the glum faces. Shh, now, I'm trying to concentrate on my tempura."

"You're the one talking." Tiffany flicked his neck with her fingertip as she stood up. He slapped her bum in return. She went to the sink to get herself a glass of water and stood watching Dakota read. She felt immensely pleased with herself, like she'd pulled off a difficult deal. Visiting Clementine and Sam had been exactly the right thing to do. Socially awkward but absolutely the right thing for her family.

Last night, while they'd been standing in the hallway about to leave, and Vid was talking on and on about spotted gum floorboards, Clementine had pulled Dakota aside, taken her hand and placed it between her own in an almost ceremonial way and said, "Your mum told me you felt bad about what happened to Ruby at your place. Dakota, I forbid you to feel bad for another minute, for another second, okay? It was my responsibility."

Tiffany had expected Dakota to say nothing, to just nod dumbly, but to her surprise, Dakota had spoken up, clearly, although her eyes had stayed fixed on her trapped hand.

"I should have told you I was going inside to read my book."

"But, see, I *knew* you'd gone inside," said Clementine. "I knew the moment you went inside, because your mum told me, so that had nothing to do with . . . anything! You weren't their babysitter! When you're older, you probably will do babysitting, and you'll be very responsible, you'll be wonderful, in fact, I know it, but my girls were *not* your responsibility that afternoon. So, you must promise me you won't worry about this anymore, because . . ." Clementine's voice had momentarily wavered. "Because I just can't bear it if you feel bad about that day too. I honestly cannot bear it."

Tiffany saw Dakota stiffen, repelled by the level of raw, grown-up emotion in Clementine's voice. Clementine released her hand and in that instant you could almost see Dakota make a decision: a decision to accept absolution and be a kid again.

And now she was back reading.

Dakota had told Tiffany that she'd given up reading as "a punishment to herself" because that was her most favorite thing in the world. "Were you going to give up reading *forever*?" Tiffany had asked her, and Dakota had shrugged. She had also admitted that she had destroyed her copy of *The Hunger Games* because that was the book she'd been reading when Ruby nearly drowned. Tiffany had considered telling her that she really shouldn't destroy her possessions, books cost money, money didn't grow on trees, etcetera but instead she said, "I'll buy you another copy," and at first Dakota said quietly, "Oh, that's okay," but when Tiffany pushed, she said, "Thanks, Mum, that would be great, because it was actually an awesome book."

Now Tiffany watched her turn the page, deep in her own world. To never once say a word about how she was really feeling for all those weeks, while her secret guilt festered. Jesus, she'd have to watch that kid like a hawk. She was like Tiffany's sister Louise, who "ran much too deep," as their mother said, while Tiffany presumably ran much too shallow.

The doorbell rang.

"I'll get it," said Tiffany, unnecessarily, as it was clear neither Vid nor Dakota was moving.

She felt a sense of déjà vu. Dakota lying on the window seat. The doorbell ringing. The morning of the barbecue.

"Hi, there, I'm—" The man on the doorstep stopped. His gaze traveled
a straight line down Tiffany's body. She wore yoga pants and an old T-shirt,
but the man was looking at her like she was wearing her schoolgirl outfit
from her dancing days. Tiffany jutted one hip and waited it out (enjoyed it,
to be frank, she was in a good mood).

His eyes returned to her face.

That'll be ten bucks, buddy.

"Hello," said the man, clearing his throat. He was in his late twenties,
very fair, and he was blushing. It was adorable. Okay, you can have it for
free.

"Hi," said Tiffany huskily, making eye contact, just to see if she could
make him blush more, which, yes, it seemed she could. The poor man was
crimson now.

"I'm Steve." He held out his hand. "Steve Lunt." He was a little posh.
One of those carefully enunciated voices you felt compelled to imitate. "My
uncle, my great-uncle, Harry Lunt, lived next door."

"Oh, right." Tiffany straightened as she shook his hand. Shit. "Hello. I'm
Tiffany. We're very sorry about your uncle."

"Well, thank you, but I actually only met him once, as a child," said
Steve. "And to be honest, he scared the life out of me."

"I didn't know he had family," said Tiffany.

"We're all in Adelaide," said Steve. His color had returned to normal
now. "And as I'm sure you're aware, Harry wasn't exactly sociable."

"Well," said Tiffany.

"We were Harry's only relatives, and my mother did her best, but it was
really just the odd Christmas card and phone call. Poor Mum would sit
there while he bellowed abuse at her."

"We, all the neighbors, we felt terrible that it took so many weeks before
we, before we realized . . ." Tiffany stopped.

"I understand you found his body," said Steve. "Must have been
upsetting."

"Yes," said Tiffany. "It was." She remembered throwing up into the sandstone pot. What had happened to that pot? Would this poor man be responsible for it? "I feel bad that we didn't keep more of an eye on him."

"I doubt he would have welcomed anyone keeping an eye on him," said

Steve. "It if makes you feel better, he apparently told my mother you were nice."

"He said we were *nice?*" Tiffany was astounded.

Steve smiled. "I think the exact words he actually used were 'nice enough.' Anyhow, I just wanted to let you know that we'll be doing a bit of work on the place before we put it on the market. Hopefully there won't be too much noise or disruption."

"Thanks," said Tiffany. She did a rough calculation on the value of Harry's place. Maybe she should make an offer? "I'm sure it will be fine. We're early risers."

"Right. Well. Good to meet you. Better get back to it."

Tiffany closed the door and thought of Harry's vulnerable bent back as he'd shuffled across the lawn to his own place. She remembered the fury in his eyes when he'd shouted at her, "Are you stupid?"

It was interesting that fury and fear could look so much the same.

68

So it looks like Mum is not going to cancel," said Erika. She'd been waiting all day for a phone call from her mother saying that she had a headache or she "didn't feel up to it" or it was too rainy, or, outrageously, that she "was catching up on a bit of housework," so she wouldn't be able to join them at Clementine's parents' house for dinner after all.

But the phone call hadn't come. In a minute they'd be picking Sylvia up and discovering what personality she'd selected for the evening.

Sylvia often went for a dreamy, bohemian persona when she was seeing Clementine's parents, as if she were an artist of some sort and they were the stuffy, suburban couple who had stepped in to help take care of her daughter when she was distracted doing her art. Another popular option was jaded, alcoholic sex kitten (channeling Elizabeth Taylor), except Sylvia didn't drink, she'd just hold her glass of water with careless elegance, as if it were a martini, and speak in a low, husky voice. Whichever personality she chose, the point was to make it clear that she was somehow special and different, and there was therefore no need to feel guilty or especially grateful for how much time Erika had spent at Clementine's home as a child.

"Oh well," said Oliver. He was in a great mood. Clementine had filled

316 | Liane Moriarty

in all the interim paperwork, she'd been for a blood test and she'd made an appointment to see the counselor at the IVF clinic. Things were progressing. Each time Clementine passed him something across the table tonight he'd probably be checking out her bone structure and imagining his superefficient sperm (tests indicated perfect motility) zipping about the petri dish with her eggs. "Clementine's parents can handle her."

Erika's phone beeped just as Oliver turned into her mother's street and her heart lifted. "Eleventh-hour reprieve!" she crowed. But it was her mother saying to let her know when they were close so that she could be waiting out front.

Erika texted back: *On approach right now.*

Her mother texted back: *Great!! xx*

Good God. Double exclamation marks and kisses. What could that mean?

"Looks like the neighbors have gotten their For Sale sign up already," said Oliver as he parked the car. "Wow," he said. "She's outdone herself."

"Told you so," said Erika. Erika's mother's front yard looked as it had the day before. Maybe worse? She couldn't remember.

"I think we need to call in the professionals," said Oliver, his eyes on the yard. "Take her out somewhere, do it while she's gone."

"She won't fall for that again," said Erika. She'd taken her mother away for the weekend once, and sent in cleaners, returning her mother to an unrecognizable, beautiful home. When they'd gotten back, her mother had slapped Erika across the face and refused to speak to her for six months because of her "betrayal." Erika had known she was betraying her. She'd felt like Judas that whole weekend.

"We'll work it out. Here she comes. She looks . . . gosh, she looks great." Oliver jumped out of the car in the rain to open the back door for Sylvia, who carried a large, white, wooden-handled umbrella and wore a beautiful, tailored cream suit, like something Jane Fonda would wear to accept a lifetime achievement award. Her hair was bouncy and shiny, she must have been to the hairdresser, and as she got in the car, all Erika could smell was perfume—nothing damp or moldy or rotting.

It was a trick. The ultimate trick. Tonight they weren't going to pretend that there was a reason why Clementine's parents had virtually adopted Erika. Tonight they were going to pretend *it had never happened at all,* and of course they would all go along with it and let her get away with it. They'd all behave as if Sylvia lived in a home that matched that beautiful brand-new outfit.

"Hello, darling," said her mother in a breathless, feminine, I'm-a-lovely-mother voice.

"You look nice," said Erika.

"Do I? Thank you," said her mother. "I called Pam earlier to ask if I could bring anything and she absolutely insisted I come empty-handed. She said something very mysterious about how the evening was in honor of you and Oliver, although she knows you both don't like to talk about it, but obviously she was forever in debt. I thought, goodness, is dear old Pam finally losing her marbles?"

Oliver cleared his throat and shot Erika a rueful half smile.

Naturally Erika hadn't said a word to her mother about what had happened at the barbecue. You would think it was a straightforward story but who knew how she'd react?

"We were at a barbecue with the next-door neighbors and Ruby fell into a fountain," said Erika. "Oliver and I sort of . . . rescued her. We had to give her CPR. She was fine."

There was silence from the backseat.

"Ruby is the littler one, right?" said Erika's mother in her regular voice. "How old is she? Two?"

"Yes," said Clementine.

"What happened? Nobody saw her fall in? Where was her mother? What was Clementine doing?"

"Nobody saw her fall in," said Erika. "It was just one of those unfortunate things."

"So . . . she wasn't breathing when you pulled her out?"

"No," said Erika. She watched Oliver's hands tighten on the steering wheel.

"The two of you worked together?"

"Oliver did compressions, I did the rescue breaths."

"How long before she responded?"

"It felt like a lifetime," said Erika.

"I bet it did," said Sylvia quietly. "I bet it did." Then she leaned forward and patted their shoulders.

"Well done," she said. "I'm very proud of you two. Very proud."

Neither Erika nor Oliver said anything, but Erika could feel their mutual happiness filling the car; they both responded like thirsty plants to water when it came to parental approval.

"So Little Miss Perfect Clementine isn't so perfect after all!" crowed Sylvia as she leaned back in her seat. There was a triumphant, bitchy edge to her voice. "Ha! What did Pam have to say about that? *My* daughter saved her grandchild's life!"

Erika sighed, and Oliver's shoulders slumped. Of course she would ruin the moment, of course she would.

"Pam is very grateful," she said flatly.

"Well, that certainly evens up the score then, doesn't it, for all that family supposedly did for you."

"They didn't *supposedly* do anything, Mum," said Erika. "Their home was a haven for me."

"A haven," snorted Sylvia.

"Yes, that's right, a haven, with running water and electricity and actual food in the refrigerator. Oh, and no rats. That was nice. The lack of rats."

"Let it go," said Oliver quietly.

"Well, all I'm saying, my darling child, is that we don't have to feel quite so grateful to them now, do we? Quite so subservient. Like they're our feudal overlords. You saved that child's life!"

"Yes, well, and now Clementine is going to donate her eggs to help us have a baby, so we're going to be back to feeling grateful to them," said Erika.

It was a mistake. As soon as she said it she knew it was a mistake.

There was a beat. Erika looked at Oliver. He shook his head as he resignedly flicked on the indicator to turn right.

"I'm sorry . . . *what* did you just say?" Sylvia leaned forward as far as her seat belt would let her.

"Dammit, Erika," sighed Oliver.

"We've been going through IVF for the last two years," said Erika. "And my eggs are . . . rotten." Because of you, she thought. Because I grew up in filth, surrounded by rot and decay and mold, so germs and spores and all manner of malignancy found their way into my body. She hadn't been at all surprised when she couldn't get pregnant. Of course her eggs had gone off. No surprises there!

"They're not 'rotten,'" said Oliver in a pained way. "Don't say that."

"You never told me you were going through IVF," said Sylvia. "Did you just forget to mention it? I'm a nurse! I could have given you support . . . advice!"

"Yeah right," said Erika.

"What do you mean, 'yeah right'?"

"We never told anyone," said Oliver. "We just kept it to ourselves."

"We're strange people," said Erika. "We know it."

"You always said you never wanted children," said Sylvia.

"I changed my mind," said Erika. You would think she'd signed a contract the way people kept reminding her of this.

"So Clementine offered to donate her eggs?" said Sylvia.

"We asked her," said Erika. "We asked her before . . . what happened with Ruby."

"But you can bet your bottom dollar that's why she's doing it," said Sylvia.

"Look, none of this is definite yet," said Oliver. "We're right at the early stages. Clementine still has to have tests, see a counselor . . ."

"It's a horrible idea," said Erika's mother. "An absolutely horrible idea. Surely there are other options."

"Sylvia," began Oliver.

"My grandchild won't really be mine!" said Sylvia.

Narcissist. That's how Erika's psychologist described her. Classic narcissist.

"My grandchild will be *Pam's* grandchild," continued Sylvia. "It's not enough that she has to take my daughter, oh no, now she can lord it over me with this: 'We're just so happy to help out, Sylvia.' So condescending and smug. It's a horrible idea! Don't do it. It will be a disaster."

"This isn't about you, Sylvia," said Oliver. Erika could hear a pulse of anger in his voice. It made her nervous. He rarely got angry, and he always spoke with such scrupulous politeness to his mother-in-law.

"Why in the world did you ask her?" said Sylvia. "Find an anonymous donor. I don't want my grandchild to have Pam's DNA! She's got those big elephantine ears! Erika! What if your child inherits Pam's ears?!"

"For heaven's sake, Mum," said Erika. "I read somewhere there's a gene associated with compulsive hoarding. I think I'd prefer my child to have big ears than become a hoarder."

"Please don't use that word. I abhor that word. It's so . . ."

"Accurate?" murmured Erika.

There was silence for a few seconds but Sylvia rallied fast.

"What will you say when Clementine comes to visit?" she said. "Oh, look, darling, here comes your real mother? Off you go and play the cello together."

"Sylvia, please," said Oliver.

"It's unnatural, that's what it is. Science has gone too far. Just because you *can* do something doesn't mean you should."

They pulled into Clementine's parents' street. It used to take Erika only ten minutes to walk here as a child, to leave all the dirt and the shame behind. Erika looked out the window as they pulled up in front of the neat Californian bungalow with its olive green front door. Just seeing that olive green front door used to make her heartbeat slow.

Oliver turned off the windshield wipers, twisted the key in the ignition, undid his seat belt and turned to look at his mother-in-law.

"Could we please not talk about this over dinner?" he said. "Could I ask you that, Sylvia?"

"Of course I won't." Sylvia lowered her voice. "Take a look at Pam's ears, though, that's all I'm saying." She caressed one earlobe. "I myself have such dainty ears."

69

"Ding, ding, ding!" Pam tapped her spoon on the side of her water glass and got to her feet. "Could I have your attention, please?"

Clementine should have known. There was going to be a speech. Of course there was. Her mother had been delivering speeches all her life. Every birthday, every holiday, every minor academic, sporting or musical achievement merited a speech.

"Oh goodness, are you going to sing for us, Pam?" said Sylvia, turning in her chair to regard Pam. She winked at Clementine.

Clementine shook her head at her. She knew that Sylvia had been a terrible mother to Erika, that she had said and done unforgivable things over the years, and that was all in addition to the hoarding problem, but Clementine had always felt traitorously affectionate toward her. She enjoyed Sylvia's subversiveness, her outlandish comments, her meandering stories and snarky, sly little digs. In contrast, her own mother always seemed so staid and earnest, like a well-meaning minister's wife. Clementine especially enjoyed seeing Sylvia's outfits. She could just as easily look like a bohemian intellectual as a Russian princess or a homeless person. (Sadly, she'd chosen "homeless person" for Erika's wedding, in order to make some long-forgotten, convoluted, pointless point.)

Tonight Sylvia looked like a lady who lunched. You would think she was going home tonight to a glossy McMansion with a banker husband.

"I hope you'll allow me the indulgence of saying a few words," said Pam. "There are two people here tonight who can only be described as—" She paused and took a deep, shaky breath. "—quiet heroes."

"Hear, hear," said Clementine's dad too loudly. He'd been drinking more than usual. Erika's mother made him nervous. Once, she'd sat next to him at a school concert, and while discussing local politics she had apparently put her hand "very close to his . . . you know what" (this was how Pam described it), causing Clementine's dad to "make the most peculiar sound, like a yelp."

"Yes, that's what they are, quiet, unassuming, unsung heroes, but heroes nonetheless," continued Pam.

"Awww." Sylvia put her head to one side in an "oh shucks" way, as if Pam were referring to her.

Erika rotated one shoulder as if she had a stiff neck. Oliver adjusted his glasses and cleared his throat. The two of them looked profoundly uncomfortable. "Why did you invite Erika's mother?" Clementine had asked Pam earlier that night.

"I thought it would be nice for Erika," Pam said defensively. "We haven't seen Sylvia for a long time, and her hoarding has gotten very bad again lately, so I thought it might be helpful."

"But Erika hates her mother," said Clementine.

"She doesn't *hate* her," Pam had said, but she'd looked upset. "Oh gosh, I probably shouldn't have invited her, you're right. Erika would have enjoyed the night more without her. You try to do the right thing, don't you? And it just doesn't always work out that way."

Now she looked brightly around the room.

"They don't want accolades. They don't want medals. They probably don't even want this speech!" She gave a merry laugh.

"I want a medal," said Holly.

"Shh, Holly," said Sam, on Holly's other side. He had barely touched the food on his plate.

"Yet some things simply cannot go unsaid," said Pam.

"But I do want a medal!" demanded Holly.

"*There is no medal,*" hissed Clementine.

"Well, why did Grandma say there was?"

"She didn't!" said Sam.

Erika's mother giggled deliciously.

"The debt of gratitude we owe Erika and Oliver is of such magnitude," said Pam, "that I cannot even begin to—"

"Could I trouble you to pass the water, Martin?" said Sylvia in a loud whisper to Clementine's father.

Pam stopped and watched her husband half-stand and awkwardly place the jug of water next to Sylvia while avoiding any eye contact whatsoever.

"Sorry, Pam," said Sylvia. "Carry on. Lovely earrings by the way."

Pam put her hand confusedly to one ear. She wore the plain gold studs she always wore. "Thank you, Sylvia. Where was I?"

"The debt of gratitude," said Sylvia helpfully as she poured herself a glass of water.

Oliver tipped back his head and studied the ceiling as if for inspiration or salvation.

"Yes, ah, the debt of gratitude," said Pam.

Ruby, who had been sitting on a cushion on the chair next to Clementine, suddenly put down her spoon with a purposeful air and slid onto the floor.

"Where are you going?" whispered Clementine.

Ruby put her hand to the side of her mouth. "Going to sit on Grandpa's lap."

"I wanted to sit on Grandpa's lap," huffed Holly. "I was actually just *about* to go and sit on Grandpa's lap."

"There is a quote," said Pam. (There always was.) She swept her hands wide, palms facing the ceiling. She liked to deliver her quotes with this particular statesmanlike gesture. "Friends are the family we chose for ourselves."

"Indeed," said Sylvia. "So true."

"I'm not sure who said it," admitted Pam. She liked to attribute her quotes. "I meant to check."

"Don't worry, Pam, we can always look it up later," said Clementine's dad.

"Oliver could check right now!" offered Sylvia. "Oliver! Where's your phone? He's so quick. Tippity-tippity-tap and he has the answer!"

"Mum," said Erika.

"What?" said Sylvia.

"Friends are the family we chose for ourselves," repeated Pam. "And I'm just so glad that Clementine and Erika chose to be friends." She glanced at Clementine and then hurriedly looked away. "Erika. Oliver. Your amazing actions that day saved our darling Ruby's life. We can obviously never truly repay you. The debt of gratitude we—"

"I think we already covered the debt of gratitude," said Sylvia. "Didn't we? Anyway, from what I hear, the debt is set to be cleared—"

"*Sylvia*," said Oliver.

Sylvia gave Clementine a roguish look. She leaned close and whispered, so that Oliver and Erika couldn't hear. "You and Oliver, hey?"

Clementine frowned. She didn't get it.

"Making a baby together!" clarified Sylvia. Her eyes sparkled maliciously.

Clementine saw that Erika's jaw was set in the manner of someone enduring a painful but necessary medical procedure.

"Erika and Oliver. We love you. We thank you. We salute you." Pam lifted her glass. "To Erika and Oliver."

There was a scramble as everyone found wine or water glasses and raised them too.

"Cheers!" cried Holly. She tried to clink her lemonade glass against Clementine's wineglass. "Cheers, Mummy!"

"Yes, cheers. Be careful, Holly," said Clementine. She could see that Holly was on the cusp of crazy. These days you could never tell what she was going to do next, and right now she was drunk on too much lemonade.

"Cheers, Daddy!" said Holly. Sam didn't register her. He still had his wineglass lifted, but his eyes were on Ruby sitting on Martin's lap, whispering something to Whisk.

"I said, *cheers*, Daddy," said Holly angrily, and she got up on her knees on her chair, and slammed her water glass so hard against her father's wineglass that it shattered in his hand.

"*Jesus!*" Sam leaped back from his seat as if he'd been shot. He turned on Holly and yelled, "That was naughty! You are a very naughty, very bad girl!"

Holly cowered. "Sorry, Daddy. It was an accident."

"It was a stupid accident!" he roared.

"Okay, that's *enough*," said Clementine.

"Oh dearie me," said Pam.

Sam stood. There was blood on his hand. For a moment the only sound was the perpetual patter of rain.

"Do you want me to take a look at that cut?" offered Sylvia.

"No," said Sam rudely. He sucked the side of his hand. He breathed heavily. "I need to get some air." He left the room. That was all Sam did these days: leave the room.

"Well! There's a little drama to spice things up," said Sylvia.

Oliver stood and began collecting the pieces of glass in the palm of his hand.

"Come sit here with me, Holly," said Erika, pushing back her chair and patting her legs, and to Clementine's surprise, Holly slid off her chair and ran to her.

"I *had* told you to be careful, Holly," said Clementine, and she knew her sharp rebuke was only because she'd been expecting the comfort of Holly's body against hers. She wanted Holly to sit on her lap, not Erika's, and that was childish. All her emotions had become tiny and twisted. She really should cancel her audition. She was too emotionally stunted to ever be a good musician. She imagined her bow screeching and scraping across the strings as if she'd suddenly become a beginner: squeaky unpleasant notes to match her squeaky, unpleasant emotions.

"Right. Well. Cups of tea? Coffee?" said Pam. "Erika brought along some very nice chocolate nuts that will go very nicely with a cup of tea. Just the ticket!"

"Isn't she clever," said Sylvia.

"I'm quite remarkable," said Erika.

As Pam began the complicated process of confirming everyone's tea and coffee orders, Clementine collected plates and took them into the kitchen. Her father followed her, carrying Ruby, who had that comfy, superior look children always got in the arms of a tall man; like a fat-cheeked little sultan.

"You okay?" said her father.

"Fine," said Clementine. "Sorry about Sam. He's just stressed about work, I think."

"Yes, he does seem stressed about the new job," said Martin. He put Ruby down as she began to wriggle. "But I think it's more than that."

"Well, it's been hard for him ever since the . . . accident," said Clementine.

She wasn't sure if she was allowed to call it an accident, if that implied she didn't consider herself responsible.

"Sam blames himself for not watching Ruby—and I think, I know, he also blames me," said Clementine. It was somehow easier to just baldly admit it to her dad, who would just take what she said at face value, rather than her mother, who would listen too intently and empathetically and filter everything through her own emotions.

"And I guess I blame him," said Clementine. "And at the same time we're both pretending we don't blame each other at all."

"Right," said her father. "Well, that's called being married. You're always blaming each other for something." He opened a kitchen cupboard and began taking out mugs. "What's the bet I'm getting the wrong ones out?" He turned to look at Clementine, holding two mugs by the handles on his fingertips. "But I reckon there's something more going on. He's not right. He isn't quite right in the head."

"Not *those* ones, Martin." Pam bustled into the kitchen. "We want the nice ones." She took the mugs off him and swiftly put them away. "Who isn't right in the head?"

"Sam," said Clementine.

"I've been saying that for weeks," said Pam.

70

"Hello again."

Tiffany lifted her umbrella to see who had spoken. She was walking through the quadrangle toward the Saint Anastasias shop to buy Dakota's uniform for next year.

It was Andrew's wife again. Of course it was. Murphy's Law would ensure that Tiffany ran into this woman and/or her husband every time she entered the school and at every school event until Dakota finished high school. It wasn't going to be at all uncomfortable. No! It was going to be freaking great. Cara and Dakota would become best friends. They'd invite them over for a barbecue. "Where did you guys meet?" the nice wife would innocently ask, and her husband would clutch his chest and drop dead of a heart attack (handy!). Except then Oliver would rush over from next door and revive him.

"Tiffany, right? I'm Lisa," said Andrew's wife. She tilted back her own battered umbrella to reveal her face. There were soft pink pouches under her eyes. One of the metal spokes of her umbrella had broken free of the fabric and was directed at her face like a weapon. "You probably don't remember me. I sat next to you at the Information Morning."

"I remember. How are you?" said Tiffany.

"Not great. This constant rain is doing my head in," said Lisa. She surveyed Tiffany. "*You* look well. Do you take some sort of secret supplement?"

"Caffeine?" said Tiffany.

"Seriously, it's a pleasure to look at you."

Tiffany laughed uneasily. Was she about to say: "I understand my husband used to pay good money just to look at you"?

"Are you buying Cara's school uniform too?" said Tiffany. She knew that the uniform shop, run by "our lovely volunteers," opened for just forty-five minutes at this time and "strictly no longer" and it was "first in, best dressed (literally!)."

Would it seem odd that she remembered Lisa's daughter's name? Suspicious?

"Actually, I'd already bought her uniform, but I'm bringing it back," said Lisa. "We're moving to Dubai for the next five years, so Cara won't be attending Saint Anastasias after all."

"Oh, well that's . . ." Tiffany tried to think of a more appropriate way to end the sentence rather than "wonderful news," although paradoxically, irrationally, she found herself feeling almost disappointed. She liked Lisa. Who actually said that? It's a pleasure to look at you. It was nice.

"How do you feel about that?" she said.

"I'm trying to feel okay about it," said Lisa. "We did the expat thing when the kids were little and it was all fine, but I just don't think I have the energy to do it again. We're very settled in Sydney and this just came out of the blue. It happened on Wednesday, the same day as the Information Morning, actually. My husband hears about some marvelous, incredible opportunity that he can't pass up or . . . or some bullshit." She put her hand to her mouth. "Probably shouldn't swear on Catholic school grounds." She looked up. "God won't like it."

"Don't you have a say in the matter?" said Tiffany.

Lisa raised a hand in defeat. "Some battles can't be won, and this is one of them. I don't think it rains much in Dubai. So that's something." She suddenly thrust out the bag she held in her hand. "Here. Take it. Got the lot there. Our kids looked about the same size. I can't be bothered going through the rigmarole of getting my money back. Roxanne Silverman runs the uniform shop. She always asks me if I've lost weight, which is her passive-aggressive way of saying I need to lose weight."

Tiffany took the bag unwillingly. "I'll pay you."

"Nope!" said Lisa. "Take it. I insist. Apparently we can afford to lose all those non-refundable deposits on school fees."

"Please," said Tiffany. "Please let me give you . . ." She put the bag at her feet and began trying to get her wallet out of her handbag while still holding her umbrella.

"I'm off. You take care," said Lisa. She turned on her heel and walked away, her umbrella blowing sideways.

"Well, thank you!" called out Tiffany.

Lisa raised her umbrella in acknowledgment and kept walking.

Tiffany watched her go. A bell rang and a babble of girlish voices rose from the nearest building like a flock of seagulls. Seagulls with nice private school–girl accents.

She thought about Lisa's husband.

Lisa's husband was a polite, softly spoken man. He had been interested in Tiffany's degree. He'd liked her schoolgirl outfit best: a green-and-white-checked uniform not dissimilar to the one still in its cellophane wrapper in the bag she now held; the one his daughter would have worn if she'd attended this school. Lisa's husband drank Baileys and milk. A girly drink, she used to tease him about it. Lisa's husband used to slip a huge wodge of tipping dollars into her garter in one go, instead of making her work for them, or worse, teasing her, as if the tipping dollars were dog biscuits. Fuck that.

Lisa's husband had taken her out a few times after work. Once he'd come to see her perform in the day and after she finished work they couldn't find anywhere open for lunch so he'd booked a hotel room "just so they could order room service." It had been a revelation to Tiffany: how you could use money to manipulate your world. When things went wrong you just waved your credit card like a magic wand. After lunch he'd gone back to work and she'd had a free hotel in the city for the night. She'd invited some of her uni friends over to stay. None of them believed she hadn't slept with him, but she hadn't. They'd just eaten club sandwiches and watched a movie. He had been a friend. She'd been like his hairdresser, except she hadn't cut his hair, she'd danced for him. Their relationship had felt wholesome.

It was maybe a whole year after that, after she'd given him a private show, that Lisa's husband had asked Tiffany, in his polite, reticent way, if she'd ever seen that movie, *Indecent Proposal*? The one with Robert Redford and Demi

Moore? The one where Robert Redford paid some obscene amount to sleep with Demi Moore?

Tiffany had seen the movie. She understood the question.

"One hundred thousand dollars," she'd told him, before he'd even asked.

She had pitched it low enough to be a possibility, but high enough so it was still a joke, a dare, a fantasy, and it didn't make her a hooker.

He hadn't hesitated. He'd said, "Will you take a check?" It was a company check, from "Something-or-other Holdings," and it was enough for the deposit on the apartment she'd bought at the auction where she'd met Vid. It had laid the foundation of her financial fortress.

She'd always told Vid that she'd never slept with any of her clients—she was a dancer, not a hooker—and it still felt true. What happened with Andrew was a one-off with a wealthy, older friend. A joke. A dare. A fun idea. She might have done it for the cost of two drinks if she'd met him in a bar and he'd made her laugh. Even after she had slept with him she'd still felt like their relationship had a kind of wholesomeness to it. They had straightforward, missionary-position sex with a condom. She had a dirtier relationship with Vid.

She remembered that afterwards, while they were in bed together, Andrew had begun to talk about a one-bedroom apartment he owned in the city, something about a trust, something about tax advantages. It took her a while to catch on that he was offering her an "opportunity," a mutually beneficial, long-term arrangement. She had politely declined. He'd said to let him know if she ever wanted to reconsider.

About six months later, he came into the club and booked her for a private show. He told her that he was moving the family overseas for a year. It wasn't long after that Tiffany finished her degree, stopped dancing and got her first full-time job.

In all her dealings with Andrew, she'd never thought of his wife. "What about the wives?" Clementine had said in the car that night. "The wives stuck at home with the kids."

Tiffany had answered with a shrug. The faceless middle-aged wives had never been her responsibility. She wished them no ill. She owed them no duty of care. They probably didn't have great bodies, but they had great credit cards.

Her deal with Andrew was the only secret she'd ever kept from Vid. She wasn't ashamed, and in all honesty she wasn't even sure it was necessary, but every time over the years when she'd gone to open her mouth and share her story, her instincts had screamed: Shut the hell up. Even her free-spirited Vid had his boundaries, and she didn't want to find out what they were by crossing them.

So, no, she'd never felt shame about what had happened with Andrew, except for right now, as she stood in the rain holding an environmentally friendly bag heavy with free expensive school uniforms, watching his tired, disappointed, chunky-around-the-middle wife head back through the rain to her black four-wheel-drive Porsche, because maybe the timing of this unexpected move to Dubai was a wonderful coincidence, but then again, maybe it wasn't.

71

It was because of the rain.

If only the rain had stopped, then Erika wouldn't be standing here right now, on a Saturday morning, in her living room with the sound of her heart thumping in her ears, feeling like she'd been arrested, her husband the policeman.

Oliver didn't really look like a policeman. He looked sad and confused. She wondered if that was the same expression he'd got on his face as a child when he found the bottles of vodka and gin his parents had hidden around the house, before he stopped believing their excited promises about giving up. (They still made extravagant promises. "We're doing Dry July!" "We're doing Sober November!")

It had happened when she was out renewing her license. She'd been in a good mood when she came home. She liked starting her weekend by ticking off those kinds of day-to-day administrative tasks that her mother had so often left undone: bills left unpaid, disconnection notices ignored, unsigned permission slips immediately lost in the maelstrom.

But then Oliver met her at the door. "We've got a leak," he said. "A roof leak. In the storeroom."

They had a small storeroom where they kept their suitcases and camping gear and skis.

"Well, that's not the end of the world, is it?" she asked, but her heart started to beat double-time. She had an inkling.

Oliver being Oliver, he'd got right onto it and had begun moving things into the hallway, and he'd come upon this old locked suitcase under a blanket. The suitcase was full, and he couldn't think what would be in there. It took him only a second to find the only unmarked key in the drawer where they kept the keys.

See. If she really was her mother's daughter, he would never have found the key.

"So I opened it," he said, and then he took her gently by the hand and led her into the dining room, where he'd laid out the entire contents of the suitcase in orderly rows, as if he were an investigator laying out evidence from a crime scene. Exhibit one. Exhibit two.

"It's just a silly habit," she said defensively, and to her horror she felt an expression like her mother's creep across her face: a furtive, sneaky look. "It's not *hoarding*, if that's what you're thinking."

"At first it just seemed like random stuff," said Oliver. "But then I recognized Ruby's sneaker." He lifted up the runner and banged it against the palm of his hand so that the colored lights flashed. "And I remembered how Clementine and Sam said that they'd lost one of her flashing shoes. It's Ruby's shoe, isn't it?"

Erika nodded, unable to speak.

"And this bracelet." He held up the chain. "It's Clementine's, right? It's the one you bought for her in Greece."

"Yes," said Erika. She felt a hot, itchy flush creep up her neck as if she were having an allergic reaction. "She didn't like it. I could tell she didn't like it."

"Everything here belongs to Clementine, doesn't it?" He picked up a pair of scissors. They were Clementine's grandmother's pearl-handled scissors. Erika couldn't even remember the day she'd taken them.

She pressed her finger to Holly's long-sleeved T-shirt with the strawberry on the front. Next to it was a tote bag with a picture of a treble clef: Clementine's first boyfriend, the French horn player, had given it to her for her twentieth birthday.

334 | Liane Moriarty

"Why?" said Oliver. "Can you tell me why?"

"It's just a habit," said Erika. She had no words to explain why. "A sort of . . . um, compulsion. There's nothing of actual value there."

Compulsion: one of those solid respectable psychological-sounding words to nicely wrap the truth: she was as mad as a hatter, as crazy as a bedbug.

Oh, she'd slept with enough crazy bedbugs in her time!

She scratched the side of her neck.

"Don't make me throw it away," she said suddenly.

"Throw it away?" said Oliver. "Are you kidding? You have to give it all *back*! You have to tell her that you've been . . . what? Pilfering her stuff? Is that what it is? Are you a kleptomaniac? Do you . . . dear God, Erika, do you shoplift?"

"Of course I don't shoplift!" She would never do anything illegal.

"Clementine must think she's going mad."

"Well, she really needs to be tidier, more organized," began Erika, but for some reason that really tipped Oliver over a precipice she hadn't realized he was balancing upon.

"What in God's name are you talking about? *She needs a friend who doesn't steal her stuff!*" shouted Oliver. He actually shouted. He'd never shouted at her before. He'd always been on her side.

She understood, of course, that what she did wasn't perhaps ordinary. It was a strange, unsavory habit, like gnawing her cuticles or picking her nose, and she knew she needed to keep it at a manageable level, but part of her had always assumed that Oliver would somehow understand, or at least accept it, the way he'd accepted everything else about her. He'd *seen her mother's house* and he still loved her. He never criticized her the way she knew some husbands criticized tiny things about their wives. "The woman is incapable of closing a cupboard door," Sam would say about Clementine. Oliver was too loyal to ever say anything like that about Erika in public, but right now he didn't just look mildly aggravated, he looked truly appalled.

The room went blurry as Erika's eyes filled with tears. He was going to leave her. She'd tried to keep her craziness confined to just one small suitcase, but deep down, she'd always suspected that his leaving one day was a foregone conclusion, and now the sight of those items laid out in all their useless, shabby glory confirmed it: She was her mother.

She felt a burst of fury, and for some reason it was directed at Clementine.

"Yeah, well, she's not that great. Clementine isn't that great," she said shakily, idiotically, childishly, but she couldn't seem to quell the flood of words. "You should have heard the things I heard her say to Sam at the barbecue. When I went upstairs! She was talking about how she felt 'repulsed' at the idea of donating her eggs to us. That's the word she used. *Repulsed.*"

Oliver didn't look at her. He picked up an ice cream scoop from the table and fiddled with the mechanism. It had a picture of a polar bear on the handle. Erika had put it in her handbag one hot day last summer, after they'd had ice creams in the backyard at Clementine's house, after she'd performed at Symphony Under the Stars. Erika had just gotten the call about another unsuccessful IVF round, but it was nothing to do with the IVF. She'd taken the first item for her collection, a shell necklace Clementine had brought back from a holiday to Fiji, when she was only thirteen years old. Where was it? There it was. Erika had to pull back her own right arm because she so badly wanted to reach over and feel its chunky, rough-edged texture in the palm of her hand.

"Why didn't you tell me?" he said.

"About this? Because I know it's weird and wrong and—"

"No. Why didn't you tell me what you overheard Clementine say?"

"I don't know." She paused. "I guess I felt embarrassed . . . I didn't want you to know that my best friend feels that way about me."

Oliver put down the ice cream scoop. There was an infinitesimal softening around his mouth, but it was enough to make Erika's legs go weak and wobbly with relief. She pulled out a chair and sat down and looked up at him, studying the faint stubble along his jawline. She remembered when they'd first sat down together to do the draw for the squash comp all those years ago. He was the clean-shaven nerd with the glasses and the pin-striped shirt frowning over the spreadsheet, taking it far too seriously, just like her, wanting it done right and done fairly. She'd looked at the stubble along his jawline, and the thought had crossed her mind: He looks like Clark Kent, but maybe he's really Superman.

Oliver sat down at the table in front of her, took off his glasses and rubbed his eyes.

"I'm your best friend, Erika," he said sadly. "Don't you know that?"

72

I'm sorry about dinner at Mum and Dad's the other night," said Clementine as she handed Erika her cup of coffee. They were in Clementine's living room with its original (but non-working) fireplace, stained-glass porthole windows and wide floorboards. When she and Sam had first seen this room they'd exchanged glinting looks of satisfaction behind the real estate agent's back. This room had *character*, and it was just so "them" (in other words, the opposite of the "modern, sterile and soulless" sort of place that Erika and Oliver went for; Clementine was beginning to wonder if her entire personality was a fabrication, nothing more than a response to Erika's personality. You are like *this*, so therefore I am like *that*.)

Right now the living room seemed dowdy and dark and very damp. She sniffed. "Can you smell the damp? We've got mold popping up everywhere. Revolting. If it doesn't stop raining soon, I don't know what we'll do."

Erika took the cup of coffee and held it in both hands as though to warm herself.

"Are you cold?" Clementine half-rose. "I could—"

"I'm fine," said Erika shortly.

Clementine sank back in her seat. "Remember when we bought this place and the building report said there was a problem with rising damp and you said we should really think twice about it, and I was all: Who cares about rising damp? Well, you were right. It's really bad. We've got to get it fixed. I got a quote from . . ."

She stopped. She was boring herself so much she couldn't even be bothered to finish the sentence. Anyway, it was all a transparent attempt at exoneration. You saved my child's life, while all I've ever done is complain about you, you are all that is good, I am all that is bad, but surely I get extra-credit points for all this self-flagellation, a reduced sentence for pleading guilty?

"The dinner at your parents' was nice," said Erika. "I enjoyed it."

"Oh, good," said Clementine. Now she felt bad. She didn't want Erika to think she meant she didn't deserve her hero's dinner. "I just meant with the broken glass and Sam storming off and . . ."

She drifted again, and drank her coffee, and waited for Erika to get to the point of why she was here. She'd called earlier and asked if she could come around. It was bad timing: Sam had taken the girls to a movie so Clementine could practice—the audition was only ten days away now, it was the final countdown—but of course, Clementine had said yes. She presumed it was something to do with the next step in the egg donation process.

Erika nodded at Clementine's cello in the corner. "Is your cello affected by all the rainy weather?"

She had that faintly defensive look she always got when she looked at Clementine's cello, as if it were a glamorous friend who made her feel inferior.

"I've been having a lot more trouble than usual with my wolf," said Clementine.

"Your wolf?" said Erika distractedly.

Clementine was surprised. She was sure that she would have talked about her cello's wolf tone with Erika before, and Erika tended to retain that sort of stuff, especially because it was something negative. She loved bad news.

"A lot of cellos have it, it's like a problem note, I guess is the simplest way to put it. It makes a horrible kind of sound, like a pneumatic drill or a toy gun," said Clementine. "I tried a wolf tone eliminator for a while but then I felt like I lost resonance and tone, so I took it off. I can deal with it, I just

have to gently squeeze the cello with my knees, and sometimes I can rear-
range the bowing to meet the wolf on the down-bow so—"

"Oh, right, yes, I remember, I think you might have mentioned it before," said Erika. She changed the subject abruptly. "By the way, while I
think of it, I found one of Ruby's shoes at my place the other day."

Erika pulled out Ruby's missing flashing-soled sneaker from her handbag and placed it on the coffee table, making the lights flash. They seemed
especially lurid in the dark room.

"I can't believe it!" Clementine snatched up the shoe and examined it.
"We looked *everywhere* for that damned shoe. It was at your place? I can't
even remember her wearing it to—"

"Good. So anyway, what I wanted to discuss today," said Erika. "The egg
donation."

"Right," said Clementine dutifully. She put the shoe back in her lap.
"Well, as you know, I've got the appointment with—"

"We've changed our mind," said Erika.

"Oh!" Clementine's mind whirled. It was the last thing she'd expected.
"How come? Because I'm really happy to—"

"Personal reasons," said Erika.

"*Personal* reasons?" It was the sort of phrase that you used with an em-
ployer.

"Yes, so I'm sorry we took up your time doing the blood tests and all
that," said Erika. "Especially when you've got your audition coming up."

"Erika," said Clementine. "What's going on?"

Erika's face was impenetrable.

"Nothing," she said. "We just don't want to go ahead."

"Is it because . . ." Clementine felt sick. "That day at the barbecue. I was
talking to Sam and at first I wasn't sure how I felt about your, ah, your request, and I'm just a bit worried that you might have overheard and you
might have misinterpreted . . ."

"I didn't hear a thing," said Erika.

"You did," said Clementine.

"Okay, I did, but it doesn't matter, it's not about that." She looked at Clementine and her eyes seemed somehow naked and raw within her folded-
up face, but Clementine was at a loss to interpret what she was feeling.

"I'm sorry," said Clementine. "I'm really sorry."

Erika lifted one shoulder: the tiniest possible shrug.

"I want to do it now," said Clementine. "Not just because of Ruby. I'd got my head around it. I feel good about it."

Was it a lie?

Maybe it was true. She was exhilarated by the possibility that deep down she was her mother's daughter, a kind, generous person after all.

"I really want to do it," said Clementine.

"It wasn't my decision," said Erika. "Oliver is the one who wants to look at other options now."

"Oh," said Clementine. "Why?"

"Personal reasons," said Erika again.

Had Erika told Oliver what she'd overheard Clementine say? The thought of kind, honorable Oliver, who had always been so unfailingly polite to Clementine, whose face lit up when he saw her children, hearing Clementine's remarks made her want to cry. She thought of the sound Oliver had made when he revived Ruby: that animal-like whimper of relief.

She put down her cup on the coffee table and slid off the couch, falling to her knees in front of Erika. The sneaker fell onto the floor. "Erika, please let me do it. Please."

"Stop that," said Erika. She looked appalled. "Get up. You're reminding me of my mother. That's exactly the sort of thing she does. That sneaker is under the couch now, by the way. You'll lose it again."

She sounded crotchety but somehow revived. The color was back in her cheeks.

Clementine found the sneaker and sat back up. She picked up her coffee, sipped it and met Erika's eyes over the rim.

"*Idiot*," said Erika.

"*Dummkopf*," muttered Clementine into her mug.

"*Arschlich*," spat out Erika. "No. That's not it. Arsch*loch*."

"Good one," said Clementine. "You big *Vollidiot*."

Erika smiled. "I forgot that one," she said. "And *verpiss dich*, by the way."

"Piss off yourself," said Clementine.

"I thought it meant 'fuck off,'" said Erika.

"You'd know better than me," said Clementine. "You're the one who got the higher mark."

"Too right I did," agreed Erika.

Clementine blinked back tears of laughter or grief, she wasn't sure which. It was strange, because she always felt that she hid herself from Erika, that she was more "herself" with her "true" friends, where the friendship flowed in an ordinary, uncomplicated, grown-up fashion (emails, phone calls, drinks, dinners, banter and jokes that everyone got), but right now it felt like none of those friends knew her the raw, ugly, childish, basic way that Erika did.

"Anyway, the truth is I'm ambivalent," said Erika. She tipped back her head and drank her coffee in virtually one gulp. It was one of her quirks. She drank coffee like she was doing a shot.

"What do you mean?"

"I never especially wanted to have children, as you know, as people keep reminding me. That's why Oliver is the one driving this. I feel ambivalent." It was like she'd only recently settled on the word "ambivalent" and wanted to use it as much as possible. She was staying on message like a politician. She pointed a warning finger at Clementine. "My ambivalence, by the way, is confidential."

"Yes, of course. But if you don't really want a baby, you should tell him! You shouldn't have a child just for him. It's your choice!"

"Yes, and I choose my marriage," said Erika. "That's my choice: my marriage." She stood up. "Oliver's dream is to have a baby and I'm not going to make him give that up." She picked up her bag. "Oh, by the way!" Her tone changed, and became brittle. "I was going through an old box of memorabilia the other day, and I found this necklace. I think it was yours."

She pulled out an extremely ugly shell necklace and held it up.

"It's not mine," said Clementine. "I always hated those necklaces."

"I'm pretty sure—well, maybe I'm wrong." Erika went to put the necklace back in the bag. "But maybe the girls would like it?"

She was giving Clementine a strange, piercing look, as if this really mattered. She was the oddest woman. "Sure. Thanks." Clementine took the necklace. She wouldn't let the girls play with it. It didn't look that clean, and it would be like wearing barbed wire around your neck.

Erika looked relieved, as if she'd wiped her hands of something. "I hope your practice goes well. Only ten days until the audition, right?"

"Right," said Clementine.

"How's it going?"

"Not that great. I've found it hard to focus. Everything that happened—Sam and I—just . . . well, you know."

"Time to knuckle down then," said Erika briskly. "This is *your* dream, *Dummkopf.*"

And then she was gone, out into the rain in her sensible shoes. No kissing or hugging goodbye because they didn't do that. The German insults had been their version of a hug.

You're off the hook, thought Clementine as she cleared the coffee mugs away. No daily injections. She thought of the "So you're thinking of becoming an egg donor!" video she'd watched yesterday, and how her own stomach had clenched in horror as she'd watched the nice, generous woman briskly inject her stomach with the drug that would cause her body to produce multiple eggs.

She sat down with her cello, picked up her bow, and focused on working her way through her chromatic scales.

Over the last few days she had been allowing an image to form in her head: an image of a little boy with Ruby's almond-shaped eyes and Oliver's jet-black hair.

The image trembled like a reflection on water and then vanished.

For heaven's sake, Clementine, how *dare* you. Her hand tightened on her bow. The image didn't even make sense because Ruby's eyes came from Sam's side of the family.

There it was again. Her friendly wolf tone. It was a truly ghastly sound. She could feel it in her teeth.

Sam always said she was overly sensitive to sounds because she was a musician, but she didn't think that was true; he was just astonishingly insensitive to them. There were only a few sounds she could feel in her teeth: her wolf tone, a certain high-pitched shriek of Holly's when Ruby had wronged her, the wailing shark alarm at Macmasters Beach.

She was suddenly transported to the last time she'd heard that shark alarm during that holiday when she was thirteen. Clementine and Erika had been in the surf together when the alarm went off. Erika was a strong swimmer, better than her. The alarm had made Clementine panicky (that *sound*) and she'd slipped as she waded toward the shore, and Erika had grabbed her arm. "I'm fine," Clementine had snapped, shrugging her off, full of that hideous rage she'd carried throughout that entire two weeks, but then, just a second later, she'd thought she felt something slippery and strange slide across one leg and she instinctively reached out for Erika. "You're okay," said Erika, calmly, kindly, soothingly, steadying her. Clementine could still see Erika's wet, white arm on hers, the salt water clinging like diamonds to her white skin, three angry red bite marks circling her thin, bony wrist like a bracelet. The fleas had come and gone in Erika's house like seasons.

Clementine dropped her bow and tried to imagine her life without Erika in it: without the aggravation, followed always by the guilt. A melody with only two notes: aggravation, guilt, aggravation, guilt. She picked up her bow and deliberately played the wolf note, over and over, letting the sound aggravate her and worm its way down her ear canal, vibrating against her eardrum, creeping into her brain, throbbing at the center of her forehead.

She stopped.

"You shouldn't put up with a wolf tone," Ainsley had told her. "Get it looked at."

When she'd tried the wolf tone eliminator, it was initially a relief. It had taken her a little while to realize that something else was gone along with her wolf. Her sound wasn't as rich. The notes surrounding the wolf tone were somehow dampened, less focused. She wondered if it was similar to how people felt when they first took anti-depressants and they lost their pain, but everything else felt muted too: flatter, duller.

In the end she decided that her wolf tone was the price she had to pay for the sound of all those centuries of time held within the red-gold curves of her cello.

Maybe Erika was her wolf tone. Maybe Clementine's life would have lacked something subtle but essential without her in it: a certain richness, a certain depth.

Or maybe not. Maybe her life would have been *great* without Erika in it.

Clementine realized she was hungry. She set aside her cello and on the way to the kitchen she picked up the horrible knobbly shell necklace and chucked it straight in the bin. She went to the fridge, got herself a tub of yogurt, went to the drawer for a spoon and the first thing she saw was the polar bear ice cream scoop that Sam had been looking for the other night. Men. It had probably been right there in front of him the whole time.

She opened the yogurt, had a mouthful. It was really very good. Creamy, as they said in the ad. She was susceptible to advertising, but really, this was very good yogurt. It reminded her of her first taste of food after fasting.

She hadn't been fasting.

There was a feeling growing within her. A twitchy feeling. She was jabbing the spoon into the yogurt and eating it too fast. She thought of the opening melody of Stravinsky's *The Rite of Spring*. The high-pitched bassoon. The strange, jerky moments building to an ecstatic unfurling. She wanted to hear that piece. She wanted to *play* that piece, because that was exactly how she felt right now. There was an upward-spiraling feeling in her chest. Was the yogurt drugged? Was it simply exquisite relief because she'd demonstrated her absolute willingness to donate her eggs but *she didn't actually have to do it*: altruism without action, it didn't get better than that!

Was it just that she'd had enough of feeling bad over what happened? She could never forget that afternoon but she could forgive herself. She could forgive Sam. If he wanted to end their marriage over this, then she would grieve him as if he'd died, but goddamn it, she'd get over it, she'd live. She'd always suspected this about herself, that right at the center of her soul was a small unbreakable stone, a cold, hard instinct for self-preservation. She'd die for her children, but no one else. She wouldn't allow one mistake, one slip of judgment, to define her life, not when Ruby was fine, not when life was there for the taking.

She thought of Erika saying: "This is your dream, *Dummkopf*."

That job was hers. That job belonged to her. She threw down the empty yogurt container, licked her fingers and headed back to her cello, not to work on her technique this time, but to play music. Somewhere along the way she'd forgotten it was about the music, the pure, uncomplicated bliss of the music.

73

He's going to steal it!" announced Holly, loud and clear.

"Shh!" said Sam. They could never get Holly to shut up during movies.

"But he is, look!"

"You're right, but . . ." Sam put a finger to his lips, although who the hell cared, the movie theater was packed with wriggly, chatty, rain-crazed kids and their frazzled parents.

Holly shoveled a handful of popcorn into her mouth and sat back, her eyes on the flickering colors of the Pixar movie. Ruby was on Sam's other side, sucking her thumb, caressing Whisk's spokes. Her eyelids drooped. She would fall asleep soon and wake up five minutes before the movie ended, demanding it be restarted.

Sam normally loved a good animation but he had no idea what this one was about. He was thinking about his job, and how much longer he could get away with coasting. He was the new guy, still "learning the ropes," but he should have had those ropes learned by now. People must be starting to notice. The head of his division had said, "Might be time to invest in an umbrella," with a quizzical look at Sam's drenched clothes yesterday. It was all going to come crashing down. Someone would say, "The weird new guy *isn't doing anything.*"

It's past crunch time, Sam. You need to get over it, to get on with it, leave a goddamned umbrella at the front door. Why did tiny things like that seem so impossible these days? Ruby's head tipped gently against his arm. He pulled up the armrest and she snuggled up to him.

Clementine was getting on with it. He'd seen something change in her after the visit from Vid and Tiffany and Dakota. "I feel better after seeing them," she'd said, "don't you?" He'd wanted to shout, "No! I feel worse! I feel much worse!"

Did he actually shout that at her? He couldn't remember. He was becoming a shouter, like his own father used to be, before age softened him.

He shifted about in his seat.

"You're wriggling," whisper-shouted Holly.

"Sorry," said Sam. The popcorn tasted like salt-and-butter-flavored cardboard but he couldn't stop eating it.

Yes, something was definitely changing in Clementine. There was a new impatience about her, a brittleness, except brittleness implied fragility and she didn't seem fragile, she seemed fed up. She wanted to move on from Ruby's accident and she was right. There was no point dwelling on it. There was no point replaying it over and over. Sam had always considered himself the more emotionally resilient one in their relationship. Clementine was the one who made too big a deal of things, who got dramatic, sometimes to the point of hysteria, over tiny things, like her auditions, for example, although of course auditions weren't tiny, they were a big deal, and nerve-racking, he got that, but she used to let them consume her. Once Sam had heard Holly telling Ruby, "Mummy is sick with an audition." And he'd laughed because it was exactly like that. An audition hit her like a virus.

But that didn't seem to be the case with this latest audition, even though it was one of the most important of her career. She wasn't saying a word about it. She was just getting on with her practice. Sam wasn't even exactly sure of the audition date, even though he knew it had to be coming up soon.

Once, he would have been able to say exactly how many days it was until an audition because that was how many days it would be until he'd be getting sex again. But that was a long time ago, when sex was still a natural, normal part of the equation, before it got complicated. It was strange how sex had gotten so complicated, because for many years he would have said it was the *least* complicated aspect of their relationship. He would have put money on it staying that way.

Right from the beginning, their very first time, it had felt so natural. Their bodies and libidos had been in perfect sync. He'd been in enough relationships to know that sex often started out awkward before it got good, but with Clementine it was straightaway *good*. There were other red flags about their relationship: he wasn't musical, she'd never even been on a date with a non-musician before; he wanted a big family, she could have been satisfied with an only child. But there was never a red flag over sex. He actually remembered thinking, in his youthful, innocent, idiotic way, that their amazing sexual compatibility was proof that they were meant to be together because that's when they were their *honest, true, raw selves*. The rest was nothing but details.

Sam and Clementine had never needed to talk about sex, and that was such a relief after Daniella, his previous girlfriend, who he had very nearly married, and who had liked to discuss and dissect their sex life, and to follow each encounter with an immediate debrief: How can we work together to achieve better outcomes next time? (She was a business consultant. She didn't use those words but he could feel their intention.) Daniella had no qualms about beginning a conversation over the breakfast table with a comment like, "When I was blowing you last night . . . ," which would make him choke on his cereal and blush like an altar boy. ("So cute!" Daniella would crow.)

He loved the fact that he and Clementine kept an element of mystery about their sex life. They treated it with a shy kind of reverence. Sex was like a beautiful secret between them.

But maybe Daniella had had the right idea all along. Maybe all that bloody reverence had been their downfall, because when their sex life slowly changed and began to seem perfunctory and rushed, they didn't have the words to talk about it. He couldn't work out if Clementine even liked sex anymore (and he didn't want to hear the answer if it was no). The idea of "performance" had begun to announce itself in his head. Everything still operated as it should but for the first time ever he'd begun to wonder how he compared to those ex-boyfriends, if their musical ability had somehow translated into sexual ability.

He had known it was probably nothing. All parents of young kids went through this. It was so common it was a cliché. There would be a renaissance, he had told himself. When both girls started sleeping reliably through the night. When they weren't so tired and stressed. He had been looking forward to the renaissance.

And then that night of the barbecue, it had seemed like Tiffany was offering them the key to the door they'd accidentally closed on themselves. She was the gorgeous ringmaster crying, "Right this way for amazing sex again, folks!" It had suddenly seemed so easy again. He'd seen it on Clementine's face. She'd seen it on his.

And then the universe had seen fit to punish them for their selfishness in the cruelest way imaginable.

He saw it again: Oliver and Erika lifting up his baby girl. He saw it a dozen times a day. A hundred times. He would never, could never, get over it. He couldn't see a way out of this. There was no *solution* here. He had to change something. Fix something. Break something. He remembered how Clementine had flinched when he talked about separating. For a moment, she'd looked like a frightened child. He felt bad, or he was aware that he *should* have felt bad, but really he felt numb and strangely detached, as if it was somebody else who was saying these cruel things to his wife.

"*Daddy*," said Holly. "You've eaten it *all*!"

Sam looked at the empty bucket of popcorn. "Sorry," he whispered. He couldn't even remember eating it.

"That's not fair!" Holly's enraged face was illuminated by the light from the screen.

"Shh," he said helplessly. His throat felt scratchy. There were tiny flakes of corn kernel stuck between his teeth.

"But I hardly got any!" Her voice rose to an unacceptable level. Someone muttered disapprovingly in the row behind.

"If you can't be quiet, we're going," said Sam in a low, shaky voice.

"Greedy Daddy!" she shouted, and she snatched the container and threw it on the aisle floor next to her. It was calculated, willful naughtiness. It couldn't be ignored.

Bloody hell. He picked up the soggy umbrella at his feet, lifted the dead weight of Ruby over one shoulder, stood, and grabbed Holly by the wrist. Something twinged painfully in his lower back.

Holly screamed blue murder as he dragged her out of her seat and into the aisle.

Consequences. He and Clementine made fun of that sort of parenting jargon, but Holly and Ruby had to learn what it had taken Sam all these years to discover: Life was all about consequences.

74

Oliver decided to go for a run in the rain.

He risked injury on the slippery footpaths, and also a relapse of his chest cold, but right now he really needed to clear his head because his wife was a common thief and as a result he would never be a father.

He was incorrectly assigning causality but he was very upset. Angry. Shocked.

He double-knotted his shoelaces, stood up, did a few stretches, opened the front door and nearly closed it again because it was raining so hard, but he couldn't bear to roam around his house while his thoughts scuttled like trapped mice.

Running would give him clarity. His nervous system would release a protein that stimulated regions of his brain related to decision making.

He took a deep breath and headed out. Vid and Tiffany were obviously entertaining. There were cars lined up in their driveway and around the cul-de-sac. They were extremely sociable people.

As Oliver ran out of the cul-de-sac he considered his own, significantly smaller social circle. It might be helpful if he could talk this through with someone, but there was no one.

He did not have the sort of friend he could call up for a "quiet beer." He was not the sort of person who said "quiet beer." He didn't actually drink beer. He had the sort of friends who drank protein shakes at the local health-food café after a 30K morning bike ride, while they discussed training schedules for the upcoming half marathon. He liked his friends, but he had no interest in hearing their personal problems and he therefore couldn't share his own. He couldn't lean over his protein shake and say, "My wife has been stealing memorabilia from her best friend since she was a kid. What do you reckon? Should I be worried?"

He would never betray Erika to another man like that anyway.

A confidential discussion with a woman might be better. Maybe if he had a sister, or a mother. Technically he did have a mother. Just not the right sort of mother. She would find Erika's stealing screamingly funny or tragically sad, depending on where the pendulum of her mood currently sat.

A car drove by and tooted at him in either a supportive or derisive way: hard to interpret.

If Erika had started hoarding, he could have handled that. He'd even mentally prepared himself for that remote possibility, in spite of her constant, obsessive de-cluttering. He'd prepared himself for depression (common while undergoing IVF), for breast cancer, for a brain tumor, for accidental death and even an office romance (he trusted her, but her managing partner was apparently a "ladies' man"), but never for this. Never for *petty thievery*. They were straight-down-the-line people. Their financial affairs were in scrupulous order. He and Erika would *welcome* a tax audit. Bring it on, they'd say to the tax office. Bring it *on*.

His glasses needed windshield wipers. He kept running while he took them and tried to dry them with the edge of his T-shirt. Useless.

She had taken Clementine's stuff, like a Dickensian pickpocket. It was unfathomable. She said she was going to stop and that she would give back what she could over a period of time, but in Oliver's world, people never stopped. His parents had said they'd stop drinking. Erika's mother had said she'd stop hoarding. They truly believed it at the time. He got that. But they couldn't stop. It was like asking them to hold their breath. They could do it for only so long before they had to gasp for air.

Another car swept by, and a teenage boy stretched almost half his body out the window in order to yell, "Loser!"

Really dangerous activity there, sport. You could get sideswiped by another car. Also bad-mannered.

He took the corner at Livingston. Twinge in that left knee again.

Right now Erika was over at Clementine's, telling her that they wouldn't need her as an egg donor after all. They had discussed it and agreed it would be polite to tell her in person. She'd invested her time doing blood tests and filling in paperwork. They didn't like to waste someone's time.

It was Oliver's decision. There were Clementine's unkind comments that Erika had overheard. *Repulsed by the idea.* Bitch, he thought, as his foot hit a puddle and water sprayed. Clementine wasn't a bitch. He was fond of Clementine, but the things she'd said had been so unkind and unnecessary.

He thought of Erika's little face (she had a small darling face) and how she must have looked when she'd stood in the hallway overhearing those awful words. His fists clenched. He felt a sudden urge to hit Sam, because he obviously couldn't hit Clementine.

The moment passed, as primal urges did. He'd never hit anyone in his life.

Anyway, even if Clementine hadn't said what she'd said, obviously Erika's relationship with her was too . . . strange? complex? dysfunctional? . . . for this to go ahead.

"Absolutely not," he'd said to Erika. "She can't be our donor. It's not happening. It's over. It's finished."

He couldn't tell if she was relieved or shattered.

He'd been so adamant, but now, as he ran, his clothes getting wetter and heavier (you would think there'd be a point of total saturation, at which they couldn't get any wetter, but apparently not), he was regretting his decision. Maybe he'd been too hasty.

It felt like another loss. Each time he thought he was doing well, avoiding the hope. Each time he told himself: I have no expectations, but with each new failure it hurt so much he understood the hope had been there after all, flitting seductively around his subconscious. It didn't get easier either. It got worse. A cumulative effect. Loss upon loss. Like the ligament strain in that left knee.

So, what now? Anonymous donor? They were so difficult to find, unless they went overseas. People were doing that. They could do that. He could do it. He could do whatever it took to have his own biological child. He just wasn't sure if Erika could. He had a terrible suspicion that if he said, "Let's forget about the baby," the first expression he'd see on her face would be relief.

His heart rate was up very high. He could hear himself puffing. He couldn't normally hear himself puffing. That chest cold had affected his fitness. He concentrated on breathing in rhythm with his footfalls.

He saw a blue car coming his way from the opposite end of the street and realized it was Erika, on her way home from seeing Clementine.

He stopped, hands on his hips, catching his breath and watching her approach. He couldn't see her face yet, but he knew exactly how she'd be driving, hunched over the wheel like a little old lady, two deep lines between her eyebrows; she didn't like driving in the rain.

Her frown was the first thing he'd noticed about her when they worked together, long before they did the squash competition draw together. He didn't know why he found it so appealing; maybe because it indicated that she took life seriously, like him, that she cared and she concentrated, she didn't just float along the surface, having a great time. He'd never told her that. Women wanted to be noticed for their eyes, not their frowns.

She must not have lingered at Clementine's after she'd delivered her news.

The car pulled up on the other side of the road. She wound down the window and bent over the passenger seat to look up at him anxiously.

"You shouldn't run in this weather!" she shouted. "You could slip! You haven't even finished your antibiotics."

He headed over to the car, opened the door and got in next to her. The car was warm. She had the heater cranked up.

Water slid off him, pooling all around him on the leather seat. He could feel it squelching. He was reminded of the night they pulled Ruby from the fountain; how they'd worked together, how they hadn't needed to talk, they'd just acted. They were a good team.

Erika sat, still hunched over the steering wheel, studying him silently, frowning ferociously.

He put his hand to the side of her face.

"Sorry," he said, going to draw it away. "I'm all wet."

But she grabbed it back and tilted her warm face into the palm of his cold hand.

75

Vid's house was full of people and music and the smell of good food, which was what he liked, what he loved. What was the point in having a big house like this unless you filled it with people?

The occasion was no occasion. What did you need an occasion for? You didn't! It was spur of the moment. He'd made some phone calls and now the house was full. It was still raining, of course, but that did not mean all the fun had to stop, they were warm and dry in here, the rain would not stop them from living their lives! They should do this more often! They should do it every weekend!

All four of his daughters were here tonight, and at this point, they were all talking to him, a rare and wonderful event. Of course, his older girls all wanted something from him but so be it. That was parenting.

Adrianna wanted him to agree to do a choreographed father-and-daughter dance at her wedding. It would be filmed and then she'd post it on YouTube. It was her dream to go viral. He would do this, of course, although he was pretending he hated the idea. (He already had a few moves in mind.)

Eva and Elena wanted money, he assumed, and of course they would get it. He'd transfer it into their accounts tonight, after they left. All that was in question was how much. He would see how their negotiating skills were developing. Eva would get hysterical within seconds. He'd been trying to explain to her that hysteria was not an effective negotiating tactic ever since she was two years old.

His baby, Dakota, didn't want anything. She was happy again, although he hadn't realized just how sad the poor little angel had gotten. Tiffany's idea of turning up at the cellist's house had been excellent, even though they had never even offered them a *drink*. It had been wonderful to see little Ruby so happy and healthy after the terribleness of that night. It had been a giant weight off his back. He had walked out of that tiny cramped house feeling straighter and lighter (also thirsty).

Clementine and Sam had been silent and strange but they had invited Dakota to Holly's birthday party! Hopefully they'd remember to feed their guests. He'd take some food along, just in case. He was hopeful they might all still be friends. Tiffany was not as hopeful as him. She said only Dakota was invited to the birthday party, not them. She said it was probably a "drop-off party." He didn't know what she was talking about. He would take meatballs, maybe. A case of champagne.

"You having fun?" said Tiffany, meeting him in the kitchen as they both collected more plates of food to pass around.

"No! Why do we do this? I just wanted a quiet night at home, and look! The house is filled with all these people wanting to be fed! How did this happen?"

"I have no idea. It's a mystery." Tiffany closed the fridge door with her hip and smiled up at him, both her hands filled with trays. "Apparently the sun is coming out tomorrow. We should invite everyone to stay the night and have a barbecue lunch tomorrow. Continue the party all weekend!"

"Excellent idea," said Vid. He knew she was joking but he was wondering if this was a possibility.

He kissed her and stuck in his tongue just to make her say, "*Vid!*" except she gave back as good as she got. She liked to surprise him. "Jesus, get a room," said his cousin, walking into the kitchen and straight out again.

Tiffany raised an eyebrow and sashayed off with an exaggerated swing of the hips just for him.

There was something else making Vid happy. To do with Tiffany. What was it? Was his mind losing its edge? No! His mind was a steel trap. Of course. That little matter of the dickhead. It was all under control. Yesterday she'd come home from Dakota's new school and said that she'd run into the wife of that old client of hers and they weren't coming to Saint Anastasias after all.

This was good because he knew she'd slept with that dickhead.

He knew it because of her left nostril.

Vid played poker once a month with a group of friends. His friend Raymond had told him years ago how poker players tried to work out each other's "tells": the little giveaways that showed when they were bluffing. Raymond said, "You, my friend, have about a dozen tells. You blink, you wink, you twitch, you virtually have a seizure, you are the worst bluffer in the world."

Vid did okay at poker, though, because he might have been the worst bluffer in the world but he had the best luck. He drew great hands. He'd always been lucky. He had great luck in business, he had many, many good friends, he'd married two gorgeous women, even if the first one had turned out to be a crazy-in-the-head bitch who'd tried to turn his daughters against him, but that was okay, because he'd got even luckier with his second wife. Walking Viagra and he loved her like crazy.

Tiffany was a great poker player. Not as lucky as him, but she could do a beautiful "poker face." It worked on him for years but then one day he broke her code.

Tiffany had a show. Her left nostril. Whenever she lied or bluffed, her left nostril quivered. Just once. A teeny-tiny movement. Like a butterfly wing.

Vid had confirmed it by studying his wife on those occasions when he knew for a fact she wasn't telling the truth. For example, when she answered Dakota's questions about Santa Claus, or when she told her sisters that she was flying economy, when really she'd booked business-class tickets. Her sisters had some strange problem with flying business class, as if it were somehow sinful.

It was conclusive. The nostril never lied. He never told Tiffany, of course, because it was very handy, his secret superpower to see straight through her poker face. (Sadly, she did not at all like the red lingerie he'd bought her for Christmas.)

So when he asked his wife, "Did you sleep with him?" all he had to do was watch her nostril, and there was the answer.

She said no but the answer was yes. Yes, she'd slept with him.

It was fine! It was no problem!

It was maybe a slight problem. Say Vid had been at a school concert and he'd seen this dickhead looking at his wife in a disrespectful way, he might have been tempted to hit him. Assault and battery that would be.

Or say he and this dickhead had ended up cooking at a sausage sizzle together (there were always sausage sizzles, even when you paid a million bucks in school fees) and the dickhead made some remark about Tiffany. It might even be an *innocent* remark, but say Vid *took it the wrong way*, because of what he knew, and say he went home and the thought got trapped in Vid's head, like thoughts sometimes did, and say, in a moment of madness, he got on the phone to his friend Ivan and arranged to have the dickhead's knees broken.

Ivan was always going on about how if Vid ever needed someone's knees broken, then Ivan was his man. Tiffany said Ivan was joking. Ivan was not joking.

But! All was good because the dickhead was safely on his way to Dubai, with his knees intact. Vid would therefore not end up in jail. He'd never knowingly broken the law, but he *could*. The potential was there: maybe not to kill, but certainly to maim, and he did not want to go to jail. The food. The *clothes*. Vid shuddered at the thought.

And for now, Vid was not in danger of breaking the law. It was lucky he was so lucky. That's why he felt happy. And Dakota's reputation at the school was safe. She could be school captain if she wanted. He was sure those people would love Dubai. Interesting place! He'd read an article just the other day about the Dubai Food Festival. They had something called "The Big Grill." It sounded amazing!

"Why do you look so happy?" said Dakota. "And goofy?"

Vid regarded his daughter, who was now in the kitchen returning an empty tray. She dimpled up at him and she looked, at that moment, extremely pretty. Hail Mary, Mother of God, please don't let her grow up as sexy as her mother.

"Because I'm happy, you know," said Vid. He lifted Dakota up under her armpits and spun her around. He couldn't spin his older daughters anymore. (Eva looked like she weighed as much as a small truck.) "Are you happy?"

"Pretty much," said Dakota. She put her mouth to his ear. "How many more minutes before I can go read my book in my room for just a little while?"

"Thirty," said Vid.

"Ten," said Dakota.

"Twenty," said Vid. "Final offer."

"Deal." Dakota held out her hand.

They shook on it. He put her back on the floor. The volume of the music at the front of the house shot up to nightclub level. Someone called out "*Whoa!*" in a scandalized tone that could only mean that Tiffany was dancing, while someone else shouted, "Where's Vid?"

"Here I come!" bellowed Vid.

It was lucky that Harry from next door was resting in peace.

76

Clementine woke to a glorious absence of sound.

All she could hear was silence, and then the familiar bubbling melody of a kookaburra's laugh. It pierced her heart, as if she'd been away from Australia for a long time and was finally home. She opened her eyes and the light felt clean and bright and imbued with significance.

"It's stopped," she said out loud to Sam. "It's finally stopped." She hadn't let herself believe the weather forecaster's promise of sunshine by Sunday. She went to wake Sam, to shake his arm, but then she saw his empty side of the bed and remembered that he wasn't there. He was asleep, as usual these days, in the study, and she felt humiliated that she'd spoken out loud. His absence this hopeful, happy morning felt freshly painful, as if it were new.

She sighed and turned over on her stomach, lifting the corner of the curtain to look at the newly minted blue sky.

They would take the kids out in the sun . . . but wait, no, they couldn't, because today she and Sam were booked in to do a first aid course at the local high school. They'd rescheduled it a few times already and she was determined they do it today. She couldn't keep on traipsing across Sydney doing those talks, solemnly telling people about the importance of first aid training, like she was some sort of school prefect for the world, handing out her little leaflets, when she'd never done one herself.

Sam's parents were going to look after the girls for the day. "It might actually be quite fun and stimulating to learn something new together!" Sam's mother had said hopefully. There was a suspicious Pam-like flavor to Joy's tone. The mothers were circling. Clementine suspected her mother had been on the phone to Sam's mother, worrying over the state of their marriage.

It was interesting how a marriage instantly became public property as soon as it looked shaky.

She looked at the clock and saw that she'd slept later than normal. It was past six but that was fine. She could fit in a solid two hours of practice before the girls woke. The audition was only a week away now. This was the home stretch. You had to time it right, like an athlete, so that you peaked on audition day. She put on her old shapeless blue cardigan over her pajamas (for some reason, the cardigan had become her practice cardigan) and went quietly downstairs. The absence of the sound of rain opened up a soaring sense of space around her, as if she'd gone from a tiny warm-up room into a concert hall. She hadn't realized how oppressive that background noise had been.

As she rosined up her bow and the dust-flecked early-morning sun created tiny glints of jewel-like light around the room, on the glass of their grandfather clock, on a picture fame, a vase, she felt a deep sense of peace about her progress. The strange thought occurred to her that she wasn't *resisting* this audition, as she had so often in the past. She wasn't wasting precious energy bemoaning the injustice of the system: the oversupply of qualified musicians on the audition circuit, the fact that auditioning was a skill entirely separate from someone's playing ability. Ruby's accident had somehow stripped her clean of what now seemed like a sort of petulant pride, of fear masquerading as outrage.

"Good morning." Sam stood at the doorway.

"Good morning." She lowered her bow. "You're up early."

"The rain has stopped," he said glumly. He yawned hugely. He looked so pale and haggard in the sunlight. She wanted to hug him and at the same time she kind of wanted to slap him. "I might take the girls to the park, so you can practice."

"We're doing that first aid course today," said Clementine. "Remember?"

"I might give that a miss," he said. Each word was a sigh, as if it were an effort just to speak. "I'll stay home with the girls. I'll do it another time. I'm not . . . feeling great."

"You're fine. You're doing it," said Clementine, as if he were one of the children. "The girls are excited about spending the day with your parents. They have plans."

He made a sound, an exhausted exhalation, like an elderly person seeing yet another flight of stairs to climb. "Fine. Whatever." He turned around and slouched off. It was like being married to an octogenarian who spoke like a teenager.

"It starts at ten!" she called out after him briskly. She felt so brisk today, she was the very *essence* of brisk, and if he didn't pull himself together soon she was going to briskly tell him that he wasn't the only one capable of throwing around dramatic, hurtful words like "separate."

77

D oesn't that look pretty," said Oliver.

"What?" said Erika. They were standing in her mother's disgusting, squelchy front yard; it seemed unlikely that there would be anything pretty to look at. She followed his gaze to her mother's liquidambar, where tiny glistening raindrops quivered on each leaf in the sunlight.

"Look at them sparkle. Like tiny diamonds!" said Oliver.

"You're in a poetic mood," said Erika. It must be because they'd had sex last night for the first time in a week.

Her eyes returned back to her mother's *stuff.* Now that the sun was out, everything looked even more depressing than it had the day she'd been here in the rain. She kicked at an unopened, soft, sagging cardboard box with an Amazon label, and the puddle of dirty water on top sloshed onto her foot. A leaf clung to her shoe and she tried to kick it off.

"What are you doing, darling? Line dancing?"

Erika's mother appeared in the front yard wearing a red-and-white polka-dotted scarf tied over her head and blue denim overalls, like a 1950s housewife ready to start spring cleaning. She stuck her thumbs into the pockets of her (brand-new-looking) overalls and kicked one leg behind the other and then out to the side while humming some twangy song.

"You're quite good at that, Sylvia," said Oliver.

"Thank you," said Sylvia. "I have a line dancing DVD somewhere if you'd like to borrow it."

"I'm sure you could put your hands on it quite easily," said Erika.

Sylvia gave a pretty little shrug. "It's no trouble." She looked around the front yard and sighed. "Goodness. What a mess. That rain was quite extraordinary, wasn't it? We've got quite a task ahead of us."

Today's choice of delusion was that Sylvia's front yard looked like this because of the *rain*.

"Well, we're not alone," said Sylvia with a brave tilt of her chin. "People across the state are out there today, mucking in, cleaning up."

"Mum," said Erika. "Those people had their houses flooded. This isn't because of a flood of rain. It's a flood of crap."

"I was watching TV this morning," continued Sylvia obliviously, "and it was so inspiring! Neighbors helping neighbors. I had tears in my eyes."

"Oh, for God's sake," said Erika.

Oliver put his hand on Erika's shoulder. "The things we cannot change," he murmured.

He was quoting the serenity prayer to her. Oliver went to Al-Anon meetings, for families of alcoholics. Erika didn't want to learn serenity.

"What's that, Oliver?" said Sylvia. "How *are* your lovely parents, by the way? Were they affected by the rain?" She was as sharp as a tack, that woman. "I haven't seen them in a while. We must all get together and have a drink."

"Mum," said Erika.

"We should," said Oliver. "Although, as you know very well, with my parents, it's more likely to be ten or twenty drinks."

"Ah, they're good fun," said Sylvia fondly.

"Yup," said Oliver. "They are that. Oh look, here comes our skip bin."

"Great. What can I do?" said Sylvia as the truck pulled into the driveway and slowly lowered the massive bin.

"Stay out of our way," said Erika.

"Yes, although you'll need me to make sure you don't accidentally throw out anything important," said Sylvia. "Do you know what I found the other day, caught up in a box of old papers? The funniest little photo of you, me and Clementine!"

"That seems unlikely," said Erika.

"What do you mean it seems unlikely? Wait till you see it! I *guarantee* you will laugh. Now just imagine if we'd thrown away that precious memory! You and Clementine must have been about twelve, I think. Clementine looks so young and pretty in it. She seemed kind of worn out the other night, to be frank, not aging well. You should take a look at it, Oliver. See what your future daughter might look like!"

Oliver's face closed down. "That's not happening now."

"What? Did she pull out on you? After *you saved her child's life?*"

"We pulled out," said Erika. "Not her. Us. We changed our mind."

"Oh," said Sylvia. "But why? That's terrible news. I'm crushed!" Erika watched in amazement as her mother conveniently forgot everything she'd said on Thursday night and made herself the victim. "You let me get my hopes up! I thought I was going to be a grandma. I was looking at those pretty little girls at Pam's place and thinking how nice it would be to have a grandchild of my own. I was thinking I could teach her how to sew, like my grandmother taught me."

"Teach her how to sew?!" spluttered Erika. "You never taught *me* how to sew!"

"You probably never asked," said Sylvia.

"I've never seen you with a needle and thread in my life."

"I'll just go pay the driver for the skip," said Oliver.

"I'll go inside and see if I can find that funny little photo," said Sylvia quickly, just in case, God forbid, anyone would expect her to pay for anything.

Erika took the opportunity to snap on some plastic gloves, bend at the knees and pick up a broken laundry basket filled with miscellaneous junk: a headless doll, a sodden beach towel, a pizza box. She carried it to the skip bin and chucked it in, hard, like a grenade. It landed with a bang against the metal. Throwing stuff out always gave her a wild, terrified feeling, as if she were running into battle screaming a war cry.

"Jeez, you've got a job ahead of you," said the skip bin guy as he folded up the yellow form Oliver had handed him and stuffed it in his back pocket. He crossed his arms across his barrel chest and studied the front yard with an expression of pure disgust.

"Want to lend a hand?" said Oliver.

"Ha ha! Nah, you're on your own there, mate. Better you than me!" He kept standing there, shaking his head, as if he were there to supervise.

"Well, on your bike then," said Erika irritably, and she heard Oliver stifle a laugh as she turned away to pick up the old Christmas tree. A Christmas tree, of all things. She couldn't remember ever having a Christmas tree growing up, and yet here was an old, mangled one with a single sad strand of gold tinsel.

The driver roared off in his truck, and Erika threw the Christmas tree in the bin while Oliver picked up a broken pedestal fan in one hand and a bag of rubbish in the other.

Her mother came out the front door triumphantly holding a tiny photo between her thumb and finger. A miracle that she'd found something.

"Look at this photo!" she said to Erika. "I guarantee it will make you laugh."

"I guarantee it won't," said Erika sourly.

Her mother leaned over and removed a tiny piece of gold tinsel from Erika's shirt. "Yes, it will. Look."

Erika took the picture. She burst out laughing. Her mother danced around, hugging herself with delight. "I told you, I told you!"

It was a grainy black-and-white picture of herself, her mother and Clementine sitting together on a roller coaster. It had been taken by one of those automatic cameras timed to capture passengers' reactions at the most terrifying moment of the roller-coaster ride. All three of them had oval-shaped mouths frozen forever mid-scream. Erika was leaning forward both hands clutching the safety bar, as if she were pushing it to go faster even as she threw her head back. Clementine had her eyes squeezed shut and her ponytail flew in a vertical line above her head like the pope's hat. Sylvia had her eyes wide open and both arms flung up in the air like a drunk girl dancing. Terrified, hilarious joy. That's what you saw in that photo. It didn't matter if it was accurate, you couldn't look at it without laughing. She and Clementine were wearing their checked school uniforms.

"See! Aren't you glad I kept it!" said Sylvia. "Show it to Clementine. See if she remembers that day! I must admit I don't actually remember that day *specifically*, but you can see how happy we were! Don't you pretend you had a terrible childhood, you had a wonderful childhood! All those roller coasters, remember? My goodness, I loved roller coasters. You did too."

Her eye was caught by something. "Oliver, what have you got there? Let

me just check that!" Oliver, who had both arms wrapped around a disintegrating cardboard box, hurried off to the skip bin, with Sylvia running
behind him calling out, "Oliver! Oh, *Oliver!*"

This was life with Sylvia: absurd, grotesque, infuriating and sometimes,
every now and then, wonderful. They were meant to be at school that day.
It was late November, summer in the air. It was Erika's twelfth birthday—
no, it was a week *after* Erika's twelfth birthday—her mother had forgotten
the actual birthday, Sylvia had difficulties with dates, but this time she'd
decided to redeem herself with a spontaneous, crazy gesture. She'd turned
up at school and taken both girls out of class for a trip to Luna Park, *without*,
by the way, Clementine's parents' permission or knowledge; it would never
happen today, and Erika was horrified now on the school's behalf. The legal
ramifications were mind-boggling.

Clementine wasn't allowed to go on a roller coaster because her mother
had a phobia about them. She had been deeply affected by the story of a
fairground ride accident in which eight people had died at a country fair,
years before Clementine and Erika were born. "They don't maintain those
machines," Pam always said. "They are *death traps*. They are accidents waiting to happen."

But Erika and Sylvia loved roller coasters, the scarier the better. No decisions, no control, no discussion: just the rush of air into your lungs and
the piercing sound of your own screams before they are snatched away by
the wind. It was one of the very few, strange, random things they had in
common: an enjoyment of scary roller-coaster rides. Not that they went on
them all that often. Erika could remember only a handful of occasions, and
this was one of them.

Erika knew Clementine had loved that day too. She had been in one of
her hectically happy moods. It was a day where Erika didn't second-guess
herself or their friendship. There had been days like those, days where her
mother was her mother and her friend was her friend.

She slid the photo into the back pocket of her jeans and watched as
Sylvia leaned so far into the skip bin to rescue something that she nearly
toppled in. She got herself back upright, adjusted her checked headscarf and
faced Oliver, hands on her hips.

"Oliver! There's nothing wrong with that fan!" she cried. "You retrieve
that for me please!"

"No can do, Sylvia," said Oliver.

Erika turned away to hide her smile. She studied the sunlight shining on the rain-speckled tree. It actually did look pretty. Like a Christmas tree.

She tipped her head back, enjoying the sun on her face, and saw the lady who lived across the road, the one who loved Jesus, but sure didn't love Sylvia. She was standing at her upstairs window, one hand on the glass as if she were cleaning it. The lady seemed to be looking straight back at Erika.

And just like that it happened: Erika remembered everything.

78

The Day of the Barbecue

Erika stood at the entrance to the backyard clutching the stack of blue china plates Vid had handed her in the kitchen. They were beautiful solid plates with intricate, patterned designs. "Willow pattern," thought Erika. She remembered that her grandmother had once had plates exactly like these. Her grandmother used to have a lot of beautiful things and Erika had no idea what had happened to any of them. They were probably lost somewhere, or broken, buried beneath the sedimentary layers of crap in her mother's house.

That was the irony: Her mother loved things so much that she had nothing.

Erika gripped the plates tighter, filled with an overwhelming desire to keep them. She imagined hugging the plates to her chest and running next door to hide them away in her own kitchen cupboard. She would not do this. Of course she would not do it. For a moment she was terrified she would do it.

She stood without moving for a moment. When she was little she used to like going into her backyard and turning round and round in circles until the world spun. That's exactly how she felt now. Why had she deliberately done that? It wasn't a nice feeling. She must be drunk. Why would Oliver's parents *choose* this feeling? Plan for it? Long for it? It was awful.

She focused on the little girls. Ruby toddled out of the gazebo holding Whisk in one hand and Holly's little blue sequined bag in the other. Holly wouldn't like that. No one was allowed to touch her rock collection. Where was Holly?

Sure enough, Holly suddenly appeared behind Ruby, shouting something Erika couldn't hear over the sound of classical music pouring again from Vid's sound system. Ruby looked over her shoulder and quickened her pace, her wings bobbing behind her. It was so cute. She looked determined to escape with her contraband.

Careful, thought Erika. Are your parents even watching you?

She looked over at the adults. Oliver was nowhere to be seen. Clementine was talking to Vid. Tiffany was talking to Sam. The four of them were just totally thrilled by each other. She and Oliver might as well not be there. They were spoiling the fun. Neither Sam nor Clementine was watching the girls right now. It was neglectful, negligent.

She watched Vid pick up a knife and pretend to conduct along to the music. She saw Clementine laugh merrily. What had she said exactly, earlier, upstairs? What was that word she'd used? "Repulsive." The idea of donating her eggs to Erika was *repulsive*. All that time she and Oliver had spent discussing it. She thought of Oliver telling their IVF doctor, "We're going to approach Erika's best friend. They're like sisters."

Like sisters. What a joke. What a lie.

Erika watched Clementine pull her hair over her shoulder as Vid fed her a spoonful of something and she leaned forward to take it. Clementine was like that princess in the fairy tale who received all those gifts from her fairy godmothers at her christening. You shall have parents who adore you! *Ding!* You shall have musical talent! *Ding!* You shall live in cleanliness and comfort! *Ding!* You shall fall pregnant naturally as soon as you feel like it and go on to give birth to two beautiful daughters! *Ding, ding!!*

One old fairy got left off the invitation list. The uninvited crone. Erika hadn't been invited to a lot of parties when she was a kid. What did the uninvited fairy do? She laid a curse of some sort. You shall prick your finger on a spinning wheel and die, so watch out for needles. But then a nice fairy stepped in and modified it. You'll just fall asleep for a hundred years. That's not too bad. Wait. It was *Sleeping Beauty*. The fairy tale was *Sleeping Beauty*!

She was really very drunk. She should move from this spot, but she didn't move.

Sleeping Beauty. Clementine did like her sleep. Sleeping bloody Beauty, that's exactly right. You're asleep right now. You're not even bothering to watch your children.

There was a sound. From somewhere. A sound trying to slide beneath the classical music pouring and tumbling from Vid's sound system.

Is Clementine performing? Of course she's not performing, Erika, you're in the neighbor's backyard, you're drunk, this is drunkenness, your brain has turned to water and your thoughts are slipping and sloshing all over the place.

She heard it again.

It was knocking. That was the sound. A rapid knock, knock, knocking. She saw her mother's face. Finger to her lips. Don't answer the door. Yes, Mum, I know what I need to do. Not make a sound. We never, ever answer the door. We don't want people to see our filthy secret. It's none of their business. How dare they knock on our door uninvited?! No courtesy. They have no right to make us feel like this. We stay very quiet and very still until they go away. Some people knock in a loud, angry, accusing way, as if they know they are being tricked and they're angry about it, but eventually they give up and go away.

Sure enough, the knocking got louder and angrier. Her mother's eyes burned with hatred. They have no right. No right.

Erika shook herself. There was no one knocking on her front door. She was at a barbecue. Where were the little girls? She saw a flash of blue in the corner of the yard. Holly sat cross-legged on the grass with her bag, carefully taking out her rocks and laying them on the ground one by one. She liked to catalog her collection at intervals.

There was a burst of laughter from the table.

Still that knocking sound. Where was it coming from?

Erika looked at the ridiculous fountain. She could see *rubbish* floating in the fountain. Someone's old coat spinning in a slow circle.

Her mother had piles and piles of coats. Big winter coats. As if they lived in Siberia, not Sydney. Well, she wasn't going to pull that coat out of the fountain. It was not her responsibility. She'd had enough of cleaning up.

Knock, knock, knock. How dare you knock on our door in that entitled way? It was coming from somewhere above her. She looked up and there was

Harry, grumpy old Harry, standing at his upstairs window as though he were pressed against it, not knocking but banging on the glass, like he was trying to escape. He saw her looking. He pointed. He jabbed his finger violently in the direction of the fountain. His mouth gaped in a silent shout. She could tell from the stance of his body and his gestures that he was angry with her. He was yelling something at her. He wanted her to clean up that rubbish. The neighbors were always angry. They always wanted her to clean up the rubbish. She wouldn't. It was not her responsibility.

She stared at the fountain, at the old pink coat turning in slow circles.

She saw Whisk lying on the side of the fountain.

That wasn't an old coat. That wasn't rubbish.

The adrenaline was like a shot to her heart. All the things she'd stolen from Clementine, but she'd never meant to do this. Her fault, her fault, her fault.

The plates fell from her hands. She screamed Clementine's name.

79

The first aid course was held at the local high school which their girls would presumably one day attend, although the thought of a time when they were old enough to go to high school felt like science fiction. Their teacher was a large, cheerful, mildly condescending woman called Jan, who reminded Clementine of an insufferable flautist she used to see each year at music camp.

Jan began the day by going around the room and asking everyone to say their name and reason for being there and, "as a fun little icebreaker exercise!" to answer the question: "If you were a vegetable, what vegetable would you be?"

They started with a muscly young personal trainer called Dale, who was there because he needed first aid training for his "PT license," and who would be a baby kale if given the choice because it was a powerhouse vegetable—at this point, he flexed an impressive biceps—and he had a baby face. "*Excellent* answer!" said Jan, looking momentarily overcome by Dale's biceps, which made Clementine feel fondly toward her.

Next was a squat middle-aged woman who was there because there had been a fatal accident at the office where she worked. A tradesman got electrocuted and the woman had never felt so useless or helpless in her life and she didn't want to ever feel that way again, even though she didn't believe it would have made a difference to the poor tradesman. "If I was a vegetable, I'd be a potato," said the woman, "obviously," and she indicated her body, and everyone laughed loudly and then stopped abruptly in case they weren't meant to laugh.

Sam was next, and he spoke up confidently and clearly, sitting casually back in his chair, his legs stretched out in front of him. He said that he and his wife—he indicated Clementine—were doing the course because they had small children. Clementine looked at him. She would have told the truth. She would have said that their daughter had nearly drowned. She was always ready to share the story, but even when they were with Ruby at the hospital Sam had avoided telling people why they were there, as if it was a deeply shameful secret. "I'd be an onion," said Sam. "Because I'm very complex. I have *layers*." That got a good laugh too, and Clementine realized that Sam did this sort of thing all the time—training workshops, team-building days—this was his jokey, blokey corporate persona. He probably always chose the onion.

When it was her turn she didn't bother saying why she was there, as Sam had covered it. She said that she'd be a tomato, because it went so well with onion, and Sam smiled, but warily, as if she were a stranger trying to come on to him, and she was reminded of the humiliation of waking up that morning and talking to him when he wasn't there.

"Aww," said everyone, except for the person behind Clementine, who said, "A tomato is a fruit."

"It's a vegetable today," said Jan crisply, and Clementine decided she was nothing like the flautist.

Once they'd gone around the class, Jan said that if she were a vegetable, she'd be an avocado because she took a while to soften up ("An avocado is a *fruit*," sighed the fruit expert behind Clementine), and she was there today because "first aid was her passion," which made Clementine feel teary. How wonderful it was that there were people in the world like Jan with a "passion" for helping strangers.

Then they got down to business, and Clementine and Sam both diligently took notes as Jan took them through the "basic life support" procedure, interspersed with stories from Jan's own first aid experience, like the

time she'd run a course and found herself in the middle of a real-life scenario when one of the participants collapsed in class. "Did you use it as a
demonstration?" asked someone. "No, I had to clear the room," said Jan.
"People started dropping like *flies*. Down they went like dominoes: bang,
bang, bang." She said this with relish, to indicate the weakness of the general
population. "That's why you've got to give everyone a job—go call the ambulance, get me some ice—or send them away, because otherwise people go
into shock. It's a traumatic event. You can suffer from post-traumatic stress.
We'll talk about that later."

Clementine glanced over at Sam to see if he was remembering their own
"traumatic event," but his face was impassive. He wrote something down in
his notepad.

Jan got Dale the muscly personal trainer to lie on the floor and then
picked two attractive young girls (carrot and cauliflower) to have a go at
putting Dale into the recovery position, which they did, and because they
were three attractive young people, it was kind of enjoyable to watch, and
when they rolled Dale over, you could see his underwear riding up under
his shorts and Jan said, "Nice to see you're wearing Calvin Klein today."

It was all good fun. It was interesting and informative, and Sam
asked intelligent questions and made the occasional well-timed joke. That's
why it was so unexpected when it happened.

Clementine had to breathe hard when Jan demonstrated CPR on a
bright blue plastic dummy of a head and torso. The rocking motion of Jan's
hands, pushing so forcefully and rapidly, brought it all back: the hard pavers
beneath her knees, Ruby's waxen cheeks and blue lips, the fairy lights wink-
ing in her peripheral vision. But she breathed through it, and when she
looked at Sam, he seemed fine.

Then Jan asked everyone to get into pairs and she gave each pair one
blue dummy and two disposable resuscitation face shields. (Jan always had
a spare disposable face shield on her key ring: that's how prepared she was
to offer her services.) They had to find a free spot on the floor where they
could lay the dummy out flat.

Jan wandered around the room checking on everyone's progress.

"Do you want to go first?" said Clementine to Sam. They were both on
their knees on either side of the dummy.

"Sure," said Sam, and he seemed fine as he methodically worked his way through the acronym Jan had just taught them: DRS ABCD, standing for Danger, Response, Send for help, Airway, Breathing, CPR and Defibrillator.

He cleared the airway, he looked, listened and felt for breathing, he commenced CPR, his locked hands pressing rhythmically on the dummy's chest, and as he did, his eyes met Clementine's and she saw a bead of sweat roll down the side of his face.

"Sam? Are you all right?" said Clementine.

He shook his head, a tiny no, but he didn't stop doing CPR compressions. His face was dead white. His eyes were bloodshot.

She didn't know what to do. "Are you . . . having chest pains?" At least they were in the right place. Jan seemed just as competent as any doctor or paramedic, and certainly more passionate.

He shook his head again.

He bent his head, pinched the dummy's nostrils and gave it two breaths. The dummy's chest rose to show that he'd done it correctly. He lifted his head and recommenced compressions and Clementine saw, with a kick-in-the-stomach sense of shock, that tears were sliding down his face and dripping onto the dummy. She'd never seen her husband cry, properly cry, not on their wedding day, not when the children were born, not when Ruby was not breathing, not when she woke up the next day. And she'd never questioned it, because she'd never seen her father cry either, and her older brothers weren't criers, they were door-slammers and wall-hitters during their angry-young-man years. Her mother got teary at times, but Clementine was the family's only true crier; she was always in floods of tears over something. Maybe all those staunch, stoic men around her had resulted in her internalizing that ancient cliché: boys don't cry, because it was absolutely astonishing to Clementine that Sam could cry like that, that his body was even capable of doing that, of producing that many tears. As she watched his tears drip onto the dummy, she felt something break inside her and a great welling of sympathy rise within her chest, and the terrible thought occurred to her that perhaps she'd always unconsciously believed that because Sam didn't cry, he therefore didn't feel, or he felt less, not as profoundly and deeply as she did. Her focus had always been on how his actions affected her feelings, as if his role was to do things *for her, to her,* and all that mattered was her emotional response to him, as if a "man" were a product or a service, and she'd finally chosen the right brand to get the right response.

Was it possible she'd never seen or truly loved him the way he deserved to be seen and loved? As a person? An ordinary, flawed, feeling person?

"Oh, *Sam.*"

He stood up so fast from his kneeling position that he nearly toppled backwards. He averted his face, rubbing his cheek hard with the heel of one hand, as if something had stung him. He turned and left the room.

80

S orry," said Clementine to the teacher. "I'll just go check on my husband. I think he's not feeling well."

"Of course," said Jan. She added, hopefully, "Let me know if you need me."

Clementine left the classroom and looked to the left. He was already nearly at the far end of the corridor. "Sam!" she called, half-running past classrooms filled with adults bettering themselves.

He seemed to pick up his pace.

"Sam!" she called again. "*Wait!*"

She followed him to a quiet, deserted passageway with a glass ceiling that connected two buildings. The walls were jammed with gray lockers. Sam suddenly stopped. He found a narrow column of space in between two blocks of lockers, the sort of hidey-hole the girls would gravitate toward, and he sat down, his back against the wall. He rested his forehead on his knees. His shoulders heaved silently. There was a round patch of sweat on his shirt. She went to touch his shoulder, but her hand hovered uncertainly for a few seconds before she changed her mind.

Instead she sat down opposite him, on the other side of the passageway, her back against the cool metal of a locker. There were squares of sunlight all the way along the corridor, like a train of sunshine. She felt strangely peaceful as she waited for Sam to stop crying, breathing in the nostalgic fragrance of high school.

At last Sam looked up, his face wet and puffy. "Sorry," he said. "Well, that was dignified."

"Are you all right?" she said.

"It was the compressions," said Sam. He ran the back of his hand across his nose and sniffed.

"I know," said Clementine.

"It felt like I was there." He used his palms to rub his cheekbones in a circular motion.

"I know," she said again.

He looked up at the ceiling and did something with his tongue as if he were trying to get food out of his teeth. The sunlight shone on the wall behind him and made his eyes look very blue in the shadowiness of his face. He looked simultaneously very young and very old, as if all the past and future versions of himself were overlaid on his face.

"I always had this idea in my head that I was good in a crisis," said Sam.

"You are good in a crisis."

"I thought if I was ever tested, if there was a fire, or a gunman or a zombie apocalypse, I'd take care of my family. I'd be the *man*." He made his voice deep and contemptuous on the word "man."

"Sam—"

"It wasn't just that I took my eyes off Ruby. It wasn't just that I was trying to open a jar of nuts to impress a bloody *stripper*, of all things, while my little girl drowned right next to me . . ." He took a deep, shaky breath. "But I didn't move. I watched another man drag my little girl from that god-awful fountain and I just stood there, like a stunned mullet."

"You did move," said Clementine. "It's just that they got there first, and they knew what they were doing. It was only a split second. It just feels like longer. And then you *did* move, I promise you, you did."

Sam lifted his shoulders. An expression of complete self-loathing crossed his face. "Anyway. I can't change what I did or didn't do. I've just got to stop thinking about it. I've got to get it out of my head. I keep replaying it, over and over and over. It's stupid, pointless. I can't work and I can't sleep, and I'm taking it out on you, and . . . I just need to pull myself together."

"Maybe," said Clementine tentatively, "you could, or we could, talk to someone. Like a professional sort of person?"

"Like a shrink," said Sam with a strained smile. "Because I'm losing my mind."

"Like a shrink," said Clementine. "Because it sounds like you are losing your mind. Just a little bit. I was thinking when the teacher mentioned post-traumatic stress earlier—"

Sam looked appalled. "Post-traumatic stress," he said. "Like a war veteran. Except I didn't come back from Iraq or Afghanistan where I saw people get blown up, no, I've just come back from a backyard barbecue."

"Where you saw your daughter nearly drown," said Clementine.

Sam closed his eyes.

"Your daughter nearly drowned," said Clementine again. "And you feel responsible."

Sam raised his eyes to the ceiling and exhaled. "I don't have post-traumatic stress syndrome, Clementine. Jesus. That's humiliating. That's pathetic."

Clementine took her phone out of her jacket pocket.

"Don't Google," pleaded Sam. "Trust me. You're always telling me to stop Googling. It never tells you anything good."

"I am *so* Googling," said Clementine, and she felt her breath quicken, because she was suddenly seeing all his behavior ever since the barbecue from a different angle, through a new lens, and she thought of her father saying the other night, "He isn't quite right in the head," and how she hadn't listened, not really, not the way you'd listen if somebody had said, "Your husband is sick."

"'Symptoms of post-traumatic stress syndrome,'" Clementine read out loud. "'Replaying of the event over and over.' You just said you do that!"

"I'm glad you're so happy about it," said Sam with a ghost of a smile.

"Sam, you're like a textbook case! Insomnia. *Yes.* Irritability. *Yes.* Solution? 'Seek treatment.'" She was speaking facetiously, ironically, kind of idiotically, as if all this were a great joke, as if none of it really mattered, as if her stomach wasn't twisting, as if she didn't feel that this was her only shot, because lately his mood could change in an instant, and in another hour he might refuse to talk about this at all, and he'd be gone again.

"Look. I don't need to 'seek treatment,'" began Sam.

"Yes, you do," said Clementine, her eyes on the phone. "Long-term effects: Divorce. Substance abuse. Are you abusing substances?"

"I'm not abusing substances," said Sam. "Stop reading that stuff. Put your phone away. Let's go back to class."

"I really think you need to talk to someone, to a professional someone," said Clementine. She'd turned into her mother. Next thing she'd be suggesting "a lovely psychologist." "Will you please talk to someone?"

Sam tipped his head back and studied the ceiling again. Finally he looked back at her.

"I might," he said.

"Good," said Clementine.

She rested her head against the locker and closed her eyes. She felt a sense of inevitability, as if her marriage were a giant ship and it was too late to change its course now—it was either going to hit the iceberg or not, and nothing she said or did right now would make any difference. If her mother had been observing this interaction, she'd tell Clementine she was wrong, that she needed to keep talking, to say everything that was on her mind, to *communicate*, to leave no possibility for misinterpretation.

If her father were here, he'd put his finger to his lips and say, "Shh."

Clementine settled for two words.

"I'm sorry," she said.

She meant, I'm sorry this happened. I'm sorry I didn't see you were going through this. I'm sorry I maybe haven't loved you the way you deserve to be loved. I'm sorry that when we faced our first crisis it showed up everything that was wrong in our marriage instead of everything that was right. I'm sorry we turned on each other instead of to each other.

"Yeah, I'm sorry too," said Sam.

81

"So in effect, Harry saved Ruby's life," said Oliver.

Erika and Oliver were walking around the block near her mother's house. The moment she remembered what had happened, she'd wanted to share it with Oliver and she certainly didn't want Sylvia overhear, so she'd insisted Oliver go for a walk with her.

"Yes," said Erika. "And no one ever thanked him. I don't think I even looked up again at his window." They walked by a young husband and wife pushing a baby in a stroller, and Erika shot them a dismissive flick of a smile to let them know there was really no need to comment upon the weather and how great it was that the rain had finally stopped.

"He would have seen that we got her out," said Oliver.

"I hope so," said Erika. "But no one ever told him that Ruby was okay. No one ever went over and said thank you. He must have thought that was pretty rude. He always thought everyone had such bad manners and he would have died thinking that was pretty much conclusive."

"I guess he could have come over and asked us," said Oliver. "If he was worried."

They both jumped over a glistening brown puddle that took up most of the footpath.

"It took me a while to work out that it was Ruby," said Erika. Her mouth felt momentarily full of marbles. "I thought it was an old coat floating in the fountain, and I was just staring at it. I had this illogical, weird idea that Harry wanted me to clean up the fountain. Ruby was drowning while I stared right at her."

Oliver said nothing for a moment before he spoke. "I always felt bad that when it happened I was hiding out in the bathroom, just looking at myself in the mirror," he said. "I think we've all got something to feel bad about that afternoon."

"Except for Harry," said Erika.

"Except for Harry," agreed Oliver.

A middle-aged woman in unflattering "active wear" came bouncing past. "Isn't it lovely to see the sun again!" she said rapturously, and she slowed down as if she wanted to discuss the sun further.

"It's fantastic!" agreed Oliver, he and Erika both upping their pace by unspoken agreement. "Have a nice day!"

"Do you think I should tell someone?" said Erika. "About what I remembered?" Now that she had the facts straight in her head, she felt an overwhelming desire to set the record straight, to submit an amended report to the authorities.

"Well. I don't see who you would tell," said Oliver. "Or how it would help."

"I could tell Clementine," said Erika, although she had absolutely no intention of doing that.

"No," said Oliver. "You can't tell Clementine. You know you can't." They had completed the block now and were coming back toward her mother's house.

"Oh, for goodness' sake," sighed Erika.

"What?" said Oliver.

"She's actually *in* the skip bin now."

82

It had stopped raining. Finally! At last! Dakota could hardly believe it. Everything about her whole life and the whole world felt entirely different.

"This is going to be so much fun," said Dakota's mum as they opened the front door and stepped outside onto the front veranda.

"I don't see why we can't *drive* there," said Dakota's dad for about the millionth time. "Why do we have to walk through the streets to get there? Like homeless people."

"Because we're so lucky to have a beautiful walk less than ten minutes away from our front door!" said her mum. She was holding Barney's leash while Barney jumped about snapping at the air, trying to catch an invisible fly.

Her mum was "practicing gratitude" lately. (Her dad said she would get over it soon, hopefully.) She had a special jar called a "happiness jar." You were meant to write down your happy memories on pieces of paper and then put them in the jar and then on New Year's Eve you went through the jar and realized all your blessings, or something. It was September so they had to get their skates on and collect a lot of happy family memories.

"But we are also lucky to have a Lexus," pointed out her dad. "We shouldn't take our Lexus for granted."

Her mum had discovered that there was a beautiful bushwalk through a national park *in their very own neighborhood*. Only a short walk away! This was a very big deal, for some reason. It was like having a window seat. Apparently Erika and Oliver from next door did this walk "all the time," and they were amazed that Dakota's mum didn't even know that it existed, and her mum had felt embarrassed by this, or so she said, although she probably hadn't, because Erika and Oliver were nice geeky people and nobody felt embarrassed in front of nice geeky people. That's why they were relaxing to be around.

"Maybe I'll meet you girls there," said her father. "I have some errands to run after. Important errands, you know."

"No way," said her mother. "Move it, move it. Jeez Louise."

Her mum was putting her dad on a health kick. (He had a giant fat hairy belly, but he could make his belly as hard as a rock if he wanted, and then he'd invite Dakota to punch him. "Harder!" he would roar like some sort of maniac. "Are you a man or a mouse?")

"What do you think, Dakota? Wouldn't you prefer to drive, eh? Much better? Much more comfortable?" said her dad. "We can stop and have ice cream after?"

"I don't mind," said Dakota. "As long as we're back by three o'clock." She was going to a *Hunger Games* party this afternoon, so none of this seemed that relevant. It was her friend Ashling's party, and Ashling's mother got really serious about themes. Presumably no one would actually *die*, she wouldn't go that far, but there would probably be some really cool archery or something.

As they walked down their driveway toward the street, they heard someone call out from Harry's old house. "Hey there!"

"Barney!" said Dakota's mum as the dog nearly yanked her arm off, straining at the leash, jumping about excitedly and barking. If Dakota could translate dog language, she reckoned he would be saying: "Another human being! How great is this!"

Her dad stopped in his tracks. "Hello!" he shouted. Like, literally shouted. Like he was calling across a mountain range, not a front yard. "How are you? Cracker of a day, isn't it?!"

Her dad was as excited as Barney to see another human. Seriously.

A man wearing a pale pink buttoned-up polo shirt and shorts came over toward them, carrying something in his arms. There was a big cleanup going on at Harry's house today. It had been strange to see pieces of furniture carried out: an old couch, a tiny television, an old, yellowing stained mattress. Dakota had looked away. It was like seeing Harry's underwear.

"Hello," said the man, sounding breathless, as if he'd run over. He spoke to Dakota's mum. "We met the other day. Steve. Steve Lunt."

"Vid! Pleased to meet you!" said her dad. "We're off for a walk, you know. We're just walking straight out our front door." He made a karate-chop motion with his hand. "That's how we roll. We are outdoorsy people."

Dakota squirmed.

"Hi, Steve," said her mum. "How's the cleanup going? This is our daughter, Dakota, by the way, and our crazy dog, Barney."

Dakota lifted her hand in the tiniest possible movement to make up for her dad's bigness and loudness. She tried not to make eye contact so he didn't feel obliged to get all chatty and fake-interested. ("What grade are you in at school?")

"Hi, Dakota," said Steve. "Actually, it's you I wanted to see. I wondered if you would like to have this old globe. Might look nice in your room?"

He held up an old-fashioned world globe on a wooden stand. It was a golden biscuity color and it had curly writing like something from an old pirate treasure map. Dakota was surprised to find that she actually wanted it very badly. She could already see it sitting on her desk, glowing gold and mysterious.

"That's really beautiful," said her mother. "But it looks like an antique. It might be worth something. You might want to get it valued."

"No, no. I want you to have it. I want it to have a good home," said Steve. He smiled at Dakota with nice white teeth and handed the globe to her.

"Thank you," she said. It was heavier than she'd expected.

"Just don't rely on it to do your geography homework," he said. He touched it with his fingertip so that it spun gently. "It shows Persia and Constantinople, instead of Iran and Istanbul."

"It is very old indeed then," said Vid. "It's a very precious thing for you to give Dakota. Thank you."

Persia. Constantinople. Dakota hugged the globe to her.

"I think it belonged to Harry's son," said Steve. He lowered his voice and turned his face slightly toward Dakota's mother, as if to avoid Dakota's hearing, although that just made Dakota listen more carefully. "It looked like his son's bedroom hadn't been touched since the day he died. My mother thinks it was at least fifty years ago. It was the eeriest thing I've ever experienced. Like going back in time. There was a book." His voice got all wonky with emotion. "*Biggles Learns to Fly.* Facedown on the bed. All his clothes still in the wardrobe."

Dakota's mother put her hand over her mouth. "Oh God. That poor, poor man."

Great. Now her mother would feel even guiltier about horrible old spitty Harry.

"We took photos," said Steve solemnly.

Dakota thought that was kind of inappropriate. Was he going to put the photos of the dead boy's room on Instagram now?

Dakota's dad was getting restless. He rattled his house keys in his pocket. "Let's put that beautiful globe safely inside, eh, Dakota?"

"Thank you," said Dakota to Steve again. "Thank you very, very much for this."

"You're very, very welcome," said Steve. "I'm sure Harry would have been happy for you to have it."

"Old Harry was very fond of Dakota," said her dad. This was such a big fat total lie, Dakota could hardly believe it. "He just maybe didn't always show it, you know." He looked at Steve. "Mate, do you need a break? Do you want to come in for a coffee? Something to eat? We've got—"

"We're going for a walk, Vid," interrupted her mother.

"Oh yes," said her dad gloomily. "I forgot for a moment."

83

The Day of the Barbecue

Harry climbed the stairs, hand over hand on the railing, like he was climbing up a rope. It was unacceptable that a man couldn't even climb his own stairs without his legs aching like they did. He'd once been as strong as an ox, and he'd always taken care of his health. He was interested in health. He kept himself up to date with things. As soon as the surgeon general released the report about lung cancer and cigarettes, Harry gave up smoking. That same day.

He knew about that food pyramid. He followed it as best he could. He did regular exercise. He took a multivitamin as recommended by his GP, who looked like he was still in high school—and maybe he was still in high school, because the multivitamin was a waste of money. It had no effect whatsoever. Every day he felt a bit worse. The manufacturers of that vitamin were laughing all the way to the bank. Harry was considering writing a letter of complaint. He averaged two to three letters of complaint a week. You had to keep corporate Australia *accountable*. When he was in the corporate world there were standards. People cared about quality. The shoddy workmanship these days was a disgrace.

He stopped halfway for a rest.

This was why old codgers had to move out of their homes into those god-awful retirement places—because they couldn't make it up their own bloody stairs. What a joke. He wasn't moving anywhere. They could carry him out in a box.

He could still hear the music from next door. Very selfish, bad-mannered people. He would call the police if necessary. He used to call the police all the time, when the son had those parties while the parents went off on their bloody river cruises in the south of bloody France. The son with the long greasy hair like a monkey. Disgusting creature.

But those people weren't there anymore, were they? He knew that. Of course he knew that. They moved out about ten years ago. He knew that perfectly well. He did a Sudoku puzzle every day. His mind was fine. It was just that he sometimes got fuzzy about time.

It was the big Arab guy or whatever nationality he was. Probably a terrorist. You couldn't tell these days. Harry had his mobile number. He had all his details carefully recorded just in case he ever needed to pass them over to the police. He kept an eye on him. The wife had said they would turn down the music but Harry strongly suspected they'd turned it up. What could you expect from a man who wore a bloody *bracelet*? The wife wasn't bad to look at but she had no class. She dressed like a whore. That girl could have learned a thing or two about class, about elegance, from Harry's wife. Elizabeth would have set her straight.

Their kid reminded Harry of Jamie. Something about the shape of her head. And something else: a kind of stillness, like a bird watcher, as if she were studying the world, carefully working it out. Jamie had been a thinker. It made Harry furious to look at that child. How dare she look like Jamie? How dare she be here when he wasn't? It enraged him. Sometimes when he looked at her, he *literally* saw red. Like a fire glow.

He kept climbing the stairs. One hand after the other on the railing. Harry used to run. He was a runner before running became trendy. *This body used to run.* He didn't recognize his own withered old legs anymore; looked like they belonged to someone else. Why had no one invented a drug to stop this happening? It couldn't be that hard. It was because the researchers were all young and they didn't know what lay ahead. They were oblivious! They thought their bodies were theirs forever and then by the time they found out, it was too late, they were retired, and their minds were all fuzzy, although Harry's mind wasn't fuzzy, he did Sudoku.

"Don't run, don't run!" Elizabeth used to shout at Jamie when he ran along the bush tracks. She was worried he'd slip, but he never slipped. He was nimble. They used to walk out the back door with a packed picnic lunch and be at the waterfall within the hour.

Now Harry was marooned in this house, like he was marooned in this body. He didn't even know if that walking track was still there, the track where Jamie used to run. He could find out, but if it was under a shopping center, he'd be angry, and if it was still there, if other kids were running along it while their mothers shouted, "Don't run! Don't run!" he'd be angrier still.

He was at the top. What a palaver to climb a flight of stairs. Now, why was he up here? What did he need?

His mind wasn't going. Sometimes he couldn't find the right word for a thing, but he remembered that sometimes Elizabeth couldn't find a word, "Where's the thingamajig," she'd say, and she'd been so young, so beautifully, gorgeously young, she had no idea how young she was, and he had no idea why he'd come upstairs.

He could *still* hear the music from next door. Even louder now. Who did they think they were? Pretending to be artsy-fartsy types. Elizabeth used to love classical music. She played the violin at school. She had more class in her little finger than that little two-bit whore had in her whole body. She'd have shown her a thing or two. How dare they play it so loud? Inconsiderate.

He imagined calling the police and telling them the neighbors were deafening him with bloody Mozart. Wasn't Mozart the deaf one? No wonder he wrote such crappy songs. Elizabeth used to laugh at his grumpiness. Elizabeth had a good sense of humor. So did Jamie. They both used to laugh at him. Once they were gone, nobody laughed at him ever again. All his funniness flew away with them.

It was the neighbors' fault he couldn't remember why he was up here. He'd got distracted. He went into Jamie's room to calm himself and turned on the light.

He looked out Jamie's window. The neighbors had all their outdoor lighting going. It was like bloody Disneyland down there.

There were two little girls running about. One of them had wings on her back like a tiny fairy. The other one was wearing an old-fashioned-looking little pink coat. Elizabeth would have liked that pink coat.

He could see the bloody dog zipping back and forth. Yip-yap-yapping. It had been digging up Harry's garden today, as happy as you please. Harry had given it a kick up the backside, to show it what's what. It wasn't a hard kick but it was true that both Elizabeth and Jamie wouldn't have laughed at that. They would have stopped speaking to him, probably. He and Elizabeth had been going to give Jamie a dog for his ninth birthday. They should have done it for his eighth.

He looked out the window. The electricity bill for all those tiny lights must be exorbitant.

He could see the people from two doors down. Oliver. Namby-pamby name but he was a nice enough bloke. You could have a sensible conversation with him. (Although he rode a bike, and wore those shiny tight black shorts. Looked like a bloody galah when he did that.) He couldn't remember his wife's name. One of those worried, skinny women.

No kids. Maybe they didn't want them. Maybe they couldn't have them. The wife didn't have good childbearing hips, that's for sure. Although now they could mix them up in test tubes.

Elizabeth would have liked a little sister for Jamie. She always looked at little girls. She liked their dresses. "Look at that little girl's pretty dress," she'd say to him, as if Harry ever gave two hoots about a little girl's pretty dress.

She was looking at a little girl that day, a little girl clutching a stick with a giant ball of fluffy pink fairy floss. Elizabeth said, "Look at that, it's nearly as big as her," but Harry had just grunted in response, because he was in a bad mood, he wanted to leave, it was a Sunday afternoon and they had a long drive back and he was thinking about work and the week ahead. The union was giving them grief. Harry didn't like Sunday nights to feel rushed. He liked to feel sorted for the week.

He hadn't wanted to drive all the way out to bum-fuck nowhere to come to this crummy little country fair. He shouldn't have said "bum-fuck nowhere" to Elizabeth, because she hated that, it really offended her, he was just thinking about the union rep, a tough bugger, that one, and the battle ahead. (The union rep came to the funeral. He hugged Harry and Harry didn't want to be hugged but he didn't want to be at his wife's funeral either.)

He should have been nicer to Elizabeth and Jamie that day. He would have been nicer if he'd known it was the last day they'd ever have together. He wouldn't have said "bum-fuck nowhere." He wouldn't have told Jamie that the games were all rigged and he was never going to win. He wouldn't have grunted when Elizabeth pointed out the little girl with the fairy floss.

But then again, he *should* have been grumpier. He should have been firmer. He should have said no when they wanted to go on that ride for the third time.

He *did* say no, but Elizabeth didn't take any notice. She grabbed Jamie's hand and said, "Just one more turn." And off they ran.

If he saw them again, he would shout at them. He would shout, "I said *no*! I was the man of the house!" Then he would hold them both in his arms and never ever let them go.

If he saw them again. Elizabeth believed in the hereafter, and Harry hoped she was right, she was right about most things, except that day she hadn't been right.

It was called the Spider. It had eight long legs with a car at the end of each leg for up to eight people. The legs went up and down, up and down, and then the whole thing spun around in a circle.

Each time they'd flown by he'd seen a brief glimpse of their pink, laughing faces, their heads flung back against the seats. It had made him feel sick.

The Spider had been built ten years earlier by an Australian manufacturer with a German name: Flugzeug Amusement Rides. Flugzeug Amusement Rides had provided only rudimentary maintenance and inspection procedures for the Spider. The company that ran the funfair was called Sullivan and Sons. Sullivan and Sons was in deep financial shit. They made staff cuts. A dedicated maintenance manager called Primo Paspaz was let go. Primo had set out his own maintenance schedule for all the rides in a red notebook. The red notebook disappeared when he lost his job. Primo thumped his fist against his knee when he testified in court. He had bright tears in his eyes.

One of the mechanical bearings malfunctioned on the Spider, and a car spun free.

All eight laughing, screaming passengers died. Five adults and three children.

The court cases dragged on for years. It consumed Harry. He still had the files: big foolscap binders filled with a story of negligence and incompetence and idiocy. Nobody ever stood up and took responsibility. Only Primo Paspaz said "I'm sorry" to Harry. He said, "It would never have happened on my watch."

People needed to take responsibility.

Harry turned away from the window and spun Jamie's globe so that all the places Jamie never got to see sped by his finger.

He looked back out the window at the neighbors. It occurred to him that if Elizabeth had lived, he would have been down there at that barbecue, because Elizabeth was so sociable, and the Arab was always inviting Harry over, as if he really wanted him to come. It was peculiar. For a moment, Harry could see it so clearly, the way this night was meant to be: Elizabeth sitting at the table enjoying the music, Harry pretending to be grumpy about it and everyone laughing, because Elizabeth made his grumpiness funny.

Harry watched the two little girls run about the yard. It seemed to be a game of chasing.

The littler one got herself up onto the side of the fountain. She was carrying a little blue handbag. She ran around the edge. The fountain was the size of a swimming pool.

"Careful there, little girl," said Harry out loud to her. "You could fall in." Was anyone even watching her?

He scanned the backyard. The other adults were all gathered around the table, not even looking at the kids. They were laughing their heads off. He couldn't hear their laughter over the music. He couldn't see Oliver, but he could see his wife, Erika, that was her name, standing on the pathway that led from the back door. She'd be able to see the little girl.

He looked back at the fountain and his heart dropped.

The little girl was gone. Had she climbed down off the wall? Then he saw it. The pink coat. Christ Almighty, she was facedown. She'd fallen in. It was like he'd made it happen by predicting it.

He looked for an adult. Where was that Erika? She must have seen it. She was standing right there with a direct line of vision.

But she was just standing there. What was the stupid woman doing?

"She's fallen in!" He banged his hands on the glass.

Oliver's wife didn't move. She just stood there. Like a statue. Her face turned away as if she didn't want to see, as if she was deliberately looking the other way. For God's sake, what was wrong with her? What was wrong with all these stupid people? My God, my God, my God.

Harry's face was hot with rage. The little girl was drowning right there in front of those idiotic, irresponsible people. Shooting was too good for them.

He tried to pull up the window so he could yell out, but it was jammed closed. It hadn't been opened in years. He banged so hard with both fists on the glass it hurt. He yelled, louder than he'd yelled in years. "She's drowning!"

Finally the woman looked up at him. Oliver's wife. Their eyes met. Thank God, thank God. "She's drowning!" screamed Harry. He jabbed his finger at the fountain. "The little girl is drowning!"

He watched her turn her head toward the fountain. Slowly. As if there were no great hurry.

And still she didn't move. The stupid, idiotic woman didn't move. She just stood there, looking at the fountain. It was like something from a nightmare. Harry heard himself sob with frustration. Time was running out.

He turned from the window and ran from the room. It was the only way. He had to be fast. He had to be nimble. He had to run next door and pull the little girl out himself. The little girl in the pink coat was drowning. Elizabeth would have loved that little girl. He could hear Elizabeth crying out, "Run, Harry, run!"

He ran from Jamie's room onto the landing. It was like he had his old body back. There was no pain. He felt exhilarated by the urgency of his mission. He was running gracefully, fluidly, like a twenty-year-old with perfect, limber knees. He could do this. He was fast. He was nimble. He'd save her.

On the second step he fell. He grabbed for the banister to save himself but it was too late, he was flying, like his wife and son.

84

It was early evening at the end of another beautiful day, and Sam was walking home from the ferry beneath an indigo sky. There had been almost a whole week of clear weather now. Everything had dried out and dried off and people had stopped discussing how nice it was to see the sun. The Big Wet was drifting away from everyone's memories on a gentle spring breeze.

Sam had just had another fairly productive day at work, so that was something. It was a little embarrassing just how much nerdy satisfaction he had achieved today from successfully completing his proposed strategic plan for preventing the further loss of market share in the now crowded sugar-free, berry-flavored caffeinated energy drink segment. He hadn't exactly composed a symphony, but it was a well-thought-out strategy that would make the company money, which would make up for the last few weeks when he'd sat at his desk being paid for doing nothing. He'd used his brain. He'd ticked off a task. It felt good.

Maybe it was all due to the amazing, magical effects of his first counseling session. After the humiliating incident at the first aid course on Sunday Clementine had arranged an appointment with a counselor after-hours on

Monday. Sam didn't ask her how she managed to get an appointment so quickly. She'd probably got her mother on the case. Pam was a big fan of counseling. She probably had one on speed-dial. Sam cringed at the thought of his mother-in-law's softly sympathetic face as Clementine told her about his *tears*, his so-called post-traumatic stress, for Christ's sake.

The counselor was a cheery, chatty little fellow, like a jockey, and he had plenty of opinions, which surprised Sam. (Weren't they meant to say enigmatic things like, "What do *you* think?") He said Sam probably did have a mild case of PTSD. He said it in the same nonchalant tone as if he'd said, "You've probably got a mild sinus infection." He reckoned Sam would need only three or four sessions "max" to "knock this on the head."

Sam had left his office almost laughing; did this guy get his qualifications online? But as he'd stood in the lift going back to the lobby, he'd been surprised to find he was experiencing just a mild sense of relief, like standing in the baggage claim area after a long flight and feeling your ears pop, when you weren't fully aware they'd been blocked. It wasn't like he felt great. Just marginally better. Maybe it was the placebo effect, or maybe it was going to happen eventually anyway, or maybe his little counselor had special powers.

Now he stopped at a pedestrian crossing and watched a woman with a baby in a stroller and a preschool-aged kid.

The baby was about one. He was sitting up, fat legs straight out in front of him, a large green leaf clutched in his chubby hand like a flag.

Was it a floating leaf that had attracted Ruby's attention that day? He imagined it, as he'd done so many times before, as maybe he was going to do for the rest of his life. He saw her climbing up onto the edge of the fountain, proud of herself, walking around the perimeter, maybe even running. Did she slip? Or did she see something she wanted? A floating leaf or an interesting-looking stick. Something that sparkled. He imagined her on her knees on the side of the fountain, in her little pink coat, her hand outstretched, and then suddenly, silently toppling in, headfirst, panicking, flailing, her lungs filling with water as she tried to scream, "Daddy!" the heavy coat dragging her down, and then, the stillness, her hair floating around her head.

For a moment Sam's world tipped and his breath caught. He concentrated on the DON'T WALK light in red, waiting for it to change to WALK. The cars zoomed by. The mother waiting next to him was talking on her mobile phone. "My shoe is falling off," whined the preschooler.

"No, it's not," said the mother distractedly as she continued to speak into the phone. "I *know*, that's the thing, I mean it would be fine if she'd just been up front about it from the beginning, but—*Lachlan, no!* Don't take off your shoe here!"

The little boy had suddenly plonked himself down on the footpath and was in the process of removing his shoe.

"He's taking off his damned shoe in the middle of the street. Lachlan, stop that. I said *stop* that." The woman bent down to drag the preschooler back to his feet. Her hand left the stroller handle. It was on a slope that led straight out onto the street.

The stroller began to roll.

"Whoops." Sam reached out one hand and caught hold of the handle.

The woman looked up.

"Jesus *Christ.*" The phone slid from beneath her head and shoulder and crashed onto the ground as she stood up fast and grabbed the stroller handle, her hand overlapping Sam's.

She looked at the traffic roaring by and then back down at the stroller.

She said, "It could have . . . he could have . . ."

"I know," said Sam. "But it's all good. It didn't." He removed his hand from under hers. She had the handle in a death grip now.

"Mummy, the phone is all cracked!" The preschooler held up the phone he'd rescued from the ground with an expression of pure horror on his face. Sam could hear a tinny voice calling out from the phone, "Hello? Hello?"

The lights changed to WALK. The woman didn't move. She was still processing it, still seeing what could have been.

"Have a good night," said Sam, and he crossed the road to go home, the sky huge and hopeful before him.

85

"Yₒu don't have to rush back to the office, do you?" said Oliver as he tucked his ears into his swimming cap—*snap, snap*—and pulled his goggles down over his eyes so he looked to Erika like a goofy alien.

They had met for their lunch break at North Sydney pool, which was within walking distance of both their offices, for their first swim after their brief "winter hiatus," as Oliver liked to call it. During the winter months they swapped their swim for a thirty-minute high-intensity cardio class at the gym.

"As long as I'm back by one thirty." Erika pulled down her own goggles so that the world turned turquoise.

"Good," said Oliver. He seemed serious.

As Erika swam her first lap, she wondered what was on his mind. Ever since his discovery of her "habit," she felt like she'd been demoted to junior partner in their marriage. He'd made her promise to talk about her "klepto-mania" with her psychologist.

"It's not kleptomania!" Erika cried. "It's just . . ."

"Stealing your friend's stuff!" finished Oliver brightly.

There was something different about Oliver lately: a kind of recklessness, except not really, because Oliver would never be reckless. Almost aggressive-ness? But not quite. Feistiness. It was not unattractive, to be honest. They were having a lot of angry sex. It was great.

She hadn't yet discussed her "kleptomania" with her psychologist because she hadn't seen her. Not-Pat had canceled a few sessions recently at the last minute. She probably had her own personal problems. Erika secretly hoped she might be forced to take a sabbatical.

As she turned her head for every second breath she looked up and saw the gray arched pylons of the Harbour Bridge soaring into the bright blue sky above them. It was an amazing place to swim. Wasn't this enough for a life? Good work, good exercise, good sex. She tumble-turned and looked for Oliver. He was way ahead of her, powering through the water; lucky it wasn't too busy, because he was swimming too fast even for the fast lane.

It would be the baby. That's what he would want to talk about. The baby was his project, and his project management skills were excellent. Now that Clementine was no longer part of the picture, he would want to "explore other options, other avenues." He would want to talk through the pros and the cons. Erika's whole body slowed in the water at the thought. Her legs felt like limp weights she was dragging along behind her.

The thought occurred to her: I'm done. I'm done with the baby project. But of course, she couldn't be done, not until Oliver was done.

This was simply the wall. Every time you ran a marathon, you hit a wall. The wall was both a physical and a mental barrier, but it could be overcome (carb-loading, hydration, focus on your technique). She swam on. It didn't *feel* like she could get past this, but that was the nature of the wall.

After their swim, they sat outside at a café in the sun, looking straight out onto the harbor, eating tuna and kale salads for their lunch. Back in their suits. Sunglasses on. Hair just slightly damp at the ends.

"I'm going to send you a link to an article," said Oliver. "I read it yester-day, and I've been thinking about it. Thinking about it a lot."

"Okay," said Erika. Some new reproductive technology. Great. It's just the wall, she told herself. Breathe.

"It's about fostering," said Oliver. "Fostering older children."

"Fostering?" Erika's fork stopped halfway to her mouth.

"It's about how hard it is," said Oliver. "It's about how people get this really romantic idea about fostering and it's not like that at all. It's about how most foster carers have no idea what they're getting themselves into. It's a brutally honest article."

"Oh," said Erika. She couldn't see his eyes because of his sunglasses. She was aware of the feeling of a tiny spark of hope quelled. "So the reason you're sending it to me is . . . ?"

"I think we should do it," said Oliver.

"You think we should do it," repeated Erika.

"I was thinking about Clementine and Sam," said Oliver. "And how Ruby's accident affected them so badly. Do you want to know why it was such a big thing for those two?" He didn't wait for an answer. "Because *nothing bad* has ever happened to them before!"

"Well," said Erika, considering. "I don't know if that's entirely—"

"But you and me, we expect the worst!" said Oliver. "We've got low expectations. We're tough. We can handle stuff!"

"Can we?" said Erika. She didn't know if she should remind him that she was in therapy.

"Everybody wants the babies," said Oliver, ignoring her. "The cute little babies. But what they really need is foster parents for the older kids. The angry ones. The broken ones." He stopped and suddenly he seemed to lose confidence. He picked up his super-food smoothie. "I just thought . . . well, I thought maybe we could consider it because maybe we'd have an understanding, or at least an inkling, of what those kids are going through." He sucked on his straw. She could see the harbor reflected in his sunglasses.

Erika ate her salad and thought of Clementine's parents. She saw Pam making up the stretcher bed for her to stay the night, yet again, flicking her wrists so that the crisp, white sheets floated in the air: the beautiful, clean fragrance of bleach was still Erika's favorite smell in the world. She saw Clementine's dad, sitting in the passenger seat of his car while Erika sat in the driver's seat for the first time. He showed her how to put her hands at "a quarter to three" on the steering wheel. "Everyone else says 'ten to two,'" he said. "But everyone else is wrong." She still drove with her hands at a quarter to three.

What was that phrase people used? Pay it forward.

"So let's say we do it," said Erika. "We take on one of these broken kids."

Oliver looked up. "Let's say we do."

"According to this article, it's going to be terrible."

"That's what it says," agreed Oliver. "Traumatic. Stressful. Awful. We might fall in love with a kid who ends up going back to a biological parent. We might have a kid with terrible behavioral issues. We might find our relationship is tested in ways we could never imagine."

Erika wiped her mouth with her napkin and stretched her arms high above her head. The sun warmed the top of her scalp, giving her a sensation of molten warmth.

"Or it might be great," she said.

"Yeah," said Oliver. He smiled. "I think it might be great."

86

D o you want distracting talk?" said Sam as he drove her into the city.
"Or calming silence?"

"I don't know," said Clementine. "I can't decide."

It was a little after ten on a Saturday morning. Her audition wasn't until
two. The ten minutes past ten leaving time had been calculated to take into
account anything that could possibly go wrong.

"I can drive myself," Clementine had told Sam last night.

"What are you talking about?" said Sam. "I always drive you to your auditions."

She thought with mild surprise: So we're still "us" then? Maybe they
were, although they still went off each night to sleep in separate rooms.

Something had changed over the last week since the first aid course;
nothing dramatic, in fact the opposite. It was as though a feeling of utter
mundanity had settled upon them, like the start of a new season, fresh and
familiar all at once. All the anger and recriminations had gone, drained
away. It reminded Clementine of that feeling when you were recovering
from being ill, when the symptoms were gone but you still felt light-headed
and peculiar.

The girls were with Clementine's parents today, and they were both in fine form. Holly had come home from school yesterday with a Merit Certificate for Excellent Behavior in Class, which Clementine suspected was really a Merit Certificate for No Longer Behaving Like a Crazy Person in Class. "The old Holly is back," her teacher had told Clementine in the playground, and she'd done a little "Phew!" swipe of the back of her hand across her forehead, which made Clementine think that Holly's behavior at school must have been much worse than she or Sam had been made aware.

Ruby had said Whisk could stay home today and have a little rest. She appeared to be losing interest in Whisk. Clementine could already see how poor Whisk was going to slip unobtrusively from their lives, like friends sometimes did.

"Okay, so there's no need to panic because we've allowed enough time for exactly this possibility," said Sam, as the traffic on the bridge came to a stop and a neon sign flashed in urgent red letters: INCIDENT AHEAD. EXPECT DELAYS.

Clementine breathed in deeply through her nostrils and out through her mouth.

"I'm fine," she said. "I'm not *thrilled*, but I'm fine."

Sam held out his palms as if in meditation. "We are Zen masters."

Clementine studied the crisp white curves of the Opera House's sails against the blue sky. Thankfully the Opera House was one of the venues where she knew she'd be given her own warm-up room, and she wouldn't have to share with other cellists, or worse, talk to the chatty ones. There were plenty of dressing rooms available, some with harbor views. It would be a comfortable, pleasant process. Her audition would be in the rarefied atmosphere of the concert hall.

She looked back at the road. The traffic inched forward past two cars with crushed front ends. There were police and an ambulance with the back doors open, and a man in a suit sat on the curb with his head in his hands.

"Erika said something the other day and it sort of stuck with me," said Clementine. She hadn't been planning to say this but all of a sudden she was saying it, as if she'd been subconsciously planning it.

"What's that?" said Sam warily.

"She said, 'I choose my marriage.'"

"She chooses her marriage. What does that mean?" said Sam. "That doesn't make sense. She chooses her marriage over what?"

"I think it does make sense," said Clementine. "It's about making a choice to make your marriage your priority, to, kind of, put that at the top of the page, as your mission statement or something."

"Clementine Hart, are you actually using soulless corporate jargon right now?" said Sam.

"Be quiet. I just want to take this opportunity to say—"

Sam snorted. "Now you sound like your mother making one of her speeches."

"I want to take this opportunity to say that I choose my marriage too."

"Um . . . thanks?"

Clementine spoke rapidly. "So, if, for example, having a third child is your heart's desire, then that's something we need to at least talk about. I can't just ignore it, or hope you'll forget about it, which was what I was doing, to be honest. I know when I asked you a couple of weeks ago you said you didn't want another child, but that was when you were still, or when we were both still, kind of . . ."

"Crazy," finished Sam for her. "Do *you* want another child?" he said.

"I really don't," said Clementine. "But if you really do, then we need to talk about it."

"What? And then we work out whether I want a baby more than you don't want a baby?" said Sam.

"Exactly," said Clementine. "I think that's exactly what we do."

"I *did* want a third child," said Sam. "But now, well, it's just not something I'm thinking about right now."

"I know," said Clementine. "I know. But we could, we might, one day, not forget, of course, but we might forgive. We might forgive ourselves. Anyway, I don't know why I brought that up today. It's not like we even . . ."

Have sex anymore. Sleep in the same bed. Say "I love you" anymore.

"I guess I just thought I should put that on the table," she said.

"Consider it tabled," said Sam.

"Great."

"You know what my heart's desire is right now?" said Sam.

"What?"

"It's for you to get this job."

"Right," said Clementine.

"I don't want you going onto that stage thinking about babies. I want you thinking about whatever it is you need to think about, intonation, pitch, *tempo*, whatever those nancy-boy ex-boyfriends of yours would have told you to think about."

"Well. I'll do my best," said Clementine. She said softly, "You're a good man, Samuel."

"I know I am. Eat your banana," said Sam.

"No," said Clementine.

"You sound just like your daughter."

"Which one?"

"Both of them, actually."

The traffic was moving freely now.

After a moment Sam cleared his throat and said, "I'd like to take this opportunity to say that I choose my marriage too."

"Oh yes, and what does that mean?"

"I have no idea. I just wanted to make my position clear."

"Maybe it means you don't want to sleep in the study anymore," suggested Clementine, her eyes on the road ahead.

"Maybe it does," said Sam.

Clementine studied his profile. "Would you like to come back?"

"I'd like to come back," said Sam. He looked over his shoulder to change lanes. "From wherever the hell I've been."

"Well," said Clementine. "You're very welcome to submit an application."

"I could audition," he said. "I have some smooth moves." He paused. "You could be blindfolded. We'll make it a blind audition so there is no possibility of bias."

She could feel a wild, raw sense of happiness growing within her. It was just silly, cheesy, flirty talk, but it was *their* silly, cheesy, flirty talk. She already knew how it would be tonight: the sweet familiarity and the sharp, clean edges because of what they'd nearly lost. She didn't know how close their marriage had gotten to hitting that iceberg—close enough to feel its icy shadow—but they'd missed it.

"Yeah, I choose my marriage." Sam swung the car to the right. "And I

also temporarily choose this illegal bus lane because I am one crazy moth-
erfucker."

Clementine reached into her bag, took out her banana and peeled it.

"You'll get a ticket," she said as she took a mouthful and waited for those natural beta-blockers to take effect, and it must have been a really good season for bananas, because it was the best banana she'd ever tasted.

87

At half past three they finally called for her.

She walked down the strip of carpet with her cello and bow to the lonely chair. She blinked in the bright, hot, white light. A woman coughed behind the black screen and it sounded a little like Ainsley.

Clementine sat. She embraced her cello. She nodded at her pianist. He smiled. She'd hired her own pianist to accompany her. Grant Morton was a grandfatherly man who lived alone with an adult daughter with Down syndrome. His wife had died the day after her fiftieth birthday, only last year, but he still had the sweetest smile of anyone she knew, and she'd been so glad he was available, because she wanted to start her audition with that sweet smile.

She was conscious of her heart beating rapidly as she tuned, but it wasn't racing out of control. She breathed and put her hand to the tiny metallic stickers stuck on the collar of her shirt.

"This is for good luck for your audition," Holly had said when they were leaving today, and she'd carefully put a purple butterfly sticker on her mother's shirt and then, with great, grown-up ceremony, she had kissed Clementine on the cheek.

"I want good luck too!" Ruby had yelled, as if good luck was a treat being handed out by Clementine, and she'd copied everything her sister had done, except her sticker was a yellow smiley face, and her kiss was very wet and peanut-buttery. Clementine could still feel its sticky imprint on her cheek.

She took one deep breath and looked at the music on her stand.

It was all there within her. The hours and hours of early-morning practice, the listening to recordings, the dozens of tiny technical decisions she'd settled upon.

She saw her little girls running about under the fairy lights, Vid throwing back his head and laughing, the chair lying on its side, Oliver's locked hands over Ruby's chest, the black shadow of the helicopter, her mother's enraged face close to hers. She saw her sixteen-year-old self standing up and walking off the stage. She saw a boy in a badly fitting tuxedo watch her pack away her cello and say, "I bet you wish you chose the flute." She saw the look of disbelief on Erika's face when Clementine first sat down opposite her in the playground.

She remembered Marianne saying, "Don't just play for them, *perform*."

She remembered Hu saying, "You have to find the balance. It's like you're walking a tightrope between technique and music."

She remembered Ainsley saying, "Yes, but at some point you just have to let go."

She lifted her bow. She let go.

88

The Night of the Barbecue

Pam and Martin pulled up in front of Erika and Oliver's neat-looking little bungalow.

"Holly might be asleep by now," said Pam to her husband. It was nearly nine o'clock.

"Might be," said Martin. "Might not be."

"That must be where it happened," said Pam. She pointed at the big house next door with dislike. All those turrets and curlicues and spires. She'd always thought it was a fussy, show-offy sort of house.

"Where what happened?" said Martin blankly.

Sometimes she could swear he had early-onset dementia.

"Where the *accident* happened," said Pam. "They were at the neighbors' house. They don't even know them that well, apparently."

"Oh," said Martin. He looked away from the house and undid his seat belt. "Right."

They got out of the car and walked up the paved pathway with its neatly trimmed edges.

"How do you feel?" she said to Martin.

"What? Me? I feel fine."

"I'm just making sure you don't have chest pains or anything, because it's times like this that people our age unexpectedly drop dead."

"*I* don't have chest pains," said Martin. "Do *you* have chest pains? You're a person of our age too."

"I play tennis three times a week," said Pam primly.

"I'm more worried about our son-in-law dropping dead of a heart attack," said Martin, shoving his hands in his pockets. "He looked terrible."

He was right, Sam had looked absolutely terrible at the hospital. It didn't seem possible that one event could have such a profound physical effect on a person. They'd seen Sam just yesterday, when he'd dropped by to help Martin move out their old washing machine, and he'd been in great form, chatting about Clementine's audition, some plan he had to help her get over her nerves, excited about his new job, but tonight he'd looked like he'd been rescued from somewhere, like those people you saw on the news wrapped in silver blankets, with red-rimmed eyes and a ghost-white pallor. He was in terrible shock, of course.

"You were very rough on Clementine," said Martin mildly as Pam pressed the doorbell and they heard its distant chime.

"She should have been watching Ruby," said Pam.

"For Christ's sake, it could have happened to anyone," said Martin.

Not me, thought Pam.

"And they *both* should have been watching," said Martin. "They made a mistake and they very nearly paid a terrible price. People make mistakes."

"Well, I know that." But in Pam's eyes, it was Clementine's mistake. That's why she was battling this terrible, unmotherly sense of rage toward her beloved daughter. She knew it would eventually recede, she sure hoped it would, and that she'd probably feel just awful about the way she'd spoken to her at the hospital, but for now she still felt very, very angry. It was the *mother's* job to watch her child. Forget feminism. Forget all that. Pam would scream about equal pay from the rooftops, but every woman knew you couldn't rely on a man to watch the children in a social situation. It was scientifically proven they couldn't do two things at the same time!

Clementine had always been too prepared to rely on Sam, but just because she was a musician, a creative person, an "artist," didn't give her the right to relinquish her responsibilities as a *mother.* Her job as a mother came first.

Sometimes Clementine got the identical distracted, dreamy expression on her face as Pam's dad used to get at the dinner table while Pam was trying to tell him something, and she wouldn't even have finished the sentence before he'd wandered off. He might have been Ernest bloody Hemingway for all Pam cared. All that time he'd spent writing that novel no one would ever read, ignoring his children, locking himself away in his study, when he could have been living. "It could have been a masterpiece," Clementine always said, as if it was a tragedy, as if *that* was the point, when it wasn't the point; the point was that Pam never got a father and Pam would have quite liked a father. Just every now and then.

What good did it do Ruby if her mother was the best cellist in the world? Clementine should have been watching. She should have been listening. She should have been *concentrating on her child*.

Of course, Clementine's music had nothing to do with what happened today. She did know that.

If Ruby didn't make it through the night, if she suffered some sort of long-term damage to her health, Pam didn't know what she'd do with all this anger. She'd have to find the strength to put it aside to be there for Clementine. Pam put her hand to her chest. Ruby was stable, she reminded herself. That rosy little plump-cheeked face. Those wicked slanting catlike eyes.

"Pam?" said Martin.

"What?" she snapped. He was studying her closely.

"You look like you're having a heart attack."

"Well, I'm not, thank you very much, I'm perfectly—" The door swung open and Oliver stood there, wearing tracksuit bottoms and a T-shirt.

"Hello, Oliver." Pam hadn't seen him in casual clothes before. Normally he wore a nice checked shirt tucked into trousers. Pam had met him on so many occasions over the years, but she'd never really gotten to know him that well. He was always so complimentary about Pam's signature dish, her carrot and walnut cake. (He seemed to have gotten it into his head that the cake was sugar-free, which was not the case, but she didn't bother to correct him; he was so skinny, a bit of sugar wouldn't hurt him.)

"Holly is just through here watching a movie," said Oliver. "She would have been very welcome to stay the night with us, of course." He said this sadly.

"Oh, she would have loved that, Oliver," said Pam. "But we were all fighting over her, you see, it's a distraction from our worry over Ruby."

"I understand you were the hero of the day," said Martin, and he held out his hand to Oliver.

Oliver went to take Martin's hand. "I don't know about—" But to Pam's surprise, her husband changed his mind about shaking hands at the last moment and instead threw his arms around Oliver in an awkward hug, thumping him on the back, probably much too hard.

Pam rubbed Oliver's arm gently to make up for Martin's thumping. "You are a hero," she said, her voice full of emotion. "You and Erika are heroes. Once Ruby is home and feeling better, we'll have you over for a special dinner. A dinner fit for heroes! I'll make that carrot cake I know you like."

"Oh, delicious, wow, that's very kind of you," said Oliver, stepping back and ducking his head like he was fourteen.

"Where is Erika?" said Pam.

"She's asleep, actually," said Oliver. "She wasn't feeling . . . quite right."

"Probably the shock," said Pam. "Everyone is feeling—well, look who's here! Hello, darling. Look at those fairy wings!"

Holly headed straight to her and buried her face in Pam's stomach.

"Hello, Grandma," she said. "I am 'exhausted.'" She lifted her fingers in quotation marks. Her funny little habit.

"Right," said Oliver. "I'll grab your rock collection, Holly."

"No. I don't want it," said Holly almost belligerently. "I *told* you I don't want it. You keep it."

"Well, I'll take care of it for you," said Oliver. "If you change your mind, you can have it back."

"Come to Grandpa, Holly." Martin held out his arms to Holly and she leaped up, her legs wrapped around his waist, her head on his shoulder. No point telling Martin not to carry her after his knee operation. He needed to carry her.

Holly fell asleep in the car and didn't wake when Martin carried her in, or even when Pam changed her into a spare pair of pajamas she kept in the house. Martin didn't see the need to change her, but Pam knew you were always so much comfier in pajamas.

But as Pam leaned to kiss her good night, Holly's eyes sprang open.

"Is Ruby dead?" she said. She was lying on her front, her head turned sideways on the pillow, a tangle of hair obscuring her face.

"No, darling," said Pam. She lifted the hair off Holly's face and smoothed it back from her forehead. "She's at the hospital. The doctors are looking after her. She's going to be fine. You go back to sleep."

Holly closed her eyes, and Pam rubbed her back.

"Grandma," whispered Holly.

"Yes, darling?" Pam was feeling tired herself now.

Holly whispered something Pam couldn't hear.

"What's that?" Pam leaned forward to listen.

"Are Mummy and Daddy very, very angry with me?" whispered Holly.

"Of course not!" said Pam. "Why would they be angry with you?"

"Because I pushed her."

Pam froze.

"I pushed Ruby," said Holly again, louder.

Pam's hand lay flat and still on Holly's back, and for a moment she didn't recognize it; it looked too old and wrinkled to belong to her.

"She took my bag of rocks," said Holly. "She was standing on the side of the fountain with my bag and she wouldn't let me have it, and it's *mine*, and I was trying to get it off her, and then I got it, and I pushed her because I felt really, really angry."

"Oh, Holly."

"I didn't mean for her to be drowned. I thought she would chase after me. Will she go to heaven? I don't want her to go to heaven."

"Did you tell anyone?" asked Pam.

"Oliver," mumbled Holly into the pillow, as if she were worried that was also a transgression. "I told Oliver."

"What did Oliver say?" said Pam.

"He said, when I see Ruby at the hospital I should whisper 'sorry' very quietly in her ear and that I should never, ever push her again."

"Ah," said Pam.

"He said it was our secret and he would never tell anyone in the whole world ever," said Holly.

He was a lovely man, Oliver. A good man. Trying to do the right thing.

But what if Holly never got that chance to whisper sorry in Ruby's ear? Ruby was stable. Ruby would not die in the night.

But if she did die, Pam refused to have her beautiful innocent granddaughter pay the price for Clementine's inattention.

"You know what, I don't think she fell in when you pushed her," she said firmly. "That probably happened later. After you ran away. She probably slipped. I think she slipped. I know she slipped. She fell, darling. You did not push her. I *know* you didn't. You were having a little argument over the bag by the fountain and poor Ruby fell in. It was just an accident. You go to sleep now."

Holly's breathing slowed.

"You just put it right out of your mind," she said. "It was an accident. A terrible accident. It wasn't your fault. It wasn't really anyone's fault."

She kept rubbing Holly's back, in ever-increasing circles, like the endless ripples created by a tiny pebble thrown in still water, and as she did she talked, she talked and talked, making the memory disappear, just like the ripples, and the funny thing was that she could feel her anger toward Clementine ebbing away as if she'd never felt it in the first place.

89

Four Months After the Barbecue

Clementine walked back from the letter box shuffling their mail and got to a plain white envelope, addressed to her. It was Erika's handwriting.

She stopped in the middle of her footpath, studying that familiar cramped scrawl. Erika wrote as if she needed to conserve space. Had she put it in the mail yesterday just before she'd left for the airport?

Erika and Oliver had flown out yesterday morning for a six-month trip. They'd both taken leave without pay from their jobs and bought around-the-world tickets. They were "flexible" with their plans, or flexible for them, as in *there were some nights where they hadn't yet booked accommodation.* Crazy stuff.

When they got back they were hoping to become long-term foster carers. They'd already begun the approval process, when all of a sudden Erika had announced (by email, not a phone call) that they were going to travel first. According to Clementine's mother, they hadn't made any particular arrangements about Sylvia. If the neighbors called the police when the house got too bad, so be it. "That's exactly what she said to me," Pam told Clementine. "'So be it.' I nearly fell off my chair."

Of course, Clementine's parents were going to keep an eye on Sylvia.

"She could have asked *me* to look in on Sylvia," Clementine had said, and her mother said, after a pause, as if she were considering her words, "She knows how busy you are."

Her friendship with Erika had been changing, shifting somehow. Weeks could go by without contact, and when Clementine called, Erika would inevitably take a few days to call back. It was like she was distancing herself; in fact, it was almost as though, and this seemed incredible, ironic, impossible, but it was almost as though Erika was *letting Clementine down gently.* She was behaving the way a kind boy behaves when he wants to let a girl know that he likes her as a friend but nothing more. Clementine was being demoted to a lower-tier level of friendship, and she was accepting this with the strangest mix of feelings: amusement, relief, maybe a touch of humiliation and a definite sense of melancholy.

She opened the envelope. There was a short note:

Dear Clementine, I got you a copy of this old photo Mum found.
Mum says it's "proof." I think she means of her great parenting.
Thought it might give you a laugh. See you in six months! Love, Erika

What photo? She'd forgotten to include the photo. But then as Clementine shook the envelope, a tiny square floated toward the ground and she caught it.

It was a black-and-white photo of herself and Erika and Sylvia on a roller coaster at Luna Park, caught at the moment they plunged over its highest precipice. Clementine remembered how staggered she'd been when Erika's mother had pulled them out of school that day. (How did she do it? Some story she invented. Sylvia could get away with anything.) Clementine had been drunk with happiness. It was outrageous! It was *living*!

She remembered how Erika had been as excited as her, what fun they'd all had, until toward the end of the day when Erika's mood inexplicably changed. On the way home she got herself all worked up about a missing library book. "I know exactly where it is," Sylvia kept saying, and Erika said, "You do not, you do not." Clementine, in her innocence, wondered why it was such a big deal. The library book would turn up, surely. After all, Sylvia never threw anything out. Stop spoiling it, Erika, she'd thought resentfully.

Clementine could relish the anarchy of that day because she was going home to order and cleanliness, to spaghetti bolognese and school bags packed the night before.

She looked closely at the photo, studying Erika's face: the pure, almost sensual abandonment with which she'd thrown back her head, laughing, screaming, her eyes closed. There was a secret wildness to Erika. It came out so rarely. She kept it under wraps. Maybe Oliver got to see it. It was like that dry, subversive sense of humor that occasionally slipped out almost by mistake. As Clementine walked back inside studying the photo, she wondered what sort of person Erika could have been, would have been, *should* have been, if she'd been given the privilege of an ordinary home. You could jump so much higher when you had somewhere safe to fall.

"What's that? What are you looking at?" asked Holly as Clementine walked in the door.

Clementine held the photo up high, away from snatching tiny fingers.

"Nothing," she said.

She looked again at the letter and saw that Erika had scrawled something in the bottom corner: *P.S. Just heard the news. Well done, Dummkopf. Knew you would.*

"Is it something 'precious'?" Holly used her fingers to give emphasis. "Precious" was the word of the moment.

"Yes," said Clementine. She looked at the tiny photo again. She'd have to keep it somewhere safe. It would be so easy to lose. "It's something precious."

Acknowledgments

Thank you so much to everyone at Flatiron Books, with special thanks as always to the wonderful Amy Einhorn, as well as to Caroline Bleeke and Marlena Bittner. Thank you also to my editors in Australia and the UK: Cate Paterson, Mathilde Imlah, Brianne Collins and Maxine Hitchcock.

Since becoming an author I've been so amazed at how kind people are when it comes to sharing their expert knowledge for fictional purposes. Thank you to Fenella for giving so incredibly generously of her time and expertise. Thank you to Rowena Macneish for patiently answering questions about life as a cellist, and to Cat Seekins for answering questions about her former life as a dancer. Thank you to Chris Jones for answering my medical questions. (As this is a book about neighbors, I would like to note that I was put in touch with Chris by his parents, Sue and Ken Jones, the loveliest next-door neighbors you could ever hope to have.) Thank you, Liz Frizell, for answering my uneducated musical questions. All mistakes are sadly mine and mine alone.

Thank you to my friends and fellow authors Ber Carroll and Dianne Blacklock for their friendship and support with this novel.

Thank you to my lovely literary agent, Faye Bender, as well as my

Australian and UK agents, Fiona Inglis and Jonathan Lloyd. Thank you to Jerry Kalajian for my entry into the wonderful world of Hollywood.

Thank you to Mum, Dad, Jaci, Kati, Fiona, Sean and Nicola, with special thanks to Kati for help with proofreading. Thank you to Adam, George and Anna for being you. I'm so lucky I got the three of you. Thank you to Anna Kuper for everything you've done for our family.

Two characters in this book are named after people in the real world. Steven Lunt was the winning bidder at the "Get in Character" fundraising auction run by CLIC Sargent Cancer Support for the Young. Robyn Byrne was the winner of the "Be Immortalised in Fiction" competition at the Sisters in Crime Australia Davitt Awards.

I've dedicated this book to my sister, the amazing novelist Jaclyn Moriarty, because I couldn't have finished this book without her help and support. Actually, I know I wouldn't have finished any of my books without Jaci.

The following books were helpful to me in my research about hoarding: *Dirty Secret: A Daughter Comes Clean About Her Mother's Compulsive Hoarding* (2011) by Jessie Sholl and *Coming Clean: A Memoir* (2014) by Kimberly Rae Miller. The website www.childrenofhoarders.com was also a great resource.

Recommend *Truly Madly Guilty* for your next book club!